Rut Bar

A HEATVERSE NOVEL

ALEXIS B. OSBORNE

Dark Moon
PUBLISHING

Editing by Lindsay York of LY Publishing

Cover © 2024 by Alexis B. Osborne

Discreet edition cover © 2024 by Alexis B. Osborne

Interior art © 2024 by Alexis B. Osborne

ISBN: 978-1-957341-24-8 (eBook)

ISBN: 978-1-957341-25-5 (Paperback)

ISBN: 978-1-957341-26-2 (Discreet Paperback)

Printed in the United States of America

First printing edition 2024

Published by

Dark Moon Publishing, Inc.

P. O. Box 2772

Poughkeepsie, New York, 12603

DarkMoonPublishing@gmail.com

For everyone who read the tag line "it's the literary equivalent of a bunch of fetish gear covered in glitter, tossed into a dumpster, and set on fire" and 1-clicked, this one's for you. You definitely don't want to read this one in public.

What is Omegaverse?

If you're unfamiliar with the omegaverse genre then here is a quick rundown of it's quirks and tropes. Omegaverse, sometimes called A/B/O or OV, is a sort of alternate reality where humans are divided into 3 dynamics: alphas, betas, and omegas.

Alphas are physically bigger and more muscular than betas and omegas. They're natural born leaders who fiercely protect their loved ones, but they can become aggressive at times and their jealous and possessive urges can sometimes get them into trouble. Each alpha give off a unique pheromones / scent / perfume that attracts omegas as a lure. An alpha claims another person as a packmate by biting a claiming bite into the juncture between the neck and shoulder. The base of an alpha's penis contains a knot which swells upon orgasm to stopper up an omega and tie the alpha and omega together for a short time for a higher chance of pregnancy. Alphas produce copious amounts of cum, and their cum is often highly nutritious to help feed an omega who doesn't eat during a heat. Alphas exposed to an omega in heat go into a rut and can become frenzied and combative against other alphas. Alphas purr to soothe distressed omegas, growl as a warning or threat to others, and bark to deliver a command. In heterosexual OV a female alpha often has a lock at the entrance of the vagina (the female version of a knot) that swells and locks onto a penis during her orgasm. In some LGBTQ OV a female alpha's clit swells into a pseudopenis, usually a smaller one than a male's, with a knot at the base and she can impregnate others.

Betas are the balanced citizens of the omegaverse. Their body size and shape varies from person to person. They don't experience the heats or ruts that omegas and alphas do and they don't have knots or locks. Sometimes they have pheromones like alphas and omegas do, but sometimes these are underdeveloped and faint. It varies widely from author to author. These are the average everyday regular humans of the omegaverse. Most OV books focus on alpha/omega pairings but beta packmates exist in many polyam romances too.

Omegas are the smaller and often more slender and submissive dynamic. Instead of menstruating, they experience estrous/heats. Heats range from a monthly occurrence to a few times a year depending on the author and the omega. Heats last for days to a week, similar to a period. While in heat, an omega becomes obsessed with finding a compatible alpha, nesting, and breeding. The delirium and increased libido of a heat may drive an omega to accept a strange alpha they normally wouldn't choose. Omegas produce a unique pheromone / scent / perfume like an alpha does. When in heat, this pheromone acts as a lure and becomes addicting to alphas and can send an alpha into rut. During heat, an omega produces excess lubricant called "slick" which helps ease the chaffing from a week-long sex marathon. An alpha's growl can trigger an omega to produce an extra gush of slick. Heats often make omegas physically warmer to the touch and sensitive to rough fabric. Omegas who have been bitten between the neck and shoulder by an alpha are considered claimed or mated. Mating is the OV equivalent of marriage and is usually permanent. Omegas are more fertile than betas. In some OV books, omegas are prone to having multiple babies rather than singles and sometimes the infants are called pups. While in heat, omegas usually don't eat except for an alpha's nutritive cum. In heterosexual OV, the alpha's knot lodges behind her pubic bone to tie them together and trap the pool of semen near the cervix to increase the chance of pregnancy. In some LGBTQ OV, a male omega has a self-lubricating anus and accepts an alpha's knot anally or they may have two holes plus a smaller penis. Mpreg, or male pregnancy, is a topic you'll sometimes find in gay MM OV. The male omega either gives birth through c-section or delivers anally or through their second hole. How MPreg works is author dependent and varies.

Pheromone preferences vary widely from alpha to alpha and omega to omega. The saying "one man's trash is another man's treasure" applies here. What smells amazing to one alpha/omega smells gross or bland to another. Many OV romances involve alphas and omegas looking for scent matches or their "fated mate" rather than dating. Alphas and omegas will scent mark each other through touch via pheromones, especially by rubbing their partner with their cheek or chin or touching their scent gland as a way to claim their "territory."

Nesting is something that omegas in heat and pregnant omegas do. It involves gathering lots of soft bedding and pillows and creating a small, cozy space that makes them feel safe. The nest is where omegas spend their heat and it can be where they'll give birth and raise their young, too. Think of it like the coziest adult pillow fort you've ever built. Omegas in heat like to make the nest smell like their alpha or pack through scent marking and sex. It's not unusual for an omega to drag her packmate's cast off clothes into the nest. If you've ever stollen a boyfriend's hoodie and worn it to bed because it smells like him then that's a good example of human nesting behavior.

Omegaverse books sometimes have shifters (like werewolves) but many of them don't. Some omegaverse books even take place with orcs or elves or in space with aliens!

The Heatverse is a non-shifter contemporary OV. There are no werewolves or shifters in this series.

Content Guide

**If you do not have triggers and you don't want to
read potential spoilers then skip this page.**

The content warnings listed below are accurate to this book but
this list may not be complete. If you have questions regarding a
specific trigger please contact the author at alexisosbornero
mance@gmail.com

Spoiler Zone - Spoiler Zone - Spoiler Zone

Rut Bar is a character driven hurt/comfort steamy contemporary
why choose MMMF omegaverse romance that contains mature
themes of: abortion (alluded to), age gap, alcohol, anal training,
babies (discussed), BDSM, blindfolds, breastfeeding (discussed
in the bonus epilogue), birth control, blood, bondage, brat
taming, breeding, cancer (discussed as a past event of a minor
character), chastity play, chronic pain, claiming bites, cock
biting, cuckolding, cum eating (consensual and non-con),
DP/DVP/TP, Daddy Dom, deceased parents, degradation play
(mild), domestic violence (minor characters), drug use (dis-

cussed), edging, exhibitionism, face fucking, Femme Dom, fisting, free use sex, foster care, gags, gangs, mafia, manipulation, orgasm denial, praise kink, pregnancy (bonus epilogue), public sex, rope, shibari, Soft Dom, somnophilia, spanking, stripping, suicide (discussed as a past event of a minor character), sword crossing, violence, and voyeurism.

Rut Bar is pregnancy/baby free in the main storyline, however these subjects are discussed at various points in the relationship. The bonus epilogue contains breeding and pregnancy.

Rut
BAR

Chapter One

VERONICA

I'M IN A ROOM FULL OF GORGEOUS HALF-NAKED ALPHAS YET nothing is going right today. What a pity.

The front door squeaks on its hinges as it opens. The sound is loud in the otherwise quiet room. All eyes turn to watch our resident himbo alpha with the body of a Greek god walk in.

"You're late," I say to Jamie. My teeth clench as I resist the urge to manhandle him to the center of the stage by his ridiculously gorgeous long blond hair. I don't know how he does it, but he always looks like he stepped off the cover of a romance novel. All he needs is a billowing, gauzy white shirt open to his lickable navel to complete the look.

"Sorry, Vee. Traffic." His smile is lazy and beautiful, his face lighting up as he looks at me. The corners of his eyes crinkle. His serene expression and calm demeanor are the norm. Nothing gets under Jamie's skin. No matter how much I bark or snap or snarl, he always looks at me with those big brown puppy eyes and smiles beautifully, then promises to do better. Then it's like he hits the reset button when he turns off his morning alarm.

He'll be late again tomorrow. And the next day. And the day after that.

"It's LA. There's always traffic." I give him an unamused stare, not that he notices or cares.

"I'll be on time for rehearsals tomorrow," he says as he slips into his empty spot in the middle of the alpha pack. "Promise."

I sigh. "Fine. But let's get on with rehearsals. I want this new set ready to go for this weekend." Pivoting, I look up at my office on the club's second floor and try to find my wayward choreographer. Enormous floor to ceiling windows keep the noise out while letting me watch the club while I'm working. "Nate!"

"Coming!" There's a metallic bang and clatter, and then a moment later Nate appears at the railing and looks over the balcony. He claps his hands together and grins before rubbing at his nose and sniffling.

Damn it. He'd better not be doing coke in the office again.

I'm gonna kill him if he is. They all know how important it is that everything goes smoothly this week, and each and every one of them seems to be set on sabotaging me.

Nate takes the stairs two at a time and stops before his pack of alpha dancers. "Good. Places, everyone." Nate's grin widens as he sniffles again. "Mike, cue the music and… three, two…"

The pack of alphas start their rehearsal, their biceps bulging and abdominals rippling. I take my cue to leave them to it. Nate does the movements with them, barking out corrections and critique as the alphas flow from one dance move to the next.

The Tarzan set is going to make the crowd lose their ever loving minds when they see it on Friday. What's better than a ripped alpha? One in nothing but a teeny tiny leather loincloth. What's better than one? A whole pack of them. Each one a different flavor to suit all tastes. We have a diverse cast here at Rut.

Jamie turns left instead of right and walks right into Margot, our resident female alpha. They collide with an audible *oomph*, and then Nate curses and yells at them to stop and reset. The pulsing music stops abruptly as Mike rewinds the track to the beginning. The cast groans softly.

I head to the bar and slap my palms on the counter. "I need the receipts from last night." *And a fucking drink.* And another week for rehearsals so they can get the new and more complex routine down. Time we don't have. The event flyers are already plastered on every streetlight and brick wall we could find.

Anthony studies me as he finishes wiping a glass dry and sets it down. "Sure thing, boss." He goes to the till and punches the drawer open, pulling the zippered pouch out from under the plastic bill divider. He hands it over.

While I rummage through it and check the contents, he pours me a drink, mixing alcohol and juice together without me having to ask. He sets it on a coaster and adds an orange slice as a garnish. The drink's a peachy pink color and there's a mashed maraschino cherry at the bottom under the ice.

"What's this one called?" I grab it and swivel the straw around and take a sip. "Oh, it's good."

He grins and goes back to wiping glasses. "Bliss on the beach."

I've never heard of it before, but then again, Anthony enjoys making his own variations of popular cocktails. He likes making everyone try a lesser known mix that becomes his signature drink of the night. He uses chalk markers to draw a picture of the drink and write out its name in fancy script on the large chalkboard that he hung above the register.

"Not sex on the beach?" I take another sip, savoring the blend of pineapple and cranberry juice with the vodka.

"If you want sex on the beach, I can do that for you," Anthony says, leaning forward on one heavily tattooed forearm.

"Let me know when you're free." He grins, flashing impossibly nice white teeth, and my heart skips a beat.

He's not hitting on me. Not really. Anthony's just a terrible flirt.

Between the tattoos, the floppy dark hair, and his baby blue eyes, my head bartender is gorgeous, and he absolutely knows it. The women who come here more than once don't care that he's a beta. Not when he smirks at them like *that*. Like he wants to throw them on the dirty floor and hike up their tight little skirts and do wicked things to them. He calls this smile the panty melter. He's not wrong. There's a reason he gets more tips than any of the other bartenders here and why he's worked here longer than the rest combined.

I frown at him because the staff is off limits, and despite his flirting, he knows that. *Don't shit where you eat.* He knows I won't call his bluff no matter how much I sometimes wonder what would happen if I did.

His grin widens to blinding levels and my traitorous pussy throbs as I push away from the bar, taking my bag of receipts and drink with me. "I'll be in my office."

"Sure thing, boss." The way he says *boss* is like an audible caress and I give a wide berth to the gyrating alpha pack so they don't catch a whiff of my growing arousal. *Talk about embarrassing.*

Once I'm safe in my office, I kick the door closed behind me until the club's rehearsal music is a dull throb that matches my growing headache. I add the bag of receipts to my never ending stack of paperwork and drain half my drink, then get to work. The music stops and starts twice as the dancers practice their new routine. I'm working on payroll for Friday's checks when someone knocks on the door.

"Come in," I snarl. I'm equal parts pissed that someone

interrupted my train of thought while doing payroll and glad for the interruption. My eyeballs ache from the computer's light.

My stomach growls and I'm reminded I skipped lunch to run errands at the bank before work. I'm expecting Anthony because he likes to bring me a plate since he knows I often forget to make myself eat. But it's not my bartender who opens the door. It's a tall, broad-shouldered alpha in a neat gray suit. His skin is light brown, and his dark hair is cropped in short curls that are shaved down to his skin on the sides in a fade.

He looks at me with rich brown eyes framed in lashes that are too long and pretty for an alpha. A hint of a five o'clock shadow with streaks of gray along his chin is already forming and a few gray hairs spot his temples.

"Can I help you?" I ask, my brow furrowing as I completely stop what I'm doing and wonder why this stranger's here and who the fuck let him up here.

"Are you Ms. Taylor?" He shuts the door behind him and sets a brown leather briefcase down on the floor.

"Yes."

"I'm Agent Hall. I'm a revenue agent for the IRS. I've come to do your audit. You've received our correspondence in the mail?"

He pulls his jacket away from his body to take a business card from the inside pocket and reaches out to hand it to me. The scent of freshly baked bread wafts in the air and makes my mouth water. As I take it, I stifle a soft whimper and my eyes flick down to the blue and white photo ID card I didn't notice hanging around his neck.

Brendan Hall, IRS Revenue Agent. It's all very official.

I slide my nail along the edge of his card and plaster a smile on my face, hoping that my hair doesn't look too crazy. I have a bad habit of running my hands through it when I'm stressed.

My naturally wavy hair gets bigger and bigger as the night progresses.

"Agent Hall, of course. Please excuse the mess. I was expecting you tomorrow."

He straightens his suit jacket, smoothing out a nonexistent wrinkle. "I finished another case earlier than expected. Did you not get my message? I called and left a voicemail."

A glance at my office phone and its blinking red light confirms his story is probably true. "Nobody's ever here before noon. It's a late night sort of place, you know. We close at two in the morning."

I eye the clutter and stacks of dirty cups. Embarrassment heats my cheeks. This is a horrible first impression to make. "Please excuse the mess. Things always get chaotic when we're rehearsing for a new act. I was going to tidy up tonight."

His smile is measured and professional, and it doesn't meet his warm brown eyes. Instead of studying my mess of a desk, he glances out the large glass windows that let me watch the floor from my office. "It's fine. Where should I set up? I only need a desk or table and an outlet."

"Set up?" Standing, I cock my head and wait for him to pull his gaze away from the pack of dancers working on their hip thrusts.

"Yes. I'll be conducting the audit here—unless your head-quarters is in an office building downtown. I find it faster to work at the place of business rather than lugging heavy boxes of files back and forth across town. The traffic, you know."

"Yeah, the traffic's a killer. Nope. No downtown office for us," I wheeze, my chest tight as I make a sweeping gesture with my hand. "You're looking at it."

His expression holds no judgment or disgust as he glances over at Nate's tidy mid-century modern desk across from mine. At least the IRS didn't send me a prude. Not everybody likes what we do here at Rut even though we're providing a valuable service people pay a lot to receive.

"Is it okay if I use that desk?" he asks.

There's no way I can refuse. Besides, it's not like Nate really uses his desk all that much. Ninety percent of his job is done on the stage floor or on his cell phone.

"Yup," I squeak and shove my wheeled chair back out of the way, harder than necessary. It rolls until it hits the window. "That would be fine." *Nate is going to kill me.*

His head dips in a nod, and he picks his briefcase up and sets it down on Nate's desk. He clicks it open, unpacking a silver laptop and charger, a pad of yellow legal paper and pens, and his own coffee mug. For a moment I expect it to say something like World's Best Dad or #1 Husband, but all it has on it is the IRS logo.

That's kind of sad.

Coffee mug... Coffee. He probably wants some.

"I don't drink coffee, but some of the dancers do," I say. "There's a pot in the… the dressing room." My brain catches up halfway through my sentence. *Fuck!* Now I need to make sure there's nothing bad in plain sight in the dressing room.

"Thank you." This time his smile reaches his eyes and I teeter totter on my heels. "Will your accountant be joining us?" he asks.

"He's, uh, out on a medical leave, but I pulled the files he said to gather. I started getting everything together when I got the first letter. Those boxes stacked over there should have everything you need."

"Great. Thank you. I'll get started, then. Pretend I'm not here. If I have questions, I'll find you."

That's exactly what I'm worried about. Because the IRS agent doing Rut's audit smells like a crusty, fluffy loaf of fresh baked bread and I want to take a huge fucking bite out of him.

Dammit. I'm suddenly regretting saving money by not extending the HVAC continuous air exchange to the office. Nate's a beta and I'm the only one who spends a lot of time here, so it didn't seem necessary. Now it seems very fucking necessary. My pussy throbs more intensely with every lungful of this alpha's scent.

I need to get out of this office.

Right. Fucking. Now.

"Make yourself at home." I run away before he can respond, gripping the railing for dear life as I take the stairs fast in my heels. At my tromping, Anthony's head whips up from where he's filling the bar's cooler with fresh ice and he raises one dark brow in question.

All but two of the dancers have gone backstage for a quick break, and I glance at my watch and groan. It's already five and our doors open in an hour.

Backstage in the dressing room, I scan the cluttered vanities and make sure there's nothing illicit out. I don't care what my employees do with their bodies on their own time as long as they show up for their shifts and work while they're here and don't bring messy drama with them, but they know better than to bring the hard stuff into my club. Not that it stops some of them. Things happen. Those employees don't last long here.

I snatch a cheetah print thong off the floor and hold it with the tips of my nails as I find Darlene at her sewing machine and add it to her pile of dirties in need of cleaning. "The IRS guy is here," I say over the furious whirr of her sewing machine.

She stops mid-stitch, pulls a lever, turns the black dress pants sideways, flicks it back down with a heavy thud, and starts sewing again without ever looking up. "What?"

"The IRS guy is here!"

"The DILF in the suit is the IRS guy?" As she talks, the pins stuck in the corner of her mouth move. She pulls the pants from the machine and snips the thread with a sharp pair of scissors. Despite the heavy fake lashes that pull her eyelids down, her eyes light up when she looks at me with a shit-eating grin.

With a strangled whine, I rummage through her stuff and find the bottle of scent nullifier she keeps on hand to freshen up the costumes. I tug the plastic cap off and shake it, then spray myself down, making a face when some of it gets in my mouth.

There. Maybe now he won't smell how damp my panties are when I have to go back up to finish payroll so I can cut everyone's checks on Friday.

"That bad?" she asks, amused.

I click the cap back onto the bottle and put it down. "I need everyone to be on their best behavior while he's here. *Best. Behavior.* Especially *you*, with your mouth."

She shrugs one shoulder and smirks as she plucks the pins from her mouth and stabs them into a hole-riddled pincushion shaped like a tomato. "Honey, I've never heard any complaints about my mouth yet."

I stare her down with a flat lipped expression, but the aging beta isn't impressed or cowed by me. Darlene's lived a fast, hard life, and a five-foot-three thirty-year-old omega doesn't make her bat a single fake eyelash.

"Best. Behavior," I stress, enunciating each word clearly. "He can make our lives *very hard* if he wants to."

"Oh, I'll bet he can," she cackles and fishes the next costume piece to repair out of her basket. It's a Spanish matador vest with a matching red thong that's missing some of its sequins. "Bet he makes a lot of things *real hard.*"

She ignores my narrowed eyes. "We need to be *nice* and *accommodating.* And *professional*," I reiterate.

"I'll be as accommodating as that alpha wants," Darlene says as she switches her black thread out for red. "Heard them say he's really tall and broad shouldered. The kind that's good for grabbing a hold of in the heat of the moment, if you know what I mean."

I sigh and give up. Darlene is harmless. Horny, menopausal, fond of making suggestive comments, but harmless. I walk away while she sews, her machine running a mile a minute as she makes her repairs in time for tonight's show.

I throw the back door open, and the dancers' conversation dies as I interrupt their break. A few are smoking, some holding cigarettes to their mouths while others hold joints or vape pens. The nonsmokers sit in the plastic folding chairs we keep by the door or they lean against the laundromat's brick wall and scarf down food from the taco truck that parks a block or two away most nights. My stomach twists with hunger at the decadent scent of charred pork and lime.

Nate is busy telling the newer guys about his time on Broadway, his hands waving as he talks, and even he pauses to look over his shoulder. His story trails off mid-sentence.

"Hey, guys. So the IRS auditor is here a day early. I'm giving everyone a heads up that he's going to be here for a while, so we need everything to go smoothly and professionally for a bit. That means go easy on the drinking. I don't want to see any illegal drugs or drug paraphernalia on the property. Weed is fine, but nothing else, okay? And absolutely *no* hooking up with customers backstage."

There's dejected murmuring, and then one of the new guys asks, "How long is he gonna be here?"

"Hopefully only a week or two."

They all groan, and I raise both of my hands in a placating gesture to shush them. "I know. Believe me, I know. We just need to put our heads down and work and get through this and then he'll be gone and things will get back to normal."

"Is Rut gonna get shut down?" a newer dancer asks, dragging his cigarette butt along the brick wall to put it out.

"No! We are not shutting down and nobody is getting fired or laid off. Audits are a very normal part of doing business. This is actually a good thing because it means we're doing well. Okay? Don't worry about it. I'm handling it. Work with Nate and practice your routine for this weekend, then get changed into your waitstaff outfit for first call. Enjoy your break."

Jamie lifts the hem of his tank top up to wipe the sweat from his brow, and the sight of his perfect washboard abs makes my mouth run dry. Where normal men have a four or six-pack, Jamie's abdomen is cut into eight boxes that make my tongue want to lick the dips between them. Before I can say something stupid or get caught staring, I turn and flee back to the safety of my office.

I must be getting close to my heat if my hormones are all over the place like this. It couldn't be coming at a worse time. Right now I can't afford to take the time off from work.

For a moment I consider going on a heat suppressant, but I really hate the way they make me feel. Bloated and weepy and so damn hungry. And then the delayed heat's twice as bad as it would have been if I just fucked through it for three days with some random alpha from Heat Buddy.

While I head back to my office, I pull up my heat tracker app and check my log. It's only been nine weeks since my last one, so it's too early. It must be the stress bringing it on sooner. Or maybe I need to get laid. How long has it been? My cobweb-covered pussy says it's been way too damn long. Probably since my last heat, if I'm being honest.

Turning a dive bar into a wildly successful alpha strip club means I meet a lot of handsome men and good-smelling alphas. It's painfully ironic I can't touch a single one of them. Either they're employees or patrons, and since Rut is my life and I spend more time here than at home, all of them are off limits. That makes it hard to date.

I'm so engrossed in my maudlin, horny thoughts that the alpha sitting at Nate's desk catches me by surprise. I scent him before I see him, his fresh baked bread scent filling the room till it smells like a goddamn bakery. A delicious bakery full of perfectly biteable treats.

My clit throbs and I squeeze my legs together to stifle it, but that only makes it worse when that extra pressure makes me feel empty and in desperate need of filling.

Fuck, he really is a DILF. There's a steady energy about him. He's broad and tall, but thick around the middle. A body meant for cuddles and comfort. Gray hair streaks the brown at his temples. Faint crinkles around his eyes show he's good natured and smiles a lot.

I have to breathe through my mouth to get past the threshold. *Does the man not use a nullifier spray? Rude.* You can't go around smelling like *that* in public. Like sex on a stick.

He looks up over the edge of his laptop as I hesitate in the doorway, his gaze holding mine until I snap out of it and shove my chair back up to my desk, plopping into it and staring at my computer screen.

What was I doing again?

Oh, yeah. Payroll.

I power through my mental fog and pick up where I left off, checking everyone's time punches and adjusting them as necessary. Jamie forgets to clock out a lot, but even though he's often late, he always stays till closing even when it's a slower night and some of the other dancers head home early. I check my calendar to compare his scheduled days against his time punches to make sure he's not missing any shifts.

Sometime later, a knock at the door drags me out of my spreadsheet hellscape and I spy Anthony standing there in the doorway. He studies the auditor, who spares him a glance and that awkward fake smile strangers give one another. Then the agent goes back to work.

"Thought you'd be hungry. Did you eat?" Anthony asks me.

"I'm starving. Thanks." My stomach growls on cue.

Anthony crosses over to my desk and finds a flat enough stack of paperwork to set down the brown bag. I dig out the to-go box and pop the lid open and look at its contents. It's a grilled chicken caesar salad, the hearty kind that's more toppings than lettuce and it's from my favorite Italian restaurant down the street. The chicken is steaming, the flakes of parmesan are enormous and it's been liberally coated in enough fresh cracked black pepper that I almost have to sneeze. It's perfect.

"You went over to Tony's?" I ask him. "Thank you. You didn't have to do that."

He leans his hip against my desk. "Someone has to take care of you since you're too busy taking care of everyone else to do it yourself. Make sure you eat a vegetable every once in a while."

My brow knits together. "I eat vegetables."

"Potatoes are a starch," he says. I open my mouth to speak, but he cuts me off. "Mushrooms don't count either. They're a fungus."

I shove my plastic fork through its plastic wrapper forcefully and stab it into my salad, taking a humongous bite of lettuce and chewing aggressively. The mouthful is too big for my jaw, but I'm too stubborn to back down. It's also delicious. Their kitchen's gotta make their own dressing or something.

We serve food at Rut, but it's typical bar food. Loaded fries and fried pickles, lots of things that come out of enormous bags from the freezer and go right into our automatic industrial fryer. After all, people aren't coming to Rut for the food.

The pepper in the caesar dressing makes my mouth burn a

little. "Happy?" I ask once I've swallowed and licked my lips clean of dressing.

"If you are, then yeah." He smiles instead of smirking.

My stomach flutters. When he stops being an asshole long enough to say something sweet like that, it's worse than the flirting.

He grabs the empty cups and plates, stacking everything in his hands in a way only people who've spent years in restaurant service seem to do. "There's bread too."

Ooh, bread. I look in the paper bag and pull out a piece of bread wrapped in foil and unwrap it. The smell of fresh baked bread covered in herb butter and garlic makes me salivate. I take a huge bite and chew, then sigh. "Thank you. What do I owe you?"

"Don't worry about it." He's already halfway out of the room. "Seeing you pleased is all the payment I need."

I frown at his back. "No, really. How much was it?"

"Nothing. Tony's my uncle, so I didn't pay anything."

Of course he is. I shouldn't be surprised because Anthony's family is humongous and they've lived here for generations.

Anthony takes the stairs down, and I swivel in my chair so I can watch him move around the club through the window. He goes back to the bar where one of the other bartenders is chopping fruit to garnish drinks.

As if he sees me watching him, he lifts his gaze and stares up at me, his lips curling into their resident bad boy smirk. *The pantymelter.* A lock of hair falls in his eyes and he reaches up, carding his fingers through it as he smooths it back into place. His stare turns into a smolder.

The distance makes enjoying this feel safer, although it's probably not. He doesn't need any encouragement. Anthony's been flirting with me for years.

He flirts with everyone.

I shudder out an exhale and swivel back to my computer and my salad, kicking my shoes off and pulling my feet up to sit cross-legged while I eat and work. I tear the garlic bread into pieces and mix it into the salad, then stab my fork through all of it like it's a salad sandwich.

God, it's so fucking good.

I've eaten the entire thing and finally finished payroll when the club's music changes abruptly from talk radio to the heavy thump of bass. The first patrons of the evening roll in, groups of omegas in business attire who want to grab a cocktail after work before heading home to their partners. They won't stay the whole night. It's too early for that crowd, but they appreciate the view.

Jamie steps out from the back, the black curtain flicking into place to obscure the back room. He walks up to their table to take their drink order.

He's oiled his body to show off every single dip and curve of his toned physique, his bare torso and thick arms on full display. I know from experience how the tight black pants—real ones, not the breakaway kind—hug his ass. Instead of a shirt, he's wearing a tiny business collar and even tinier tie that doesn't make it past his nipples. White shirt cuffs wrap around his wrists, and cufflinks with Rut's logo catch the light as he scrawls on his order pad.

The omegas eat it up, blushing and whispering to one another as he scribbles their orders down on his notepad and takes it over to the bar. They turn in their seats to watch his ass while he walks away. The door opens, and my bouncer Dan lets in a few more omegas, a couple of women and a slender man. Their group sits at the bar.

I watch the entire scene with a smile, proud of what we've all done. It's been hard work, but the results are worth it. My mom would be happy for me once she got over the shock of it all. A rut bar designed specifically for omegas instead of alphas. It's genius.

I'm seriously thinking of opening another location. Miami? Vegas? New York City? The possibilities are endless. I break into goosebumps just thinking about it.

A snap breaks me out of my thoughts as I swivel away from the window. The auditor stares down at his ink splattered hand, the remnants of his broken pen sitting on his legal pad. He looks up sheepishly and pulls an actual honest-to-goodness handker-chief from his pocket, then wipes the worst of the ink off. Rather than doing him any good, he ends up smearing most of it around.

He wraps up his broken pen and drops it all into Nate's trash can. "Well, I guess that's my cue to head home for the night." He packs up his things, unplugging his charger from the wall and closing his laptop. When he's done, he latches his briefcase and goes to leave before hesitating in the doorway.

"I'll… see you at noon tomorrow?" he asks.

Spurred into motion, I stand up and follow him to the stairs. "Noon. Right. I'll be here. Let me walk you out."

"That's unnecessary, but thank you. I can see myself out."

"Oh, uh…" I bite my lip, worried I'm about to offend him. "I'm so sorry, but we don't allow unmated alphas who aren't staff to wander around during omegas' hour. It's omega members only until seven and then the doors open to the public. Wait, are you mated?"

I flick my gaze down to what little of his throat I can see above his shirt collar and then down to his ink stained hand. No ring, and if he has a bite mark, it's hidden by his suit.

"No. I'm not mated." His broad shoulders stiffen as I follow behind him. We stop at the top of the stairs. "Wait, you're serving customers, but you're not open to the public right now?"

"Omegas only, yes," I answer.

"Wouldn't that be considered discrimination? If you're open to the public at all, then you're not really a private club."

My lips firm and I take a deep breath as I get ready for the speech I've had to recite so many times in the past couple of years. "Under the federal civil rights laws and the Omega Protection Act of 1978, private clubs, religious organizations, and nonprofits are allowed to discriminate based on sex, gender, and dynamic. The amendment in 1981 added new protections for organizations for omegas and women where there are safety concerns. You've heard of female-only gyms and women's and omegas' shelters, right? It's the same concept. Right now, from six to seven, we're only open to omega club members and all our proceeds go to support omega shelters. At seven, the doors open to the public."

He blinks at me until it's uncomfortable, even with the thump of the music filling the silence. "You're running a nonprofit within your business?"

My eyes widen. "No! God, no. That would be illegal. A for-profit company can't own a nonprofit because a nonprofit can't technically be owned. No. The nonprofit that I run owns Rut."

His mouth opens and closes a few times, and then his shoulders round.

I think I've broken my tax auditor.

"It's all outlined in my paperwork," I say, getting worried. Did he not read my detailed letter I sent them along with my certificate of formation?

His expression shutters, his jaw twitching as he clenches his teeth. "I took this assignment from another agent who went out on maternity leave. That information wasn't in her notes. I'll… see you at noon. We can go over it tomorrow."

We reach the main floor and wade through the thickening crowd. My bouncer Dan barely looks up at us as he keeps his eyes on the growing line of betas and alphas forming at the velvet rope, waiting for the club to fully open so they can mingle with horny omegas.

They stare at us with assessing looks while my tax auditor walks away. Worry gnaws at me. Maybe I'm wrong and I've fucked it all up and it's all going to be ruined now. It'll be all my fault for thinking I was being clever.

Did I mess up the paperwork? Not fill something out correctly? It's times like this when I wish I could call Harvey and get reassurance that audits are completely normal and every successful business goes through this. But the last thing I want to do is bother him while his wife's dealing with chemo.

"Everything okay, Miss Vee?" Dan asks.

I paste a fake smile on my face. "Everything's fine." And then I head to the bar.

I need a fucking drink.

Chapter Two

BRENDAN

IT'S ANOTHER AFTERNOON OF SHEER FUCKING TORTURE AS I stare at numbers on a spreadsheet and add them quickly in my head. It should be easy. I've always been good with numbers, and I can do this in my sleep, but I keep getting distracted before I reach the bottom.

I keep looking at the same lines. Because all I can think about is juicy dripping oranges.

Not orange juice from a carton—or worse, that fake orange from a plastic jug that's nowhere near the real thing—but the orchard-ripened kind. The sort I used to pick and eat fresh whenever we flew to Florida to visit grandma. The kind of orange that sprays bitter oils in the air when you peel it, slowly revealing its soft white rind and the delicate segments full of juicy vesicles ready to pop in your mouth and run down your throat and… All the blood rushes to my cock until I fidget and adjust my pants so they're not strangling my chub.

This. Is. Fucking. Torture.

I'm thankful the desk is wooden, not glass, otherwise I'd have a lot of explaining to do about why I keep getting an erection. Someone knocks on the door jamb and Veronica—Vee as the staff affectionately calls her—says they can enter without looking up from her computer.

The beta bartender with the tattoos stares me down as he steps over the threshold, two fancy drinks complete with pink straws in hand. The drinks are two different colors, the bottom yellow and the top turquoise blue. "Thought you'd like to try today's signature drink."

"Hmm?" She stops running her fingers through her hair—something she does a lot—and looks up. The ever-present crease between her brows smooths out as she smiles at the sight of him.

A radiant fucking smile.

Her pheromones thicken in the air. My cock twitches again, and I bite back a groan. My teeth grind from the effort.

The beta grins like he knows I'm hard from one whiff of her excitement. I'd worry he could detect my spike of pheromones despite the expensive nullifier lotion I've slathered on, except he has a beta's blunted sense of smell. There's no way.

If Vee can't scent me, then he can't either. Clearly he's got a thing for her.

I drop my attention back to my work to let him see I'm not a threat. He can stake all the claims he wants. I won't fight him for her. What are we, cavemen? I scratch the calculated total onto the bottom of my worksheet.

"Thanks," she says as she takes the drink from him.

Instead of drinking the other one himself, he takes those five steps to his right and sets it on my borrowed desk. I frown at it. There's an orange slice, and a cherry stabbed through with a toothpick perched on the rim of the frosted glass. "I'm on the clock, but thank you."

"It's a mocktail, and I'd like your impartial opinion. Sometimes I suspect Vee goes too easy on me. Let me know what you think."

She takes a sip of her drink, the sound noisy as the ice cubes clink against the glass. I glance up in time to see her cheeks hollowing as she sucks. A drop of pre-cum soaks into my boxer briefs as I imagine her sucking on something else. Vee makes a happy omega chirp, her smile widening.

"It's great," she says. "What's this one called?"

"Lick her right."

Vee blushes, her mouth dropping open, and then she laughs nervously. "No, it's not. You made that one up."

The bartender shakes his head and grins at her. "I didn't. Look it up if you don't believe me."

She rolls her eyes. "Nice try. If I type that into the search bar, all I'm gonna get is a bunch of porn and virus pop ups and that's the last thing I need to be using the company computer for. It's like you're trying to get me into trouble."

"What's the point of being the boss if you can't break a few rules?" he counters.

I'm forgotten about as they flirt. The bartender rakes his artfully tousled hair back and all I can wonder is how long he takes to look like he rolled out of bed after pleasuring a good woman all night long. I've never been able to perfect that post sex aesthetic.

"Google it up when you get home," the bartender says, snagging her empty glass from her. "And call me if you find anything interesting."

She bites the bright red cherry off the toothpick with her pink lips and chews it. "Hmm."

I get back to my sums until the room falls silent and I realize he's asked me a question. "Well?" he asks again. "I hope you're not too much of a *big bad alpha* to drink a fruity beverage."

A gut instinct tells me he's used to getting what he wants, and he won't leave me alone until he gets it. Sometimes it's easier to play along. Get it over with. If he's trying to goad me into reacting, it won't work. I'm a professional.

I grab the drink and take a small sip to make sure it really doesn't have any alcohol in it. It doesn't, so I suck in a deeper pull, enjoying the mix of orange, peach, and pineapple.

"It's good."

Good doesn't cover it. It's a tropical paradise in a glass. I can practically feel the warm sand under my feet and the breeze in my hair. My mind wanders to the mental image of licking it off her stomach as he pours it down her naked body in a body shot, the cocktail mingling with her own natural orange essence until I can't tell what's the drink and what's her as I lick her pussy. His grin tips into a smirk as if he can read my filthy thoughts.

"Just good?" He arches a brow and taps the empty glass against his thigh. "Come on. Surely you can do better than that. Give me a word that's not monosyllabic. I deal with enough grunts and one-word answers from the alpha dancers."

"Anthony," Vee chides, frowning at her bartender.

"It's fine," I interrupt before things can get out of hand. I'm going to be here for a few weeks. This paperwork and Janet's half-assed notes are a nightmare. The last thing I want is for things to be more tense than they normally are during someone's first audit. If letting the bartender tease me in this one-sided competition makes my life easier, then I can play along.

"Delectable," I tell him. "Or is that two syllables too many?"

"No, that's perfect. Delectable… I couldn't agree more. That's what I'm going to write on my menu board." He flicks his eyes to my glass. "Drink up. You wouldn't want to waste a single drop."

And then he's gone. I stare at the empty doorway before shaking my head and getting back to work. The drink sits forgotten as I wade back into the familiar realm of numbers where everything makes sense.

People are confusing. Numbers don't lie.

"Let me know if anyone bothers you," Ms. Taylor says, interrupting me from my work. "Or if I bother you. Sometimes I don't realize I'm humming until someone points it out."

The sum I was building in my head disappears like a cloud scattered on the wind. Normally the interruption would bother me—that's why I work in the field instead of next to my noisy cubicle neighbor Sharon—but the excuse to catch the omega's wide, honest eyes and take in the stubborn tilt of her chin soothes the irritation. She's so fucking pretty.

She gives me a polite smile, and I'm hit with the sudden urge to say something that makes her smile at me like she looks at the bartender.

Stop. You can't flirt with her.

Against my better judgment, my mouth opens before my brain can stop me. "There's nothing you could do that would bother me."

I hold her gaze, keeping her attention on me. It feels good to have it. She's a beautiful woman. Of course it's pleasant to have her attention. And that's all this is. Base attraction to a pretty little omega because it's been too long since I went on a date.

Her mouth softens and she blinks before she recovers, her cheeks pinkening with a delicate blush. "Oh," she exhales in a soft puff of air.

The bloom of her perfume fills the room, and I clench my hand tight until my pen creaks. *Don't break another one, idiot.* It took an entire bottle of rubbing alcohol to get the stains out.

"I'm used to working around distractions, I mean," I add. She can't know that's not what I meant at all. It's unprofessional conduct.

"Oh. Yes, of course." She gives me a strained, polite smile.

Well, at least my half-mast erection dies. We both go back to our own work until the noise from the club reaches a crescendo of female screaming that's louder than the thumping club music. Veronica doesn't glance up from her computer. I guess this sort of thing is pretty common in a place like this? How does she not go deaf?

She pushes away from her computer. *Is she going to go check on the club? Flirt with her bartender?*

My chest pinches at the thought, although I understand it's stupid. I have no claim over her and even if I wanted to, I can't. I shouldn't want her attention like this. Shouldn't imagine licking cocktails out of her navel or burrowing my face in her cunt. Fucking her up against the large glass windows that look out on her club.

Shouldn't, shouldn't, shouldn't. But that forbiddenness makes the fantasies harder to resist.

Half an hour passes and I barely make any progress as I crosscheck receipts to expenses on her first quarter reporting. My mind keeps getting distracted by her juicy citrus scent.

I'm constantly aware of her in my periphery. Every sigh, every carding of her fingers through her hair, every creak of her chair. She likes to tuck herself into a ball and sit cross-legged, her shoes kicked off. The intimacy of witnessing such a small thing makes me long to slip out of my jacket and do the same.

My hand is halfway to the first button of my jacket before I realize this is madness. I reach for the folder containing her 501c paperwork instead. I've read the same three paragraphs a dozen times before I'm forced to admit this is going nowhere fast.

It's not cowardice if it's for her benefit. That's what I tell myself anyway when I gather up her incorporation paperwork and January's documents and collate them into a folder I shove into my briefcase.

"I'm going to head to the office. I forgot something I need," I tell her as I rise and avoid looking at her.

"Oh, okay. Have a good night."

This time, she lets me head down alone. The club is nearly wall to wall with patrons. The omegas are five deep as they ring the raised dais that acts as a stage where three muscular and nearly naked alphas dance with synchronicity. They're dressed as cowboys, but they've forgotten their jeans underneath their chaps. Big silver and turquoise belt buckles draw the eye to their tiny and well-stuffed paisley printed thongs.

One after another, they take their cowboy hats off and fling them into the crowd. And then one steps forward, the spotlight tightening as he reaches for his hip and uncoils a rope. He makes a show of stretching it between his hands, his arms splayed wide as he shows off his bulging arms and pecs, then turns so his audience can glimpse his broad back and bare ass.

The dancer ties the rope into a lasso and whips it over his head, and the omegas scream. I'm awestruck by the show as much as the rest of the crowd is. While there are some omegas sitting at tables or hanging at the bar, mingling with the alphas and betas in the crowd, most are ringed around the stage watching the floor show.

It's no wonder Veronica hit her first five-million-dollar year. This club is a goldmine. In college, I hung out at my fair share of rut bars, but I've never seen one packed with so many betas and omegas. Normally, the alphas outnumber the omegas ten to one. At Rut, it seems like a more normal mix of dynamics.

The crowd's energy peaks, and I'm pulled from my thoughts as the alpha dancer lassos a woman at the front of the crowd and makes a show of reeling her in. She giggles and blushes as he helps her on stage so he can treat her to a private dance that's not so private. They sway like lovers, and he's careful to keep his touch to her hands and arms as he guides her hands over his abdominals. After a brief moment of hesitation, she touches him in earnest.

That's my cue to leave. I slip out the door and let it bang shut behind me. The noise dies down to a dull roar as the thick door keeps the worst of it contained. The mountain of a man who guards the club's door nods at me, and the line of patrons waiting behind the red velvet rope perk up at the prospect that their entry is coming soon.

Once I'm safely ensconced in my car, I drag in a deep breath, hold it, then exhale slowly until I settle. "Don't be stupid," I tell myself. It's not like I could compete for her even if I wanted to.

The alphas who work for her are built. Young. Healthy. Their bodies are whole. They've honed their physique at the gym and chiseled it to perfection. They're in their prime and they're handsome.

The young beta bartender who clearly wants her has that bad boy edge to his looks that drives women wild. He looks like he's in his late twenties, much closer to her in age than my forty-one.

I can't compete. I spend more time behind a desk than at the gym and my body shows it. I've gone soft around the middle from too much takeout and not enough sit-ups. Even if I wanted to get back into shape again, it's hard to do at this age without intense exercise, which hurts too damn much.

It's fine. It's not like I want her attention anyway. Scent compatibility doesn't guarantee a good relationship. *Remember how things ended with Jenna.*

With my spirit completely crushed, I slot my keys into the ignition and turn the engine over, then pull out into traffic.

It takes me over an hour for me to get home, where I promptly strip and collapse into bed in only my underwear. I'm too old to be coming home this close to midnight. Before I'm fully rested, I'm awake as the sun rises and prods me from sleep. Half dead to the world, somehow I make it through a shower. When my jacket is buttoned and my hair has been sufficiently combed into order, I head to the office.

"Morning," Andrea says from the front desk. A ringing phone interrupts whatever she was about to say next.

"Good morning." I leave her to it and head to my desk, unpacking my files from my briefcase and pulling out my coffee mug. Hopefully the pot is fresh. I'm going to need it to get through the day.

Mark sees me and uses his coffee cup to wave. "Oh, hey, Brendan. What are you doing back so soon? Aren't you doing a field case?" He cuts in front of me to nab the last of the coffee and sets the stained but empty pot back on the burner.

"I am. It's a distracting place, though."

"Yeah, I'll bet it is," Mark says. He blows on his hot black coffee and takes a sip. "It's that bar called Rut, right? My girl's been trying to get me to take her there for forever, but I don't know, man. I'm not really interested in seeing a bunch of dudes' junk waving in my face."

I remember how the blond alpha dancer's barely concealed cock jumped inside the too small thong underwear as he gyrated on stage. The half-naked alphas weren't the thing distracting me, but I'm not planning to elaborate on that to Mark. "Mmm. I'm gonna try to get through the more important paperwork here."

"See ya," he says as he shoves his hand in his pocket and walks out while sipping his coffee.

I sigh and dig out the huge tin of grounds that we keep in the cabinet and scoop some into a fresh filter. After a few minutes, the water's heated enough that coffee percolates into the pot. My fingers tap against the counter as I wait for it to finish brewing, then click it over from brew to warm.

The first sip makes me human again, although it burns my tongue. I settle at my desk and get to work, checking over Veronica's nonprofit paperwork. I can't say that a nonprofit running a for-profit rut bar is something I've ever come across before. It's not that unusual for nonprofits to run for-profit businesses, but usually they're closely related entities. I'm not sure what a rut bar has to do with… omega protection services?

The paperwork is vague and I make notes for questions to ask Veronica the next time I see her. If she loses her 501c status, then her taxes just got a hell of a lot more complicated and I'm looking at several months of work instead of two or three. That's not in either of our best interest. The longer I'm there, the more I have to smell how delicious she is.

Sharon pokes her head over the cubicle divider. "Oh, hey, you're back! I knew I heard a noise. I thought you were out in the field again?"

The banality of polite office conversation makes my eye twitch. "That's right. I'm taking over one of Janet's cases while she's out on leave."

Sharon's eyes light up, and I realize my mistake too late. *Fuck.* Sharon goes into a long winded and mostly one-sided conversation about the latest news regarding Janet's birth. I learn all about the baby boy Janet just had—six pounds, seven ounces and twenty-one inches—and then Sharon moves onto her own experiences as she recounts her own birthing stories and the harsh adjustments to life with a newborn as a first-time mom.

"—and it's so hard to find a good daycare around here that doesn't—"

I nod dutifully and make faint conversational noises whenever there's a lull as I pack my briefcase back up. Why did I ever hope that I'd get some work done at the office? You'd think by now I'd know better. Sharon probably wouldn't stop talking if I croaked and died right at her feet. She'd keep going and only notice something was wrong hours later when it was time to go home and I didn't walk out with her. I snap the briefcase closed and stand, straightening my jacket.

"Sorry to interrupt," I lie. "But I have to get back out there. I only came back for my…" I grab the nearest thing on my desk without looking. "Got it!"

"Stapler?" she asks, perplexed.

"Yes." I put the stapler in my jacket pocket. "Would you believe they don't have one? So weird. See you later, Sharon."

Before she can start up again, I hurry toward the door.

If I'm not going to get any work done because of the distractions, then I may as well look at a pretty little omega while I'm unproductive. Anything is better than Sharon's prattling. That woman wouldn't know brevity if it tripped her.

Chapter Three

VERONICA

REHEARSALS GO BETTER TODAY THAN THEY DID TWO DAYS AGO, and I'm feeling better about tonight's unveiling of Rut's new act. Hopefully it won't be a disaster that makes the patrons ask for their door fee back.

"Okay! Places, everyone!" Nate yells over the music. "Let's reset. Cue the music from the top. On three, two…" Nate moves into the first part of the choreography while my dancers do their first dress rehearsal. "Now hip dips. That's right. Knock knock, who's there? Thighs, that's who. Slap on three, two… Good. Now walk away. Show them what they'll be missing… and come back, you've changed your mind. Feel yourself. Show off those abs and chest. Hold yourself. The jungle gets cold without your omega to warm you. Good, now fall back so Jamie can take the center. Here's your solo, Jamie. Make it personal. Don't forget to connect with your audience."

Jamie stares at me as he practices and I stand there and pretend to be a crowd of screaming omegas for him. Some dancers do fine without a fake audience, but others need their practice to be more realistic. He reaches a hand inside his faux leather loincloth and palms the base of his cock as he makes slow hip swivels. There's a peek of trimmed hair as the loincloth dips while he strokes himself until his bulge is more pronounced.

"No pubes, Jamie. We'll lose our liquor license," I bark.

He flashes me a sad puppy smile that says *sorry* and pulls his hand out of his loincloth, then moves back into his solo routine. When he drops to the floor in a dolphin dive that drags his package along the floor in a sort of pseudo push-up, there's a loud ripping sound.

"Oops," Jamie says as he goes completely still.

Nate groans and puts his hands on top of his head and the other dancers shift on their feet. Our DJ cuts the music.

"It's fine," I reassure them. "This is why we do dress rehearsals. Let's go get your costume sorted, Jamie. You can switch into regular underwear and get back to rehearsals while Darlene fixes it."

Jamie pops up, the movement making his loincloth tilt precariously as the faux leather string holding the sides together sags. He presses the front down to keep himself covered and hops down from the stage. The back of the loincloth hangs, and I have to stare at his gloriously sculpted bare ass the entire way to Darlene's costuming closet.

She peers over her machine at us, one pencil thin eyebrow raised as she takes in the damage.

"Please tell me you can fix it in the next half-hour," I say.

"Hmm. Let me see it. Strip."

"Sorry, Miss Darlene." Jamie hooks a thumb in the good side and shoves the loincloth down his thighs so he can hand it to her. "The string snapped when I was humping the stage."

While Darlene inspects the broken costume, I sort through the pile of freshly laundered thongs until I find the ones with his name written on the inside. I hand it to him while keeping my eyes firmly above his nipples. "Here."

"Thanks, Miss Vee." He steps into it and tugs it up, reaching inside to pull himself into place. "I'm sorry I broke it."

Once his cock is covered, I can breathe again. "It's fine." I drag a hand through my hair. "Accidents happen. What do you think?" I ask my seamstress.

"It's the fake leather. There's no stretch to it. I can sew the front and back together with brown elastic. It won't be as pretty, but it'll hold. I can make it nicer tomorrow. Sew fake leather on top, but leave the sides open so it can still flex."

"Sounds good. All right, Jamie, get back to it. We'll bring you the costume when it's finished."

He leaves us, and Darlene snips the broken fake leather away and picks at the stitches. "He rips more costumes than any of the other dancers," I say under my breath.

"It's because he's a grower," Darlene says. She switches her machine to brown thread and digs around in a drawer for brown elastic. "He's got a lot more to swing around when he's hard. Funny how that happens mostly during dress rehearsals when you're watching him dance."

I frown at her. "What's *that* supposed to mean?"

She gives me a wry face and doesn't answer my question. The whirr of her machine fills the silence until she pulls the fixed piece free and snips the threads. "Here."

"Thanks." The loincloth is still warm from his body heat and saturated in his suntan lotion scent. It should smell bad, like chemicals and minerals, but it's coconuts and joy instead. Warm summer sun with a hint of salt. The scent reminds me of all the days we spent at the beach until Mom got sick and we traded beach days for hospital stays.

With one hand gripping the black curtain divider, I pause and glance over my shoulder. Darlene is busy sorting through her bolts of fabric to dig out the fake leather. I know I shouldn't do it. I shouldn't bring the loin cloth up to my nose to drag his scent in deeper, but my omega urges are too close to the surface from being in preheat. From being trapped in a tiny room with a compatible alpha for days. I can't ignore them.

I ball the loincloth into my hand and pretend to scratch an itch on my nose. A groan swells in my throat and I strangle it before it can turn into an actual purr. Before I get caught and teased, I force my hand with the costume back down and push through the curtain.

My dancers are back to their routine, and Nate snaps out their cues as he drills them with the mercilessness that makes our cabaret show one of the best on the West Coast. Jamie sticks out like a sore thumb with his black thong compared to all the others. With their brown leather loincloths and Margot's leather fringed bikini and their summer sun-kissed skin, it's like they stepped right off a movie set. They stomp their feet together and bang their fists against their sternums, and then they all kneel around Jamie and raise their arms as he prepares for the grand finale.

Jamie throws his head back, flexes until his abdominals and pecs look like you could bounce a quarter off them, and gives us his best Tarzan yell. It echoes in the enormous space until it's deafening.

The omegas are going to eat this act up with a spoon. This is probably Nate's best work to date. Even the Singing in the Rain set that we installed a very expensive rain simulator for doesn't compare to this routine. There's raw, primal energy here. My alphas look like they're ready to toss an omega over their shoulder and run off into the tree line.

It's perfect.

I clap around the loincloth still balled in my fist and my cheeks hurting from how hard I'm grinning. The dancers break from their positions and follow Nate out back to take a well-earned break while Jamie hangs back.

"Here's your costume," I say as I hand it to him. He takes it, but he doesn't follow the dancers like I expect him to.

"Do you have a minute?" Jamie asks. He won't meet my eyes and he's fidgeting with the costume in his hands.

My first thought is that he knows. He knows I nuzzled his costume like some creepy pervert. But there's no way he could know that. My heart races in my chest as a thousand possibilities run through my mind.

"Can we talk somewhere private?" he asks again when I don't respond.

Oh, shit. He's going to quit. My most popular dancer is going to quit and then the show will fall apart and I'll fail my audit and Rut will shut down, and then what the hell am I going to do with my life?

"Of course," I say, covering my inner meltdown with a blanket of professionalism. "Do you want to get dressed and meet me in my office?"

He nods, hesitates, then walks away. I watch him go, then catch Anthony eyeing us with interest. He's cleaning glasses at the bar and he arches one brow at me in a silent question. I shrug, then head up the stairs. The IRS agent glances up from his stack of paperwork, and I mentally curse because I forgot he was here today.

The scent of coconuts and sunshine makes me turn in time to see Jamie climb the stairs behind me. Faded blue jeans are slung low on his hips and he's wearing a pair of brown flip flops and that's it. No shirt. He probably didn't change out of his work thong either. *Why did he throw on clothes so fast? But this is a good sign, right? If he was about to walk out on me, he'd have gotten fully dressed.*

"Could you give us a few minutes, Agent Hall?" I ask as I head to my desk and perch on its edge.

"Of course. And just Brendan is fine. This is a good time for a dinner break, actually."

"Thank you. The taco truck two blocks down is the best one in the neighborhood. And there's a little park with benches not too far from it."

"That sounds perfect." Brendan pats his stomach over his jacket and smiles. "I love tacos." He glances between me and the still shirtless Jamie and looks the alpha up and down. "I'll be back in a half-hour."

They nod at one another in that weird way that alphas do when they're sizing each other up. I ignore them and sit, ignoring the heat creeping up my neck. Was that thirty-minute remark insinuating something? A warning? Does he think I brought Jamie up here to fuck?

Brendan pulls the door closed behind him and I'm tempted to tell him to leave it open, but Jamie asked for privacy and his comfort is more important than avoiding looking suspicious.

Jamie pulls a chair out and sits, his knee almost touching mine. God, he's tall. I'm torn between moving away from where I'm leaning so I can sit, which risks this conversation feeling scary and important, and needing to put distance between us.

His suntan lotion scent is filling the room, and somehow it's mingling with Brendan's fresh bread scent deliciously. Coconut bread. I've seen it being sold at the Jamaican restaurant by my place, but I can't recall if I've ever had it. My mouth waters. I bet it's delicious.

"What can I do for you?" I ask to break the ice.

"It's more what I can do for you," Jamie says. "Anthony told me I should ask if you need help over the next few days. Because of the tax dude."

I wait for him to elaborate, but he never does. If Jamie recognizes the uncomfortable silence, he doesn't seem disturbed by it. "Help me with what?" I ask. He can't possibly think there's anything he can do to help with the audit. Jamie is sweet, and he is my best dancer, but I don't get the idea he's good with excel spreadsheets.

"Your heat," Jamie answers.

I blink, not quite sure I heard that correctly. "My what now?"

"Your heat. You're…" He pauses as if he's just now realizing what he said to me. "I can smell it's coming. We all can. He thought… I mean… We thought you might want help. Because of the tax man."

"You thought I might want you to help me through my… my heat because of the IRS audit?" I'm more baffled than upset.

"Yeah. Because you always come back so crabby after your heats. We thought you might like to be relaxed this time."

My jaw drops, and all of my cool professionalism goes out the window. "Crabby?" The word comes out as a squeak. *My staff is discussing my heat cycles?* Mortification and irritation war with one another inside me.

Jamie panics and raises his hands in supplication, his eyes wide. "I didn't mean it in a bad way."

"There's a good way to take being called *crabby*?" I ask.

He drags in a deep breath and sighs, then lowers his hands to his thighs. "Sorry. I'm not good at words. You practically live at Rut. The club is your life. We all know how hard you work. And with Harvey being out, Anthony says there's extra work being dumped on you and you'll need help. We want to help you. You don't have to do this alone."

"You want to help me through my heat," I reiterate. Perhaps if I say it enough times, he'll understand how inappropriate his offer is.

"Yeah. I'm a good cook. Anthony can clean and… and do

laundry and stuff. When was the last time you let someone take care of you?"

"Oh." Mortification wins. He was offering to help me do laundry and here I was thinking about licking his cum off his abs. My face heats, and I clear my throat and glance away. "That's actually pretty sweet. Inappropriate, but sweet. I can't take you up on your offer, Jamie. You're my employee. I'm your boss. That wouldn't be right."

Because when the full force of my heat hits me, I won't have the forethought to stick hard and fast to my no-employees rule. Especially not with Jamie. I've had a crush on him for years. I'd end up begging for his knot, and then how would I ever stare him in the eye again after it was over?

I sigh. "It's a nice gesture, but I can't."

"Okay," he says. "Then I quit."

"*What?!*" I screech and push away from the desk so fast my heel skitters between two tiles. My ankle rolls and I nearly fall over. Jamie's hand engulfs my thighs to keep me from breaking my face on the ceramic. "You can't quit! Darren's your alternate, and he's out because of his broken clavicle. No one else has learned the king of the jungle role. We haven't practiced it with anyone else."

"I'm sorry!" He holds his hands up again. "I don't really want to quit. I thought that might… I don't know, make things easier? When I can't decide what I want, sometimes I flip a coin and then I know how I feel. If I'm happy or sad. I'm sorry, Miss Vee. I didn't mean to scare you."

His hands massage my thighs and liquid heat pools in my belly. I sag against my desk as relief washes through me. It's okay. He's not leaving me.

It feels like I've aged ten years in two minutes. My hand snags on a snarl as I run it through my hair until it puffs around my shoulders. "Okay. You're not quitting. You'll dance in the show tonight. It's fine. Everything is fine."

He grabs my hand before I can make my hair even bigger. "It's all good. We all want Rut to do well. We love it here. There's a lot of workplaces that say they're like a family but that's not really true, you know? But for Rut, it is. When we get sick, you still pay us. When Patrick wanted to go back to school, you helped him with his paper.

"You help so many omegas. My sister's an omega. If she needed it, I'd want someone like you around to help her. You close the club on Christmas so we can be with our families when you could make a lot of money instead. You care about this club, and us, and we care about you. We want to help. Please let us help you. Anthony says you shouldn't have to suffer through your heat alone."

My eyes grow hot and scratchy with unshed tears. When was the last time anyone ever said such nice things about me? "I really do appreciate it, but I can't. It's not appropriate. I would ask you to do things that a boss shouldn't ask their employee to do. I would never let that happen."

Jamie gives me those sad puppy eyes, but nods. His chair scrapes against the floor as he stands. "I understand." He opens his mouth to say something, but the abrupt change in the club's music makes him pause. He hooks a thumb toward the stairs. "I should get changed into my waiter's uniform. Sorry I harshed the vibes."

"It's fine. I… appreciate your offer. It was sweet."

He leaves without another word. I move to the window and track his progress, watching him take the stairs two at a time until he hits the floor and bypasses the first rush of omega guests, chatting with them briefly before heading to the back and into the dressing room.

Anthony's stare from his place at the bar is hot along my

skin. My hands press hard into the glass as I wonder what else my bartender has been saying behind my back.

Not your business. Get back to work.

And I do. At some point, Brendan comes back and sits at Nate's desk. We ignore each other as we work in a comfortable silence. I've finished printing out the last of the bi-weekly paychecks when Anthony interrupts me to set down a plate of food. I can't bring myself to peek at him as I murmur my thanks and ignore his hovering until he leaves.

It's the crowd's eruption of cheers that finally pulls me from my work. The familiar beat of the Tarzan set's music pulses through the room. Now *this* I have to see. I push away from my desk and roll my chair over to the window.

The first night that a new act unveils is special. The crowd's reaction will tell me if this is one we should keep in the rotation or let go after a few weeks.

My pack of alpha dancers burst onto the stage as the drumming speeds up. The omegas see the itty-bitty leather loincloths and baby oiled muscles and they lose their damn minds. A tall, curvy redhead in a white bridal sash gets jostled to the front of the crowd and Jamie latches onto her, making her his target in the audience.

He stares at her as he dances, his gaze always coming back to her after he's done with one move before he moves onto the next. When it's time for his signature move, he drops to the stage right in front of her and moves like he's fucking the floor.

The play of the stage lights makes his body downright glisten. He's so oiled up that for a moment I worry one of them is going to slip. It happens sometimes when they do the floor moves. The bride covers her face with her hands, but not her eyes. She's still looking, and so is Jamie as he works hard to make her feel special on her special night.

Good. The bachelorette package is expensive. Any bride

who comes to Rut for her naughty night out gets the VIP treatment.

When he's done, he pops up and sticks the landing. He sinks back into the pack and I let out an anxious breath. They finish their dance and drop to their knees around him. The light makes his long blond hair gleam like molten gold.

Jamie throws his head back, and the music dims as he lets out a Tarzan yell that shakes the rafters.

There's absolute silence for a few stunned seconds, and then cheering so loud that my ears ring. A grin splits my face as the dancers parade across the edge of the stage, stopping long enough to accept their tips as patrons shove dollar bills into their loincloths.

When one of the drunk omegas gets too frisky and tries to shove her hand down a loincloth, her friends drag her away to a booth in the back of the club.

I pull my phone from my pocket and send Anthony a text telling him to cut her off. After a moment, he pulls his phone from his back pocket, reads the screen, scans the crowd to find the booth, then looks up at me and nods.

"Wow, they really liked that set," Brendan says, interrupting my thoughts.

"Yeah, they did. Nate's a genius. I'm pretty sure that Rut wouldn't be half as successful as it is if we hadn't snatched him up. He was working on Broadway before he joined us."

"How'd you manage that?" he asks.

"His boyfriend landed an acting job, so they moved out here. The bar isn't far from where they live, so they ended up drinking here occasionally. Sometimes they like to pick up a new friend for the night, you know. He turned my job offer down three times before he finally caved. I give him full artistic control, and he gives me a better routine every month."

"It seems like this work is a lot more complicated than I thought it would be," he says.

I glance over my shoulder and smile. "What, you thought it was just G-strings and dollar bills and a little wiggling?"

His face reddens, and my smile grows. "Uh… yeah. Kind of," he admits. "I've never been to a rut bar like this before. I mean, I've been to them. When I was younger. Not now. But those were more like…"

"Dive bar sausage fests?" I tease him.

He barks out a laugh, the sound warm and comforting. "Yeah. That's an apt description. You've really built something amazing here."

Embarrassed but pleased, I duck my head and steal one last glimpse of the crowded club. "We really have."

I push away from the window and stare at my computer as I try to remember what I was doing before the set started. *Right. Paychecks.* I pull up the payroll application and make sure it all transferred over to the spreadsheet where I track the business expenses.

"Have a good evening," Brendan says as he gathers up his things. "I'll see you tomorrow."

"See you tomorrow."

My food is cold by the time I get to eat, but I scarf it down anyway as I take a quick break before looking at the supply order Darlene sent me. The total at the bottom makes me groan, but I know every dollar spent on Nate's over-the-top costumes comes back to us in drinks and entry fees.

After all, omegas don't come to Rut for the half-naked alphas. They come for the show. The experience. There's nothing wrong with good old-fashioned stripping, but this is different. It's more. Every set doesn't just tell a story, it sells a dream. A fantasy.

The music cuts off and the lights brighten, and I glance out the office's vast windows to see the stragglers being ushered out. It's past the last call, but we still have a half hour to get everyone out so we can close by the ordinance time. Everyone will want their paychecks.

I grab the stack and head downstairs, handing them out one by one as clothed dancers walk past and wish me a good night.

"Go home," Anthony says to Cassie, one of the other bartenders. "I've got this." He hauls a black bag of trash from the plastic bin and ties it off.

"Are you sure?" Cassie asks, but she's already taking her black waist apron off and hanging it up on its hook.

"I'm sure. Don't you have a test tomorrow? Go get some sleep," he says.

"Thanks," she says to both him and me as I hand over her paycheck while she grabs her purse.

The only check left is Jamie's. I check the back room, but it's empty, so I wander over to the bar. "Have you seen Jamie?" I ask Anthony. "I need to give him his check." Did he dip out early to avoid me and forget it was payday?

Shit. Things are already weird, and I haven't done anything wrong.

"He's around here somewhere," Anthony says while he hauls another bag of trash toward the back door. "His car's still in the lot."

I check everywhere backstage until the only place left is the main bathroom. *Why would he use that one?* That one is for customers. The staff use the private one in the back.

I pause outside the door when I hear a giggle, and then my vision goes red around the edges. *He wouldn't. No. Not Jamie. He never... Not once has he ever...*

I push the men's door open with too much force and it

bangs against the wall with a sharp crack. Sure enough, the bathroom's only stall has four feet underneath the divider. The woman in the stall with him is on her knees in front of him, and I can guess what they're doing.

Chapter Four

VERONICA

"THE BAR IS CLOSED," I SAY, MY VOICE FROSTY AND MY WORDS clipped. "It's time to go."

The drunk woman on her knees gasps and scrambles to her feet. Jamie reaches down to help her onto her spindly stilettos. There's fabric rustling and then the stall door clicks open and an embarrassed curvy redhead who is suspiciously missing her white bridal sash slips past me.

Her gaze is cast down with shame, as it should be. She pushes past me without a word and I let the door go so it can shut behind me once she's gone.

Jamie's low-slung jeans are still unzipped but at least he's wearing a shirt now. Judging from the impressive bulge in his pants, he's still hard. Good. That means this drunken blowjob didn't get very far.

"What was the *one thing* I asked you guys not to do while the auditor is here?" I seethe.

The skin between his brows creases. "No illegal drugs?"

My jaw aches from the way I'm clenching my teeth. "The other one thing, Jamie. The one that's relevant to this particular situation."

The silence stretches as he thinks. "No… no fooling around with customers backstage? But we're not backstage. The bathroom is next to the stage."

I reach up and pinch between my brows to stifle the headache that's brewing. If it was anyone but Jamie, I'd call their behavior insubordinate, but Jamie is… Jamie is a golden retriever in human form. He's sweet, loyal, caring, and he takes direction well, but you have to be very clear or he doesn't always get it.

"The location wasn't the point," I say. "The *no sleeping with customers* was the point. I don't care if it's behind the bar or on the stage or in the bathroom or backstage. Do. Not. Fuck. Customers."

"While the tax dude is here, yeah. I thought he left?" Jamie asks, tilting his head like he's honestly confused.

"What if he forgot something and came back?" I ask, my voice raising. "Yesterday he showed up holding a stapler before we were open. Why would you…"

This feels like a betrayal, but that's stupid. I'm his boss. He's my dancer. That's it. It doesn't matter that he's a scent match. He's off limits.

I pinch the bridge of my nose and sigh. *No. It's not my business.* It's not my place to ask why he'd do this to me. It isn't personal.

The dancers get horny from all the omega perfumes and lust swirling in the air and I don't mind if someone wants to sneak off to a dark corner and let off some steam so long as they're discrete and I can pretend I don't know it's happening. They're adults. They can decide what to do with their own bodies.

As long as money's not exchanging hands for sex, then it's all good. But not while the fucking IRS is breathing down my neck and looking for a reason to shut us down.

"You don't want me," he whispers.

"What?" I drop my hand and study him, my heart dropping into my stomach at the expression of devastation on his beautiful face.

"You don't want me. I offered to… It's fine. I'm not trying to guilt trip you or coerce you or do any of those things you aren't supposed to do to omegas, but… it hurt to hear it, Vee. I thought… I don't know. I thought maybe this would make me forget how much my chest hurts right now. Even if it was only for a few minutes. At first I didn't know what that woman meant and then… Well, I figured why not? Because I can smell you everywhere all over the club, and it's driving me insane. All I can think about is falling to my knees for you. Do you have any idea how good you smell?"

"My scent's been compared to floor cleaner and furniture polish," I tell him.

"You smell like the ripest, sweetest, juiciest orange that was ever plucked, and I'm dying of thirst whenever I'm near you. It kills me a little inside, knowing you don't feel the same way about me after all this time. I'm so stupid." He drags his hands through his hair and rakes it away from his face. "Why do you think I took this job?"

"It pays well?" I say, but it comes out as more of a question than the statement I intended it to be.

"The pay is pretty good, but I made more money pro surfing."

"What?" I had no idea he surfed. I don't know much about his personal life outside of the club, actually. And he's been with me since the early days, almost since our doors first opened.

"Yeah, some competitions pay a lot in prizes. Plus, there are sponsorships. And I taught lessons too. One time I got a brand deal for a board wax that still pays pretty good every month. My money guy says I'm pretty set, but I don't like being stuck in the house all day and I'm too old for the circuits. I've got mad respect for the dudes still hitting the competition waves, but that's not for me anymore. I like my little slice of beach and this. Dancing at Rut gives me something to do when I'm done surfing in the morning. And all the dancing is good cardio."

He catches my eye. "Plus I get to see you. I like seeing your face every day. I'd like to see it every day forever if you'll let me."

He likes seeing my face every day, is my first thought, followed quickly by, *and that's why he's always late.* Because he's surfing before work.

I lean against the bathroom wall for support because suddenly it feels like the rug's been pulled out from under my feet. This isn't a brief infatuation or an offer to be heat fuck buddies. It's not an offer to do my laundry, either. That was a bullshit excuse. He knew what would happen if I let him into my nest during a heat. We both did.

That's why I had to say no.

And that's why he wanted me to say yes.

His expression is devastated, and I put that kicked puppy look on his face. I feel like the worst sort of person in the world. It might not seem so bad if I wasn't actually attracted to him, but I am.

And it's not only because he's hot, but also because he's sweet and thoughtful.

He offers to walk me to my car so I'm not alone in the parking lot late at night. He's always so cheerful even when I'm in a shit mood. And he makes the other dancers laugh. Being around him feels good. Easy. Natural.

"You work at Rut for *me*?" I ask.

"Yeah. There's nothing I wouldn't do for you," he says.

We're both silent as I digest this. It's like the planets are realigning in my universe. This hulking, gorgeous alpha—the one whom half of LA wants to fuck and the other half wants to be—said he wants to fall to his knees before me.

And maybe it's the preheat or being bathed in Brendan's pheromones for days that's wrecking my self-control, but that's exactly where I want him. *Stop it.* Once the idea's in my head, I can't get it out. *You can't.* The idea of Jamie on his knees for me crowds out every other thought. *It's wrong.*

My tastes are… peculiar. Could he actually swallow his pride and do it? Most alphas won't. They get too caught up in the idea of what an alpha should be. They take the dynamic stuff too seriously with their endless posturing and pecking order bullshit. But Jamie is easygoing. He's never balked at following my lead or refused a command. The alpha staff who aren't okay taking orders from an omega don't last long at Rut.

But taking orders from a boss and taking orders from a lover are different situations. If I tell him what I want, what I expect, he'll balk like all the others. Once he's refused, shown me his repulsion, I can finally get over this crush. Chalk it up to pheromone driven nonsense.

This is a bad idea.

A terrible one.

It's probably not going to end well.

But I realize I'm going to do it anyway, and a calmness settles over me now that I have a plan. He won't give up until I show him exactly why he doesn't really want me. And a part of me wants to see how far he'll go. There's only so much temptation one omega can resist.

When I tell him what I want from him and he says no, then it's not my fault this didn't work. Things can go back to how they've been.

"You want me?" I ask him.

"Yes." His eyes light up with hope. "More than anything."

"Then prove it," I command. My heart knocks against my ribs as he stares at me with those puppy dog eyes. "Get on your knees and crawl to me, alpha."

If he thinks the command is odd, he doesn't question it. Jamie sinks to his knees on the bathroom floor and goes down on his hands, and then he crawls. The entire time he does the humiliating gesture, his attention never wavers. I search his face for a hint of disgust or anger but find none of that.

Oh, shit.

Instead, he stares up at me like I'm a goddess he wants to worship.

I'm so fucked.

Because I really like the way he looks when he's on his knees at my feet.

When he's right there, he sits on his haunches and reaches for me. I lean back against the wall and lift a leg, setting my heel onto his thigh and pressing lightly till the point digs in enough so he knows I'm serious. "Did I say you could touch me?"

"No." He shakes his head to emphasize the point, his collarbone-length hair moving over his shoulders with the movement.

His gaze is adoring, as if he'd kneel on this bathroom floor all day if it pleased me. It wouldn't. Hard floors hurt after a while. I'd never want to hurt him like that, but having that sort of control over someone is a heady thought all the same.

I need to scare him off before I do something really stupid I can't take back.

"Very good, pet. Now let's discuss the ground rules. You'll tell me if I do something you don't like. Your homework will be to think about and write up a list of things you do and don't enjoy. I expect to have it in my hand when the club opens."

Jamie nods in agreement. "I can do that."

Fuck. Is he serious? "Are you seeing anyone?" I ask.

"Anthony. It's been going on for over a year now."

His cheeks tint pink, and I forget how to breathe for a moment. The sight of him kneeling at my feet and blushing makes my pelvis tighten. I didn't know both of them were bi, but now I can't get the thought of them together out of my head. What a sight that would be. One dark and slim, the other fair and broad. They'd be a beautiful study of contrasts.

"How did *that* happen?" I ask before I can stop myself. They're such opposites. Jamie is sweet and kind and gentle. Anthony is charming, a little bratty at times, and intense. If Jamie is a Golden Retriever in human form, then Anthony is a German Shepherd.

"My car broke down and his cousin owns a foreign car shop. My car is vintage, so parts aren't always easy to find. Anthony gave me rides while they were fixing it. We started hanging out."

"Is it serious?"

Jamie nods. "He's pack, but he wants to wait and find the rest before committing."

My breath hitches at the idea of Anthony sprawled out on a bed with Jamie's teeth marks decorating his throat. *What is a bite mark over a tattoo like?*

I close my eyes and take a breath before I can get too distracted. I'm not really doing this… am I? He's not balking. He's calling my bluff and—God help me—I'm trying to remember why it's such a bad idea. He's a consenting adult.

Is he really serious, though? Or are they like Nate and his boyfriend? Only looking for a fun weekend threesome?

"I'd have expectations," I warn him.

Jamie nods and waits, obedient and patient.

"I don't ask my partners for exclusivity but I don't want to be blindsided either if a lover comes to the club. All I ask is for you to respect that Rut is my home. There will be absolutely no more bathroom hook ups with customers." I think of how literal Jamie can be and rephrase it, "No hookups with customers at all. Could you handle that?"

He nods and his lips stretch into a serene smile. "Yes. I want us to help you through your heat."

Us. Him and Anthony. My nipples tighten as I picture myself sandwiched between them. Am I really doing this? It breaks all of my rules. Maybe if I weren't so close to preheat, I could stuff these feelings back down, but... I can't. Being forced into the proximity of Brendan's pheromones over the past several days has left me in a perpetual state of horny. I can't deny I want them.

"Please, Miss Vee," Jamie begs. "Please give us a chance. We won't make you sorry."

I know I should tell him to get off the floor and to forget this brief lapse in judgment happened... but the words get stuck in my throat. No matter how hard I try to force myself to say them, they won't come out. The truth is, I want them. I have for a long time. And the build up of his sweet coconut pheromones in such a small space is making it so damn hard to remember why I should say no.

Jamie leans his face against my thigh, breaking the *no touching* command, but he keeps his hands to himself so I let it go. My heel digs into him as he leans, but either he doesn't seem to notice, or he doesn't care.

"Please, Miss Vee. I'll be so good for you."

My failure to snap at him must make him bold because he nuzzles my inner thigh. His cheek rubs against me where the hem of my pencil skirt rides up my leg. He's scent marking me.

My brain short circuits, and each thought feels molasses

thick. I try to stay on track, but it's impossible when his hot breath ghosts over the sensitive skin of my thigh. "What's your safe word?"

He shrugs and closes his eyes and drags in a noisy inhale, his nostrils flaring as he scents me. When his eyes open, they're darkened with lust, and the bulge in his still-unzipped pants looks painfully hard.

"Hmm?" he hums, distracted.

"I don't play without safe words, pet."

"I don't have one. How do I get one?"

"You can use the traffic light system if you don't have your own. It's easy to remember. Green for go, yellow for slow down, red for stop. If you can't speak, you'll tap something or make a noise three times. Do you understand?"

He nods, his face still pressed against my thigh, and his lips drag against my skin with the movement. That's probably good enough, but I'd like the verbal confirmation. I press my foot down on his thigh until the heel digs in harder. "Tell me you understand, Jamie."

Jamie groans and lets his eyes close, his head tipped back to bare his throat to me in a submissive gesture that's so at odds with his alpha dynamic. The tanned expanse of his bare, unmarked throat makes my clit throb and moisture pool in my panties. I want to cover that throat with kisses and licks. Suck my temporary mark into it until his skin is purple. I can't. He has to appear attainable for the customers. That's what the fantasy we sell them is all about. But I still want to.

"Green. Greengreengreen. Miss Vee, can I lick your pussy now? Please?"

I don't know what I love more—the sight of him kneeling at my feet or his begging. With the knowledge this is a bad idea but I'm going to do it anyway, I reach down and grab the hem of my fitted skirt. It takes some wiggling until it's bunched around my hips. My shoulders press against the bathroom wall as I thrust my pelvis toward his face. Maybe once we've worked it out of our systems we can all move on.

"Since you asked so nicely, I'll let you pleasure me," I say. "You can use anything but your hands."

Jamie leans forward and presses his nose to my juncture. His hot breath fans my cloth covered pussy as he scents me. He rubs his cheek against my inner thigh until we're both covered in each other's scent. Orange and coconut sunshine mix into a delicious blend that makes me ache.

His nose brushes against the seam of my sex, the fabric sticking to the dampness pooling there as he pushes the fabric up. The broad flat of his tongue licks across my panties, the sensation dulled and teasing.

"Hmm. That's good." My hands tangle in his hair as I stroke his head between my thighs and pet him while he licks me. He's savoring me. When was the last time someone gave me pleasure while getting none in return? I must be greedy, because I want more.

His tongue swipes again and the fabric tugs against my swelling clit, but it's still only a tease. A delicious torment. My wetness soaks my panties as he presses lower, the fabric straining against my hole. It's not quite slick, but I'm probably close enough to my heat that I'm sweeter than normal.

There's a building ache in my pelvis that demands satisfaction. A desire to be filled. Stretched. Tonight, he's earning his place in my bed.

"More," I demand, scratching my nails over his scalp until he shivers.

He doesn't nudge my panties aside and sink his tongue into me like I expect. Instead, Jamie shifts and presses a kiss to my hip bone. And then he grabs the side of my panties with his teeth and tilts his neck to drag them down the curve of my ass.

Oh. Ohhhhh, fuck. That's hot.

My panties are lopsided, so he moves to the other side, hooking the fabric with his mouth and contorting to pull them down. They're twisting up and rolling around my upper thighs, but the angle is too awkward to continue as we are. The foot I still have pressed to his thigh keeps my hips slanted too much for him to work them off me easily. Jamie adjusts his posture and reaches.

"No hands," I remind him.

His eyes snap to mine, and he nods. "No hands."

He folds his arms behind his back, and I bite back a groan at the sight of him with his arms restrained behind him. One day I'll tie him like that for real. Bind his powerful arms behind his back with leather cuffs and steel. Hobble him so he has no choice but to be creative as he pleases me. He's doing such a good job by taking my panties off with his teeth. He's more eager than I thought.

It's a slow, difficult thing, but he never complains or questions why I like this. Why I'm an omega who's been wired wrong. Bossy. Bitchy. Hard. A perfectionist who's more alpha-like in temperament than the traditional submissive personality that my dynamic says I should have instead.

He does what he's told. Jamie pulls, works, and wiggles my panties down to my ankles and then I decide to help him. I lean my weight against the wall and lift one foot at a time so he can take them off me completely.

This is so much better than I could have wished for or demanded. I thought he'd nudge them aside and work his tongue beyond the gusset. I never expected him to spend ten minutes painstakingly baring me. The way he uses his lips and teeth and tongue to work the fabric off me is almost reverential.

With my panties off and my skirt bunched around my waist,

there's no hiding myself from him as he stares at me. He's eye level with my pussy and the look on his face is pure hunger.

"May I lick you, Ma'am?" he asks, his voice thick with desire. And then he waits for my answer.

The sense of power and control is intoxicating. He's more than twice my size, but I'm the one in charge. He's been very good, and good boys deserve a treat. "Yes. Lick me until I come on your tongue."

He presses a tender kiss to my mound first, then nuzzles his face between my legs. His tongue is warm and wet against me as he licks my seam, lapping up the wetness gathered there. He groans and licks deeper. The first brush of his tongue against my swollen clit makes my hips jerk against his face. *There!*

Jamie pulls away until I firm my hand on his head and nudge his head back into place where it belongs. "More. Make me come. I'm giving you what you begged for, pet."

"Thank you, Ma'am," he sighs against my mound and goes back to licking. His lips wrap around my clit as he sucks it into his mouth and wiggles his tongue under my hood, peeling it back to expose all of me for him.

It feels so good, and with every lap of his tongue and suck on my clit I forget why I fought this so hard. Why I've been such a masochist by denying myself this for so long.

"Fuck, that's good. Hmm. More, pet. Don't stop." My pussy aches to be filled, and I regret that he's not allowed to use his hands. I need more. Need him deeper. Need him to fill me. But not his cock. Not tonight. This is his apology for trying to get a stranger to blow him a few hours after he asked to help me with my heat. I'm still mad about that.

"More," I tell him. "I want you deeper." My nails dig into his shoulder as I use him for balance and lift my foot from his thigh to drape it over his other shoulder. The new position opens me up and spreads my slick folds for him to worship as he works to obey me.

His tongue slicks down to my hole and pushes in, and my head hits the wall as my eyes slide shut and a groan rips out of me. There's no sting or stretch like there would be with an alpha's cock, only a gentle filling that's enough to ease the growing ache inside me. His nose rubs against my clit as he feasts and spears me with his tongue in a pantomime of fucking.

My hand goes into his hair and I whimper as my pelvis tightens with the first inkling of my building release. My fingers tangle and tighten in his locks, pulling enough to remind him who's in charge without hurting him. His tongue fucks me faster, the hot and heavy puff of his breath against me making my clit throb in time with every exhalation.

"I'm close." *So close.* "Don't stop." My focus on the world narrows until the pleasure building between my legs is the only thing that matters. The incessant need for release can't be ignored or denied. We're too far gone to stop.

The creak of the bathroom door opening doesn't bother my lust-drunk mind. Footsteps on tile are enough to make me glance up as Anthony steps into the bathroom while my world unravels.

My walls clamp down on Jamie's tongue and I forget how to breathe as I come with a cry that turns into a ragged moan. My ankle wobbles as I struggle to maintain my balance on these heels. If the wall wasn't at my back and Jamie wasn't half propping me up, I might keel right over and curl up for a good, long nap once my pussy stops quivering.

Bright blue eyes fringed by impossibly long dark lashes stare at me while my body spasms with aftershocks, my clit throbbing against Jamie's face as he licks me clean. Anthony smiles as he looks over at us and takes in the sight we make. "He's good with his mouth."

Fuck. We're caught. In my distraction, I forgot Anthony might still be here. *What should I do?*

"Isn't he?" Anthony asks, one brow arching.

"What?" I grab the hem of my skirt and tug it down to cover myself.

Jamie leans back on his heels and smiles up at us, his face slick with my fluids and his smile wide. "She tastes good."

"Oh?" Anthony asks. "I want a taste." He grins.

Chapter Five

VERONICA

I slide my leg off Jamie's shoulder and tug my skirt down to cover myself as he leans up, his big body stretching. Anthony meets him halfway, and they press their mouths together in an open, sloppy kiss. Their tongues tangle as Anthony laps my arousal from Jamie's lips and mouth.

Anthony pulls away, smiling. "Hmm. Now *that* is what I'd call decadent," Anthony says. He presses one last kiss to Jamie's mouth. "Hey, babe."

"Hey."

Then Anthony stands up straight and turns his attention to me. With one arm leaned against the wall over my head, he leans in and gives me a Cheshire grin. "Did he do a good job?"

With my preheat hormones satisfied, guilt and doubt creep back in and make me hesitant. This was a lapse in judgment. It never should have happened. Especially since they're dating.

So fucking irresponsible. I know better than to trust a guy's word that their partner's cool with it. Whatever the fallout is, I deserve it for thinking with my pussy. "He did."

Anthony nods. "He's good with his hands, but he's even

better with his mouth." The sound of a belt buckle clinking open is loud in the otherwise silent room.

I glance down and watch Anthony unbutton and unzip his black jeans. He's not wearing underwear. He frees his cock and fists the base, sliding his hand up and down the shaft to plump it. It's average in thickness for a beta, but long, with a slender ruddy head that flares at the corona. My breath catches at the sight of the silver piercing looped through the opening. A bead of clear pre-cum is already pearling at his pierced tip. I've never been with a guy who was pierced down there before.

"What are you doing?"

"He's good at sucking cock too, aren't you, babe?" Anthony asks.

"I am. I'm a good cocksucker."

Jamie leans toward Anthony. He doesn't flinch when Anthony taps that pierced cock against his lips three times until the pre-cum dribbles and smears. He opens and sucks the tip into his mouth, his eyes going half-lidded, and then he bobs with practiced, familiar movements.

Anthony sighs and his hips cant back and forth as they find their rhythm. But his eyes are on me as he fucks his boyfriend's mouth on the floor of Rut's bathroom.

"He's so pretty with a cock in his mouth, isn't he?" Anthony asks.

I squirm under the attention, unsure of what to say. So I settle on the truth. "He's beautiful."

I watch Jamie suck on that cock. His cheeks hollow, and Anthony grunts. They make wet, slurping sounds together. And then my view is obscured as Anthony leans in and hovers his mouth over mine, close enough to feel his breath on my lips without them touching. My heart knocks against my ribs and my breathing shallows as he waits.

"Are you always in charge?" he asks, his voice controlled

and steady despite the uptick in his breathing as Jamie swallows him down.

I lick my lips, and a small thrill goes through me when his eyes follow the movement. "Usually." *Where did that husky, seductive voice come from?*

He reaches up, his movements slow so I have time to move away, and drags two fingers gently along the side of my face. His hand moves down to my neck, then slides around to the back and up. He grabs a fistful of hair and gets a good enough squeeze so I know he has me.

"I'm always in charge," Anthony says.

I wait for the usual panic of being trapped and pinned to come, but it never does. Because he's a beta? Because I've known him for years? Or because he's only a couple of inches taller than me and I think he could take me? I'm not sure, but I'm not scared.

My nipples tighten into hard little peaks that scrape against my bra and ache. It's a strange sensation to go from topspace to subspace. I can't say that I've ever experienced one right after another before.

It's dizzying. Subspace makes my thoughts hazy and sluggish.

"In the bedroom, maybe," I say. "I'm not interested in being told what to do outside of that."

"Hmm… Are you sure about that?" Anthony asks. "Sometimes you like it when I'm pushy. Like when you're not taking proper care of yourself."

I ignore Jamie's slurping sounds and Anthony's grip in my hair. But I can't ignore the smell of them. On their own, they're great. Together, they're breathtaking. Jamie's coconut and Anthony's cherry blend together enchantingly.

"I take care of myself fine," I argue.

His grip softens and turns into stroking along the back of

my neck. He teases the sensitive skin behind my ears. "But we could take care of you better. If you'll let us." Anthony leans down, his lips a breath away. "The question is, will you let us? Or are you too scared you'll like it?"

"This is a bad idea." What was I thinking? I wasn't. I can blame it on pheromones or preheat or jealousy, but I wasn't thinking straight. Not with my head, anyway. We shouldn't do this. What I've already done is bad enough, but taking it further will only make it worse.

"Then why are you leaning into me?"

"I'm not, I…" I am.

I'm stretching up on my toes to get closer. My nostrils flare as I drag his scent in deeper with each breath. It's the tiny bath-room. There's nowhere to get away from their pheromones. And my omega urges have been dredged too close to the surface for me to stay rational while in the thick of them.

Anthony tilts his head and his nose brushes against mine. "I think you are. I think you want this, but it scares you, so you're fighting it. I think you want us as badly as we want you."

"We shouldn't… I shouldn't have…"

"Then tell me to stop. But you better mean it, Vee."

He leans down slowly. Fingertips run up the side of my neck and skim over my earlobes. My nipples scrape against my bra and I do my best to block out the filthy noises Jamie's making down below. I can't deny how much they excite me. How they leave my pussy slippery. How much my body wants this even if it's crazy and wrong. But my lips don't want to form the five short words that will end this. *I want you to stop.* Because I don't.

Anthony's mouth comes down to mine in a gentle kiss that's so different from what I expected. I'm pinned against the wall, but I could still get away if I wanted to. I know from experience my elbows are bony and my stilettos can do some real damage.

I've had to do it before when a guy got too insistent and didn't want to listen.

The gentleness of the kiss lulls me, makes me pliant as the kiss deepens. Intensifies until I can't think of anything else. Anthony ravages my mouth. Steals my breath and all sense of reason. He leaves me panting and my clit throbbing. My panties are somewhere on the floor, and slickness makes a mess of me again as arousal gathers between my legs. Despite my protests, I return it.

When I lean into the kiss, Anthony twists his tongue around mine. He groans, and I swallow the sound. Wet sucking sounds make my thighs slippery, and when our kiss breaks, I study the agony etched into Anthony's face.

"Stop, babe," he says to Jamie. "I won't come until I'm inside her."

It's such a presumptuous statement. So cocky. But his confidence is attractive.

It doesn't matter that I've just had an orgasm. The preheat makes me ready for another, and suddenly the idea of being stretched by that cock and learning how his piercing feels down there is way too tempting to say no.

We shouldn't do this. I'm their boss. They're my employees. But, God, it's gonna be so damn good while we do it.

"Do you have a condom?" I ask him.

"Don't need one. We both got checked last week." He uses his free hand to drag the edge of my blouse from the waistband of my skirt and then he moves onto the buttons.

"You either need condoms or papers. I'm on the pill and I've tested negative, but you still need one or the other." There's a lot of fucking that happens in this bar, and while I've never seen Anthony or Jamie hook up with a patron before today's interlude I interrupted, a person can never be too safe.

"Here." He pulls a folded up sheet of paper from his back

pocket and hands it to me. Then he goes back to what he was doing. He pops the buttons free one by one until the shirt falls open.

The papers crinkle as I unfold them and read the print out from a lab. There's a line of negatives down both pages, one for each of them. I frown as I read through them. "Do you always carry medical documents around on the off chance you might need them?"

"What can I say?" He grins and pops the final button apart. "I'm a regular Boy Scout. Satisfied?"

Before I can answer, Anthony turns his attention to my chest. I expect him to go right for my breasts, but he teases me with whisper light touches of his fingertips over my stomach and collarbone. He grazes the edge of my bra. The tickling is infuriating as much as it's tantalizing. When he finally glides a hand over one breast and its painfully hard-tipped peak, I groan and press it more firmly into his hand. The papers fall from my hand, forgotten.

Jamie groans. "I want to watch. Let me watch, please."

"You'll do more than watch," Anthony says. "You'll be her mattress. Lie down, babe."

Jamie lies down on the bathroom floor, and his hands go to his jeans. He finishes unzipping them and shoves them down. He's not wearing any underwear either.

His huge alpha cock is rock hard and dripping. It slaps against his stomach with unwieldy fullness. It bulges at the base before narrowing toward the tip. His balls are big and his pubic hair is neatly trimmed, so everything is all on display. The wrinkles of excess skin at the base of his shaft show that he'll have an impressive knot when he comes. Darlene's statement that he's a grower, not a shower, is true.

Anthony tugs the cup of my bra down until my breast spills out of it. He curls over me to lick his tongue across the tip.

"Brown. I've been wondering if your nipples were brown or pink," he says.

He sucks the peak into his mouth, the pleasure traveling straight through my body to my pulsing clit. His teeth graze the sensitive area, and I moan and bury my fingers in his messy hair. He nips me and I gasp, and then he lets my nipple go with a wet pop and tugs me away from the wall.

"You've been thinking about my nipples?"

I teeter on my heels until he steadies me. He's a flurry of activity as he tugs my shirt all the way free of my skirt and pulls it from me.

"Every single day." His eyes devour me. "God, you're so fucking pretty. On your knees for me, pretty girl. I'll make you feel so damn good."

He nudges and pushes me down so I'm straddling Jamie, then leans over the both of us until we're positioned exactly as he wants. He's demanding, and my mind is made of cotton batting. Fuzzy and soft.

How long has it been since I felt safe enough with a lover to let go? Lose myself in the moment and enjoy it? It's not like I remember much of what happens with the alphas I meet on Heat Buddy. Those hookups are brief and they're not usually memorable. Once they realize I'm not their dream omega, they can't wait to leave fast enough.

Anthony positions us both like we're dolls until Jamie's cock sits between my spread lips, his crown kissing my clit. Moisture pools between us, and I don't know if it's my arousal or his. Probably both of ours.

"Is this okay?" I ask Jamie.

Jamie trembles and nods as I rock and rub my clit against him, using him to find my pleasure.

There's a ripping sound as Anthony grabs my bunched up skirt and hikes it higher. I'm past caring about the state of my wardrobe when he kneels behind me and hard steel slides against my warm core. I gasp and rock forward and Jamie curses under his breath, his eyes squeezed shut. The veins in his neck pop from strain.

Am I too heavy? "I think I'm hurting him," I say as I move to get off Jamie.

Anthony's fingers tighten on my hips as he keeps me in place. "I can promise you that you're not hurting him in a way he doesn't fucking love. Isn't that right, babe?"

Jamie nods and cracks his eyes open, and from this distance I see that they're not brown like I've always thought, but hazel. "Please use me, Ma'am. I'm good. I'll use my safe word if I need to, I promise."

I nibble on my lower lip and nod, then settle.

"You picked a safe word with her?" Anthony asks, his tone curious.

"Yeah," Jamie says. "Green, yellow, and red."

"Interesting," Anthony says softly. "Are those your safe words too?"

I look over my shoulder and nod. "Yes. What do you normally use?"

"No, stop, don't," he says in a calm voice.

I shrug and hate how admitting this makes me a bit self-conscious. "Sometimes pretending to resist can be fun. But don't pin me down. I hate that."

His expression is calculating. As if he's trying to rethink a conclusion he's already made. "Interesting. Okay. You got it. I'll ignore your protests unless you use a safe word."

To distract him from thinking about this too deeply, I wiggle my hips so his piercing's teasing my hole, but his tight grip on my hips keeps me from impaling myself on his length. He won't let me fuck myself on his cock because he's the one in control right now, and I… I like it more than I thought I would.

"Are you waiting for a formal invitation?" I ask.

"Hmm," he says, his fingers digging in until they make divots in my skin.

Anthony's piercing has warmed up since he's been slicking it through my wet folds. His tip presses at my entrance and he surges, sinking in with two insistent thrusts. I'm so wet, there's nothing to stop his glide as he pushes in all the way to the root and pauses there.

"Oh, fuck yes," I moan and drop my head.

His cock is perfect. Not too big or too small or too thick. Enough to make me full without struggling to take him outside of the delirium of a cock-crazy heat or an extensive warmup.

"Fuck," he grunts, his hands heavy on my hips as he tilts my ass high, then reaches up to nudge my shoulders down so I'm flush against Jamie's front. The alpha's cock twitches and jumps against my clit when Anthony gives an experimental thrust. "So fucking good. Your cunt is heaven, Vee. Are you ready?"

I don't know why he's asking, because he's already started. He makes slow, lazy thrusts that hit the end of me and press. "Mmhmm."

He pulls back and thrusts hard, his groin snapping against my ass with a loud slap of skin against skin. The force of it drags me over Jamie's trapped cock, the bump of his crown and bulging veins adding texture to the rough slide.

"Oh, God," I say and suck in a breath. My palms grip Jamie's muscular shoulders as I ride him while my bartender fucks me on the dirty bathroom floor.

"That's good," Anthony chatters. "That is top-shelf pussy. I knew it would be. Such a fucking tease walking around in those tight skirts and high heels. Smelling so fucking good. So juicy and goddamn biteable. Do you get off on teasing an entire room full of alphas with that sweet arousal? That slick? Knowing everyone coming here wants a taste?"

I frown. "That's not why they come to Rut. I'm not the reason—"

His hand comes down on my ass in a spank that's more sound than pain. I startle and yelp and jerk against Jamie, who groans, his hard cock trapped underneath me. The poor alpha is subjected to my every movement and none of them are careful, but he hasn't used his safeword, so I force myself to relax.

"Do you have any idea how special you are?" Anthony asks. His hands tighten on my ass and he spreads my cheeks. His pace slows to something more savory.

"I'm really not special, I—"

Anthony fists my hair again and drags my head back, making my spine arch and all my body weight come down on Jamie's cock as he tugs me off balance. "Don't you ever say anything bad about yourself where I can hear it. Do you understand me?" His hips snap and he thrusts deep.

"I…" I don't know what he wants from me. This isn't the sort of dirty talk I'm used to hearing.

"This is special, decadent, top-shelf pussy and you are a thoughtful, kind, and caring woman." He punctuates every couple of words with a thrust that makes it hard to follow the conversation.

"People usually call me a bitch."

Anthony stills and grunts, then leans down so his lips are by my ear. "Words like that are going to earn a bad girl a punishment. Is that what you want, baby? For me to spank those filthy words right out of your mouth?"

Baby? While I think about it, I move. I glide my pussy over Jamie's cock, rocking Anthony's in deeper. "Which word? Bitch?"

He growls in my ear and I go still, some primal part of my

brain taking over. It's not an alpha bark, but it makes the omega side of me—the part I squash so ruthlessly because weakness is shame—want to bare my neck all the same. "You must need your mouth washed out with cum after saying such filthy things."

I suppress a laugh and frown. "Don't you mean soap?"

"No." He presses a chaste kiss to the corner of my mouth, then pulls out of me. "I definitely did not mean soap. Take your spanking like a good girl and I'll let you come on my cock."

I whine at the loss of him and regret all of my teasing. Anthony tugs my hips until my ass is in the air. Jamie reaches up and cards my hair from my face, gathering it to the back of my neck and cradling it out of the way.

A hand comes down on my ass and rocks me forward, and I grunt from the heavy impact. "No warmup?" I ask.

He brings his palm down on the other cheek with an equally thuddy slap. "Warmups are for good girls. Naughty girls get spanked so hard they think about their lesson every time they sit the next day."

Oh, fuck. I like his dark promise. It makes my body taut with anticipation.

"Will you take your lesson like a good girl?" he asks.

I barely think about it before I agree. "Yes."

Anthony makes good on his promise and spanks me until the skin is hot, each slap like jagged glass. Despite the force of the spanking, he's competent, and that's sexy as hell. He keeps the blows to the curve of my ass and the dreaded, beautiful sweet spot. There's nothing worse than an amateur spanker getting your hip bone because they can't tell the difference.

This hurts too, but deliciously. It's been a while since a guy did more than give me one or two halfhearted slaps when I asked for it during sex. But Anthony? Anthony is ruthless. The strikes get heavier until we both know I'll bruise. I bite my lip and grunt with the next hard blow.

It's only because I've worked with him for so long and I trust him that I'm able to let go and enjoy this. The man who force feeds me vegetables because he's worried I don't eat enough of them isn't going to actually hurt me. And if he does, I'll stab him with my stiletto and run. I'm fast when I need to be and ruthless when it counts. I've had to fight before when another foster thought he could take advantage since we lived together.

The next spank breaks the dam, and tears roll down my cheeks as all the stress and worry and panic leaves me in a flood of oxytocin and endorphin-saturated tears. He rubs me down, the sensation equal parts comforting and agony, as the over-sensitized skin tingles and burns.

"Say *thank you, Daddy*," Anthony orders.

"I'm not saying that."

"No?" He rubs me again, but this time with his short nails. The scrape of them on the overly-sensitive skin makes all my nerves light up. "That's a pity. But I guess if you want more…"

I gasp, and he drags his nails over my glowing buttocks harder. I can't take more, but I'll be damned if I use my safe word the first time we play together. Especially not over something like a spanking.

"What do you say? Do you want more, or are you done?" he asks.

"Thank you, D-Daddy," I stumble over the unfamiliar words.

I've never called anyone that before. If it were someone other than Anthony, I'd have probably laughed myself hoarse. There's something about his energy, his dark vibe, that speaks of control and comfort. Like a collared tiger. Well trained, safe for the most part, but with an undercurrent of caged violence that makes petting it exciting.

"You're welcome, baby."

My reward is the kiss of his cock at my entrance, and I sigh with satisfaction when he hits the end of me and does it again. He sinks home and stretches me as I go limp and lie on top of Jamie.

I use the alpha as my mattress. Jamie's chest rises and falls underneath my cheek, and his cock drags against my clit as Anthony fucks me, his hips slamming against my smarting ass. The smacks turn the pain into delicious pleasure.

My pelvis tightens as need coils, but it's still too far out of reach. I've never had multiple orgasms outside of a heat and I already came, so the next one is going to be more difficult. I need more stimulation than this slow, luxurious drag. Need him to fuck me so hard I can't think. If I start thinking, I'll worry about how I've made a huge mistake I don't want to stop and can't take back.

"Fuck me harder," I order.

He grunts and quickens his pace. Every smack of his pelvis against my bruised ass lights my nerves up like a Christmas tree, and Jamie's slippery, hard cock adds enough pressure on my clit that I'm getting there.

"Damn, that's good, baby. Squeeze my cock. Your pussy's so fucking tight. I love the way you clamp onto me, like you don't want to let me go. Don't worry, baby. I'm not going anywhere until I've stuffed this pretty pussy so full of cream it's dripping."

"I'm—fuck, right there—God, don't stop," I pant.

"Anthony, I'm close," Jamie says. "I can't hold it back."

"Then don't, babe. Come for me."

Jamie tenses underneath me, and his knot knocks against my hole where Anthony's buried deep. The alpha comes with a grunt, and wetness makes us both sticky as he spills his seed all over his belly and soaks me too.

Anthony chuckles again and leans back to get a deeper angle as he fucks me harder, each thrust dragging me over Jamie's cock from knot to head. The bumps make my toes curl so hard that one of my heels falls off my foot.

"One day I'm gonna find your birth control pills and throw them out," Anthony says. "Then I'm gonna make him watch me put a baby in you."

Alarm flickers through me as I panic until I remember I'm on the pill and this is only preheat. "Are you insane?"

Even if I found my pack and I wanted to—and I don't—I can't have a baby right now. This is a pivotal moment for the club. Everything is riding on this audit and the next couple of years. Everything else has to wait.

"Been called worse." Anthony chuckles, his cock jumping with each laugh as he continues to fuck me. "Don't pretend you hate the idea. You got wetter. Listen to how wet this pussy is at the thought of me putting a baby in it one day."

Despite my denials, my pussy tightens down on his cock. Typical omega breeding kink. We're sluts for cum. Obsessed with finding safety in a partner or a pack and pumping out babies to keep them engaged. It's in our fucking genes. Hard-wired into our essence and reinforced one love-obsessed book or movie at a time.

The idea of Anthony trying to knock me up while Jamie watches makes my clit throb with every drag over the alpha's cock. There's only one surefire way to keep an alpha from breeding an omega during a heat and that's abstinence. Alpha semen is aggressive. Hyperfertile. When both alphas and betas are present, it'll always win.

"I'll wear you down one day," Anthony boasts. "I always

get what I want in the end. You'd look so pretty all bit up and bred. Like you're ours."

Despite my irritation with him, I moan as I come. My walls clamp down on Anthony's cock to milk the cum from his balls. He stutters out a curse and follows me, his thrusts slowing and working deeper. His cock pulses as it fills me.

I'm dripping when he finishes and pulls out. He orders me to squeeze and work it out so he can watch. All three of us are a sticky, sweaty, blissed-out mess.

For the first time in forever, I'm not anxious or stressed. Not thinking about payroll or spreadsheets or beer orders. I'm not worried about the audit or Rut getting shut down. Anthony drops a kiss to the base of my neck, the place where a bite goes, then pulls away.

He slides my shoe back onto my foot and helps me stand.

"That was perfect, baby."

His praise leaves my body warm and loose and my head confused.

When I'm vertical, I notice the smarting in my knees. I'm getting too old for floor sex. Anthony draws me into his arms and kisses me, then lets me go so he can help Jamie up off the floor.

I wiggle my skirt down and button my sticky shirt while I make my excuses and flee before things can get weird. What was hot five minutes ago is rapidly cooling and congealing.

Tomorrow will be awkward and full of regrets for all of us. Things will be different now. For better or worse. Probably worse, knowing my luck.

I make it to my car before them and peel out of the nearly empty lot, driving home in a haze of muscle memory and shame. I'm no better than the bride-to-be who got caught trying to blow the stripper.

I broke my rule not once, but twice. And tomorrow I'll have

to face that. It might not be too late. They got a nice orgasm, worked their boss lady fantasy out of their systems, and now we can all pretend this never happened. Things will go back to exactly how they were.

I wouldn't be good for them anyway. I work too much and I'm never home. Boyfriends always want more and end up leaving when they realize I won't budge. I'm not restructuring my entire life around a man or two. I'm definitely not settling down and popping out babies like a good little omega.

My reddened ass smarts the entire drive home, and when I undress while the shower's heating, I realize I forgot to grab my underwear off the floor.

I'll have to get to Rut early in the morning to make sure someone doesn't find them before I can hide them. The bar's advanced pheromone filtering system will make sure nobody can smell what we did last night, but even industrial-grade HEPA filters won't work on arousal-soaked fabric.

I go up on my tiptoes and angle my head to get a better look at my ass in the fogging bathroom mirror. The darkness shadowing my skin tells me the bruises are going to be glorious. I brush my fingertips over the skin and think of them before telling myself to stop.

It was a one-time lapse in judgment. Jamie might be infatuated or have a crush, but I'd only disappoint him when he realized that Rut is my life. I'm married to it. It's my baby. And I'm not sure there's room for anything else.

Nobody actually wants to come in second place.

I'm a bad omega.

Chapter Six

ANTHONY

"WILL YOU COME OVER?" JAMIE ASKS WHEN WE GET TO OUR cars in the parking lot. His pink cheeks are barely visible in the harsh fluorescent street lighting. It takes a lot for him to gather up the courage to ask for things, so I don't ever deny him when he does it.

"Of course, babe," I say, looking at him fondly when he smiles. "You need more cuddles?"

I need to talk to Vee about proper aftercare. She didn't stick around for hers or Jamie's, and both scenarios are unacceptable. She seems to think she doesn't deserve the affection she's earned after a good, hard fuck, and that thought makes my chest ache for her. Our girl deserves better. "I'll follow you."

The roads aren't empty even though it's nearly three in the morning. LA is a town that never fully sleeps. The bars and clubs are empty, but that doesn't mean people go home.

Jamie's place is closer to the club than my apartment. And nicer. Plus it's a single-family home. The beachside shack, a tiny sunny yellow house that was built right in the sand, is cozy and comfortable. His neighbors' houses are right on top of him, and his lot is the size of a postage stamp, but who needs a yard when the entire ocean is only a few steps away?

He pulls his old turquoise VW van into his single-car garage, and I park in the driveway behind him. I meet him inside his dark garage and grab him by his belt loops, pulling him against me and fisting my hand in his shirt to force him to bend until his mouth is right where I want it—fitted to mine. The pose is aggressive, but my kiss is gentle as I slide my lips against his and claim his mouth as *mine*.

Jamie is the first to pull away with a low laugh. He reaches past me and up behind my head. "At least let me get the garage closed before you maul me."

"Worried someone might see?" I tease him. "Don't want your neighbors watching the big, strong alpha getting on his knees for a beta?"

The metal door click-clacks and bangs as he rolls it down until gravity carries it the rest of the way and it crashes shut. We only have a minute of light before the garage door opener's timer runs out. "No. You know I don't care about that, babe," Jamie says. "But I'm exhausted from the show and I'd rather do this in bed."

"Lead the way." I reach around and smack his ass, then follow him inside.

We fill our bellies with cold Chinese leftovers, then take a quick shower together. His sweatpants are too big on me, so I cinch the waist tight and roll the band until they're snug on my slimmer hips. He's offered me a drawer to keep my things, but I enjoy wearing his stuff. It's soft, and it smells like him.

In bed, Jamie is the little spoon. I wrap my arm around him and go up on the other elbow so I can see his face while we talk.

"You did a good job today," I tell him, enjoying the way he blushes with the praise. "Good work, babe." I slide my hand up and down his arm and wiggle against him until there's no space between us.

"Thanks." Jamie lays his hand over mine and threads his fingers with mine. "At one point I thought I messed it all up, but you were right."

"So what do you think?" I ask him.

"It's her. I knew it would be, but… it's really her. I can feel it. Smell it. Taste it."

It's the answer I expected. We've talked about this for months now. "She won't make it easy to court her. Vee seems determined to do the opposite of what society thinks an omega should be and do."

Jamie threads his hand with mine and presses it to his flat stomach. "I know. That's what I love about her. And she's so pretty and smart."

"What did she say about helping her through her heat?" I ask.

"Ah… I'm sorry. That's the part I messed up. I told you that you should do it. I never know what to say to her. She's just so pretty that I forget what I'm supposed to say and then the words come out, but they're wrong. Half the time I don't remember what I said."

"It can't have gone that badly," I insist, smoothing a lock of hair off her face. "She let you eat her out."

He snorts, his belly moving under my hand with the rapid movement. "It was bad. I quit Rut."

"What?" I sit up so I can see him better and the guilty look on his face makes my heart drop into my stomach. "What happened?"

Jamie waves his hand in the air for dramatic emphasis. "She said she'd never let me help her with her heat while I worked for her."

A headache forms between my eyes, and I let his hand go so

I can pinch the bridge of my nose. "So you quit. Okay… We can fix this. It's okay," I reassure him. "I'll talk to her when Rut opens."

He rolls over so he's facing me, his eyes wide and sad. "I took it back right away. You should have seen her, she almost cried! I felt horrible. I'm the worst alpha ever. I almost made my omega cry. And then I…" Jamie scrubs a hand over his face and he looks near to tears himself.

It's probably the subdrop making things seem worse than they are. She ended up in our arms tonight, so whatever happened, it's salvageable. I can fix this. I know it.

"Hey, it's okay." I rub his shoulder and brush his hair from his face. "She let you lick her, right? If she hated you, she wouldn't have done that."

"Really?" he asks, his voice watery and thin.

"Really. And you're not a bad alpha. If you were, I wouldn't love you."

His smile is slow and weak, but hopeful. "I love you too. So you can fix it?"

"I'll fix it. I promise. Want to tell me what happened with the redhead?"

Jamie sighs. "She cornered me and told me there was something I had to see in the bathroom. By the time I realized there was nothing wrong, she already had her hand in my pants. And then, I don't know, I guess all the pheromones got to me and I thought if Vee was never gonna be with us… She smelled okay. I thought maybe we needed to try with someone else. I'm sorry. Are you mad?"

I bite back a comment that fooling around with a bride at her bachelorette party isn't a good way to meet omegas. It'll only make him feel bad and it won't change anything. But I don't like that he was cornered and felt like he had to go along with what some stranger wanted. That's not okay. If that bride had been a guy, I'd have kicked his ass.

"That's assault," I tell Jamie.

"What? I never… I wouldn't."

"Not from you," I say before he gets too confused and worked up. "From her. She shouldn't have touched you like that. I'm not mad, babe. We've talked about it enough. The only way we're going to find the others is if we're flexible. But I knew it was weird that you were gone for so long. I should have looked for you sooner. But then Vee came downstairs and I got distracted watching her. I'm sorry I let that happen. I'll talk to Dan about the redhead. She'll probably be too embarrassed to come back, at least for a while."

Jamie gives me an odd look. "I doubt it. They touch us all the time. I'm used to it."

"That doesn't make it right." Neither of us pushes the subject anymore, and when the silence grows uncomfortable and Jamie's expression is far too serious, I distract him. "I have a treat for you."

"A treat?" he asks. His face lights up with pleasure, and I grin.

I slip from the bed and find my discarded jeans on the floor and pull the waded up fabric from the back pocket. I hold it up for him to see. My trophy from tonight's success.

"Are those…" He's breathless and struck dumb.

Vee's panties are tiny and ballet slipper pink with sheer lace along on the top and leg holes. I slingshot it at Jamie, and it hits him dead center in his chest. He palms it reverentially, then brings it to his nose and drags in her scent. It's soaked with her pheromones and pleasure, and the combination makes him purr.

I love seeing him happy like this. Content. I wish I was enough to keep him satisfied, but he needs a pack. So that's what we're building.

"I thought you'd like a souvenir," I say as I climb back into bed and grab it from him. His fingers tighten with an alpha's urge to lay claim, and then he remembers himself and lets go. His gray sweatpants bulge with the proof of his happiness. I stroke a hand over his erection until he thickens to fullness. He's got such a nice cock.

"Look at how hard you're getting for me." I grin.

"Thank you," Jamie says while I tug the waistband of his sweats down until his thick cock bobs free.

I wrap the pink fabric around his cock and stroke him once, savoring the way his nostrils flare and his eyes go unfocused. He's so delightfully responsive. So perfectly receptive to my every whim. He might not understand why I enjoy dominating him so much—Jamie doesn't have a dominant bone in his body —but he appreciates the aftermath. We both do.

"You like that, babe?" I ask. "You like knowing I stole these for you? How something that touched her pussy all day is stroking your cock? This is the closest your cock's ever been to her pussy, hasn't it?"

He nods, his hips twitching with the urge to thrust and fuck the ring of my fingers and the panties wrapped around his cock. "Yes. Feels so good. Smells good too."

"I got to fuck that sweet, juicy pussy tonight, and you had to watch. It must drive you mad, babe, knowing all you get to do is watch while I fuck our omega. I should have made you get on your knees and lick her cunt juice off my cock. Made you blow me, knowing she came all over it. You'd like that, wouldn't you?"

"Yes," he pants, his pre-cum soaking the fabric and staining the pale pink dark.

"Look at you getting her panties all dirty." I tsk and tug harder, faster, until his abdominals flex and tense with every belly-fluttering movement as he fucks the tight ring of my hand.

I palm his heavy sack and tease over the base of his cock where his knot is swelling. He's already close. Her preheat pheromones must be driving him mad with need.

"I'm so bad," he groans, lost in the fantasy. In his cravings. He loves this.

"Such a bad boy," I agree. And I love this too. I love pushing all of his kinky buttons. Riling him up.

My boyfriend is addicted to shame. Humiliation. He needs it. Needs to be put in those deep, dark fears of his so he can face them with someone safe. Someone who'd never use those secret thoughts to actually hurt him. So he can come out of the scene and know he's still loved despite those intrusive thoughts. Cherished.

He shudders as I pump my hand. Seeing him unravel is delicious. My sweet, kind, loyal alpha. Undone by a scrap of fabric and a wisp of a barky omega. What will he do when I unveil the next phase of our plans to court her? I grin whenever I think about it.

From the way his nostrils flare and he grunts with every rise of his hips, I know he's close. I could slow down. Stop. Order him to flip onto his belly and present his ass for me like he's the omega. Claim him and ride him hard. Make him come harder than anyone else ever did. And he would do it. Because he's perfect. Because he's mine.

My grip tightens as I tug and twirl and twist with my wrist. After all these months, I can read his body like an open book. Salty, musky, coconutty pre-cum slides down my knuckles and soaks into Vee's underwear.

When my alpha is seconds away from coming, I lean down close and press my lips to his ear. He's panting hard. "One day, when she's bitten and claimed and ours, I'm gonna make you watch me breed her. And there will be nothing you can do to stop me. I'll tie you down if I have to. I'll make you raise my baby."

"Oh, f-fuck." Jamie gasps and his thrusts turn into a languid rolling movement as the first splash of his cum dribbles down my fingers. His swelling knot bumps against my thumb and index finger. I grab it with my other hand and crush it tight, mimicking the knot squeeze my beta body can't produce.

My reward is another splash of coconut-scented cum. There's so much of it, so much more than normal. It must be her preheat pheromones triggering him. I can't wait to see him in a rut from her heat. Desperate, yet denied. He'll be radiant with his unmet desire. And the fallout of finally releasing him will be resplendent.

"Bad boy," I tease him as I grab a tissue from his nightstand and wipe the cum from my hands and then his stomach. "You've made such a mess. Let's get you cleaned up." Once we're both clean, I fold the panties up carefully and set them aside on the nightstand for later. I have plans for those.

"What about you?" he asks, but his voice is already sleepy and he yawns.

It's late. Well past our bedtime. And Jamie wakes up at an ungodly hour, no matter how little sleep he got the night before. I tug his waistband up and press a kiss to the corner of his mouth.

"I'll take a rain check. You can thank me in the morning."

"It's morning now," he says in protest, but it's halfhearted and he's already falling asleep.

"Go to sleep, babe. I'm satisfied by holding you."

I tug the blankets over the both of us and curl myself around his powerful body. At some point in the night he'll be so hot he's impossible to cuddle, but for now it's a pleasant warmth. And I love holding him while he sleeps.

THE SMELL OF COFFEE RIGHT BY MY NOSE WAKES ME, AND I grunt and fling an arm over my eyes to shield them from the sun. Why the fuck are his curtains so ridiculously sheer? "It's too early."

Jamie chuckles, and the bed dips as he sits, and then a hand ruffles through my hair. "It's nine. You said you wanted to get to Rut early today."

I heave a weary sigh, then crack my eyes open and regret it immediately. "You're right. Thanks for waking me." I take the hot mug from him and sip it gingerly. The first hit of caffeine is almost as good as the first cigarette of the day. "What time did you get up?"

"Six."

"Masochist." I scrub a hand down my face and wipe the crust from my eyes.

He chuckles and rises to shower and dress, and I take a moment to appreciate the view as he strips his wetsuit off and hangs it up. God, he's gorgeous. His blond hair is wet and dark from the ocean, and he's still absolutely delicious after only three hours of sleep. I don't know how he does it. No matter what position I sleep in, I always look like a depressed goblin nightmare boy first thing in the morning.

I drag my sorry ass out of bed before the temptation to roll over and go back to sleep can claim me. While he showers, I throw on my dirty clothes from last night and head out to his balcony with my cigarettes and coffee.

The ocean might not be as fun for me to swim in as Jamie finds it, but the view sure is nice. An elderly couple dressed in matching pink polo shirts and white visors walks by and waves. I return the gesture with my coffee mug before I drain it. The wind tousles my hair and I shake my head to get it out of my face.

"Those'll kill you," Jamie says behind me.

"Not fast enough." Our routine is familiar. The words never change, and that's comforting in its own way, even if it's scary. I've never done *forever* before. It's nice, though. Especially with Jamie. He's the only alpha I've ever met who doesn't, on some level, think he's better than me because of our dynamics.

I flick the ash into the ceramic ashtray he bought for me and placed here where I like to smoke. We've never spoken of its appearance, but I know it wasn't there the first night he brought me to his home.

"Do you want a protein shake?" he asks as he heads back inside to the kitchen. Jamie pulls out his blender, then rifles through his fridge.

"Now *that* shit will kill you." I snub my cigarette out, then pull the sliding glass door shut behind me until it latches.

"How?" he asks, his nose crinkling with amused confusion as he looks back at me.

"Sadness." I plant a kiss on his cheek, mindful of my cigarette and coffee breath and my dire need of a toothbrush, then grab my things. "See ya later, babe."

"You're not riding in with me?" he asks.

"Not today. Got work to do. Love ya."

"I love you too."

There's not enough time to stop by my apartment if I want to get to Rut early so I drive straight to the club. I should probably keep a change of clothes and a toothbrush in my car if this is going to keep happening.

I hope it happens again.

Rush hour traffic is almost done at this hour. That's one perk of this job. The main perk is working with Veronica. Now all I need is to figure out how to get the stubborn omega to bend. My fingers tap with the rhythm of the radio as I pull into the parking lot and park in my usual spot.

I'm the first one here. *Good.* I pull my visor down, flip the mirror open, and run a hand through my hair until it's less insane-looking, and then I head inside with the help of my key. I flip the lights on and make sure everything's in order, and then I take the stairs to her office two at a time. I have the key to this door too, since I have to come in early sometimes to take keg deliveries.

There's only the faintest hint of her orangey scent since the fans have been working for hours to exhaust all the pheromones. I cross to her desk and flop into her chair, then pull her drawers open one by one. When I find one that has personal effects in it, including what looks like a brand new bottle of scent-nullifying body spray, I grin.

Perfect.

I pick the bottle up, lay her panties down and spread them out so the first thing she'll see and scent is Jamie's enormous cum stain, and then I spray her desk down with the nullifier, shove the bottle into the back of the drawer, and shut it. When she digs around for her nullifier, she's going to find her present instead.

"That was easy." I lock her office and head downstairs to start prep work and throw some food in the fryer because I'm fucking starving and my hard work's earned a treat. With my phone synced to the speakers, I blast some music and get to work.

There's a lot of planning and prep we have to do if we want to make Vee admit how much she needs her pack.

Chapter Seven

VERONICA

EITHER I'M BLOATED FROM PREHEAT OR I NEED TO LAY OFF THE bread because this skirt is so tight it scrapes across every single bruise that Anthony spanked into me last night.

Such a fucking tease walking around in those tight skirts and high heels.

His words from last night haunt me this morning. I realize my hips are swaying suggestively as I walk, and I force myself to stop as I reach the back door of Rut. The door's propped open with an empty keg and music is blasting, but it's not the kind we play for customers.

A guitar riff with a heavy bass and lyrics that seem more like warbles than words assault me. I slide my sunglasses up onto the top of my head and let my eyes adjust to the dark.

"Why is the door propped open?" I ask.

Anthony looks up from his prep station where he's busy cutting up fruit. He gives me a lazy smile. His bright blue eyes drift toward the bathroom door, and then he looks back down at his knife where he's making his cut. "Thought you'd want to make sure it was all aired out."

Guess we're not pretending it never happened.

A blush heats my face and neck. Mentally, I curse. When was the last time I blushed? I'm losing my edge. I turn away before he can get a good look and tease me. I ignore him and make my way up to my office. In my distraction, I plop down into my seat and hiss through my teeth.

Ouuuuch.

How the fuck did I forget my ass got spanked until it was black and blue? The initial burst of pain blooms into a dull ache that radiates through my entire pelvis. My clit throbs, and I drop my head back and groan. It's been way too long since I played that hard. I've become a newbie again. I'm making rookie mistakes here.

I kick my heels off under my desk and curl my legs up, which takes the pressure off the worst spots, although the extra tight skirt makes it not as comfortable as I'm used to. But I refuse to stand all day. I'll have to whiteknuckle through it.

There's over a dozen emails already waiting for me, so I work through them until footsteps on the stairs make me look up. The IRS agent Brendan appears at the top of the stairs.

"Good morning," I say. "I'm surprised to see you here on a Saturday. No days off with the IRS?"

He straightens his tie. It's navy, with tiny gold dots patterned across it. "I could say the same for you." Brendan smiles as he sets his briefcase down on his borrowed desk, then sits.

"No rest for the wicked," I answer blithely. "Weekends and holidays come with the territory. You'd be surprised how packed we get on Easter."

I think of the set we did with the alphas dressed as bunnies, complete with floppy ears and fuzzy cottontails glued to their white thongs. The omegas went completely feral over the egg hunt. One out of every ten eggs contained a solo dance token they could redeem from the dancer of their choice. The fire department shut us down that night for overcrowding, and we were packed for a solid three months afterward. It was the best publicity we didn't have to pay for.

"Easter? Sounds blasphemous." His grin softens the words so they're teasing instead of judgmental.

"Jesus wasn't the only thing rising that night," I say suggestively. The second the words are out of my mouth, I'm flooded with horror and shame. *What if he's super religious?*

"Oh my God. I'm so sorry." I press my hand to my mouth to stop myself from making it worse and saying anything else. I have a terrible sense of humor, and sometimes it comes out at the absolute worst moments.

Fuck. I'm going to fail this audit because of bad erection jokes.

Brendan unbuttons his suit and slips the jacket off, swinging it so he can drape it over the back of his chair. He unbuttons his sleeves and rolls them up his forearms. "It's fine. I went to Catholic school."

Fuckityfuckingfuck. My IRS agent is Catholic, and I made a dead Jesus boner joke. If I believed in it, I'd say I'm going to burn in hell.

"It's fine, really. I do have to fail your audit now, though." His smile slips and his face changes into a serious mask.

I squeak and scramble out of my chair, slapping my hands down on my desk. Adrenaline floods my system, but it doesn't know if I'm about to fight him or fall to my knees and blow him. Maybe if I suck his soul right out of his cock, he'll rubber stamp my audit and give Rut a pass. God knows I've done worse things for Rut than a BJ.

Brendan holds his hands up in the air. "Kidding! I'm kidding. You're fine. I'm a lapsed Catholic. Too much kneeling for my bad knee."

The air and fight go out of me at the same time, and I sink into my seat hard, only to wince and hiss in a breath.

"Are you okay?" His brow knits with worry and something about his eyes sharpens. It's such a distinct alpha move. Like he's scanning for danger as if a predator broke into the bar and he needs to find a spear. He probably doesn't realize he's doing it.

"I'm fine. It's…" I can't tell him I fucked both my bartender and my lead dancer last night and got my ass spanked black and blue. "I have cramps." Alphas never argue with an omega about cramps.

"Oh." He clears his throat and then he busies himself with work. He pulls a manilla folder of documents out of his brief-case, and I can't stop staring at the jutting veins on his bare forearms.

Oh, fuck me. There's nothing sexier than a guy in a business shirt with the sleeves rolled up to his elbows. My clit throbs in time to match the smarting of my ass and I flail blindly for the drawer with my new extra-strength nullifier spray. The drawer contents rattle around as I jerk it open a little too hard. I reach for it, but my fingers brush against fabric instead.

What the…

The panties I lost last night are in my drawer, and I know for a fact I'm not the one who put them there. Now that the drawer is open, the scent that soaked into them last night is permeating the room. The first hint of orange and coconut sunshine and tart cherries assaults me. It won't be long before Brendan smells it too. Before he learns what I did last night.

I slam the drawer shut, then realize that's only a stopgap measure. It's only a matter of time before the smell leaks from this drawer and the entire bar knows what I did last night after the rest of the crew left.

I have to destroy the evidence.

Brendan glances at me and frowns as I jerk the drawer back open and ball up the cum-stained panties. Dammit. My skirt doesn't have pockets. *Why the fuck does women's clothing not come with motherfucking pockets?* I fight back the urge to release a primal scream.

If I blast them with nullifier, he'll hear the misting nozzle and wonder why I'm spraying down my desk drawer. Palming them and walking them out would make less noise. Will he scent it, though? How good is his sense of smell? He's an alpha. His sense of smell is as good as mine.

I'm taking too long. I have to get them out of here. It's worth the risk.

I palm the pheromone-soaked panties and hide them at my side and try to walk nonchalantly toward the door. For a moment, I debate whether I should make up some excuse about why I'm leaving the room. Then I realize that's silly because this is my bar and I'm the boss and I can do what I want.

And that includes fucking my own employees, I guess. Since that's something I do now. Fuck. I'm such an idiot. A horny, stupid idiot.

My heels click clack against the stairs, and Anthony glances up from his cutting. He eyes the hint of pink in my clenched fist, then leans over and says something to Emma. His lips curl into a grin and she nods.

What is he telling her?

My stomach drops like it's in free fall. This was a huge mistake, and now I'm going to pay for it. Emma takes her apron off and heads to the back of the bar. I stalk around the bar counter, slap the panties against Anthony's chest, and shove him backward so he stumbles into the tiny storeroom where we keep the extra cases of imported beer and bottles of liquor.

"If you want to play seven minutes in heaven, all you have to do is ask, baby," he says, his eyes half-lidded and sultry.

I shush him before someone can hear us and grope for the door, closing it behind us so nobody will overhear our conversation. "When we're at the bar and someone might hear you, I'm the boss, not baby. Got it?"

He arches one brow, but wisely stays silent.

"How the fuck did my panties end up in my desk drawer?" I ask. "Because I know for a fact I didn't put them there."

"I stole them and brought them home, and then I used them to jerk Jamie off. Then I came to work early so I could put them in your desk before anyone got here. For safekeeping. You're welcome. Don't worry, I know how to take care of you."

For the second time this morning, I flush, but this time it's with anger. "I don't need to be taken care of. I've been doing it all by myself since I was fourteen."

Anthony's face softens with pity, and the expression makes my rage turn incandescent. "You don't have to do it alone anymore," he says. "We want to help. We care about you."

"I don't need you to take care of me, Anthony. I need you as a bartender, yes. But not… Last night was a mistake."

"You don't need us, but you need nullifying spray the minute you get to work?" he asks, calling me out.

My jaw snaps shut, and Anthony leans forward, crowding me. My back hits the closet door, and he traps me with an arm pressed above my head. I'm caged unless I grope for the doorknob and open it, which will send us both tumbling.

"What did you need the nullifying spray for? Were you thinking about last night? About how I fucked that sweet little pussy until it quivered on my cock? How we made Jamie watch me fuck you? Your pussy sliding over his cock? How good his mouth felt when he ate up all your delicious slick? Did you think about us every single time you sat down today on your sore little bottom?"

The flickering overhead bulb gives his face and tattoos

shadows that make this conversation feel even more dangerous. He's too damn attractive for his own good. Or mine.

"That's none of your fucking business," I protest a little too weakly. My body has no qualms about his closeness. My nipples tighten and press against my bra until they're aching. My panties will be as wet with slick as last night's pair was if this doesn't stop.

"I think it is. I think your pussy's wet right now from thinking about it." His hand brushes my thigh and slips up my skirt, rucking up the tight fabric, and I shimmy my legs to dislodge him. All my wiggling does is make his grip firmer. More insistent.

"We can't do this," I tell him. His hand shoves its way higher. He brushes the seam of my sex, and I nearly whimper from that minimal contact.

"Then use your safe word… baby." He curls his hand to cup me, and my pussy throbs against his hand. "Because your pussy is calling you a liar. I can feel how much you want me with every throb."

My breath catches when he strokes a single finger up and down my seam with a teasing, featherlight touch. "Someone could walk in, Anthony, we have to… to stop. You can't. I can't. Oh, God." *Why does this feel so good?*

"I sent Emma to the store to buy more oranges. We're gonna need them for tonight's special cocktail. Do you want to hear what it is?" He caresses my slit through the fabric from top to bottom until the damp material clings to me.

"It's called a Sloe Comfortable Screw Up Against The Wall."

I curl my hands in his shirt to push him away, but somehow I end up pulling him closer instead. My hips move in time with his taunting exploration. My clit swells, and the urge to trap his hand between my legs and grind until I come grips me.

"You have to stop." This is madness. Forbidden. I'm his boss. And I desperately want him—need him—to finger fuck me to completion. Right fucking now.

"If you really want me to stop, say the magic word. Or…" He pulls his phone from his back pocket and shows me a timer counting down. Eleven minutes and forty-three seconds. "That's how long you have to come before she gets back."

Oh, fuck. For some unfathomable reason, I find that hot. That he sent her away so he could get me alone. That he knows how long it takes to walk to the small grocer around the corner. How he's controlling the entirety of our interaction and has been since yesterday.

It's manipulative.

Calculating.

But it's also tomorrow, and he still wants me. Yesterday, they had me. If this was only about putting a notch on a bedpost, he wouldn't have his hand up my skirt. He engineered an excuse to get me alone again. To tease me. When was the last time someone put effort into fucking me beyond sending me a DM that says *heyyy wyd* at two in the morning?

"Tick tock," he teases me, still stroking me.

I should be horrified and walk away. Say no. But I can't. Preheat's left me empty and needy. The stretch from him last night wasn't enough. I ache to be used so roughly that I'm sore for days.

"Tick tock," he says, his middle finger tapping my cloth-covered clit.

This is a bad idea. The stupidest. But I've never been someone who backed down from a challenge, and I don't intend to start today.

I tip my chin up and meet his half-lidded gaze and he grins. "Then you'd better work harder," I tell him, throwing down the gauntlet.

"Hmm." Anthony stops what he's doing, and I bite back a whine at the loss of him and his delicious friction. He hikes my tight skirt up and shoves his hand in my panties. The first kiss of his skin against mine is torture and bliss. He strokes me, plays with me, and spreads my wetness with a leisurely pace that won't make me come in eleven minutes.

"I didn't hear a *please* or a *Daddy* in there, baby. And you begged so prettily last night. Don't be cruel. Don't deny me."

Pride is a hard pill to swallow, but he evades every movement I make to rub my clit against his fingers. If I push, he pulls away. If I rub faster, his touch lightens. He controls my orgasm, and I'll need to beg him for the pleasure of it.

I hate that I love it.

"Please." The word is a bit less stilted and embarrassing this morning, and that's unsettling. I don't like how easily he makes it come from my lips.

"Please… what?" He arches a brow, his lips tipped in a demented grin.

His stupid, arrogant ass is going to get us caught. Fighting him, fighting this, won't end with anything but my frustration. I clench my teeth and give in. "Please make me come, Daddy." It comes out stilted and strange.

"Good girl." Anthony drops his head to my shoulder and his fingers come alive. They stroke and tease and delve. He zeroes in on my clit with uncanny precision and rolls the tender nub in furious circles.

"Oh, God." I tighten my grip on his shirt as I focus on holding on for this ride he's taking me on. My pussy makes slick, wet sounds as he fucks his fingers through my folds. He dips lower, then in.

Two fingers slide inside and curl as he finds the perfect spot on my front wall and rubs it again. The base of his thumb grinds against my clit with every stroke, and my world feels like it's about to shatter. My pelvis tightens until the aching need for release travels all the way to my spine. My breaths turn into panting gasps as I cling to him and whimper.

"You're so wet, baby. What made you so wet and needy this morning?" His pace is steady as he fingers me until I can barely think. All of my focus, my entire world, narrows down to the way we're joined. His weight shores me up when my legs tremble and my ankles wobble.

"You did," I confess. "Every time I sat, I thought of you spanking me. Of J-Jamie watching. And then... hng, oh, fuck. There. Don't stop. Please, I need to come."

"And then?" he asks. "What else?"

"The IRS agent roll-rolled up his sleeves." I gasp and arch against him, my lungs as tight as the coil of tension in my pelvis. He balances me on the precipice of release and what's probably only seconds drags on until it feels like an eternity.

"Every time I see you at that desk I want to bend you over it."

There's a noise as something heavy lands on a hard surface nearby. "Tony?" Emma calls out. "Huh. Maybe he went to the bathroom."

Irrational jealousy bites at me. She calls him Tony?

You can't fire her because he's friendly with his coworkers.

I swallow down my gasps and whimpers. His timer hasn't gone off yet. Either he miscalculated or he lied. Did he do this on purpose so we'd get caught? Either seems possible. It's Anthony.

But my stupid omega hindbrain is more worried about her use of a nickname for him. I should be worried about getting caught fucking my employee, not about two employees becoming friends.

Anthony slaps a hand over my mouth to stifle my whimpers, but his fingers never slow their pace inside me. They don't stop like they should. My release builds and builds until I know it's going to wreck me when it hits.

This is wrong, but it's far too late to care.

"I bet the IRS agent thinks of bending you over your desk too," he whispers directly into my ear.

The thought of Brendan—buttoned-up, straight-laced IRS agent Brendan—bending me over my desk is enough to tip me over the edge. My walls crash down as my pussy spasms around his hand. The milking contractions squeeze his buried fingers and tug on my clit. I'm grateful for the hand cupped over my mouth. It's a reminder to reclaim some restraint and stop acting so wantonly. I barely hold back my moans even with his muffling.

Anthony removes his hand and captures my mouth with a kiss while my body pulses with aftershocks. He pulls his fingers free with a wet suck and tugs my panties down. The air is cold against my hot slit.

The sound of his zipper sliding down is far too loud. *We can't. What if she hears it? What is he doing?* The slap of skin against skin makes it fairly obvious what he's doing. He's jerking off.

He kisses me until I'm dizzy as he palms his cock and works it. His breathing comes faster, and so do his strokes. All I can think of is that she'll hear it. This is it—we're going to get caught. It's exhilarating. Like cresting the top of a rollercoaster and facing the long drop. You know it's coming, yet it's still a surprise when it happens.

The head of his cock hits my wet folds as he tugs, and then his breathing shudders. His hips cant. His hard cock thrusts between my legs, fucking through my wet folds and rubbing against my overly sensitized clit with every pass. The hardness of his cold piercing and the warmth of his skin are a distracting combination. My pussy wants him to turn me and pull my hips up and sink deep inside.

It doesn't matter that I already came. I want more. Need it with an intensity that frightens me. I've never been so horny before.

What's wrong with me? I've never had such a lapse in self-control before. It's like sitting in that office for days, trapped in a fish bowl of Brendan's delicious alpha pheromones, has rotted my brain.

Anthony works me like my pussy is a sleeve, his cock sliding between my labia. My wetness makes loud smacking sounds as he moves faster. His breathing grows heavy. Emma is going to hear us. She's going to open that door and see Anthony's cock sliding between my thighs as he uses me to jerk himself off. She's going to see my skirt rucked up around my waist and my panties pulled down my thighs. The black and blue marks he spanked all over my ass.

A part of me wants her to. I want her to see me staking a claim. Know he's off limits to her. That he's mine, now. Emma and her nickname for him can fuck right off.

His pace picks up, the wet smacks obscene and loud. I ache for him. I'm needy and empty. Anthony groans and buries his face in my hair. He grabs my ass, his fingers digging into the bruises until I have to choke off my gasp. His cockhead and piercing stroke against my swollen clit, and a second, smaller orgasm makes me flutter. I bite my lip to hold back my loud moan and throw my arms around his neck to hang on before I fall over.

Lips crash down on mine and my teeth cut into my lip a bit. He kisses me like he's feral. Desperate.

Anthony comes with a stifled groan and I feel him shuddering as he finds his release. We break our kiss and he tilts his forehead against mine. Our breaths are synched and now that he's come, we're both slowing down. My prickly heart thaws a bit at the weirdly intimate moment.

"Here's your present for being such a good girl, baby," he whispers. "I'm going to check later, and if I found that you took them off, I'm going to bend you over no matter where we are or who can see and I'll fill your pretty little pussy up till it's bursting."

His words don't make any sense until he grabs the edges of my panties and hikes them up. The cold, wet fabric against my heated flesh is a shock. That's too much wetness. He… Did he just shoot his cum into my panties and tug them back up?

My eyes widen. "What do you think you're doing?" I hiss as softly as I can.

Anthony pinches my chin between his thumb and forefinger and tilts my face up. "I mean it, baby. Wherever we are. Whoever is there with us. If I palm your ass and I don't feel a panty line or if I lift your skirt to check and it's not there, I will bend you over and fuck you raw and breed your cunt until you're dripping. I don't care if the whole fucking world has to watch me fuck you for you to know that you and this pretty pussy are mine now. I will shout it from the rooftop for the entirety of Los Angeles to bear witness to, if that's what it takes to convince you we want you and we mean it. Forever. Till death do us part."

My stomach squirms. *It's unease,* I tell myself. Not anticipation. Not yearning.

I don't want *this*. Forever. Shit. I'm not meant for forever. Nobody keeps me for that long.

I work better alone.

He slaps his palm against my cunt, the wet fabric squelching, and I flinch.

All I can think of is how long sperm live and how fast they can travel and I can't remember if I took my pill this morning.

No, I did. I always do. I'm meticulous about it. But there's a bit of doubt that leaves me uneasy. That can't happen. My heat's coming too early.

My mouth drops open and closes twice before I figure out what I want to say. Some way to wrestle control back in this unwieldy whatever the fuck this is. It's not a relationship. It's business with benefits.

"Grab something and go out there," I tell him. "Get Emma away from the bar so I can slip out."

His face hardens as if he's disappointed in me, and the idea I might deserve it stings. "Okay, baby. I don't mind doing this again tomorrow. And the day after. And the next. I'll breed your pussy every day until you realize we mean every word. We want you for keeps."

Anthony zips up his jeans and buttons them. He searches the wall and picks up a bottle of the concentrated food-safe disinfectant we use to clean the glasses and dishes with. I stand aside and let him leave. He talks to Emma, says something that makes her laugh, and then a few minutes later they walk away.

Jealousy pricks at me. What did he say that made her laugh like that? Is that her normal laugh, or is she flirting with him right now?

The cum and arousal-soaked fabric clings to my pussy, and now that I've come twice and I'm no longer aroused, the sensation is irritating. There's no way that I can work all day with these panties on. Especially not once they get crusty.

While his beta pheromones are so mild that most omegas and alphas won't be able to pick them up on me without being extremely close, they'll still be able to scent my slick.

In the staff's private bathroom backstage, I strip them off and pee, then wet a paper towel and clean myself up as best as I can. I shove the panties to the bottom of the trash can and grab the bottle of nullifier spray we keep there for anyone who needs to use it. I spray myself and the bathroom, then the trash can too for good measure. So long as nobody goes digging, I might get away with this.

He wasn't lying. I know Anthony well enough to know that when he makes a promise, he keeps it. If he finds out I've ditched my cum soaked panties, he'll try to bend me over and fuck me even if that means the entire bar has to watch. He's crazy enough to do it. I'd have to use my safe word to get him to stop.

I'll simply have to avoid him for the rest of the night.

I wash my hands, check my hair, and straighten out my wrinkled clothes, then leave the bathroom to see if all the dancers are here for practice yet.

Chapter Eight

JAMIE

I STEP OFFSTAGE AND BLINK TO CLEAR THE SPOTS FROM MY vision. The bright stage lights are blinding and hot. It takes a moment for my eyes to adjust to the dark club. The next song queues and another act starts while I take my break. Once I'm backstage, I pull the folded and crinkled bills from my lederhosen short shorts and compile them into a tidy pile of cash.

"Thirsty?" Anthony asks from behind me.

I shove the bills into my money bag and lock it up in my locker, then turn and take the drink from him. *He's always taking care of me like this.* "Thanks. You always know exactly what I need."

The first sip is so refreshing that I sigh and close my eyes as I suck down a longer gulp. He's mixed lemonade with orange juice and a splash of cherry syrup, and the combination makes me want to kiss him. But we're at work. It's only the middle of the shift so there's still too many people around. He doesn't want everyone to know we're together. Not yet.

"That's me," he says wryly, "I always aim to please."

He sounds like he doesn't mean what he's saying, but I know it's true. Anthony works hard to keep me happy. He's the only one who ever made me comfortable enough to fully explore being submissive. Everyone looks at me and sees an alpha and has an idea of who I should be or what I should act like, but Anthony lets me be myself. Lets me figure out what that means for me.

I give him a smile. "You do."

The straw makes a loud sound as I suck up the rest of the drink and slip the embroidered lederhosen straps off my shoulders where they're digging. They hang around my thighs when I let them drop, and my chest warms with satisfaction when Anthony's eyes follow the movement.

He'll never admit it, but he appreciates my alpha physique. As a beta, he'd have to train himself to death inside a gym to achieve what my dynamic makes almost effortless. It's hard to take pride in it, though, when it comes so naturally. As long as I get enough protein and exercise, I'll always look like this until I'm old and gray. Until my testosterone level eventually drops.

But we always want what we can't have. Or that's what my mom says anyway. And she's the smartest person I know other than Vee and Anthony.

I like his wiry strength. The sleek lines of his more subtle, toned muscles. The dark ink that covers almost every inch of his skin from knuckle to neck to navel. I'm too scared of the needles and the pain to get a tattoo. *We always want what we can't have.*

"And you do," I say, agreeing with the statement I know he doesn't quite believe. But he does. He pleases me immensely. I'm not sure I've ever been as happy as I am lately, except after that one time I rode a tasty fifty-footer off the coast of Portugal and didn't wipe out. With our omega in sight, we're one step closer to finding our pack. We're one step closer to feeling complete.

His pale blue eyes flash with some dark emotion, as if he

can read my thoughts. It's scary yet thrilling whenever he does it. I glance around the dressing room and find it empty. The backdoor is propped open with an empty keg so I know a few dancers are out back, clearing their noses and catching their breath. Everyone else is on stage making money. Darlene's working in her office, but I know from experience she won't hear us over the sound leaking from the stage and the hum of her sewing machine if we keep our voices low.

"Is everything… okay?" I ask him, my belly all fluttery with nerves. I'm not really sure what I'm asking though. Is Anthony really okay with opening our relationship up? A threesome or a casual fling aren't the same as a pack. Packs are work. They're hard, but rewarding. Most betas don't feel the urge to pack up like alphas and omegas do, and some of them like the fantasy more than the reality. *Are we still okay?*

Am I doing my part, or am I messing this up? I panicked yesterday and quit and nearly ruined all of his careful plans. I'm not good at stuff like this. Not like he is.

Anthony glances at people and knows how they tick. I'm… handsome. Strong. Sweet. A nice guy. All the things people say about you when what they really mean is *not smart*. Normally, that stuff doesn't bother me, but I don't want to wreck this before we get started. If this all hinged on me, we never would have made it this far.

Are we going to scare her off or make her so mad we have to leave Rut? I don't want to go. I didn't know how much I'd like working here when I took the job. And I don't want to mess this up and get Anthony fired. I could always go back to surfing. Maybe open a board rental shack on the beach and really lean into teaching so I don't have to leave for competitions and be away so much. But Anthony can't afford to be jobless unless he calls his family and he's too proud to ask for help, especially not from an alpha. Not even if I'm his boyfriend. Probably especially because I'm his boyfriend.

"Yeah. Of course it is. Why wouldn't it be?" Anthony asks, his expression guarded.

"She didn't watch rehearsals today. She always watches, at least for a few minutes. Did something happen?"

"I fingered her in the supply closet."

My cock twitches inside the tight costume, and I reach down to adjust it. Anthony's gaze follows my hand, his lips twisting up at one corner.

"You… you did?" I ask.

That's good. Real good. If she let him finger her, then that means she's interested in more than a one time thing. A low purr starts in my chest, but I squash the rumble before it can become audible.

"Yeah. She came all over my fingers. Made a mess of my hand with her sweet slick. And then I gave her a present."

I groan from the strain of holding my purr back, and my costume strangles my bulge as I think of Anthony licking her sweet cream off his fingers. Maybe he'll let me watch next time. Let me lick it off his fingers. "What sort of present?"

"Well," he drawls, and leans one arm on the lockers behind me, invading my space. He leans up and I curl down to meet him so he can drop his voice to a whisper. "I pulled her panties down and inched her tight little skirt up."

My breath catches and I nod while I keep an eye on the back door. "And then?"

"Then I unzipped my jeans and pulled out my cock and I stroked it with the hand covered in her slick."

I clench my jaw and hold back a deeper, throatier groan. Is his cock still covered in her scent? I want to drop to my knees and shove my head in his groin and sniff. I want to pull his cock out and lick it clean, but I can't. We're at work. Nobody's supposed to know we're dating. He said we have to be on the downlow for now.

My cock kicks as the costume becomes strangling and my next adjustment is more of a stroke. I want him to describe it to me. The whole thing. I need to hear every single detail. "And then what'd you do?"

Anthony's voice drops into a low, seductive tone that's almost a purr. "I slid my cock through all that slick and used her. Covered her panties in cum and pulled them back up because I wanted her to know that even if her hot little pussy doesn't take my cock, it's still my cum that's going to fill her sweet little hole."

"Oh, fuck," I moan under my breath and close my eyes as I picture it. Vee with her skirt rucked up and her panties askew. Anthony's cum splattered along the gusset. His tattooed hands tugging the delicate fabric up until his cream smears all over her wet pussy. She'll have already come—because Anthony is a gentleman when it matters and I know he let her come first—so her cheeks will be pink.

I can't explain why I'm like this. Why I enjoy knowing he's gotten further with her than I have. Why I like watching him take her while I'm there, used but forgotten. It's humiliating, and that's why I love it. If all of this happens and she still wants me, it means I'm good enough. All of the bad things happened, but she didn't leave. I'm good enough to stay for, even though I'm not good at being an alpha.

"I wish I could have seen it," I admit.

"It gets better," Anthony says, grinning. "I told her if she takes them off before the end of the night that I'm going to fuck her whenever and wherever I find out they're gone."

My swollen head scrapes against the non-stretchy fake leather of my costume and I want to reach in and pull my cock out. I'm so hard it hurts. "Do you think she will?" As much as I know she'll hate it—or pretend to hate it—I'd give anything to watch him bend her over the bar and fuck her with everyone looking.

"Oh, she already has." Anthony's lips curl in a grin that's terrifying. "Her panty line is gone. That's why I came to find you."

My chest feels light while my cock feels as heavy and thick as a club. "When?" *Can we do it now?*

"It's time for phase two. Come on—and don't forget to bring your glass."

I follow Anthony, and we head to the staff bathroom rather than the black curtain. He urges me inside and fits himself in there with me. It's tight. The door's lock clicking into place is loud. The minute it's secure, he's on me.

Fingers dig into muscle as he grabs me by the neck and pulls me down for a hard kiss that borders on feral. Teeth nip at my lower lip until my mouth slackens. His tongue invades my mouth while his hand sinks beyond the waistband of my costume. The first brush of his fingertip over my leaking slit makes me shiver. This is urgent. Rough. Demanding.

Whatever he wants from me, from my body, he'll take without asking. And I'm all too eager to give it. Whatever he wants from me is his to take, because I'm his. The same way he's mine. *My packmate.*

Was this what he was like with Vee this morning, or did he finger fuck her gently? Did he drag her orgasm out with tender strokes so she'd know who was in charge? Or did he finger her hard, his hand moving impossibly fast with all the skills learned from his brief stint as a guitarist in a local band that was pretty good but didn't quite make it?

He breaks the rough kiss and knocks his forehead against mine, his fingers tangling in my hair and squeezing to the point of pain while his other hand palms me tight and tugs. "Think of her pussy, babe," he whispers. "Think of that glistening, wet pussy, all pink and sweet. Remember how it felt on your lips? The velvety slide of her skin against yours? The way she gushed and filled your mouth? Your mouth will give her more pleasure than this cock ever could," he says as he squeezes tighter until I groan.

Yes. I love knowing he was satisfying her and I didn't know it was happening. It's the absolute loss of control. It would be easy to choose jealousy or anger. Instead, I give in. I find the peace in the submission. When I submit, I don't have to worry about being perfect or the best alpha. I can simply be myself. Anthony tells me there's nothing wrong with me being wired this way. Every day, I work hard to believe him.

"Her pussy was so wet for me."

Pre-cum leaks freely as pressure tightens in my groin. I can almost feel my balls swelling with cum. With useless sperm. There's no hole here to breed, only the tight ring of my beta lover's hand as he strokes me and whispers delicious filth in my ear.

"She tasted so good on my tongue."

I sigh, my hips bucking from the urge to stand still. To surrender. It's hard to fight the alpha urge to rut. To claim. To fuck and fill and breed. Denying it is the sweetest of torments.

It's agonizing bliss.

"She's going to taste even better when I fill her pussy up with cum, then sit her on your face," Anthony promises.

"F-fuck." God, I want that. I want to savor the both of them together, their pheromones mixing. Tart cherries and sweet orange. My hard beta and my harder omega. Seeing her mellow and sweeten after he makes her come will be so satisfying. "Yes. I want that."

"But first," he says, and I groan. "First, my darling, sweet alpha, I need something from you." He lets go of my hair and my scalp aches, the pain adding to my pleasure as my orgasm swells and grows.

"Anything," I pant, my balls so tight they feel like they'll burst.

His grip is furiously tight and his pace is fast. He strangles my cock more than he tugs it. My knot begins to swell from every strike of the flat side of his fist against my groin as he jerks me off in Rut's bathroom. I lick my lips and squeeze my eyes shut and focus on delaying my orgasm until he lets me come.

"You can have anything you want," I promise.

"I need you to hold this glass."

Surprise makes me open my eyes and I see the empty glass he holds out to me. I take it and frown, my mind too lust drunk to keep up with the sudden change in topics. "What do you want me to do with it?"

He nudges my hand and the glass lower and tilts it so my cockhead is pointing at its rim. "I want you to come. As much as you can. Fill it for your omega, alpha. Feed her."

His words and his grip make me come undone. My control snaps like a broken rubber band and my hips buck up, forcing his grip lower so he squeezes me from knot to tip. Milking me. My knot swells with the first jet of cum, and we both stare as white ropes of semen coat the melting ice cubes and strike the walls of the glass. Everything pulses as bliss washes over me and Anthony crushes my knot with one hand and tugs my shaft with his other.

My cum covers the ice cubes like heavy cream.

She's going to drink it. He's going to give it to her, and she's going to drink my cum and then a part of me will be inside her. Nourishing her in a way she obviously denies herself. He jerks me five more times until the pulsing eruptions slow and my knot is completely blown.

"That's the most I've ever seen you come," Anthony says, his voice impressed.

I pant and catch my breath, my low purr stuttering in my chest. "It's her slick. She's so close to her heat. It drives me crazy. I *swear* I can practically smell her right now."

I've never summoned phantom smells of omega pussy from memory before. Is this because she's mine? Is that why I can smell her so strongly right now? It's like she's here in this bathroom with us.

"Hmm." Anthony scrapes the cool, smooth edge of the glass under my glans, and I grunt from the odd sensation. It's weird, but not awful. "All right," he says. "That'll do it."

"Do you really think she'll want to drink it?"

Anthony shrugs. "What she doesn't know won't hurt her. Besides, it's not really different from swallowing after a blowjob."

My stomach squirms because that doesn't sit right. "Are you sure? Shouldn't you ask?" I'm pretty sure you're supposed to ask for something like this.

"Vee needs it, but she's too stubborn to admit it. She's spent years suppressing all of her natural urges. Denying herself. Hurting herself in the process too. She forgets to eat. Works too much. Doesn't take a single day off until she absolutely has to. Then she comes back from her heats as spitting mad as a wet cat. Why? Because she chooses safe alphas who don't threaten her. Ones who will never be able to satisfy her. Not like we can. Like we will."

"Hmm." It's true, but I still don't know if it's okay.

"She just needs a nudge in the right direction," he adds. "Then it's up to her to take that first step. And this is going to be our nudge. Besides, she needs the pheromones. She's been starving herself of a scent match for years, and the toll that takes is awful. I read an article last week about pheromone rejection syndrome. It's unpleasant stuff. Causes reduced fertility, sleep cycle issues, hair loss, weight loss, fainting, headaches… The list goes on. Being in such close proximity to a scent match for this long without acting on it isn't good for her."

"That's bad." I didn't know I was hurting her by staying close. All I wanted was to see her pretty face every day. If I couldn't have her, at least I knew she was okay.

"When was the last time you saw her laugh or have fun?" Anthony asks.

I rack my brain, but I can't remember. "I don't know."

"Exactly. So think of it like medicine. We're keeping our girl happy and healthy. When she's feeling less stubborn for no damn good reason, she'll take it right from the source. But for now, we'll have to bottle it."

I look down at the cum-covered ice in the glass. "That's not a bottle, babe, that's a glass."

Anthony fights off a smile. "You're right."

Okay. "Can I watch?" I ask him.

My knot shrinks and my cock deflates. Without the heat and slick of an omega or fist, its inflation is brief. Will she ever let me knot her? I'm not opposed to begging. I like it, actually.

He chuckles and washes his hands at the sink while I tuck my soft cock away and fix my costume. "Fine," he says. "But if you come up to the office with me, she'll get suspicious. You can watch through the window. Your next set is in two minutes. Better hurry." Anthony presses a kiss to my lips and leaves me to change.

Two minutes isn't long to change, and some costumes are hard to put on. I'm not the only dancer in the break room now and a few of the other alphas throw confused glances my way, and then I see their nostrils flaring as they scent what we did.

Our secret might be out. I'll have to tell Anthony later. He was the one who insisted we keep things quiet. I don't care if everyone knows we're together.

My face heats as I do my best to ignore them, pulling the lederhosen short shorts off and shoving them into the dirties bag for cleaning. I grab my next costume and step into the thong. Red, orange, and yellow sequins have been sewn onto it to look like a flickering flame. I step into the long yellow pants and latch the waist, then slip the suspenders over my shoulders and grab the yellow fireman's helmet off the stand.

Nate glares at me as I slide into my spot back stage and wait for my cue. "You barely made it."

"Sorry, Nate."

His eyes flick down to my pants and the lack of a bulge, and his upper lip practically curls with displeasure. "Do something about that. You've worked here long enough to know you're not supposed to fuck around until after we're done for the night. What are they gonna think if they go to tip you and you're as limp as wilted lettuce? They're gonna think you don't want them."

"Sorry, Nate. I'll fix it."

I ignore him and shove my hand inside my pants and grip my wrung-out cock. I think of Anthony and Vee. Of her joining the crowd around the stage. He'll come behind her and use the throng of people to hide the way he palms her ass.

The cum drenched panties he told her not to take off are gone, so he makes good on his promise. He kicks her feet wide and slides his hand up her bare thigh, pushing his fingers into her as he fucks her with his hand while I dance and watch them.

Anyone in the crowd could look over and see too if they only paid attention. If they saw how close he was standing. How pink her cheeks grew and her hips wiggled as he got her wet and ready. The crush of people gets so thick on Saturday nights that they might not notice when he unzips his pants and bends her forward a bit, pushing into her hot pussy right there.

But I hope they do. I want them to inhale the thick perfume of her arousal. I want them to see him fuck her and make her scream when she comes. I want to dance on stage for her, eating up every inch of the sight of her getting fucked by my beta while I'm powerless to leave the stage and join them. My cock fills my hand as I get lost in the fantasy.

"Better. All right, that's your cue. Go," Nate says. He slaps me on my mostly bare back. My skin crawls from the contact as the jarring makes me tug my fluffed cock harder than necessary.

The music swells and the crowd's energy pulses, and I burst through the hidden seam in the black curtain and I dance. The omegas grow wild. They siphon off our untapped sexual energy and feed it back to us. Whoever said omegas were the weaker, more submissive of the three dynamics clearly never met a whole pack of them.

There are about thirty omegas huddled together alongside some betas, their money thrust into the air as they scream and yell to be heard over the music. Thirty to one. They would tear me apart in their frenzy if they could. They'd scratch and claw and bite each other in their heat delirium to claim a virile alpha caught alone and unaware.

Their perfumes blast my nose in an olfactory assault. Someone in the crowd smells like the fourth of July, like fireworks and gunpowder, and the scent is so acrid and sharp I almost sneeze and ruin my footing. Flowers and fruit and sweets and woodsy notes make a nauseating potpourri.

Think of oranges and cherries, I tell myself.

My cock jerks against the tight bright yellow pants and an omega screams. Working a thumb under my suspender, I don't forget to smile out at the crowd and gyrate suggestively as I smack it against my chest before I slide it down my arm and move to the other one.

As the song reaches its first crescendo, I grip the pants by the hidden velcro seam on the sides and tug. It breaks away like it's designed to, and I twirl it up in the air before tossing it behind me. I've learned not to toss it forward into the crowd. When you do that, some of the costume pieces go missing and then Darlene gets mad. I don't like it when Darlene gets mad at me. She makes the thongs too tight if you really piss her off.

From the corner of my vision, I see movement at the bar. Anthony lifts the wooden counter and steps away, dropping it down behind him, and then he heads to the stairs. I do hip thrusts while he takes them one by one, my hands slapping onto my thighs to draw attention to my groin.

I barely pay attention to the crowd as I turn, so I'm in profile and do body rolls. Anthony disappears inside the office, and I hold my breath until he reappears by Vee's desk. The stage lights are blinding and her office is dark. All I can see is the glow of her computer and her outline. He leans against her desk and hands her the glass. I forget how to breathe when she lifts it toward her face.

There's hardly any detail. Only the shadowy outline of her body against the bright glow. Yet it's the most erotic thing I've ever seen.

If only I were there. If only I could see it better. Closer. Watch his cocktail made with my cum slide down her throat and fill her belly. Alpha cum is highly nutritious. It has to be for omegas to survive off it alone, plus water for days to a week at a time during their heat. Can't have the omegas wasting away, after all. You can't breed omegas who are underweight.

While I stroke my raging erection through my sequin-covered thong, I think of my omega. And I dance. The crowd's screams fade into noise, and I barely register the song's end.

I do my required tour of the stage and slip through their grasping, clawing touches. Folded money gets shoved in my too tight thong, and when one omega gets too frisky, I turn around so they can load up the back. If I have to choose between them groping my cock or my ass, I'll always choose my ass. Before they're ready to be done with me, I leave the stage.

None of them excite or tempt me.

There's only one omega I want.

Chapter Nine

VERONICA

"Oh, God. This is good. You should make this tomorrow's signature drink."

Anthony's grin widens, and he looks far too happy with himself. "It's the fresh coconut cream. You can't beat getting something right from the tap rather than out of a bottle."

I frown, but take another sip. "You bought fresh coconut?"

"Mmhmm. Locally sourced."

That sounds expensive. But if it makes the drinks this good… we can charge extra to make up for the expense. God knows the omegas will pay for it. They love anything that seems luxurious, and the alphas and betas who bring or meet them here don't mind financing it. If I could bottle whatever's making this so fucking delicious, I'd be a millionaire.

"None for me today?" Brendan asks, his voice teasing and light.

Anthony twists to glance back at the IRS agent camping out at Nate's desk. "Not today, but maybe if you beg me nicely…"

"Anthony," I chide him, warning him to stop.

"What?" he asks, feigning innocence.

I give him a look that says *be professional or get out of my office.*

He kicks away from where he's leaning against my desk, and his eyes drop to my skirt as if he can see through it with x-ray vision. Like he's Superman instead of a handsome pain in my ass.

I squirm in my seat and try to pretend I'm not going commando right now. He can't tell. There's no way. This skirt is black. My clit throbs from the way I'm squeezing my thighs together.

"I'll leave you two to it," Anthony says. He heads toward the door, then pauses at Nate's desk. He looks the confused IRS agent up and down, practically eye fucking him. "I hope you do."

"Pardon?" Brendan asks.

"Beg me for it. The buttoned-up ones are always the kinkiest." Anthony grins back at me and leaves before I can do more than let my jaw hit the floor.

"Agent Hall, I am so sorry," I say as I rise from my seat and slap my hands on my desk. "Please let me apologize for my bartender's inappropriate behavior. I'll talk to him."

"It's fine," he says. "Don't trouble yourself." He's so embarrassed that he's blushing, his light brown skin reddening. He ducks his head over his paperwork.

I exhale sharply and plop back down in my seat, wincing at the contact of it with my bruised ass. Wet lips rub together, and I spend the next minute trying to figure out if it's leftover arousal from earlier or if my preheat has transitioned over to the first stage of heat.

It's coming on too fast to be normal. Likely because I'm being hot boxed by his pheromones. Already, my clothes seem extra annoying. My skirt is too tight. My heels pinch my toes too much.

The tag inside my shirt collar rubs. I'm crawling out of my skin… and there's far too much work left to do. I won't be able to put it off too much longer, though. I'll have to take a few days off to deal with my heat unless I stop by the twenty-four-hour pharmacy tonight.

So why does the thought of going on suppressants fill me with such dread? Yes, it's annoying. But it's bearable. It's an option.

I take another sip of my drink to cool myself down. Each sip softens my rough edges until my pounding headache eases and I can think again.

If Anthony wasn't the best bartender in the entire city, I'd probably write his behavior up. At the very least he'd get a verbal reprimand. But knowing him, he'd pay me back for it twice and I… I think I'd let him. And now that we've fucked, disciplining him professionally will be awkward as hell. He could claim sexual harassment.

What the fuck have I done?

I sip the rest of my drink while I spiral. Creamy coconut and pineapple and white rum should make another boring piña colada, but he's made it absolutely decadent. It must be the fresh coconut cream. It tastes like sitting in a sunbeam on a Caribbean beach. There's no other way to describe it. I feel better than I've felt in years. Less anxious and irritated by everything.

Before I'm ready for it to end, I've drained the glass, and I set it down on a stack of old paperwork. The coldness of the blended drink helps with the heat symptoms. I don't feel in danger of overheating or crawling out of my skin anymore.

As if he knows my glass is empty and I was thinking something nice about him, my cell phone lights up and Anthony's name scrolls across it. My heart flutters traitorously. "What is it?" I answer a bit too sharply.

"One of the customers ordered an angel shot, but I'm all out of the syrup I need."

My heart goes from fluttering to hammering in my chest. It doesn't matter how many times we do this—and we've done this far too many times for my liking—it never gets easier. "I'll handle it." I hang up with him and dial the shelter's secret line.

Moriah answers, her voice thick with sleep. "Veronica?" It's almost midnight and far past her bedtime.

"I have one. Bring the van."

"Sugar," she says, because she never curses. "Okay. Rob! Wake up. Get the van. No, I don't know where your shoes are. Leave them. We don't have time. Wear your slippers. Nobody's gonna see your feet and they won't care if they do. Here's the keys. Veronica, we're coming. We'll be there in fifteen."

Thank God they live close. I stand up and wiggle my feet back into my heels, then run my fingers through my hair until it's more sleek than frizz. I unbutton my blouse and shrug out of it until I'm down to my lace trimmed camisole and tight skirt.

"Is everything okay?" Brendan asks as he watches me primp and fuss so I look more like one of my customers than the owner. This is why I wear skirts and heels every day. If I dressed comfortably, I wouldn't be able to blend with the crowd.

"Everything's fine," I tell him. "But I have to go handle something."

"Are you sure? You sound... Is there anything I can help with?"

I ignore him and pull the bottom drawer of my desk open and dig out the bottle of bright blue mixture we keep ready. I unscrew the cap and pour its contents into a tumbler, then head for the stairs.

Anthony's eyes snap to mine, and then he looks at a tiny blonde omega in a bright pink dress. It's tight and short and her hair is curled and big. I thread through the crowd and make sure I don't lose track of her as people cut across my path and bump into me.

There's an alpha standing behind her at their spot at the bar. He's tall and broad as all of them are, with light brown hair and dark eyes and tanned white skin. His clothes are designer and sleek. Expensive. A silver-colored watch peeks out from the edge of his black button up. I'm sure that whatever brand it is, it's real and expensive.

He leans down to say something to her, his hand on her hip, and as she turns, I see the amount of makeup she's wearing. It's thick, especially around her eyes. Her concealer can't quite hide the dark shadowing underneath. It's easy to spot the particular sort of eye makeup that covers a black eye when you know what to watch for. The blonde nods at something he says in her ear.

The alpha barks for Anthony to hurry while my bartender makes a show of looking through a big cardboard box full of extra mixers and syrups. The crowd jostles me, and I use the energy to fall into the omega and shower her with my tumbler of watery blue dye.

She gasps and her alpha barks something, his words lost in the noise but the tone of his command loud enough to make the omegas around us flinch. "Gawd, I'm ssosorry!" I slur, pretending to be drunk. I grab a napkin from the bar counter and make a show of patting her stained dress and wiping her arm dry.

"Look at what you did, you stupid bitch. This is silk," her dickhead alpha says. He plucks at his shirt and scowls at me.

"We sshould go tah the bathroom!" I yell over the music. I clutch her by her forearm and teeter on my heels.

"Go!" her alpha barks at her. "Get cleaned up. You're

embarrassing me!" He holds his arm up to inspect the droplets splashed all over his silk shirt.

"I'm sorry, baby," she says.

"This way. It's back here." The omega lets me pull her through the club toward the back, but we don't stop into the main bathroom that the customers use. I glance at the bar and, satisfied that her alpha is busy yelling at Anthony and isn't looking, I lead her to the black curtain that separates the front of the club from the back.

"Come on," I say, dropping the drunk act once the curtain closes behind us.

"Where are we going?" she asks. Her steps slow as she looks around the dressing room.

A few of my dancers are in various states of undress as they change outfits. All of them watch us pass as we head to the back of the club. I peek out the back door, but there's no van yet. Good. It gives us a few minutes to talk.

"Do you have any children?" I ask her.

She shakes her head and looks at the black curtain, lines of worry etching furrows into her face.

"He won't follow us," I tell her. "And if he does, he'll regret it. Can one of you go tell Nate to stall? The rest of you watch the curtain. He's tall and white with tan skin, brown hair, and dark eyes and he's wearing a gray silk shirt. If you see him coming back here, lay him out cold."

Margot nods and motions for two of the other alphas to follow her. I rummage through the cubby screwed onto the wall and fish out one of the white envelopes we keep there. It doesn't have much in it. Only some business cards and pamphlets about domestic violence and advocacy groups for victims of violence.

The police officers we work with will help her get her stuff from her alpha's house. The shelter will take care of the rest.

They'll help her get somewhere new to live. Out of the city or out of the state, if that's what it takes. If her family is somewhere else, they'll get her there. She'll be safe now.

"Do you have a claiming bite?" I ask her. "It's okay if you do. But it changes how we approach things."

"No. He said I had to earn it first."

I barely resist the urge to roll my eyes. "That's good. It makes things easier. An older beta couple is going to come and drive you somewhere safe. I trust them, and I need you to trust me right now. We have doctors who can look at you if you need one, and an officer we trust who can help you—"

"The cops can't help me," she interrupts me.

Well, shit. That means one of two things. Either he's in some sort of organized crime, or he's law enforcement. I scan what I can see of her, but I don't see the usual tattoos and markings of a trafficked victim, although sometimes they're hidden. "Okay."

"I'm sorry... He's going to hurt you. He's going to... I should go back before he gets angrier." She looks near tears.

"I'm not worried about being hurt. Do you *want* to go back?" It kills me to ask, but not everyone who asks for an angel shot is actually ready to leave once the idea of leaving becomes real.

You can't force someone to get help, no matter how desperately they need it. That's why we run the play like this. We could walk through that curtain and pretend we were fixing her dress and he would never know. Everyone knows girls take forever in the bathroom, especially at a crowded bar where there's a line.

She's quiet for a moment that seems to stretch for eternity, and then she shakes her head. "No." The omega shivers and her eyes get glassy with unshed tears.

"How dangerous?" I ask so I know what to expect.

"Extremely. I'm sorry."

"Connected or a cop?"

"He's in a gang. I hear him talk to them in Russian sometimes."

"How high up? What does he do for them?"

"He sells drugs. I found a bag of pills in his closet. That's when he gave me this." She points to her black eye hiding under the concealer.

"Oh." I breathe a sigh of relief. "That's good." If he's distributing pills like molly or oxy, then he's not that high in the organization. If he's even a fully pledged member at all. He might just be some well-connected asshole. Important gang members don't deal with low-level shit like small bags of pills.

She gives me a confused, worried face.

"How do you feel about hiking?" I ask her while I ignore the distressed stink to her cinnamon scent. On a good day, she probably smells like Christmas, but right now it's more like burnt snickerdoodles.

"Hiking?" Her brow furrows. "It's okay. I like taking walks, I guess. Or I used to."

Before this alphahole ruined her life.

Headlights light up the dark alley as a white wedding cake delivery van pulls up and idles. A woman with gray hair braided away from her face hops out. Her pajama pants are tucked into black combat boots, and she's thrown an old bomber jacket over her hoodie.

"This is Moriah," I say, sweeping a hand out to the beta. "And her husband Rob. They're going to take you and get you where you need to go. We only have two rules. You don't tell anyone about our process and you wear your blindfold for the entire car ride until Moriah tells you that you can take it off."

"What about my parents?" she asks. The omega takes the blindfold from Moriah and stares at it with wide eyes.

"Your family will be in a lot more danger if they know where you are, and so would our whole organization. We can't help *anyone* if our safehouse locations get leaked. We'll get a message to them saying you're safe once you're settled. Think of this as a chance to start over. Wipe the slate clean. Are you ready to start your new life?"

She hesitates again, and then her face hardens with resolve and she nods. We help her get into the van and tie her blindfold, then throw a pillowcase over her head to be certain. Her breathing picks up and her chest heaves, but it's out of fear more than a need for oxygen. She clutches the envelope to her chest like it's a lifeline. She'll be fine.

"Thank you," she says, her words muffled, and then we slide the door closed.

Once she's secured, I turn to Moriah. "Take her to the mountain house. He'll forget about her in three months."

The beta nods and hugs me, then gets in the van and they drive away.

I watch them leave, then wait another five minutes to be certain they're gone. I never got the omega's name, which is for the best. The less one hand knows what the other is doing, the better. After her five-minute head start is up, I pull out my phone and call Dan. He answers on the fourth ring.

"What's up, Vee? Everything okay?" he asks.

"I need you to be Tiny right now. Meet me at the bar."

Dan hangs up without answering. He doesn't need to. We both know what happens next. I walk back through the curtain and find Nate on stage. He has three dancers competing in some sort of fake contest that involves a half-empty pitcher of beer, a chair, and a wiffle ball. The rest of my alphas are spread out throughout the club, ready in case there's trouble.

My bouncer cuts through the people like the mountain that he is. His normally sweet smile is replaced with a scowl that would make my knees knock together if I didn't know he was a marshmallow underneath that gruff ex-biker aesthetic. I use my chin to point toward the alpha, who's still at the bar with Anthony.

Dan lays a hand on the alpha's shoulder and the unsuspecting man meets my bouncer's alter ego, Tiny. "Your welcome has been revoked. Get the fuck out."

"What the fuck, man? Get your hand off me or I'll—" The alpha never gets to finish his sentence.

Dan closes a hand around his throat and cuts his tirade off as he lifts the alpha onto his tiptoes. The alpha swings and grapples, but it's like trying to wrestle a grizzly. You're gonna lose and all you'll do is piss off the grizzly. But the alpha doesn't seem to recognize that he's no longer the biggest threat in the room.

The people who notice the commotion make a hole and then Dan kicks the front door open and tosses the man out onto the street. The alpha lands on the sidewalk hard and people gasp, backing away from the scene.

"Stay the fuck off our property," Tiny growls, "or you're gonna see how mad I can get."

When the front door shuts, my blood is still pumping through my veins. I'm electrified. Is there anything better than knowing I took an abused omega away from an alphahole?

I turn to Anthony and raise a brow. "You got his photo?"

"Did you doubt that I would?" Anthony asks. He grabs his phone and a minute later, mine chirps and I get to stare at the alpha's smarmy, smug face. I wish I could see him now, see the fear in his eyes, but it's better if I don't reveal myself now that our hand is tipped. Is he giving Dan trouble? Is the alpha meeting the business end of Tiny's fists? I wish I could watch. I love it when Tiny grinds an alpha's face into the floor.

Pure elation and adrenaline flood my system. Now that the

need for subterfuge is over, I'm left with the rush. It's like I stepped off a roller coaster. Like I can do anything.

"That's gonna go great on the wall with the others. Good work." I turn around and bump into an alpha, who reaches up and steadies me on my heels.

The familiar scent of warm, freshly baked bread fills my nose and teases my senses. They're already in overdrive from my fight-or-flight system triggered. "It's you," he says. "You're the bar that's helping the—"

Fuck.

I grab his tie and wind it around my hand and yank his head down. The fabric—burgundy with thin gold stripes—pulls taut and his words get cut off mid-sentence as I choke him. I press my lips to his ear. "If you blow my club's cover, it will be your life's biggest regret. Not your boring little desk job. Not your off the rack suits that don't quite fit you. Not your sad little corporate coffee mug. Me. I will ruin you. I will make you regret the day you crossed my threshold. Am I crystal clear?"

His hand cups my hip, and I tense and get ready for him to grab me or push me away, but all he does is hold it there as I choke the air from him. After another yank on his tie to prove my point, I ease my grip and let him breathe.

"Everything okay?" Anthony asks from my side. I didn't see him join us.

Patrons near us give us wary looks, but the rest of the club is oblivious. The omegas closest to the stage are too busy trying to toss a wiffle ball into a beer pitcher while it's balanced on an alpha dancer's erection.

Brendan stares down at me with brown eyes blown dark, his pupils wide with lust. The crowd surges, and he's shoved against me. My leg slots between his, and it brushes against a bulge that shouldn't be there. His eyes slide halfway shut and he shivers. I eye the impressive erection tenting his pants underneath the edge of his suit jacket.

Oh. He likes it. Anthony was right. The buttoned-up ones really are the kinkiest.

Realization floods through me as I come back to my senses. Ah, shit. I choked my IRS agent and threatened him with pain and suffering, and… and I think he *really* liked it.

Brendan reaches for his tie and loosens it. His face is red. Is that all from the choking, or is that embarrassment too? Shame and arousal are a potent mix.

"Everything is fine," I say before things can escalate anymore. *Shitshitshit.* I didn't mean to do that. It was the endorphins flooding my system, the adrenaline making me think I'm invulnerable.

I am so epicly fucked. The IRS is going to throw me in tax jail or something. Does the IRS have jail?

Brendan's nostrils flare as he inhales, and then he purrs. It's a deep rumbling sound that reminds me of 16 wheelers on the highway. The sound chokes off before it can get really started. He coughs to clear his throat and drops his eyes.

"Fine," he agrees. "Everything is fine. I'm going to… Excuse me."

Anthony and I watch the IRS agent slip through the crowd and head to the stairs. I should follow him to apologize or explain, but that would probably make things worse. Nothing good comes from an alpha who's cornered and threatened.

"Did he pop a fear boner?" Anthony asks.

I sigh and close my eyes and pray to the universe to grant me patience. "Yeah."

"Huh. This is working out even better than I could have planned."

"What does *that* mean?" I ask, rounding on Anthony for an explanation.

Anthony gives me a tilted grin, then reaches around me to cup my ass. He grabs it, his fingers digging into the exact spots where he spanked the deepest bruises. *Motherfucker.* He grabbed those spots on purpose. "Where are your panties? I can't find a line."

I remember his promise—threat—and blush. "No! This doesn't count! These are extenuating circumstances."

"I don't remember allowing for stipulations."

Anthony's grin is full of wicked promises.

Chapter Ten

VERONICA

ANTHONY SMIRKS. "YOU CAN'T SAY I'M NOT GOOD TO YOU. I'll give you a choice." He leans down so he can whisper his next words without the entire club hearing as he shouts to be heard over the music. "Either I can ruck your skirt up right now and fuck you right here, right now, on the dance floor, or you'll stay after closing and I get to do anything I want to you."

"Define anything," I demand, because there's a lot of stuff I don't like and he and I haven't had a discussion about hard limits yet. We haven't done much talking at all, actually. We're like horny teenagers discovering orgasms for the first time. It's ridiculous.

"No," he says, shutting down my demand. "Make your choice."

I bite back a scream while his fingers rub the crack of my ass. They press until the skirt fabric sticks to my wet mound. One finger slips over my cleft and rubs the seam of my pussy. God, when did I get so wet? It's gotta be slick from my upcoming heat. There's no way I'd normally like this… this manhandling.

"Tick tock," he says just as he works lower and his thumb

brushes the bare skin along the inside of my knee. "Decide now or I'll decide for you."

"Fine! Later. Within reason."

He laughs and gives my tender ass a squeeze, then lets me go. "Deal. See you later, boss. Agent Hall might need you right now. I think he's got a crush."

He's wrong. But arguing with Anthony will only make him more insistent that he's right.

I head to the stairs and climb them without once looking over my shoulder to find Anthony in the crowd. I expect to push open the door and find my IRS agent furiously packing up his things. Instead, he's sitting at his desk and working. His red ears give him away as the color of his warm brown skin deepens when I step over the threshold.

The door creaks as I swing it shut so the music dampens to a dull thump. "Agent Hall, I have to apologize for my behavior. I should not have touched you like that. The extent and inner workings of my nonprofit are a mystery even to most of my own employees. People only know what they have to know to play their role. I trust you'll understand that secrecy is necessary when dealing with sensitive things like omega shelters. I would appreciate your discretion."

There. That sounded professional.

He looks up by the end of my apology speech, and I see his eyes are back to normal. "Call me Brendan, please. And I understand. Surprise made me speak without thinking."

I nod and take a deep breath. "That's still no excuse for putting my hands on you like that." Although he seemed to have enjoyed it. I think of the horrible things I whispered to him in the moment and wince.

"Your protective urges were close to the surface. It's understandable," he says.

When he says nothing else after that, I cross to my desk and sit. *Well. That went better than I thought it would.* I nudge the desk drawer, the one I keep the angel shot in, closed with my foot, and stare at it as I let myself get lost in thought.

She's probably made it to the first safehouse by now. It's really more of a pit stop to make sure she doesn't need urgent attention before they hit the road again. They'll be feeding her and letting her shower and change clothes before they make the second leg of their journey. No matter what the fallout of today ends up costing us, we did a good thing, and that's what matters.

"I have three sisters," Brendan says, breaking me out of my thoughts.

"Excuse me?"

He twirls his pen in his hand and eyes his coffee mug, the one I called sad. "I have three sisters. Two of them are omegas. What you're doing is important. I would want someone like you to be around to help them if they needed it."

"Thank you." Maybe he really understands. Maybe I won't be put into handcuffs in the morning. *Assaulting a federal employee... Fuck.*

And then I think of the reckless promise I made to Anthony. The one I'll no doubt regret tomorrow. I might end up in handcuffs anyway if that crazy beta has his way.

Trepidation makes my belly squirm.

We work in a tense silence that eases when nothing else unsavory happens, and then when last call comes, Brendan stands and packs up his things. He stayed later tonight than he ever had before. *Is he getting used to our schedule?*

"Good night, Veronica." He nods at me as he snaps his briefcase shut.

"Good night, Brendan."

At the doorway, he pauses with one hand on the trim. He

looks over his shoulder. "You've built something really amazing here."

Nerves flutter back to life before turning into something molten at his praise. I must be more starved for attention than I realized, because I don't want him to stop. I want him to keep telling me how good I am, how great Rut is, with his deep, fatherly voice.

"Thank you."

"See you later," he promises. His smile is genuine, and he raps his knuckles against the trim before leaving. I watch his descent down the stairs until I can't see him anymore.

That's a good sign, right?

I save my documents and shut down my computer. Dan secures the building and walks the staff out to their cars in case the disgruntled alpha comes back. "Want me to walk you out, Miss Vee?" he asks.

"No, but thanks, Dan. You go home to your mates. Anthony and I are… going to do inventory."

He grunts and looks at Jamie, who's seated at the bar and drinking what looks like lemonade.

"Jamie volunteered to help… count bottles," I supply. The excuse is weak, but Dan doesn't talk much, let alone ask questions. Before I met his mates at the one-year anniversary party and saw him interact with them, I didn't know he knew words that weren't monosyllabic. I didn't hire him for his elocution, after all.

My bouncer grunts again and leaves, and I do a last sweep to make sure there are no stragglers. Once I'm sure it's empty, I sit on the padded stool next to Jamie and try to look unaffected, but my heart is beating against my ribs like a bird battering its wings against its cage. I can't help but feel like I've made a deal with a devil.

"Well?" I ask, arching a brow. May as well get this over with.

"Have a drink." Anthony slides another piña colada over to me, and all I can think about is how I didn't hear him use the blender.

"Another one?" I ask, frowning, but I'm already reaching for it before actively thinking about it. My mouth waters as I look at the condensation sliding down the curved glass. There's a wedge of pineapple balanced on the rim. It looks delicious as fuck.

"You were right. We'll talk about boundaries while you relax," Anthony says. "It's been a crazy day and you've more than earned it."

Oh. That's actually sweet of him. "Sure." I swivel the straw and wrap my lips around it and suck, nearly groaning with the first splash of pineapple and coconut and chipped ice on my tongue. "Seriously, what do you put in these? Crack?"

"No." He grins and throws a bar towel over his shoulder, then crosses his arms over his chest. "Absolutely no illegal drugs in it. But I'm glad you like it. It's Jamie's special recipe, actually."

"It is?" I swivel on my stool to observe the alpha dancer whose cheeks are pink. His eyes are glued to my lips, where they wrap around the straw. "This is your recipe? It's fantastic. You should work on the daily drink specials with Anthony. What else can you make?"

"Uhhh…" Jamie scratches the side of his face. "I don't remember the names."

He doesn't remember the names of his own cocktail mixes? "Umm… okay."

"Blue Hawaiian. That's tomorrow's drink," Anthony says. "Now, let's talk about limits."

"Fine." I get ready for my usual speech, the one I give to all the alphas I pick from Heat Buddy whenever I need one. "I prefer to top, but on the rare occasions when I switch, I enjoy spanking, clamps, flogging, and light pain. Nothing heavy and zero bondage. No permanent marks or body modifications."

He nods. "So choking, hair pulling, and calling you my pretty cum slut are all fine?"

I shrug one shoulder and stir my drink with the straw. "Yeah." Words don't bother me. It's actions that matter.

"We already established you don't mind a bit of rough handling. Jamie and I have a free use situation going on. Can I wake you up with my cock in you?"

If I decide to let them help me with my heat, that's the least of my concerns. When I'm in a bout of heat delirium, I won't care. "Sure. But don't take that to mean you can do anything you want all the time. Work and play are separate. When it comes to work, I'm still your boss."

He's still for a moment, then he nods. "Fine by me."

"And we need to talk about this public sex kink of yours."

"Oh yeah?" He arches a brow and leans his elbows on the bar top.

"Yeah."

Reaching over his prep station, I flick a finger and nudge one of his tiny mason jars toward him to annoy him. He likes to experiment with his own herb and fruit-infused liquors before he makes big batches for the bar. This one has blueberries in it. It smells like paint stripper to me, but he insists they're classy and he needs them for his top-shelf gin cocktails. He hates it when anyone else touches them.

"If you take it too far, I'll castrate you and wear your balls in this jar like it's a necklace."

Anthony lines them up again. "You're gonna need a bigger jar," he says, noncommittal.

I laugh, and then the crinkling of the skin around his eyes as he smiles makes me feel things I'm not comfortable naming. "So is this all you wanted to do with your carte blanche card? Talk?" My pelvis tightens with anticipation.

He fiddles with the berry jar until it's perfectly in place and wipes his station clean. "Yes."

Wait, what? I square my shoulders and try to see through this new play of his. "Really?"

Anthony takes his black server apron off and hangs it on its hook. "Really. But if you're saying that you want me to bend you over this bar and fuck you till you forget your name, all you have to do is ask nicely, baby. Don't forget the *please* and *Daddy*."

A shiver rolls through my body, and I fight the urge to squirm in my seat as I stare at him. "You would *love* that, wouldn't you?" It's bad enough that I've ever begged him for anything before without having my nose shoved in it after. *That's just fucking rude.*

"So would you." He leans onto his forearms on the counter and gives me his panty melter grin. "I can promise you this. I'll never do anything you don't love, whether you enjoy admitting it or not."

Ooh, boy. I thought it was good before, but after having his cock in me... That look is absolutely devastating. "Hmm." I drain the rest of my drink and nudge the empty glass toward him. He may have gotten me to call him Daddy, but I'm still the one in charge. During play, it's the submissive who holds the actual power. Who determines the limits and end of a scene.

Anthony doesn't make a fuss as he snags the empty glass and washes it in the sink along with Jamie's empty lemonade glass. "I know nights like tonight normally take a lot out of you," he says as he rinses the suds off and dips them in disinfectant, then lays them out on the rubber bar mat to dry. "Figured you'd need a calm end to the night to unwind."

He's right. Except… he's not. I feel fine. Better than fine, actually. Normally, whenever we have to bundle an omega out to safety, I'm emotionally wrung out once the initial adrenaline rush fades. Sometimes if the alpha puts up a big fight and my bouncer and dancers have to get more involved, I hide in my office until the shaking passes.

Too many bad memories triggered by all the growling and fighting. Being a teenager in foster care wasn't easy. Being a girl and presenting as an omega was even worse. Between other teenage fosters and my foster mother's abusive asshole boyfriend of the month, some of them thought they could put their hands on me and get away with it. Those who tried quickly found out they were wrong.

But right now I'm good. I'm feeling better than I have in weeks. "Huh."

"What's wrong?" Jamie asks, his expression pinched with concern.

"Nothing," I say. "I'm… good." It's like the rush of energy you get when you take one of those sketchy vitamin shots they sell at gas stations. My tension headache is gone. I'm energized, despite the late hour. The worst of my preheat symptoms have faded into the background, easy to ignore for now. It's like I got a second wind. "I feel better than I have in a long time."

"That's good. I'm really glad to hear that." He smiles, a real one rather than a lurid grin. "You should go get some rest. It's been a long day. Walk her to her car, babe," Anthony says.

Jamie slips off his stool, and I grab my purse and keys and follow him out. Our parking lot is well lit and we have a state-of-the-art security system, but he still glances around as if that alpha from earlier is lurking in the shadows with a baseball bat. It's happened before. But tonight, the coast is clear.

I press the unlock button on my key fob until my car beeps, and Jamie pushes ahead to get my door for me. It's awkward because I'm not used to it, but kind of charming coming from the sweet blond alpha. "Thank you." I slip inside and buckle my seat belt, but he leans on the door frame instead of closing the door right away.

"I'm not good with words," Jamie says as he tucks his hair behind his ear. "But I really like you, Vee, and I wanted you to know because if I don't say something, I think I'll regret it for the rest of my life."

"Jamie," I sigh and tap my fingers on the steering wheel to stall.

"You don't like me?" he asks, his voice wavering.

"It's not that." Because I do. He's sweet, genuine, and kind. When he stares at me like he can't get his fill of looking at me, I feel amazing. Like I'm capable of anything. And his scent drives me wild. I can't get enough of it. I want to dig my nose into his neck and live there. It makes me remember happier, better times, when things were so simple. I took those days for granted until they were gone. Now the memory of them is bittersweet.

"I'm not pack material," I tell him. "Rut is my life. I work sixteen-hour days, seven days a week. Half the time I barely remember to eat. I'm allergic to being told what to do, and I have dreams. Big ones. Ambitions that keep me from being a good girlfriend who remembers to text back or call or keep plans when work stuff comes up. I can't think about settling down and having kids right now because there's so much work to do. I'll disappoint you."

Because I always do. Rut will always be the first and biggest love of my life. The work we're doing matters more than my own personal happiness. On the surface, we give omegas a safe space for them to be free and wild. Where their needs are catered to at the expense of alphas for a change. And underneath that, we help the ones who need it the most. The abused. Trafficking victims. The runaways. The ones who are suffering.

"So you're hurting me by saying no because you don't want to hurt me by saying yes?" he asks, his face scrunched with thought.

If it were anyone other than Jamie, I'd say they were arguing, but he seems to be genuinely trying to piece things together. I give him a rueful smile. "A little hurt now compared to a big hurt later, yes."

He frowns and tilts his head. "But isn't that taking away my choice? What if I want to risk the big hurt because I think it's worth it? Because I think *you're* worth it."

I open my mouth to argue that I'm really not worth it, but he cuts me off as if he can't keep the words contained now that he's found them, "I drink the *respect women juice*, Vee, but this has bad vibes. It seems like you're making my choice for me and that's not fair. I choose to try. If you'll have me. If you don't think I'm weird or stupid or a weak alpha."

"You're not a weak alpha, Jamie. Being submissive in bed doesn't make you a bad alpha."

"It doesn't?" The hopeful look on his face rips my heart into a hundred jagged pieces. Who hurt him? I want to stomp on their balls with my stilettos.

Submissiveness isn't bad unless it's forced. But I can imagine that most omegas don't understand his urges. Most alphas don't understand mine. "Do you think I'm being weak when Anthony has me call him Daddy?"

He shakes his head, long blond hair sliding over his broad shoulders. "No. I think it's hot."

"It's fun. A make-believe fantasy. We're all consenting adults."

He nods. "Then you're okay too. You're not a bad omega if… uh… if that's what you're thinking when you're with us. It's play."

My grip tightens on my car keys until the metal teeth dig into my palms. It's easy to say these things about him, but it's harder to believe them about myself. "I don't know. Sometimes I think the way I like to treat people isn't always healthy or fair. I can be controlling. Demanding. Jealous."

"You'd want me to stop seeing Anthony?" he asks, his tone horrified.

"No! No, that's not what I meant. I mean that if you're serious, I would want to keep things closed. Only us. We would decide things as a group, but I don't do casual unless it's only for heat relief. I won't have a threesome if you bring some girl home from the bar. I don't want to deal with hookups and swinging and group play at parties. If you look at another omega, I'll want to claw their eyes out."

"Oh," he says, his smile returning. "Okay."

I arch a brow and wait for him to continue, but he doesn't. "That's it? You're okay with that?"

"Yeah. Anthony's always asking why we should have to live our lives according to someone else's rules. He says we don't have to listen to the people who say that alphas like me and betas like him and omegas like you are wrong. That we shouldn't care what they think, not if it means we're right for each other.

"It's like learning to stand up on your board in the water when all you've done is practice on the beach. You won't know if you can do it until you try. And if you wipe out, you try to stand up again until one day you get it. You get to ride your first tasty wave, and you know you're never going to stop now that you can do it. So can we try? I want to stand up on the surfboard with you."

I can't help but smile at his odd metaphor. It's so distinctly Jamie. But I'm less like a surfer and more like the ocean itself. Cold. Unforgiving. My ambitions have drowned the hopes and dreams of others to the point where it doesn't seem worth it to keep trying.

There's no white picket fence and two point five kids and a golden retriever in my immediate future. When people leave, all you have are things. I aim to have a lot of things. Too much to fit into a garbage bag when the temporary family who welcomed me and said all the right things they're supposed to say eventually showed me the door because my presence was more trouble than it was worth.

"Oh, I know!" Jamie slaps his palm against the roof of my car. He grins. "Audition us!"

"Audition you to become my boyfriends?" It's not the strangest request I've ever had, but it's up there.

Normally when I tell the alphas I occasionally hook up with that I'm only looking for a one and done, they're content to fuck and get out. Some of them can't leave fast enough once my heat breaks. It's better that way. Less messy and uncomfortable.

"Yeah," he says. "Let us get you through this heat. Give us until the next one to prove we'll be a good pack."

I'm not sure if it's the fatigue because it's almost three in the morning or because I'm flying high after rescuing an omega today, but I'm tired of fighting this. So I give in.

My heat is coming whether I have someone to help me through it or not. Maybe I'll get a few orgasms out of it. And when they see what a shitty girlfriend I am after, they'll decide it was fun and I won't have to feel bad about it when things end naturally. It'll be awkward, but it's going to be awkward no matter what. There's no avoiding that now.

"Okay," I say.

Jamie's face is blank for a moment, and then his eyes round and his eyebrows climb. "Really? You mean it?"

"Yeah." I slot my keys in the engine and start my car. Before he can get too excited, I decide to lay down the first of many house rules. "Don't get your hopes up. I'm sure you'll regret it in a month. No hard feelings when you do. You'll still have jobs." Seeing them at work after things go south will be rough. It's a stupid move I know I'm going to regret, yet it seems I'm going to do it, anyway.

"Yes, Ma'am," he says, cheerfully. "Vee, can I kiss you?"

My answer pops out before it passes through my filter. "Only if you get on your knees for me."

He obeys the command instantly and sinks to his knees in the parking lot. It can't be comfortable. The surface is rough with gravel and debris and needs to be resealed next year. I leave him hanging and wait to see what he does.

Jamie stares up at me as if I hung the moon and stars in the sky. The power he's willing to give me is heady and scary at the same time. I'll be responsible for him as the dominant to his submissive, and I'm not that great at caring for my things. I can't keep a spider plant alive, and they're supposed to be unkillable. I went through three before giving up and finally getting a plastic one.

Once he's proven he won't take what hasn't been offered, I cup his strong, square jaw in my hands and drag his face closer. His lips are soft and pliant underneath mine, and my belly flutters as his sweet pheromones wash over me.

I have the urge to scent mark him. To tell the world he's mine. Why shouldn't I? Just because he's only mine for three months doesn't mean I can't enjoy him while it lasts.

I break the kiss and turn his face to the side so I can rub my cheek against his. He holds still, but he breaks into a purr while

I do it. Unlike Brendan's loud diesel truck purr, Jamie's is smoother. When cheek rubbing isn't enough, I reach a hand under the collar of his T-shirt and rub it over the large primary scent gland in his neck.

His purr stutters, and he groans, and then he gives me his neck. Bends it submissively to give me better access. A thrill runs through me at the sight of his stretched out neck and everything that it means. I want to dip my head down and nip at him. Suck my mark into the skin there for everyone to see that he's mine.

But he's one of my dancers. I can't. He has to stay pristine. Attainable. That's the entire illusion of Rut. Dozens of alphas wait on the omegas who patronize it. If they're visibly mated or claimed, it kills the fantasy.

Have some restraint, I berate myself. Restraint is good. I focus more on keeping control of myself and my teeth as I lean away from Jamie and take in his blissed-out expression. I savor the beautiful picture of surrender he makes. He's so fucking handsome on his knees for me.

"I won't forbid you from masturbating." *Yet.* "But you have to ask me for permission first and occasionally I might tell you no, not right now. If I do, it will be for a good reason, but you'll have to trust me. Is that clear, pet?"

"What about when I'm with Anthony?" he asks. "Sometimes he comes over after work or on our days off."

"That's fine. Anthony and I will discuss how we're going to handle this when we're not all together. Is that still okay with you?"

I wait for the first inkling of horror or regret on his face, but there's only a dreamy smile. The tension in my shoulders bleeds out. "Good night, pet. Text me when you get home so I know you're home safe and text me first thing when you wake up."

"Okay, Miss Vee. Good night." Jamie stands and closes my

door for me, then watches me pull out of the parking lot so I can head home.

I can't believe we're doing this.

It's crazy. Stupid. Reckless. But I can't stop smiling while I drive.

Chapter Eleven

VERONICA

I GO THROUGH MY ROUTINE IN A DAZE AS I GET HOME AND I plug my phone onto its charger and strip so I can take a shower. I check the fridge as if groceries have suddenly bought themselves and been magically put away. Its meager contents haven't changed since last night.

I really need to get to the store, but with my heat coming there doesn't seem to be much point. It's not like I'll eat while I'm delirious. Takeout and breakfast items will have to hold me over for a bit until after it's over. I eat dry cereal because my milk is spoiled, and then I shower. The plastic half-gallon jug makes glugging sounds as I dump its soured contents down the sink and toss it into my recycling bin.

When I'm cleaned and dressed in my softest pajamas, I slip into bed and punch the pillows into place. It takes a few minutes to get comfortable and I have that vaguely restless sensation growing under my skin again. It will only get worse over the next few days. I'm not at the hot and scratchy stage yet, but I can't get comfortable either.

An orgasm usually helps. I drag my wand from the nightstand and pull up my favorite site, finding a video that'll do.

Five minutes later, aftershocks spasm through me and dopamine floods my brain, smoothing out my jagged edges. Heaviness presses me deeper into my nest and I shut my eyes, curling up on my side.

My phone dings when I'm on the cusp of falling asleep.

Who the fuck is texting me at this hour?

And then I remember. I smile and unlock my phone, but instead of a sweet good night message from Jamie, it's a photo of him with his mouth full of cock and a familiar, tattooed hand smoothing his blond hair out of his face.

ANTHONY

Jamie would call to say good night but his mouth is busy keeping my cock warm for you

VERONICA

What a thoughtful pet

That was my exact thought

Good boys deserve treats, don't you think?

What sort of treat did you have in mind?

The breakfast of champions. Come to work early if you want to come.

Good night

Good night baby

I don't confirm if I'll be there early because I haven't decided yet. The obstinate part of me wants to stroll into work fifteen minutes late to prove a point. But isn't that biting off your nose to spite your face? Will losing an orgasm be worth the pettiness of resisting what's becoming inevitable?

I'm still deliberating the pros and cons when I fall asleep.

My phone's text message chime wakes me at the ass crack of dawn, and I blink, bleary-eyed, as I try to focus on anything but the insides of my eyelids.

I grope for my phone and read the time. It's half-past six. *What in the actual fuck?*

JAMIE

Good morning

VERONICA

What are you doing awake so early, pet?

Surfing

Do you surf everyday?

Yeah if the weather is good

What makes it good surfing weather?

Wind speed and direction

Fall and spring are the best because of the Santa Ana wind

There weren't a lot of waves today but I don't mind

It's nice to float too

You still need to sleep at some point

You were up late and now you're up early

That isn't good for you

I've never really slept more than 5 hours even when I was a kid

It drove my mother nuts

Oh the wind is finally picking up

Have fun pet

See you soon Ma'am

I roll over and snuggle under the warm covers and go back to sleep until my alarm blares and wakes me at a more reasonable ten in the morning. Normally I'd hit snooze for a while, but today I'm motivated to get to work early.

After I pee and brush my teeth, I throw my closet door open and consider my wardrobe options. I dress and run through my morning routine and commute in a blur of auto pilot and muscle memory.

It's gonna be a good day today.

BOTH OF THEIR CARS ARE ALREADY IN THE PARKING LOT WHEN I pull into my spot and park. I cut the engine and smile to myself, then head in. Their conversation stops mid-sentence as they stare and the attention feels good.

Both of their eyes travel down my body, but each one gets stuck on a different area. Anthony is staring at my legs. I'm wearing shiny black silk hosiery that gleam under the light. Jamie's gaze is stuck further south. I don't wear my red-bottom heels very often. They're insanely painful. But the expression on Jamie's face makes the pain worth it.

I push my sunglasses up on my head and set my purse on the bar top. "Hello, boys. I hope you both brought your appetites with you today because you have promises to fulfill."

I smile, my red lips curving up in a smug grin as their eyes travel up over the short black pencil skirt—mid thigh today instead of knee length like usual—and the sheer black Peter Pan-collar shirt I wear tucked into it. When more people get here, I'll throw on the camisole I shoved in my purse, but for right now I enjoy the way they devour the peek of my red lace bra underneath the sheer black shirt.

"We're starving, baby," Anthony says. "Come, give Daddy some sugar."

It's a test. He's waiting to see if I'll take orders from him when I'm not half out of my mind from horniness and my defenses are lowered. But this is what I want. I've decided to give into temptation for this heat. Afterward, we'll see what happens.

I saunter forward and let my hips sway with the movement. Anthony's wearing faded blue jeans and a gray short-sleeve Henley with the top two buttons undone. It's enough to see the peek of his chest tattoo above the collar. I close the distance between us and set my hands on his chest, using him for stability as I stretch up and press a chaste kiss to his mouth.

He pinches my jaw between his thumb and forefinger and tilts my chin back so I'm staring up at him through my lashes. "Am I gonna mess up your lipstick if I kiss you for real, baby?"

"It's a stain." But it was surprisingly sweet of him to worry about it.

"Then kiss me like you mean it," Anthony orders.

I throw my arms around his neck for more support as I go up on tiptoes and kiss him fully on the mouth. His response to the kiss is harsh, demanding, yet I find it comforting. As if he's desperate to have me.

His arms come around me, and he gets two good handfuls of ass and squeezes. The pain from my spanking is mild now. I heal quickly, especially this close to a heat, and the bruises weren't that deep to begin with. The blue and purple have faded to a sickly yellow green. The pain is more of an ache, a pleasant reminder of his attention every time I sit. Anthony deepens the kiss and groans against my mouth, and I swallow his hungry, yearning noises.

He nips my lower lip, then lets me go and passes me to Jamie, who's been waiting patiently. He's taller, so I can't quite get my arms all the way around his neck, but I can loop them over his shoulders.

"Good morning, pet."

"Good morning, Ma'am."

I make him do the bending. Jamie's kiss is gentle and patient. He follows my lead, softening when I do, then opening his mouth so I can push my tongue inside and slide it against his. His hands cup my back with enough force that I know he's there, but not enough to be demanding or grabbing.

Both men leave me breathless in their study of contrasts.

I make a happy hum against his mouth and pull away. What a pleasant way to start the day. It's certainly putting me in a better mood than normal. Mornings and I aren't friends. But I don't mind that Jamie woke me up so early to show me his time on the beach. I enjoyed having a private, intimate moment that's only the two of us. Anthony's personality is so vibrant, so big, that sometimes when all of us are together, it seems like Jamie gets lost in the background.

"Was I good?" Jamie asks.

"You are. I'm happy." I run my thumb along his clean-shaven jaw and scrape my nails over the coarse beard hair that's already growing back. It's all that testosterone flooding his alpha system.

"Can I please you some more?" he asks.

My belly swoops with anticipation. "Yes. I think that's a good idea. You were very good last night and this morning. You did everything I told you to. Good behavior earns rewards. Would you like your reward now, pet?"

He nods.

"Good." I unwrap myself from around him. "Come."

He follows me to the bar, and his hands open and close in fists as I grab the edge of my short skirt and inch the fabric up. It'll wrinkle, but this will be worth it.

Both of them are speechless when they see what I'm wearing underneath. Instead of pantyhose covering my pelvis, the stockings end at the tops of my thighs. A vintage suspender belt with eight metal tabs holds them up. Black silk panties go over all of it. Easy on, easy off. It baffles me when people get it backward and wear their panties underneath the garter belt. The entire point of a crotchless system is easy access.

I scoot a bar stool aside and lean against the bar. Then I spread my legs apart and lean back on my elbows. I arch a brow and shift until I'm comfortable. "Well? Please me."

"Yes, Ma'am." Jamie gets down on his knees before me and starts his worship with kisses up and down my legs. He drops them on my thighs, calves, and ankles. He presses one to the tops of my heels.

"That's good, pet, but you can do better." I thread my fingers through his hair and grip him by the head and drag his face toward where I want it most—between my legs. The place where I've been aching to be touched since last night.

He shoves his nose against my fabric covered mound and drags in a deep breath that makes his eyes flutter shut. Jamie purrs and nuzzles my pussy, and I close my eyes and tip my head back as I give in and focus on the sensations.

"Hmm. That's good, but I want more. Pull my panties down and lick me. You can use your hands this time. Yes, that's right." The fabric digs into my thighs where he's rolled them down, but the slide of his tongue along my seam makes up for it.

Quick licks tease me and long swipes of his tongue make me sigh. When he nudges the hood back from my clit and sucks it into his mouth, my mind empties of all thought other than the sensations he brings to life between my legs. Each suck and pull and swipe brings me closer to the cusp as everything inside me tightens, but it's not enough. This close to my heat, I'm aching to be filled more than normal. My pussy is so empty.

When Jamie's tongue licks lower and dips inside my entrance, his throaty purr makes my spine arch. I bury my hand in his hair and press his face harder against my mound. I've never had an alpha purr while eating me out. Why has no one ever offered before? It's amazing. "Do that again."

He purrs while he sucks and licks me, while his tongue pierces my hole with tentative thrusts and his lips round around my clit. "That's good, pet. Very good. But I know you can do better. Give me more."

My hips rise to meet him and my hand keeps him steady as I crush him to my body. Worries about if I'm hurting him or if he can breathe fades away. All that matters is the wave of pleasure swelling within me and the delicious throb of my clit against his lips. My breath catches and I let out a throaty hum. So close. A bit more and then my world can shatter.

"That's enough," Anthony says.

Jamie's movements stop abruptly, like he's a windup doll whose cranking has run out. My swelling orgasm stalls and sputters out. I lift my head from where it's dropped back and glare at Anthony for messing with my orgasm right when I was on the cusp.

Anthony is closer than he was before. I didn't hear him move when I was enraptured with the skill of my pet alpha's mouth. Anthony stands over the kneeling Jamie and reaches out, gripping me by the back of my neck. He spins me around and keeps me from faltering as I get my heels under me and try not to knee Jamie in the nose or step on him. That's only fun if I mean to do it.

"Hands on the bar, baby. It's time to feed our boy breakfast."

Confusion makes me slow, because I already was. Isn't this what they meant? Anthony takes full advantage of it and pushes my shoulders down. A foot kicks my legs apart, and I have to lean on the counter to avoid falling over from the shock of it.

"Down," Anthony orders, but his fingers dig into my hip and keep me from moving.

When Jamie's broad shoulder knocks into my leg, getting

comfortable at my feet, I realize what they're doing. Jamie curls himself up tight on the floor between two stools. His large hands grip my legs to steady me as he plants himself between them.

The sounds of a belt buckle being undone and a fly unzipping are loud in the silent room. Anthony still has a hold on my neck as he undoes his pants one handed. Something blunt nudges at my entrance, and then he surges inside of me and buries his cock in deep to the hilt in a single smooth thrust that steals my breath.

"He got you nice and ready for me, baby. He's such a good boy, isn't he?" Anthony asks. "Such a talented tongue."

"So good," I agree as my hips arch back to meet Anthony's thrusts until our skin slaps together with dull smacks. "Such a… a good boy. Oh, fuck."

Jamie's mouth is on me again while Anthony rails into me from behind. My palms squeak against the shiny countertop with every jarring slap. There's no gentle warmup from the beta. He goes from entering me to pounding my cervix with every snap of his hips. His cock fills me completely. Stretches my walls.

If I weren't already aroused from Jamie eating me out, this would hurt. It's wonderful. Exactly what I need with my heat riding me so close.

Anthony slides his hand up my neck until it's buried in my hair. He cards his fingers through the strands at my nape and grabs a handful, squeezing, and then he tugs me where he wants me until my spine arches. It's either comply or rip out hair, so I go where he moves me. My pelvis tilts so he can thrust deeper, his cock burrowing a home for itself inside my cunt, and Jamie's tongue follows. It never stops lapping.

Jamie licks through my folds and teases my clit. He sucks the nub into his mouth, and then he purrs and I'm lost. My dignity takes a backseat because my pleasure is the only thing that matters right now and I want to come. Need to. Desperately.

"Fuck," I mutter as my eyes squeeze shut and I revel in the sensations. "It's so good. Fuck me harder. Make me come. I want to come on your cock."

He groans from behind me and his thrusts turn into brutal poundings. If the bar weren't holding me up and Jamie weren't keeping my trembling legs from buckling, I would be a puddle on the floor.

"Such a bossy bottom. Fuck, baby. I kind of love it when you make demands. Especially when you beg me to cream this sweet little pussy. We're gonna feed our boy so well, baby. He needs his protein, don't you, babe?"

Jamie makes a noise of agreement that's muffled because his head is still smashed between my thighs. His tongue licks over where Anthony and I are joined. He teases my stretched entrance and laps over my swollen clit. And then he purrs and I'm lost again.

All I am is neediness. The need to come. The need for complete and utter acceptance. And I wonder if I've found that or if our house of cards will come crashing down after and make everything beyond awkward.

A scuffing noise makes Anthony's brutal pounding rhythm falter, and my swirling orgasm stalls out again before it can be realized. I release a frustrated noise and try to turn my head to look and see what's wrong, but Anthony's grip tightens in my hair as he keeps me where he wants me, even though he isn't moving.

"I am so sorry," a familiar voice says from somewhere behind us. I know that voice. "I was running errands and saw the door open so I thought… I mean, I left something here last night, so I… You know what? It doesn't matter. I'm sorry. I'll go. Forget I was here."

"Why?" Anthony asks. "Pull up a stool, Agent Hall." Anthony kicks a stool a few inches to the side and its legs scrape against the floor. It teeters and nearly falls over. "Why don't you join us? We love an audience."

Oh, fuck.

Chapter Twelve

VERONICA

My entire body clenches with panic. Anthony grunts, since his cock is still buried deep inside of me. Of all the people to walk in on us fucking, it had to be the IRS agent who's not even supposed to be here today because it's Sunday.

"Anthony, that's eno—" My protest gets cut off when he pulls my head to the side, then shoves two fingers in my mouth and pins my tongue down.

I'm gonna fucking kill him.

Anthony makes a tsking sound. "You didn't list exhibitionism as one of your hard limits. You should have been more thorough yesterday when we were negotiating. But if you want me to tell him to leave, then I want something in return. I want you to let Jamie fuck your cute little ass."

I give Anthony a murderous glare that promises pain and retribution, but all the cocky beta does is grin and chuckle as if he likes it. His cock bouncing inside me with the movement of his diaphragm. Jamie's alpha cock is massive. There's no way it's going anywhere near that hole.

"No? Don't tell me you've never done anal before. Your ass is so perfectly fuckable."

"The lady said no," Brendan growls. He sounds five seconds away from tackling my bratty bartender.

That's the last thing I need. My mumbled protests are incomprehensible as I try to talk around Anthony's fingers. He's five seconds away from getting bitten.

Anthony huffs. "The lady likes to protest so she doesn't have to feel guilty about giving in when it comes to something she needs, but doesn't want to admit. She didn't use her safe word."

"Maybe," Brendan says. "But I need to hear it from her, and then I'll go."

Instead of stopping, Anthony pulls his hips back and slides forward and Jamie goes back to licking my clit. Anthony's other thumb ghosts over my asshole, and my pussy tightens in response.

"If she hated it, she wouldn't be getting wetter right now."

My eyelids flutter and my breath comes out in ragged pants. We can't be doing this with the IRS agent watching. But Anthony has no such qualms, and neither does Jamie. They both go back to fucking me, and I don't hear footsteps walking away. With Anthony's tight grip on my chin and his fingers in my mouth, I can't swivel my head to check.

"Still, I really must insist," Brendan says. "Or we're going to have a problem."

Anthony grunts, and his thighs hit against my ass with a loud smack. My body makes filthy noises as he fucks me in front of our audience. Loud squelches and wet sounds.

"Fuck, baby, your pussy's practically strangling my cock. I love how you pretend you hate this. But your body is honest even when you're lying to everyone and yourself. This pussy doesn't lie. It's so fucking wet for me. Tell the nice IRS agent I'm not doing anything you don't absolutely fucking enjoy."

His fingers slip from my mouth and trace a wet line over my jaw.

"Remember when I told you there's a line between work and play?" I ask him.

"Not her safe word," he says to Brendan, then shoves his fingers back into my mouth. His momentum never stops.

I clamp my teeth closed enough to make him aware I might be bottoming but I'm never defenseless. He's lucky I hate using my safe word. I know I shouldn't, but it feels like giving up. Sometimes I'm too stubborn for my own good.

Anthony chuckles. "Well, I guess if this is my last day with balls, I should make it really count." He lets out a satisfied moan as if he's savoring this. "I think you enjoy making him see you get fucked while he knows he can't touch you. What do you think, baby? Think you can get him hot enough that he unbuttons his collar a bit? Maybe he'll pull that thick alpha cock out and jerk off while he watches me nail you to the bar. Watch your pussy drip with my cum while Jamie laps up all my cream."

Anthony drives his dick in deeper, making me go up higher on my tip toes. "You can't see your IRS agent right now, but he's hard. That's a big bulge in his pants. I bet his alpha cock is huge. Big enough to make you think you're splitting in two if him and Jamie knot both of your holes while I fuck your throat. Oh, fuck. Yeah, clamp down on me, baby. That's good. Is that what you want? A cock for every slutty hole?"

His dirty talk is deplorable. Absolutely filthy. For some unfathomable reason, I don't hate it. The picture he paints makes me groan around his fingers. The head of his cock batters at my cervix as if he's knocking for entry. He'd probably try to fuck his way deeper if it were physically possible. Jamie sucks my clit into his mouth and purrs and I'm lost again. The room loses meaning and fades from my thoughts until coming is the only thing I care about.

Anthony pulls his fingers from my mouth and my head drops until my forehead rests against the bar. Its surface is cool and smooth against my heated skin. For the third time this morning, my pleasure swells until it's nearly at that point of no return. I want it. Desperately. I need it. I *have* to come.

"If you edge me one more fucking time today…" I growl.

Anthony grunts out a laugh and his cock twitches with his next thrust. "I can't fill you up with cum if I don't have balls, baby. But I'll buy you a pretty necklace if that's what you want. Until then, I've got what you need right here. Here you go. Take it. Don't look away, Agent Hall. She's too pretty not to stare at when she comes. I'm gonna make her drip all over his mouth. Oh, fuck, that's good. Now, Jamie. Do it now." He lets out a deep and ragged moan. "I'm gonna come."

Jamie breaks out in a deep, rolling purr that unravels me in seconds. I come, my walls crashing down to milk Anthony's jerking, pulsing cock, while my IRS agent watches our depravity. I whimper as the aftershocks zip through me like tiny lightning strikes.

I'm sure the universe will make me pay for this moment of pleasure later, but right now I can't bring myself to care. Anthony pulls his cock out and grabs my buttocks, spreading my cheeks apart. "Push, baby. Jamie's earned his breakfast."

I'm too spent to argue. With my head pressed to the bar, I can pretend that my IRS agent isn't seeing me push my bartender's cum out of my pussy so my stripper can lap it up. Jamie's tongue licks at my messy cunt, and when that isn't enough, he pushes his tongue inside and cleans me thoroughly.

My pussy is sensitive and tired and a few of his swipes are too much, but he gentles his strokes whenever I flinch or twitch or gasp. Jamie cleans me of cum and slick and then he tugs my panties up and pulls my skirt down so I'm covered.

His cheek nuzzles my inner thigh. He's scent marking me back.

"Now that's a good way to start the day," Anthony says. "Wakes you up better than coffee." He brings his hand down on my ass, and I yelp and straighten up. I untangle myself from Jamie and try not to glance at Brendan. If I look at my IRS agent right now, I'll probably have a mental breakdown.

"Anthony," I warn him.

Unrepentant, Anthony grins and steals a kiss from me before I can react. "Don't be mad, baby. Everyone here liked it. See how hard Agent Hall is? I bet he's gonna rush home so he can jerk off while he thinks about how good your pussy smells. I bet he wishes he got a lick before Jamie cleaned you up."

My lips press together with displeasure as I put a hand to Anthony's chest and push him away. He stands there, unmoving for a moment in our unspoken power play, then lets me go.

Finally, I meet Brendan's eye and try to maintain a mask of composure. "Brendan, I'm—"

"It's fine," Brendan interrupts. His eyes are dilated, the pupils so large that his warm brown eyes are nearly black. "It's my fault for not knocking or calling first. And for, uh… staying. I just needed to know you were okay." He waves his hand as if to clear the air. "I'll see you tomorrow."

"You're off tonight, right?" Anthony calls out to Brendan's retreating back.

Brendan pauses, his shoulders squaring, and he turns to face us slowly. I get a good look at him and see that he's not in one of his suits. He's wearing dark washed jeans and a black T-shirt. His casual clothes fit him better. Instead of the bulky, boxy lines of his suit, I can see the breadth of his shoulders and the slight curve of a big body gone soft with age. He looks like he's made for cuddling. Strong, but in a comforting way.

"I am," Brendan says.

"You should come by as a customer," Anthony says. "You might find the show you're looking for."

Brendan tilts his head and frowns. "I'm not gay, if that's what you're asking. Not that there's anything wrong with it. Just… not really my thing."

"What are you doing?" I hiss at Anthony under my breath.

Anthony ignores me. He pulls me against his side and sets a proprietary hand on my hip. His thumb draws circles that make my pussy tingle even though it's sore. "Not *really* your thing or *not* your thing? Those are two different statements," he says.

Brendan fidgets and frowns. "Umm…"

"Got it," Anthony says. "You might have fooled around in college once or twice, but you've never dated a man. Probably didn't get much further than fumbling hands or a sloppy blowjob. A mouth's a mouth, right?"

I slap a hand over my face and groan because I can't bear to see this trainwreck. There doesn't seem to be any stopping it unless I gag my mouthy beta who doesn't know when to quit.

What did I do to deserve this?

"Nobody's gonna make you do anything you don't thoroughly enjoy," Anthony says. "Come by tonight if you're curious."

Brendan doesn't answer as he turns and leaves, the door banging into the metal keg behind him as it tries to bounce closed. I rub at the growing ache in my head. My feet hurt. I need to wash up, and we need to put the filter on high to get rid of the scent of our sex before the rest of the staff arrive.

Anthony and I need to have words.

"What the fuck was that?" I ask him as I step away from them both so Jamie can rise from his place on the floor. Jamie adjusts the bulge in his pants, and I realize that we've forgotten about him once more.

"He wants you," Jamie says. "I can smell it."

"That's not true. Not every guy who comes to Rut wants to fuck me. And he's not even here because he wants to be. He's doing a job. A job we need him to do well. I shouldn't have to explain that sexually harassing him is bad for business. Do you feel good about risking everything I've built here over the last five years for an orgasm? Was it worth it?"

Jamie has the decency to appear chastised, but Anthony's face is a mask of perfect neutrality. "You want him too," is all Anthony says in his defense.

"W-what? That's…" Impossible. A bad idea. I try to deny it, but the words get stuck.

Anthony does up his pants and finger combs his hair into place. "I'm working on getting him for you. Because there's nothing I wouldn't do for you. Even if that means bringing a relative stranger into this when things are tenuous at best. You don't make it easy to court you, Vee."

That's his idea of courtship? I blink in stunned silence. *Of course it is.* He's only a couple years younger than me, either twenty-seven or twenty-eight, but in some ways he's a lot younger. It doesn't excuse his behavior, but it makes sense. I grew up hard and fast because I had to. There was no other option but to survive or fail. Still, that doesn't mean I can let this stand.

"If you endanger Rut, you won't like me," I warn him. "You won't enjoy the response you'll get."

"You're right. And I'm sorry. I pushed it too far." He hangs his head and nervously drags his hand through his already straightened hair. He's silent as we all adjust to this abrupt shift in mood.

"But I'm also not wrong," he says. "You work with a lot of

alphas and nobody's made you perfume as hard as you have in the last few days," Anthony says. "Don't blame it on your heat either. Everyone can smell your interest."

Fuck. I don't know what to do with that. *Everyone can smell me?* I thought I was doing an okay job hiding it.

"It's okay," Anthony says when I'm too stunned to finish my sentence. "Jamie likes the way he smells too. And I enjoy ruffling his uptight attitude. He might be pack material. I still need to figure out a few things, but he has the potential to be promising."

"That's ridiculous," I wheeze. He's our IRS agent. We can't fuck our fucking IRS agent who is fucking *auditing* the bar. And Anthony's not the person in charge of putting my pack together. I am. If I even want one.

"Is it ridiculous?" Anthony asks. "So your pussy's not getting wet right now at the thought of having him under you? His scent rubbed all over your naked body? Him and Jamie teasing each other while you watch their show? I could stick my hand up your skirt and check if your panties are wet."

Anthony reaches for me, but I dance away from him and scowl. "That's enough."

"There's nothing wrong with wanting the comfort and security of a pack. But you're not ready yet. I didn't mean to push it this soon. How about this? If he doesn't come tonight, I won't bring it up again. Promise."

He holds a pinky out to me, and I stare at it before I realize what he wants. A pinky promise. It's so silly and juvenile and the gesture throws me mentally off balance. My irritation fizzles out.

Arguing with Anthony is like trying to push a boulder up a hill. The boulder always rolls back down into the gutter no matter how high you get it toward the peak.

It's not like it really matters. There's no way that Brendan is coming tonight after we traumatized him. He's probably calling the IRS office right now and getting our case reassigned. I am *definitely* going to IRS jail for unrestrained horniness.

"Fine," I sigh. "But when Brendan doesn't show up, you'll learn how to behave in public."

Anthony grins. "Okay. And when he does, I want your promise that you'll give him a fair trial. If you don't like him or he's not a good match, fine. But if he is, don't cut your nose off to spite your face."

He wiggles his pinky in the air. I bat it away, and then I ignore the both of them so I can head into the back. We need to clean up and run the fans on high exhaust before everyone gets here.

While they stay downstairs to get started working, I hide in my office. But I can't focus on my paperwork.

My phone buzzes, and I see that it's a text from Jamie asking for permission to come. *Poor guy.* We really left him hanging and I feel guilty. It's not fun when everyone in the room gets to come but you. I enjoy leveraging orgasm denial, but only to edge the pleasure higher. Not as a punishment. I roll my chair to the windows and examine the club, but they're nowhere in sight.

I text back a confirmation and he sends me a pink sparkling heart emoji in return. My lips curl with a smile. Is he thinking about me while he's stroking his cock? Is Anthony helping? I wish I were there, but I don't trust myself around them when the rest of my employees are due at work any minute. I've never had such an egregious lapse in self-control than the last several days. Ever since Brendan showed up, if I'm being honest.

We can't afford to get caught. Two employees getting caught fooling around is different than the boss fucking both of them.

I hang my head in my hands and wonder what the fuck I'm doing. This is crazy. A few minutes later, my phone buzzes again. It's Jamie saying thank you and calling me Ma'am again. My body feels tingly and my sore pussy attempts to boot and rally for a round two it won't get.

I don't know why the fuck I'm really letting all of this happen, but the truth is, I'm powerless to stop it. *I want them.*

If I'm honest with myself, I've wanted them for a while now. Years. And I can't remember why I ever thought that saying *no* but keeping them around was a viable long term option. The longer you deny a scent match, the worse the craving gets. It's simple biology.

This won't end well. But I'm not sure what's worse. Not trying at all and knowing I'm a coward, or trying, but having it crash and burn around me anyway.

Deep down, I didn't realize a sliver of me is still hoping for some sort of fairy tale happy ending. Those sorts of stories aren't meant for me. Life taught me early the world is full of disappointments and everyone leaves in the end. The only one you can really rely on is yourself.

Look at the omegas I help. They try, and they still don't get their happily ever after with their alpha or pack. The very people who are meant to protect them are the ones perpetrating their violence.

But Anthony is right. The three of them do feel like pack material, even if I'm trying so damn hard to suppress these useless omega urges.

Grumbling, I push these confusing thoughts away and dig through my desk for my extra strength nullifying spray. I'm gonna need to spray myself down like I'm in a hazmat decontamination.

Chapter Thirteen

BRENDAN

THE PARKING LOT IS PACKED BY THE TIME I ARRIVE WELL AFTER the doors opened. I find a spot after some circling and then sit in the car for twenty minutes while I work up the courage to get out and walk over.

"What the fuck am I doing?" I ask my reflection as I check myself in the mirror. I should go home. Jerk off for the fourth time today, pop some ibuprofen, and go to bed. But I can't stop thinking about how damn good they all are together. It should be illegal for people to be this beautiful and smell this good.

There's no way they actually want *me*. Maybe twenty years ago, but now?

"I'm a moron," I say as I open the door and get out. My car door slams shut behind me, and I click the lock on my fob and shove my keys in my jacket. This has to be a joke. I'll show up and they'll laugh and then I'll have to call the office tomorrow and tell my supervisor they need to reassign this case to someone else, but I can't explain why.

There's a line of people waiting at the door and they barely glance at me, other than a quick assessment to see who's joining the throng.

"Hey, IRS man," the enormous bouncer says, making me stop mid-step as I head toward the back of the line.

"Uh, yeah?" I turn and crane my head up because he keeps going and going. The alpha who guards the door is a brick house of a man. He's got to be over six and a half feet tall and nearly three hundred pounds of muscle and bulk. The faded leather vest he's wearing is covered in motorcycle patches. A name tag that ironically says Tiny is sewn over his heart.

"Brendan is fine. It's Dan, right?" I ask. It always pays to be polite to an alpha who could knock you on your ass while barely trying. In my glory days, I might have put up a good fight, but after I tore my knee and lost my scholarship, I've never been quite the same. Long days spent at a desk for years have finished me.

Why do you think they'd want you, the bitter voice in the back of my mind asks, *when there's a room full of healthy, powerful alphas she could summon to their bed with the crook of her finger?*

Dan nods and unlocks the hook on the red velvet rope. "Go on, man. No cover for you. Enjoy your time at Rut."

The line of people waiting to get in protest at me cutting ahead, but a sharp look from the burly alpha makes them quiet down. I wait for the bouncer to hook the rope back together and laugh before I can get inside, but he doesn't.

"Thank you." I shove my hands in my pockets and duck inside. Rut is so different when there are customers here. Like night and day. Talk radio and workplace banter have been replaced with dance music and the thump of bass. The lights are down and the floors are sticky from spilled drinks.

Neon decorations that I hardly notice when I'm leaving here, bleary-eyed after staring at computer screens and paperwork all day, now stand out to me. With the dim lighting and neon, the club is transformed. Bright colors break up the normally grungy black and gray walls and floor, and the luxe furniture keep it from looking low class. There's a crystal chandelier I've never noticed before and it reflects the neon signs around the room as it twinkles.

Padded faux leather chairs surround tables and velvet couches make groups of seating along the walls at the back. Every inch of the bar is social media snapshot worthy once the mood lighting is in place. The performance stage and the seating that rings it dominate the room, but there's a row of curtained private booths in the back and a stripper pole on a tiny raised stage. I wonder if they do private performances or if this is their version of the champagne room you find at seedier places around town.

The bar is crowded, especially at the end near the stage. One of the alpha dancers, a Black man with dark brown skin and long twisted locs tied away from his face, dances and strips while dressed as a fallen angel. Huge white wings that fade to black extend from his back. He's wearing tiny black rubber shorts that show off his impressive package. A black and silver leather harness crisscrosses over his chest while hiding nothing.

Something prickles at my awareness, and I swing my gaze around until I see what the cause is. There's a spot open at the bar, and that bartender, Anthony, is staring at me. We make eye contact and he grins, and then he reaches one tattoo-covered arm up and slicks his wild, dark waves out of his face.

His bright blue eyes never waver. They're captivating, but I'm not sure if that's a good thing. Something tells me Anthony is used to getting what he wants and he's not afraid to use his bad boy sex appeal to get it.

The trouble is, I don't know what he wants from me and I'm not sure finding out will be good for me.

I go to the bar like I'm pulled to him with a magnetic force I don't understand. I lean against the countertop and remember watching Veronica get fucked over it a few hours ago. My nostrils flare, trying to scent her, but it's been hours and there's no trace left.

"Did you bring it?" Anthony asks, shouting over the noise to be heard.

I reach into my back pocket and pull out the folded-up sheet of paper I put there this afternoon. I'm not sure how he got my phone number and I almost didn't follow his directions to go to a walk-in clinic that offers same-day test results. It felt like a joke. But the *what if* of it kept bugging me.

"Here. All negative."

Anthony reads the paper and instead of passing it back, he pockets it. "Good. So are we. Want a drink?"

"Sure." After today, I could use one.

He leaves without asking me what kind of drink I want, and a moment later he returns and sets a tall, curvy glass full of something pink down in front of me. He scoops ice into the frosted glass, then spears two cherries on a long toothpick and sets the garnish on top. The next thing he adds is a sprinkle of shaved coconut. He sets the drink down on a napkin and pushes it to the center where I can reach it.

When I go to take it, his hand covers mine to stop me. He leans over the bar and smirks. "If you drink this, you're saying *yes*."

My palm grows damp against the cold glass as condensation gathers from the warmth of the packed bar. "What's in it?"

"It's a very special recipe Jamie and I both came up with especially for you."

My suspicion grows along with his smile. "What, did you spit in it?" I don't understand this man. First he's staking his claim and posturing to warn me away, and then he's telling me to go get tested and promising it'll be worth my time. I don't know what to believe.

"If you want my spit, all you have to do is ask nicely for a kiss." Anthony plops a tiny black straw into the drink and gives it a stir. "No spit, I promise. But there will definitely be fluids swapping tonight if you take this drink. You're here. So are you in? All in? Because if you're not, then you should leave and we'll see you tomorrow, Agent Hall. I won't let you walk into her bedroom and risk everything we're building here if you're going to walk out of her life once your audit's done. Vee isn't some random hole for you to get your dick wet. She's special."

Agent Hall. The thing that used to fill me with pride leaves me tired now. Even if this strange offer is only for one night, do I want to say no? No is safe. Boring. Tedious. *Agent Hall* is a very boring man. Anthony makes me remember the guy, the alpha, I used to be before one kick shattered my knee and broke my dreams along with it.

It's funny how fast your life can change. One decision alters the course forever.

When did I get so... complacent? So dull and dependable? *Agent Hall* is going to die of old age and boredom. I'd like to remember what the old Brendan, the varsity soccer player with a full ride scholarship to UCLA, was like. I want to be that guy again.

I don't know if Veronica is as serious about trying this as Anthony seems to think she is, but I know I've never smelled anyone like her. I've never been an omega-crazy kind of alpha before. But she makes my mouth water and my self-control feels gossamer thin, so if there's a chance that this is for real and not a joke...

I tug the glass free from his grasp and raise the straw to my lips before I can overthink things to death. The first splash of lemonade, coconut cream, and cherry syrup floods my mouth and makes my jaw pinch before my mouth waters. Then I notice the rum and vodka. It's strong. On my empty stomach, this one drink might be enough to fuck me up. It's been a while since I had more than a beer with dinner while watching a game.

"How is it?" Anthony asks, his eyes lighting up. Patrons on either side of me make bids for his attention, but he ignores them all.

Being on the receiving end of his complete attention is exciting, but it also seems kind of dangerous. He's probably the most unhinged, feral beta I've ever met. If I couldn't detect his lack of obvious pheromones, I'd swear he was a smaller than average alpha.

"It's good."

"Oh, come on now." He puts his chin on his palm and pouts. "You can do better than that. Give me a fancy word, smart guy."

My chest puffs a bit from the mild praise and I wrack my mind for the most pretentious word I know. "Ambrosial."

Anthony laughs and the woman next to me practically melts against the bar top. I can smell the thick, cloying scent of her sweet pea pheromones. My nose wrinkles from the olfactory assault. Except for that very brief confrontation yesterday, I haven't been outside of Veronica's office while the bar was this busy.

"How do you stand it?" I ask him while looking around. I tap my nose so he knows what I mean.

He taps his nose and shrugs. "Beta, remember?" He turns to the omega next to me and tilts his head. "What do you want, doll?"

"I'll have whatever you'll gimme, handsome," the drunk omega slurs. "And a drink too." Her attempt to be provocative falls flat when she moves to pose herself better and stumbles against the bar.

Anthony sets a glass of water down in front of her and ignores her pouting. "Go on," he tells me. "Jamie's set is next."

I take the hint and my drink and get lost in the crowd and make my way toward the stage. I can't bear to wade into the throng of horny, perfuming omegas. I have no idea how the other alphas in the room stand it. This place is insane. It's unlike any rut bar I've been to before.

The omegas are eight deep around the stage. The alphas who brought some of them here, and the others who came to bring some of them home, all line the walls like a living fence of testosterone.

I join the other alphas and ignore their snickering as I drink my girly pink drink. It's delicious, and I don't care what color it is. The air is easier to breathe here, and when I look up, I see there are extra vents in the ceiling. I understand why the alphas hang out along the rim where it's safe from the jumble of competing pheromones.

I wonder if this is by design. I wouldn't put it past her. Veronica seems whip smart. I'll bet if I showed the floor plans to an HVAC guy, he'd tell me she angled the vents on purpose so that the alphas would flock to the sidelines, leaving the stage area clear of them. The omegas don't seem to mind packing up in the center, even though their scents make a nauseating blend. I feel bad for the alpha dancers on that stage. That's got to be a miserable job.

The fallen angel leaves the stage in nothing but his wings and a spike studded black thong stuffed with money. The MC comes out and talks fast into the microphone. The lighting changes and there's another burst of announcements, and then the omegas scream.

Jamie bursts through the split black curtain and starts his set. He's dressed in a Scottish kilt, complete with knee-high socks and boots and the leather belt pouch positioned right over his groin. He seems to have forgotten his shirt, though, because the extra swath of plaid tossed over his shoulder is the only thing covering his muscular, oiled chest. With his long hair and sun kissed skin, he looks like he stepped off the cover of a Highlander romance novel.

The omegas lose it.

He dances for a bit, each pose getting more and more suggestive, and then he unwinds his plaid. I'm surprised the costume is real instead of something sewn together and quick to take off, but this is Veronica we're talking about. I've never met someone so driven, so fierce, before. Of course she'd put one of her exotic dancers in an authentic, traditional kilt.

All I can think of is how long it must take him to get into this costume, only to take it all off a few minutes later. It seems like a lot of work for me, but from the reaction of the omegas at his feet, they appreciate it. There's a lot of money flying toward the stage.

When his song finishes and he's down to only the leather waist purse and a nude-colored thong, he makes his way around the stage and lets them shove their money into his underwear. They're rabid, tiny things as they stroke his purse, his legs, his abs. When one tries to sneak a hand under his purse to grope his cock, he turns away and moves further down the stage. The spurned omegas whine at the loss of him.

Huh. So much for the idea omegas are the submissive, meek dynamic. This group of omegas would likely storm the stage and carry him off if they thought they could get away with it.

Is this what makes Rut so special? I thought it was because of her secret omega rescue business, but this bar is more than a carefully constructed front. It's an omega oasis. I'm ashamed of my alpha brethren that none of us ever thought to make alpha strip clubs a thing, but I'm also glad we didn't. We probably would have found a way to ruin it.

Jamie steps off the stage, but a man with dark hair meets him at the curtains before he can go through it. He shifts and I see him in profile. It's Anthony. They bend their heads together, and then they both turn in unison. Jamie finds me in the crowd and smiles, and I almost drop my drink. They're both so handsome it hurts. The practically nude alpha gives me a tiny wave, then listens to something Anthony says and finally he disappears behind the curtain.

While Anthony stalks across the club, I drain my drink and eat the cherries off their stems.

"Come on," Anthony says.

He walks past me without waiting for my answer. I set my empty glass down on a table and follow him. "Where are we going?" I have to ask twice to be heard over the MC's announcement and the screams that follow. There's a lot of bawdy jokes about firemen and their hoses and then something about bringing the heat followed by making it rain.

"You'll see," Anthony says. We pause at the bar long enough for him to bend under the counter and grab a pitcher of something light blue and a stack of red plastic cups. A few people shout their drink orders, but Anthony ignores them and gives a signal to the two other bartenders working.

We walk to the back and climb the stairs to the office. Veronica looks up from her paperwork. "Is everything okay?" she asks.

"Everything's fine," Anthony says, "except for one thing. You haven't had a night off in months. Come on, baby. Let's take a break."

She sighs and runs her hands through her hair. "I have to get the next order sheet together. You know, it would help if you made your drink specials in advance. I could plan when to order these special liquors and have one big monthly order instead of these weekly ones. I don't know what half of this stuff is. I spend so much time deciphering your chicken scratch writing and googling things to make sure I order the right shit. I mean, what the fuck is rose water? How do they get water out of a rose? And why would anyone drink it?" Her nose scrunches as she rants and waves her arms around with jerky, angry movements.

Anthony hands me the drink pitcher and cups and walks behind her desk. He grabs the back of her chair and physically drags her away from her computer.

"Hey!" she shouts.

He rolls her into the center of the room and then slaps his hands down on her armrests and leans into her personal space. "I'll do the ordering tomorrow. Since I know exactly what I want and how much to buy, it won't take me that long. There. Now your evening is free. And we," he motions between us, "are going to play a game."

Veronica leans back until her chair creaks. "What sort of game?" Her voice is full of suspicion.

Anthony grins and stands up, then grabs the pitcher and all but one of the red cups from me. "The best kind. Truth or dare."

Chapter Fourteen

BRENDAN

ANTHONY POURS BRIGHT BLUE ALCOHOL INTO OUR CUPS AND then pulls over the room's three other chairs until they form a circle.

"Don't start without me," Jamie says from the doorway as he joins us. He's changed into street clothes, a pair of brown shorts with frayed edges, thong sandals, and a faded white hoodie with a Japanese block print of a sun setting over an ocean full of waves. He's scraped his hair up into a messy topknot, but a few of the shorter pieces frame his face. Jamie takes his seat and then his drink.

"All right, here are the rules," Anthony says as he turns his chair around and straddles it. "We're playing truth or dare. We'll go around in a circle and you have to pick either truth or dare, and if you don't like your question or order, you have to drink before we'll give you another option."

"Uh-huh," Veronica says with narrowed eyes. "You're going to order me to strip and blow you."

Anthony grins and shrugs mockingly. "Then I guess you're gonna be drinking a lot, baby. But fair is fair and you get to do it to us too. I have a feeling the game will get easier the longer we play it."

"You mean the drunker we get," she says. "And they say chivalry is dead."

"If you want a white knight, baby, I'm not your man. That's what they're for. But if you need the heads of your enemies on a pike, you've got my number. All I need is a name. Okay, is everyone good with it?"

One by one, they all turn to me expectantly. "Yeah, I'm good," I say. "I don't have anything to hide."

Anthony grips the back of his chair and his drink and grins. "Good. I choose Vee."

"Shocking," she deadpans.

"Truth or dare, baby?"

She hesitates for a few seconds before she decides. "Truth."

If Anthony is disappointed by her answer, he doesn't show it. "When was your last relationship? And I don't mean a casual thing or a fuck buddy or a hook up. A real relationship. Living together or staying over and cooking dinner and going on cute dates and shit."

Her face scrunches, and she takes a while to answer. "I was... twenty-two? That'd be eight years ago."

God, she's only thirty. I'm forty-one. I'm a dirty old man for lusting after her.

She looks around the room and folds her arms over her chest with her drink cradled in the crook of her arm. "What? I'm married to my work. It's hard to date when you never have any free time. My turn now, right? I choose Anthony."

"Shocking," he says with a smile, parroting her.

"Truth or dare?" she asks him.

"Dare."

"Shit, okay." She takes a while to think. "Okay, I've got it. Show us the most embarrassing photo on your phone."

"Ooh, naughty. I like it." Anthony pulls his phone from his back pocket and swipes until he finds it. He shows us what looks like an old photo of a little boy with short brown hair and bright blue eyes dressed as a Catholic altar boy in the black cassock and white surplice.

"That is not what I was expecting," Vee says as she takes the phone from him so she can really study the picture. Her lips curl in a tiny smile that softens her face as she hands it back.

"Church is a big deal for my family," Anthony says. "But I only go for Easter, Christmas, weddings, and funerals, much to my ma's complete and utter horror. All right, you're next, Jamie. Pick someone."

"Brendan," Jamie says. "Truth or dare?"

My pulse quickens as I wonder what dare they'd come up with, but I'm not sure I'm brave enough. Or drunk enough. I see why Anthony made the pitcher of booze now. "Truth."

"How did you end up working as an accountant?" Jamie asks.

I guess I shouldn't be surprised by the question. It's more commonly asked than I'd thought it would be. It's true that most alphas tend to enjoy more physical or demanding or authoritative jobs. Like construction or surgery or being a corporate executive. White-collar desk jobs are often seen as beta work, although there's no law about it.

"I played soccer in school and it seemed promising. I got a full ride athletic scholarship to UCLA. Then halfway through my high school senior year, only a few weeks before Christmas, I took a stray kick that shattered my knee in three places and tore my ACL. I lost my scholarship and any chance at going pro in college. I had to have surgery, and that took a few months and a lot of physical therapy to heal."

I avoid looking at them as I finish my story. Seeing the pity on people's faces gets old. "I was kind of lost and pretty depressed after. Soccer was all I'd ever wanted to do. But I've always been good with math. I can skim a page and add it all in my head. So I taped up a bunch of math related careers on my dart board and threw one. Went to school for whatever it landed on. I got my bachelors, then got my CPA. I worked in public practice for a while, then applied for the IRS."

The plastic cup dents in my grip, and I force myself to relax. "The pay is fine. You could make more money in LA if you had the right practice and good connections, but the benefits and pension can't be beat. I think after seeing how quickly you can lose everything, it made me want that security and peace of mind."

"Oh, man, that sucks hard," Jamie says. "I don't know what I'd do if I couldn't surf."

I study him, and suddenly everything about him makes sense. His golden tanned white skin. The sun-kissed blond hair with long beachy waves. His cut physique, but calm demeanor. Alphas run hot-blooded and competitive—the bigger they are, the worse they usually get—but that isn't the vibe I've caught from him. He's mellow for an alpha of his size. I don't think I've ever met an uptight surfer.

"You'd figure it out," I say, "but I hope you never have to. All right, so it's my turn now. I choose you, Anthony. Truth or dare?"

Anthony's icy blue eyes glitter with amusement. "I'm not sure you're ready for anything but the truth yet, so let's do that."

There are a million things I could ask him, but there's only one question I really need answered. "What is all of this? What's going on and how do I fit into it?"

"That's three questions, but I'll answer them all if you drain your cup. Drink up."

I glance in my cup and guess that it's barely more than a

double shot's worth of liquor mixed with juice. Despite its blue coloring, it tastes like lemons and oranges. I drain the cup and hold it out so he can refill it from his frosted pitcher.

"Vee doesn't think she needs a pack," he says, "and we're working diligently to prove her wrong one load of cum at a time. So you could call this a courtship, I guess. As far as how you fit into things… I suppose that's up to you."

"You want me to potentially join the pack you're forming?" I ask as I glance over at Jamie. They already have an alpha. Handsome, fit, and younger than me. Whole. Why would they want me when they could have *him*?

But it sounds like this isn't an either-or thing and that's what makes it even more confusing. I don't think I've ever known a pack with more than one alpha in it. I'm sure it's happened before—no two packs are ever the same—but it's got to be fairly unusual. Most alphas can't stand the competition of another alpha's presence when they're lost in a rut.

Anthony tsks and shakes his head, but smiles. "It's not your turn right now. All right, I choose you, Brendan. Truth or dare?"

There's a dark gleam in his eyes I don't fully trust. I remember his questions earlier and his statement that he won't make me do anything I don't want to, but… He's practically a stranger and I'm not quite sure I trust him that much yet. I'm also drunker than I thought I was because the tip of my nose has gone numb. "Truth."

"What's your deepest, darkest kink?" he asks.

Oh, that's easy. It's not something I advertise, but I'm not embarrassed by it, either. "I like rope."

The energy in the room turns tense and I glance around, confused about what I've said that's made them look at each other like that. I can't imagine these three being shocked by some shibari. They don't exactly scream *vanilla*. "What?"

"Rope, as in tying people down?" Vee asks, her voice

deceptively neutral. Her words don't match her body language. Her lips are thinned and her shoulders are square and stiff. I'm not sure what I said wrong, but it was obviously the wrong answer.

I shrug. "Sometimes, but it's more about the aesthetics. You know it's probably easier to show you instead of trying to explain it." I pull my phone out and open the hidden folder that contains my portfolio of work. I hand the phone to Anthony because he's the closest. He swipes through the album for a bit, then gives it to Veronica.

"Oh. I see what you mean." She relaxes, and the tension in the room mellows. "The symmetry is pretty. Who's the model?"

"A fetish model I met in a dungeon once. I ran into her again at a house party in the valley."

"I never pegged you as a dungeon-going sort of guy," Veronica teases me.

"You haven't pegged me at all yet," I say, and then immediately regret it. The words slipped out before I could stop them. I'm way drunker than I thought. I eye the bright blue liquor in the party cup, then give Anthony an assessing stare. "What the fuck is in this?"

He grins and rests his chin on his forearms where they're folded along the back of the chair. "I call this one *truth serum*. It seemed appropriate for the game."

I blush and scratch my nails through my hair as I avoid looking at Veronica right now. "The photos of her wearing the dress made of rope are from the party. It took over an hour to tie. I enjoyed working with her because she's a rope bunny, so we both get into the zone and she lets me do my thing. Some of the more complicated designs take hours of prep, so I hate tying up brats who only want to wiggle out and escape. That's not my thing."

"So she's not your girlfriend?" Veronica asks, looking up from the photos.

I laugh. "No. She'd be more interested in you than me. Steph's a beta lesbian with a very protective female alpha named Allie. They go to parties to pick up a third when the mood for a threesome strikes them."

"Oh." Veronica says as she looks at the photo on the screen again, then passes the phone to Jamie, who flips through them briefly before returning it to me. "Now it's my turn, I think. Jamie, truth or dare?"

"Dare," he says with no hesitation.

Veronica bites her lip and uncrosses her legs, then crosses them the other way. "I dare you to give me a foot massage."

Jamie rises from his seat and sits on the floor. He wedges his plastic cup in his folded legs, then pulls her heels off one after the other and sets them down neatly. He takes one of her stocking covered feet and kneads them.

She melts in her chair. Veronica leans back and props her other foot on his thigh as he digs his thumbs into the balls of her feet until she moans. "Oh, fuck. That's good. How'd you get so good at this?"

The alpha dancer presses a kiss to the inside of her thigh, and then he does something to her toes that makes a bone pop and she sighs. "I had to learn how after taking this job. Sometimes my feet are so sore by the end of my shift that I can't sleep until I've worked the kinks out. Okay, I think it's my turn. Truth or dare, babe?" he asks, looking at Anthony.

"Oh, definitely dare," Anthony answers.

"I dare you... to kiss someone in this room who you're attracted to."

Anthony sets his cup on the floor, then stands. "So many choices." He glances around the room, looking between them, and then his attention fixates on me and my breath catches when I realize he's serious and nobody is laughing or making jokes.

"Me?" Is Anthony serious when he says he wants to kiss me?

"Yeah," Anthony shrugs. "I kind of dig the fifties sitcom dad vibe. Plus, you've got a hidden wild streak that I think could be fun. Remember what I said earlier?"

Nobody will make me do anything I don't want to do. I take time to think about it and work through the repercussions. Fucking around with the person I'm auditing is a terrible idea, but... Anthony is an employee. It's bad. But it wouldn't be as bad as if I pulled Veronica onto my lap and sank her down on my knot like I so desperately want to.

I meant what I said earlier too. I'm not really into men, but I can't say I'm perfectly straight, either. There was too much experimentation in high school and college for that to be true. And there's something magnetic about Anthony's cocky attitude.

He's so confident it's hard not to be impressed. He's a beta. Shorter, smaller, physically weaker. But I've never met a beta who was so ballsy and downright dominant before. It's intriguing and part of me wants to see how far he'll go.

So my preference might be for women, but I can't deny there's a spark of interest there.

"Okay," I say, then swallow hard when he stalks across the room.

Anthony leans over me and grabs my chair's armrests so I'm caged in my seat. He stares at me until my stomach flutters with the good kind of nerves, and then he dips his head until his lips barely brush against mine. It's almost a kiss, but not quite, and it takes me a few seconds to realize he's waiting for me to balk and change my mind.

I let my eyes slide closed and tilt my head to close the

distance between our mouths and the beta gives me a deep and aching kiss that's sweeter than I expected. After a brief hesitation, my lips soften and I kiss him back until the rest of the room fades away. When all the blood leaves my body to pool in my groin and my cock twitches to life against my briefs, he finally pulls away.

Anthony cups my jaw and scrapes his thumb over the stubble growing on my chin. "You're a good kisser, papa bear."

The nickname stuns me, but I don't mind it. Anthony lets me go and saunters back to his chair, where he sits. "Your turn," he says to me.

"Right." I can't reach down and adjust my strangled cock without all of them knowing exactly how hard I got from kissing another man. One who's practically a stranger to me. I've only known them a week, and I'm still trying to figure out how I took this assignment and ended up right here, right now, in this surreal moment that feels like it should be a dream. "Truth or dare, Jamie?"

"Truth," he answers from his spot on the floor. He's still rubbing Veronica's feet, except his massage has worked its way up her ankles and calves. I can't blame him. I wouldn't want to let go of her either if our situations were reversed.

"Would having another alpha in your pack bother you?" I ask him.

"No," he answers immediately. "As long as you're good to Miss Vee, I want whatever would make her happy."

I would like to call him a liar, to say that two alphas in one pack would be like oil and water… but I can't. I'm struck by the sudden realization that I don't want to shoulder him out of the way so I can rub her feet instead, but to join him.

I was a competitive, arrogant alphahole before my injury hobbled me, and I lost everything. My scholarship. A promising career. Almost all of my friends. Now, however… I could see myself sitting on the floor next to the big blond alpha and rubbing one of her feet after a long, hard day while he does the other.

"My turn," Anthony declares with far too much glee. "Vee, truth or dare?"

"Truth," she answers without even looking. She's slung her head over the back of her chair and her ass is barely perched on her seat as Jamie works higher up her legs.

"How have you been on your own since you were fourteen?"

She sucks in a breath and her eyes pop open as she stares at the ceiling. She's silent for way too long until it's uncomfortable. "Hand me my drink," she says to Jamie. When he does, she drains it in a single gulp. "That's not a story you want to hear at a party, Anthony. Dare."

Chapter Fifteen

BRENDAN

"I choose dare instead," Veronica says.

"Okay, baby." He fishes something egg-shaped and purple out of his pocket. "I dare you to wear this for the rest of the night." He passes it to Jamie, and the alpha holds it up for her to inspect.

"Are you kidding?" She exhales loudly, but takes the remote control vibrator egg with a mulish expression. "Fine. Let me up, pet, so I can go use the bathroom."

"No." Anthony's one-word command is so sharp it's almost a bark. "That wasn't part of the dare. Do it here so we can watch. How else will I know you're being a good girl and wearing it? And don't forget, baby. I'll check later, and if you take that vibrator out before I make you come, you know there will be consequences."

Veronica glares at him and her nostrils flare, but she reaches for the hem of her skirt and wiggles it up until we can all see her panties. Jamie leans back on his elbows to get a better view as she holds the vibrator egg in one hand and shoves her other hand down into her panties.

The sight of her hand rubbing and sliding over her pussy,

her knuckles tenting the shiny black fabric, is so erotic that a drop of pre-cum soaks my boxers as I watch her make herself wet. Her hips buck against her rubbing and she sighs, then moves lower and works two fingers in until they squelch.

Once she's deemed herself wet enough, she tugs her gusset aside and I see the pink petals of her wet sex. The purple silicone toy spreads her lips apart as she guides it in until it disappears from sight, swallowed up by her pussy. The juicy orange scent of her pheromones makes my knot ache to pop.

She snaps her panties back into place and wiggles her skirt down her thighs. "Happy?"

"Immensely," Anthony says as he pulls a remote from his pocket and hits a button.

Veronica jumps in her seat and bites off a strangled moan as she grips the edges of her seat and squirms. "Oh, fuck. Shit. Goddamn it, Anthony."

"Your new little friend stays in until I say so," he says. "Unless you beg me for a cock instead. You don't want to break the sacred covenant of truth or dare, do you? I didn't take you for a quitter, baby."

When she gives him a withering stare, he taps the remote again, and she bites her lip and jerks in her seat. "You… are… such an asshole… sometimes," she pants between clenched teeth.

"Hmm. Maybe it's not enough. You're still grumpy. Let's try a different vibration setting. I think the next one is a pulsing one." He clicks the remote and her hips twitch as she sucks in a breath.

"I should have known better than to play this fucking game with you."

Anthony chuckles and hits another button, and Veronica forgets how to speak. She melts in her chair, her head thrown back. She spreads her legs wide and grips the fabric of her skirt in one hand and twists. Her knuckles blanche.

"T-turn it down," she begs. "It's too much. I can't take it."

"Turn it down… what? Oh, I'm sorry. I thought you were asking Daddy for a favor. Baby girls who make mouthy demands don't get their way. That would reinforce their bad behavior."

"Are you trying to train me like a dog?" she asks, her voice incredulous. Veronica bites her bottom lip and lets out a moan that's more of a wail. "Turn it down, Daddy. Please. Please turn it down. It's too much. I can't take it."

He presses the remote again, and the crease between her eyebrows smooths out. "There you go, baby. See? I can be generous. I'll keep it to a dull roar if you're good and if you're very good, I'll let you come before midnight. Now, it's your turn. Pick someone."

"Truth or dare, Daddy," she says as she locks eyes with him and glares.

Anthony grins and palms the remote. "Dare."

"I dare you to go fuck yourself," she snaps.

"Sure." Anthony stands and steps away from his chair. Once he's in the center of our circle, he unbuckles his belt and undoes his jeans, sliding the zipper free. He reaches in and pulls out his cock and strokes it from root to tip, playing with his head until it hardens. The big silver ring looped through his slit surprises me, but I guess it shouldn't. Half his body is covered in tattoos. Why wouldn't his cock be pierced?

Anthony squeezes and strokes until a bead of clear fluid swells at the slit in his head. He walks over to Veronica and stands at her side while Jamie stares up at them both from the floor.

"What are you doing?" she asks him, her eyes flicking over to meet mine briefly. Her cheeks pinken with a delicate blush.

"I'm fucking myself," Anthony says. "Like you dared me to. But if you've decided you want to be a good girl and suck my cock, I'd be willing to forgive the lapse in sacred truth or dare rules."

"I told you this would end in blowjobs," she says, trying hard not to smile.

Anthony grins and tugs harder, the slap of his skin growing louder. "You're the one who told me to fuck myself. I'm exhibiting good… What's the word I'm looking for, Brendan?" He looks over his shoulder at me while he tugs his cock harder, faster, and his piercing catches the light.

"Sportsmanlike behavior?"

"Right." Anthony nods and returns his focus to her. "That's me. A total team player. But if you don't want to suck my cock in front of your IRS agent, that's okay, baby. All you have to do is open those pretty red lips. I've got good aim. If you swallow, I'll let you come before midnight. If you don't… And remember, if I check and find that my toy isn't nestled in that sweet little cunt, what am I going to do?" He presses buttons on the remote with one hand while his other one never pauses as he jerks off inches from her face.

Veronica flinches and squeezes her eyes shut. "It's not going to happen. I can take whatever you throw my way."

Oh, fucking hell. These are the craziest, horniest people I've ever met. But I can't deny that I like it. My sensitive head rubs against my boxers and tight jeans.

I want to follow in the bartender's footsteps and fish my cock out and jerk off. But I don't. I sit there and suffer while I watch them flirt instead.

Jamie must feel the same, because he's lying on one elbow while his other hand strokes his erection over his pants.

"It's your choice, baby. How badly do you want to come? Are you gonna be a good girl and swallow?" He taps the remote again and her hips jerk in time with whatever buzzing pulse he's sending to the toy deep inside her.

She fights it, her jaw twitching and teeth clenching, until she can't hold out any longer. Veronica parts her lips and her hips rock with an electronically driven rhythm.

God, she's gorgeous. She's pretty, with gentle curves and enough tits to palm. Her white skin is pale like she rarely sees the sun. She'd be so pretty in nothing but rope. She'd be even prettier in nothing but my rope marks.

I want to bind her skin tight, then unwind it and lick every single indentation in her skin. I want to cover her in rope marks and reveal them one by one, kissing each divot as I uncoil it from her body, its dry length softened by the oils from her skin.

Veronica's whimpers drive me wild. Her orange scent drips into the room until it's all I can smell. Orange, and coconut, and a faint whiff of cherries. I'm still not sure how my scent fits in with theirs. Anthony grunts and thrusts into his hand with every downward stroke on his cock.

When Jamie tugs the band of his shorts down and pulls out an impressive alpha cock, I can't deny myself anymore. I guess we're all really doing this.

I work my zipper down and pull my cock free through the opening of my clothes. I stroke my hard length and catch the pearling pre-cum with my thumb, working it around my tip with circles.

When her hips grind as she searches for friction, I thrust into my hand and pretend I'm sinking it into her warm, slick depth. She's close to her heat. Unbearably close. There's a sweetness to her scent that wasn't there a few days ago when I first arrived.

I tighten my grip around my cock and fuck the ring of my fingers until there's no option except to come. My knot begins to swell and bump against my hand. So I reach down with the other and cup it, squeezing.

Anthony glances at me, but I'm too far gone to be embarrassed at getting caught to stop. He holds eye contact with me as we both work our cocks and there's something strangely erotic about it.

"Fuck, baby. See what you're doing to them."

Veronica follows his order with lust-dark eyes and lets out a mewling whimper. Whatever hesitation she felt before is gone. She's lost in her pursuit of pleasure. Her hips rock faster and the points of her breasts tent her shirt. She bites her lower lip and stares up at Anthony as he towers over her, his cockhead brushing against her mouth until her lips part.

"You're driving them wild with the need to have you," Anthony says. "Look at those big alpha cocks. Those fat knots. I bet they're both dying to sink those cocks inside you and knot you good and fill you up. Breed you raw. He's negative—I checked his papers. You'll let him come in you, because we all know how badly you need it. Crave it. Look at them."

She follows his command and looks at Jamie, first, where he's sprawled at her feet. Veronica moves a stocking covered foot over him and gently kicks his hand from his cock. She pins it to his belly and presses. He grunts, his empty hand opening and closing around nothing, and rocks his hips up into her foot as she steps on his cock. Her tiny foot barely covers him from knot to tip.

Veronica reaches down and shoves her hand between her legs and grinds against it, the movement traveling down her body to where Jamie's pinned under her. Coconut-scented pre-cum darkens his light-colored hoodie. He doesn't seem to mind her rough treatment. If anything, the alpha's cock grows harder, his knot so swollen it's almost ready to fully pop.

She turns her attention to me, but I'm too caught up in the

way her hand works between her thighs to feel embarrassed. Later tonight, I'll probably lie in bed and regret this moment, but right now I can't. I don't. I want to come—need to come—and I want to see her bare pussy again when I do it.

If I can't lick her, fill her, knot her, then I'll drink my fill of her with my eyes and fuck my hand while I drag her almost-in-heat thick scent so deep into my sinuses that I'll be smelling oranges for weeks. Even when her audit's done and I've moved onto the next assignment. She's going to live in my head rent free for the rest of my life.

Anthony slaps the head of his cock against the side of her face, and that gets her attention. He grins and keeps tugging. "I bet with enough training you can take them both, one in that wet pussy and one in that tight little ass. Brendan's bigger. He'll have to fill your pussy, and that's good. Because Jamie doesn't deserve to knot your pussy, right? He'd be better off watching us all rut and breed your greedy cunt, knowing we can please you better than his puny knot ever could. Isn't that right, babe?"

"If you don't stop, Ma'am, I'm going to come." Jamie drags in a deep breath and holds it. A purr rumbles in his chest.

"No," she says, her voice strained. Her heel digs into his knot and the veins in his neck bulge as his hips buck against her heel, digging the point in deeper. "Not yet, pet. You come last."

My lust-thick mind is struggling to pick up the nuances of their muddled pack dynamics and relationships, and I'm still not a hundred percent sure where I fit into it. I slow my hand until the edge of release fades and I can think. I'm not a bottom bitch, not that there's anything wrong with it. *Someone's* got to be on the bottom. And it looks like that someone is Jamie.

I spread my legs wide, lounging, and channel some of the guy I used to be so long ago. "I want to see her pussy again. Show me."

Anthony grins at me and stops what he's doing to reach

down and knock her other knee wider. He ignores her gasp and protests as he pulls her hand from her panties, grabs the delicate fabric, and rips. The elastic string holding the front and back together snaps with the flick of his wrist.

"Those were my favorite pair!" she whines.

Her skin is pink where the fabric rubbed her hips before it tore, and it almost looks like a rope mark. My cock pulses in my hand and my balls feel tight. Swollen. Ready to be emptied.

He pulls the remote control from his pocket and clicks it. Her back arches and she whines.

"I'll buy you a dozen more, baby. Pretty ones. Sparkly ones. Lacy ones. Panties without a crotch at all. I'll rip every single pair off you and buy you a dozen more. Spread those legs, baby. Your alpha wants to watch you come."

Her alpha. Hers. The thought alone is almost enough to make me lose it and come right then, even without seeing her pink lips and slick hole and swollen clit. "Fuck," I groan under my breath, slowing my hand and edging myself again. I will not come. Not yet. I'm not some teenager with no self-control.

"Let me see that pretty pussy, sweetheart," I tell her, my voice deep from the strain of holding back.

Veronica picks her free foot up and puts it on the edge of her seat. She drops her knee to the armrest and the movement puts her beautiful pussy on full display. She knocks Anthony's hand away, then returns hers between her legs.

I memorize every slide and rub she makes as she plays with her clit. She dips her fingers into her toy-stuffed hole and wets them, drags them up. She slides her hood back and rubs circles around her clit. Her hips chase the movement of her hand. The toy makes a noxious buzzing noise, but her sweet whimpers and whines nearly drown it out.

Anthony's reward for her is the smack of his cockhead against the corner of her mouth as he jerks his cock until his breathing comes hard and fast. Something about his posture, his tugging, changes, and she and I both realize at the same time that he's about to come.

"Open and swallow, baby, or I'm gonna come on your face. Your choice," he says.

Veronica tilts her head back to stare up at him, then drops her mouth open and sticks out her tongue. Her fingers slick through her pussy and her toy buzzes as she waits for him to shoot his load past her red lips.

"Fuck, you're so pretty," he moans. "So fucking perfect. Makes me want to defile you."

Anthony's head drops forward and his cock pulses. A rope of wet cum lashes across her waiting tongue. He grunts and tugs, his breathing ragged, and he works another spurt free. "That's good. Swallow it all. Take your medicine like a good omega. Don't waste any." He shakes his cock and a few more drops land on her tongue.

Veronica licks the head of his cock, her pink tongue dragging over his silver piercing, and Anthony curses. When her red lips wrap around his crown and her cheeks hollow, he spits out a string of foreign words that run together. I think it's Italian.

"Good girl, baby." Anthony rakes her hair from her flushed face and pulls his softening cock from her mouth with a wet pop. "Are you still hungry? Keep playing with that pretty pussy. I'm gonna get you more cum."

He tucks his cock away and does up his jeans, then glances between Jamie and me with predatory intent. It's an expression that promises so much while saying nothing at all. My cock jumps in my hand and the knot of tension swelling in my root tells me I can't hold back much longer unless I edge myself again.

And I really don't want to.

I want to come while she's still playing with her pussy so I can see with no distractions the exact moment she comes undone. Is she a moaner? A screamer? I want the entire club to hear her cries of pleasure. To know we're the ones dragging her to this edge and drowning her in bliss. I want them to smell her sweet, breedable cunt and know they can't have her.

There are dozens of alphas downstairs, and none of them matter. The only two who matter are in this room with her. Because for some reason, a quirk of genetics or a twist of fate, we're a scent match and she's picked us. Maybe she hasn't fully accepted it yet, but God, I want her to.

The wet sounds her pussy makes and her keening whine keep me close to that precipice. Anthony crosses the room to me and kneels between my legs. My tugging slows from confusion until he puts his hands on my knees and his mouth softens. He licks his lips and looks up at me with bright blue eyes through thick, dark lashes. His eyes are far too pretty for my old heart to take.

I recall his words from earlier. *A mouth is a mouth.*

I squeeze my thickening knot and grunt, nodding.

When his warm, wet lips wrap around my cock and his hand nudges mine aside so he can take control, I almost come right then. He sucks like a hoover and I swear he's trying to pull my spine out through my cock.

Veronica and Jamie both groan at the same time and my hips snap to shove my cock deeper into his mouth. If he's going to suck my cock, he's going to take it to the knot. We settle into a rhythm and his tongue slides up and down my sensitive underside, dipping into my weeping slit. I pump in and out, watching his cheeks hollow and my growing knot swelling against his lips.

"Fuck, why is that so hot?" Veronica asks in a low voice.

"I know, right?" Jamie whispers back.

Knowing how much they like watching me fuck Anthony's

bratty mouth makes it easier to let go and fully immerse myself in the slide of his tongue and the squeeze of his hand. I rest a hand on his head. Lightly, not demanding, because I have manners.

And I think if anyone tried to take something from Anthony that he didn't want to give, they'd meet the business end of his teeth. I like my dick being in one piece. I don't mind some pain during sex, but not *there*. He makes a throaty sound around his mouthful and I take that as encouragement, or at least acceptance.

His head bobs up and down on my length and I stare at Veronica's slick, pink pussy until my knot pops in his clenching fingers and he angles me to catch my cum on his tongue. I grunt when I come, my balls unloading with thick pulses into his mouth. It's a big load because I edged myself so many times and she's so close to her heat. Each stalled orgasm fills me to the point of pain until all the pressure bursts into a messy spurt of seed.

Cum leaks from the corners of his mouth as he struggles to contain it all without swallowing like his reflexes demand. But that would defeat the point. Because my cum's not for him, he's only the vessel.

Anthony pulls off my softening cock and lets my knot go. I groan from the absence of his heat. But the pleasure I get from watching him get up and go to her kills my sense of loss. He leans over her and grabs her face in his hand. Tilts her head back. His hand slides down to her throat to keep her like that.

He bends the rest of the way and presses his lips to hers. I watch her throat bob against his thumb as he passes my cum to her and she swallows. She moans into his mouth and nearly rises out of her seat. She would have if he didn't have her by the throat. Anthony's grip keeps her seated with her hand, rubbing furious circles around her clit and the toy buzzing in her pussy.

She moans again, deeper this time, and then she comes. It's my cum that pushes her over the edge into bliss.

Her back arches and her hips take on a life of their own as she bucks against her hand and spreads her legs wider. Jamie grunts from where her foot grinds against his hard cock in her carelessness. She's not paying attention to him, but that only seems to make him harder.

His hips move against her crushing foot, and he scrambles to get his hoodie shoved up his torso in time as he comes all over his belly. White ropes of it drip and roll down the divots of his abs. Jamie's chest rumbles with a purr as he goes limp on the floor.

Anthony swallows each of her delicious whimpers as she shivers and twitches with aftershocks. She purrs. Her omega purr rattles from disuse before smoothing out as her throat warms up. It's the most erotic thing I've ever heard or seen in my life.

My cock twitches as it tries to rally for another round, but I'm spent. I'm not in a rut so I can't come again yet, but my body knows that her heat is so fucking close, so it tries.

"That was so good, baby," Anthony praises her as he clicks the remote and the toy's buzzing stops. She sags against her chair and he follows her so he can stroke her. He runs his hands over her hair and face and breasts and then lightly over her thighs and finally her pussy. She jerks away from his touch, probably too sensitive, and her purr stutters.

Anthony slaps her right on her mound and grins when she gasps and jerks against him. "Hold still, baby. Let me take care of you. That's my good girl. Relax. I know what you need." He dips a finger and thumb inside her pussy and takes out the purple toy. It disappears into his pocket.

The beta leaves her limp and pleased and purring as he kneels by the equally collapsed Jamie and presses a kiss to the alpha's mouth. Fingers run over the alpha's messy stomach. Anthony stands and holds those cum-drenched fingers up to her mouth.

"Open, baby." He shoves his fingers and Jamie's cum past her red lips and whispers praise when she sucks his fingers clean. Twice more he repeats this until Jamie's stomach is as clean as it will get without soap and water and her contented omega purr rumbles to a stop.

"Whose house are we going to have your heat in, baby? Yours? Jamie's? My place is too small. It's coming soon. Probably tomorrow."

"Tomorrow," Jamie agrees.

Silently, I agree with him. She's right on the cusp. And she probably wouldn't have let us do anything like we just did if she wasn't so close to her heat already. The closer she gets, the less she'll care about anything but being knotted.

Although, with her Domme tendencies, I'm not sure what her heat will be like. I wouldn't mind letting the little goddess ride my knot rather than feeding it into her doggy style. As long as it's in her sweet orange-scented pussy, I don't care about positions.

The prospect of her heat fills me with excitement until reality comes crashing down and I realize there's no way that I can join them. I'm auditing her, for God's sake. If the IRS finds out I've had a lapse in judgment and fucked her, my whole case will get thrown out and she'll have to go through the process again, but with someone else. Someone who isn't me. Someone who doesn't understand why she's doing what she's doing. And I can't let that happen.

The world needs more places like Rut in it. And that's exactly why I can't join them for her heat. It doesn't matter how much I want it. How much my instincts say I *need* to knot and breed her and lap up her pheromones.

Being an alpha means doing the hard things, and sometimes that means knowing you don't get what you want. And I want her. I've tried to fight it, fight this intense attraction, but I can't.

But this isn't the time. Not yet. It won't kill me to wait out this one heat. Not when the benefit of waiting outweighs the risk of getting my dick covered in her slick.

"My place is too small," she says while she puts her feet on the floor and tugs her skirt down her thighs.

"No big fancy condo or house down in the valley?" Anthony asks.

"No. I'm hardly ever there except to shower and change and sleep, so what's the point? All my money goes back into Rut."

That's true. She barely pays herself the wage she should be compared to what Rut's earning. I have to talk to her about that because under paying herself won't help her businesses in the long run. Looks too suspicious. The last thing she needs is to put her S Corp status in jeopardy.

"My place," Jamie says. "If you don't mind leaving your nest." He sits up and tugs his hoodie down, but he seems content to stay at her feet as long as he can nuzzle his cheek against her knee. She reaches down and runs her fingers through his hair, and I'm struck with the urge to have her scratch her nails over my scalp too.

"It's not much of a nest," she says. "Like I said, I'm rarely there."

"We'll handle it," Anthony promises. "You don't have to worry about anything but showing up." He drops a kiss into her hair, then fixes his clothes and buckles his belt. Jamie and I both put ourselves right as well.

I open my mouth to tell them I'll have to abstain when there's a disturbance somewhere outside. There's loud shouting. Angry. Male. Alphas.

Something's wrong in the bar.

Chapter Sixteen

BRENDAN

My hackles rise, and I'm struck with the urge to either pick her up and run her somewhere safe or go down there and beat a man half to death. My head spins and I realize I'm standing up on instinct.

Oh, fuck. They weren't kidding. The mood swings an alpha gets when they're around a scent match omega near their heat is insane.

The sound of glass shattering makes me growl, and even Jamie seems on edge.

"What the fuck?" Veronica curses as she pops out of her chair and runs to the bank of floor-to-ceiling windows.

"Shit," Anthony says, following her. "Is that the alpha from yesterday fighting Dan?"

"Fuck!" she yells. "I forgot to print his picture and post it. Dan's training a new guy on the door."

There's another crash and then the sound of wooden furniture splintering. Omegas scream and a few alphas roar.

"Someone's getting fired," Anthony says under his breath.

"No, it's my fault," she says. "I let myself get distracted. Fuck, why the hell did I have to wear my highest heels today?"

Veronica shoves her feet into her red-bottom stilettos, then goes to her desk and pulls open a drawer. She takes out something rectangular and black and clicks a button that makes an arc of electricity flash as it crackles menacingly.

"No," Anthony growls as he catches her by the waist and swings her around like they're dancing. He stops her before she can stomp off toward the door. "I am not letting you go out into a room full of half-drunk, blood-lusting alphas one day away from your heat with only a stun gun for protection. Where did you even get that thing? They're illegal for civilians."

"This is *my* bar, Anthony. *Mine!* I won't let them ruin it."

When she attempts to struggle free, he lifts her off the ground and pushes her into the circle of Jamie's arms. He lets her go, but takes her stun gun with him. "Keep her here. Do *not* let her leave this room under any circumstances. I don't care if you have to sit on her to stop her. Her feet do not touch those stairs. That is a direct fucking order."

"Got it," Jamie says, his arms straining to keep her trapped without hurting her. She wiggles like a fish on a hook.

"Let me handle this," Anthony says. And then he stalks to the door to make good on that threat.

Veronica gives up after a few minutes of useless struggling, then pleading, then cursing that goes ignored. I follow as far as the top of the stairs and watch the drama unfolding from the balcony. The scene below is pure chaos.

Four male alphas cluster together in a somewhat organized pack. Two keep the enormous bouncer busy while the third hands the trainee his ass. It's the fourth, the one from yesterday, who is causing most of the ruckus. He picks a chair up and throws it into the crowd. One of the alpha dancers catches it and keeps it from crashing into the huddled mass of screaming omegas behind her.

Whatever alphahole put a bunch of omegas in danger like

this is borderline feral and needs to be locked away. Sirens ring in the distance. Thankfully it sounds like someone already called the police. The alpha dancers, some practically nude and others still in their costumes, pull omegas and betas to the sidelines while alpha patrons form a living wall between them.

Anthony cuts through the crowd with single-minded precision, dodging flailing limbs and improv weapons. He shoves a stumbling alpha who got caught in the ruckus away. Then he makes a beeline for the leader of the disgruntled alphas and darts in while the larger male turns to grab another chair.

A swift, well-placed kick to the back of a knee makes the larger male scream in agony and I flinch because I know how that feels. The alpha falters and nearly goes down, but his rage and adrenaline are too high for him to give up now.

The alpha spins and raises the chair over his head, and I hold my breath as I wait for it to come down on Anthony and take the smaller beta down. That alpha's gonna kill him. My chest is tight. I feel impotent and useless as I stand here and watch, but I'm better use up here guarding her door. What good would I be in the thick of a fight? Outside of a few halfhearted high school brawls, I'm not someone who gets into fights.

I can throw a punch, but I'm no MMA fighter.

Apparently Anthony is.

He grabs the chair mid-swing and rotates with it, using the momentum to throw the bulkier, slower alpha off balance. When the alpha passes him, he aims a kick to the dead center of the man's back and I wince at the kidney shot.

The alpha goes down, but tries to get up. When that fails, he flips onto his back and tries to kick at the beta. Anthony grabs him by the foot and twists the already injured knee, then slings the stun gun up in an arc from the strap dangling on his wrist. He lights it up on the alpha's exposed ankle.

The alpha screams and goes rigid, and Anthony keeps the

stun gun live and crackling for a horrifying amount of time. The alpha's screams are filled with rage and pain, and his next kick dislodges the stun gun from its contact. It connects with Anthony's shoulder. The blow knocks the stun gun away and pushes Anthony back.

I wince and wait for someone to intervene, to rush in and help the beta wrestle the alpha back down, but nobody does. The alpha staggers up, but Anthony rushes in and throws a punch that connects on the jaw. He doesn't stop at one. He hits him repeatedly, one jab connecting right after the other in a brutal flurry. After a particularly hard swing, the alpha's head snaps to the other side, and he goes completely still for a moment, and then he goes down like a dropped sack of bricks.

By now, the huge bearded bouncer has finished with his two. They're unconscious on the floor, and he spins and looks to see where he's needed next. The fourth alpha is on his knees with his hands in the air.

That's what the room looks like when the police arrive. Officers in bulky black tactical gear push into the crowd and get people to make way with the crackling ends of their stun batons. Now that everything is under control, I go back into the office to give Veronica and Jamie a rundown of what's happened.

She's not going to like it. The bar is trashed. But everyone is okay and the alphas who did this won't get away with it. It'll all be okay.

Veronica

My beautiful bar is a disaster.

I run my fingers through my hair and scrape it away from my face as I watch the police cars peel away and leave us alone. Now that it's completely empty—the alphas who ran amok taken away into custody—I can survey the full extent of the damage.

There's glass everywhere and a few of the chairs and bar stools are little more than firewood. It looks like one of the alphas threw a chair right out of Rut's main window. A third of the alcohol behind the bar is broken and spilled all over the floor.

None of the customers or dancers were seriously hurt, so I take my losses with grace. It's stuff. Stuff can be replaced. I remind myself that's what insurance is for.

I walk outside and let the muggy evening air clear my sinuses as I go find Anthony. He's sitting in the back of an ambulance while a cute beta EMT tries to talk him into going to the hospital to get an x-ray of his shoulder and hand.

"You should go," I tell him, crossing my arms over my chest.

"Nah," he says. "I've had worse. A little ice and ibuprofen and I'll be fine." He looks at me and gives me a halfhearted version of his signature panty melter smile. "You should see the other guy."

I would laugh, but my heart hurts too much to find any of this situation funny. Anthony is right, though. Aside from some shadowing on his shoulder that's going to turn into a nasty bruise and his bloodied knuckles, he's okay.

I'm drained, but it's going to be hours before this mess is sorted. We have to take photos and save the security footage for the insurance company, then board up the broken window and sweep up the glass. I'll be lucky if we get home before dawn.

Sighing, I nod and watch the EMT slap a disposable ice

pack into his hand. She looks between us and shrugs. "I can't make you go, but if it's still hurting after a few days, you'll want to go get that looked at."

"I'll be fine," he says. "I've got stuff to do that doesn't involve sitting in a hospital for hours for them to tell me I'm fine and to put ice on it and take some ibuprofen. I can do that at home."

It's my heat that he doesn't want to risk missing. He's too stubborn to risk a doctor telling him he's got a hairline fracture that needs surgery if it means he'll miss my heat. It's so asinine that I want to slap him upside the back of his head for being so stupid, but my insides feel too soft and fuzzy to stay mad at him for long.

The truth is, he stepped up. Protected the bar and the other staff. Minimized damage and took down the threat swiftly. I can't help but be impressed.

He did it for me. Got hurt for me, risked his life for me. He was outnumbered by bigger alphas, yet he didn't hesitate. He got into the fray and fixed it.

And he said he wasn't my white knight.

"Where did you learn to fight like that?" I ask.

"I have seven siblings and thirty-two cousins." He shrugs. "Eventually you learn how to stop getting your ass kicked."

"I'll trade you," the EMT says, handing him a fresh square of gauze for his bleeding knuckles. She takes the old ones with her blue gloves and discards them in a bag of trash.

Rationally I know that he needs to go get looked at and missing one heat won't matter in the long run, but the omega instincts I work so hard to squash make me tremble with antici-pation at taking this strong, stubborn, battered beta into my nest. He's a good defender. He'll be a great nest guardian one day. And right now, it doesn't matter that I have zero plans to have a baby anytime soon. That insidious omega instinct is always there. It simmers under the surface, ready to rise at any moment. My ovaries are holding up a flashing neon sign that says *pick this one!*

And I'm getting really fucking tired of saying no to this man when all I really want is to say yes.

I open my mouth to tell him to stop being stupid and go get looked at, but he hooks an arm around my waist so he can tug me against him. He buries his face in my neck and the faint scent of cherries makes me lose all sense of reason.

"Are you sure you'll be fine?" I ask.

"I'm fine," he mumbles against my collarbone. "But if you wanna kiss it and make it better…"

Despite my heart ache, anger, and fear, he makes me laugh. I card my fingers through his hair and neaten the unruly waves.

I was so angry at first when he manhandled me and kept me from defending my bar, but seeing the damage those alphas wrought and the state they're going to the hospital in soothes the sting. He fucked them up good. Between their injuries and the charges we're pressing, I hope this is the last we'll see of that alphahole and his stupid friends.

"Let's go home," he says. He sits upright, and the EMT comes back with a form for him to sign.

After he's signed them, he hops out of the back of the ambulance and ditches his ice pack in their rig. He puts his uninjured hand between my shoulders and steers me toward the parking lot.

"Wait," I say, "I need to call the insurance company and take photos and then we have to board up the window, and—"

"And that's what your staff is for. It's not like they're gonna be dancing or bartending for the rest of the night anyway. They can handle boarding up the window and taking photos and then everyone can pitch in and clean. You can call the insurance company from home. Come on. Hey, Jamie! We're going home. Get your van."

"But—"

Anthony shuts me up with a kiss, and my hormones are running so high that it almost works. It nearly makes me forget the mountain of paperwork I have to do. "It's actually decent timing if you think about it. Now you can take a break from work for your heat without feeling guilty about missing anything because there is absolutely *nothing* you need to do over the next few days while Rut is shut down for repairs. I'll check in with Dan every single day, I promise. Leave your car, Vee. We'll figure it out later."

It's reasonable, and deep down I know that the only reason I want to say no is because it wasn't my idea. But he's right. There's no reason the others can't sweep up broken glass and mop up spilled alcohol. If I hurry, I can get the insurance report filed and get a new front window ordered before my first bout of heat delirium makes me knot-drunk and useless. I blow out a breath that leaves me feeling weary. "Fine."

Jamie and Brendan both meet us in the parking lot, and Jamie unlocks his vintage van with his key. Brendan's shoved his hands in his pockets, and he stands there awkwardly next to the van while we all climb in. "Veronica, I'm sorry about the state of the club. I'll let the office know you'll be closed temporarily for repairs."

My stomach sinks with the intuition that he's not coming with us. And then I'm irritated, because why should I care? He's basically a stranger. I've only known him for a week. I only care because I'm in preheat and I like the way he smells.

It's stupid omega instincts, that's all. I've lived my entire life without them and I don't need them now. So I do what I'm good at. I shove those useless yearning feelings down and ignore them while I pretend that his subtle rejection doesn't hurt one bit. "Thank you, Agent Hall."

Brendan winces at the not-so-subtle reminder of his place and Jamie finally picks up on what's happening. Jamie leans out the driver's side window. "Are you gonna follow in your car?"

"No, I…" Brendan looks between us all. "I can't. At least not right now while the audit's happening. Maybe after it's over, if…"

If it's not too late. If we still want him to join. If we haven't formed a pack without him. Not that I'm saying we're a real pack or anything, but… It's getting harder to remember why I ever wanted to say no.

Why am I fighting this when all of my instincts scream they're mine?

"We'll let you know when Rut reopens," Anthony says.

"Let's go," I order as I yank the van door open.

Chapter Seventeen

VERONICA

I PULL THE VAN'S SLIDING DOOR CLOSED BEHIND ME AND buckle my seatbelt. It's only when the latch clicks that Jamie puts his van in gear and backs out of his spot. I give Jamie my address and he puts it into his phone and follows the GPS.

While we make the drive, I call the insurance company and get a claim started. Once we've pulled up outside of my place, I realize I don't want them to see where I live. My apartment is a tiny disaster. There's rotting takeout in the fridge and used underwear on the bedroom floor. I haven't run a vacuum in forever. I don't think I've dusted since I moved in. What's the point when I'm only there to sleep and do laundry?

Before they can get out of the car, I've already hopped out and slid the door closed. "I'll only be a few minutes," I say through the open window. Jamie pauses mid-unbuckling and I pin Anthony to his seat with a stare and a wordless command. Thankfully he heeds it.

My keys jingle as I pull them from my bag and unlock the door, slipping inside and going straight to the hall closet where I keep a duffel bag. I shove the things I'll need inside. Lots of panties, a clean bra, a loose sundress, a pair of shorts and a top, my softest pajamas, flip-flops, my birth control, and some toiletries.

I eye the contents of my nightstand and hesitate, then grab what I need. I bury the knotting vibrator at the bottom of the bag, then shove my laptop, charger, and phone charger on top. Hopefully during one of my heat delirium lulls I can get some work done. On my way out, I grab my favorite pillow and my softest blanket.

It's a struggle to carry everything out to the car, and when Jamie sees I can't get the door open with my hands full, he hops out and takes it all from me. "Thanks," I tell him as I tuck my hair behind my ear.

"No problem." Jamie says, a goofy grin on his face.

We all get back in, and Anthony turns in his seat to eye me and the bag and bedding shoved around my legs. "Are you hungry?" he asks.

The thought of eating makes my stomach revolt. "No, but I wouldn't mind a drink." Heats make me so damn thirsty. It takes a lot of fluid to make all that slick, and it's easy to get dehydrated when you're lost in it.

"Let's grab burgers," Anthony says to Jamie. "There's a drive-thru up ahead."

The In-N-Out isn't too busy at this time of night on a Sunday. While they order at the window and wait for food, I use my phone to send emails to three window companies for quotes. Anthony hands me a drink and I take it without looking and suck down what turns out to be a Cherry Coke. It's cold and refreshing, and the artificial cherry flavor reminds me of his pheromones. I'm sure he picked it on purpose.

They eat while they drive and I resist the urge to crack a window because the smell of their food is turning my stomach. Then the first cramp hits low in my belly. I'm grateful I changed my sexy panties out for a pair of full-coverage slick panties. I suck in air and breathe through the cramp until it passes with a gush of slick that soaks the super absorbent gusset. A few minutes later, a second one hits me. This one is longer and more painful and I can't bite back my whimper as I fidget in my seat.

Jamie stops mid-sentence in his conversation with Anthony and he lets out a deep, rumbling purr that makes the tension in my pelvis melt into liquid heat. The cramp eases, and so does my grip on the edge of my seat.

"We're almost there, baby," Anthony says as he turns in his seat.

"I'm fine." I am not fine. I need dick. I need to ride a fat cock and come until the bottled up need inside me bursts and floods me with a sweet relief of dopamine.

My slick panties work overtime as I fidget while I look out the window and count the palm trees we pass to distract myself. I'm not sure why this heat is starting off so strong. It could be their proximity. Or it's because my omega instincts swear these men are pack and my body is tired of being denied what it wants. Of smelling them from afar, knowing they were so close but untouchable.

Well, I've touched them. I've done more than that. And my instincts won't let me keep denying what a part of me has known—and feared—for years.

Needing people makes you vulnerable, and right now I need them so much it fucking hurts.

"It hurts," I whimper and fidget again as the ache to be filled becomes a tangible, terrible thing.

"I wish I was back there with you, baby," Anthony says. "But we're almost there. Can you hold out or do you need Jamie to pull over?"

The thought of them pulling over so they can fuck this need right out of me on the side of the road makes my thighs tremble.

But right now, I want the safety and certainty of an enclosed space more than anything else. I bite my lip until the overwhelming urge lets up and shake my head.

"I can wait." It's a lie. The next wave is already building, but I make it true through sheer determination.

I'm barely paying attention to where we're going as Jamie drives us to his place while I fight the urge to shove my hand down my slick panties. It wouldn't take much to get off right now.

And with the way his old van rumbles, I'm already halfway there. A little more than halfway there. My thighs clench and the pressure on my swollen pussy and the vibrations of the rumbly van set me off. A shallow, empty orgasm washes through me and leaves me breathing hard.

Jamie drives closer and closer to the beach until he turns away from the pier and heads down the side street into a historic neighborhood. The multi-million-dollar mini-mansions fade into tiny beachfront cottages and shacks that still probably cost a cool million or more. He turns into the short driveway of a cute little yellow shack and then he hits his garage remote and we idle as the door rolls up enough so he can pull in and park.

Holy shit.

My alpha dancer lives in a million-dollar historic beach house. So what the fuck is he doing working at Rut?

The distraction and orgasm are enough for me to find a lull. The roiling need simmers below my surface once more. A warning that my chokehold on my self-control is nearly spent. Next time won't be so easy.

"I'll get your bag," Jamie says as he hops out and slides my door open. He grabs it from my feet and drags it up his shoulder while the garage door rolls back down.

"I want to look at your hand," I tell Anthony. I turn to Jamie and ask him, "Do you have a first aid kit?"

"Yeah, it's in the bathroom." Jamie leads the way and we follow.

My head swivels as he leads us through the house to a guest bathroom off the hallway. My gut clenches with longing at the soaked in scents layered in this house. Anthony comes over often. His smell is almost as embedded in this home as Jamie's is, and the tension coiled between my legs eases.

Pack.

This house smells like pack. Like safety. Affection and comfort. Cozy spring mornings full of sunshine and our mingled scents as we make love in that huge bed and an ocean breeze makes the sheer white curtains flutter.

All three of us pile into the tiled bathroom even though it's a tight fit. Jamie digs in the cabinet under the sink and pulls out a white first aid kit with a red cross printed on it. He pops the lid open and I take a moment to appreciate how well stocked it is.

"All right, let's get that off," I say, pointing to Anthony's bandage. The EMT slapped a white dressing over it, but the edges are already peeling up from him using his hand and flexing it.

"You gonna nurse me back to health, baby?" Anthony asks, his tone teasing as he grins. He rips the bandage off with no delicacy at all and the wound on his middle knuckle re-opens. It beads red with blood as the scab pulls off with the dressing.

I ignore his antics and point at the lidded toilet. "Sit. And try not to open every single one of your wounds. Do you think you can manage to behave for two fucking seconds?"

He sits and drapes his busted hand over the white countertop, and I turn the tap on so the water can warm up while I pour some hydrogen peroxide onto some clean gauze and lay it over the open skin on his knuckles. "This will probably sting," I tell him while I'm already doing it.

Anthony doesn't so much as flinch. He watches me wet

another piece of gauze, then wipe the trickling blood off his hand and clean his skin. After the peroxide has cleaned his wounds, I peel the gauze away to check that it looks clean and it's stopped bleeding.

"Think it'll scar?" he asks.

The edge of the rose tattoo on his hand might be affected, since one of the flower leaves extends to his knuckles. "Maybe." He might have to go back to his artist when it's healed and get the ink touched up.

"Good." His other arm curls around me, his hand sliding down to cup my ass. He grabs a handful and squeezes.

"Good?" I toss the pink-tinged gauze into the trash and grab the bacitracin. "Your tattoo might be fucked up."

He shrugs and tilts his head so he can watch me squeeze the antiseptic ointment over his broken skin. "I'll wear the scar proudly, because it means I kept you safe. Nothing else matters. You're worth a few scars, Vee. You're worth a whole damn lot of them."

My heart squeezes in my chest, even when his hand begins to grope and fondle. He's trying to distract me and it's nearly working, but I'm not done gently scolding him. I pop the wrapper on a roll of stretchy gauze fabric and wrap it around his hand. "You got in the way of me protecting my bar, Anthony. I don't mind taking orders in the bedroom—that's playtime—but when it comes to the rest of my life, I'm the one in control of it. If you can't handle that…"

"No."

I stop winding the gauze around his hand and try to pull back, but his grip on my ass tightens to keep me trapped between his knees. "No?" I ask.

"I know you're the boss. I don't care if you wear the pants at work so long as you let me tug them down so I can fuck you sometimes. But when it comes to your safety, we will never let you put yourself in harm's way. Not when one of us could be your shield instead. I know you don't think you need or want protection, but you've got us. Whether you like it or not. Get used to it, Vee. We're not fucking going anywhere."

An intense longing I haven't felt in years rips through me and leaves me feeling breathless and shaky. Deep down, I'm scared. Afraid that I'll open myself up, let my defenses down, need them, and then they'll leave. I haven't needed anyone in years. But now I sort of want to, and that's frightening.

Because loving them would be so easy. But sooner or later, everyone leaves me. They'll get disappointed when I can't give them whatever it is they want from me. They always do. But I'm tired of being good and saying no. Of denying myself. It's the heat making my self-control weak, or the sight of his battle-torn skin and the knowledge that he got hurt for *me*, but my omega instincts are clamoring for me to claim them both. My sweet, trustworthy alpha and my hard, dependable beta.

If they want to set themselves on fire, then we'll all burn.

I finish wrapping the gauze roll around his hand and tie it in place, winching it down harder than is strictly necessary. Still, he doesn't flinch. His groping hand kneads my ass, then moves to pass teasing strokes in the dip between my cheeks. He can't quite touch my pussy unless he goes under my skirt, but he tries.

"I guess you're gonna keep getting hurt then. I didn't take you for a masochist," I say.

Anthony's lips twist in a lopsided grin. His grip tightens, and he tugs me forward. Not that there's anywhere to go. His chin wedges between my breasts and he tips his head back to keep eye contact. "For you, baby, I don't mind it. You're worth all the pain in the world. Now give Daddy his medicine."

I cup his face in my hands and tilt his head back more, then curl down so I can press a tender kiss to his lips. Despite the chaste contact of our mouths, it's deep, and it leaves me breathless when I pull away.

"Fine. It's clear that I can't talk either of you into your senses, but I'm serious, Anthony. I make my life choices no matter what we do when we play." I run a nail down his throat and chest and tap him directly over his heart where the crucifix on his tattooed rosary is inked. "And you two are going to be in charge of making sure I get my pills. If you fuck with my birth control, you will *not* like the consequences. Lapsed Catholic or not. Understand?"

"Of course, baby. Don't worry. I'll make sure you get your pills. But the minute you tell me you want a baby, I'm gonna bend you over and put one in you."

My pussy clenches at the threat. One that's more of a promise, and I have to remind my traitorous body that we do not want a baby right now. I swear, the heat makes my ovaries practically cry with mourning at the thought they won't get their way this cycle. *Stupid omega breeding fetish.*

"Fine."

"Yeah?" Anthony asks, his eyes lighting up.

And then it hits me what I distractedly agreed to, and I blush as I pull out of his grip and use the first aid kit as an excuse to ignore him. I put the unused supplies inside and organize it so it'll close, then latch it shut. "Don't get cocky," I warn him. "I'm not saying yes to anything like that. It'll be years before I can think about having a family."

My suppressed instincts try to rise to the surface. I scrub a hand over my face. *God, what's wrong with me?* It's the heat. It always messes with my head. Makes me irrational. Makes me want things I can't have. "And heat talk doesn't count as consent. I'm telling you right now while I'm rational, and I expect you to respect that or this will be over."

"I know, baby. Don't worry. Daddy will take care of you."

Anthony smiles, but it's not as reassuring as he probably intends. It'll have to do.

"All done?" Jamie asks, pointing to the first aid kit.

"Yes, thanks." I slide it over to him so he can put it away. I've made myself as clear as I can get.

"Do you want a tour?" Jamie asks. "So you know where things are?"

I'm not sure I'll be seeing much of anything but the bedroom, but I'm still curious. "I would love one."

Jamie tells me all about the house as he leads me through it. It's an old Craftsman beach bungalow that his grandfather ordered from a catalog and built from a kit he pulled off the train. Warm, honey colored wood beams frame the ceiling and the entire house has been painted in soft creams and white.

His furniture is large and sturdy, the kind built especially for alphas who are often bigger and heavier and need the extra support, but lived-in. Framed family photos of a bunch of freckled, towheaded kids cover the walls. The pictures range from vintage to modern, and I wonder if any of these are nieces and nephews. He mentioned siblings. One or more of them might have kids. Do they come here for vacation? Family beach trips to fun uncle Jamie's house?

The furniture is used and comfortable, but the polished floors gleam. There's sand embedded in the rug by the porch and front door and an enormous surfboard leans against a corner. It's too dark outside to see the ocean, but his view of the beach must be magnificent. It makes me wonder again what he's doing working at Rut.

Jamie shows me the kitchen and tells me where the various things like cups and silverware are, but I'm barely listening. My brain is too busy trying to put together this puzzle.

What can I offer them? That nasty inner voice that tells me I'm only wanted because I'm an omega or they want the bar.

I've made Rut into a success against all odds, but I don't want either to be true. I can't believe that Jamie would be capable of that sort of duplicity, and he's the opposite of an alphahole. Anthony, though…

Anthony could absolutely be capable of that sort of duplicity, but my intuition tells me that isn't it. Maybe he really does just want to get laid. I've denied him for years, and now he's worn me down. For some guys who view themselves as players, especially insecure betas, it's all about the chase and conquest. Getting an omega pheromone-hooked can become a game.

But we've already fucked. If all he wanted was to spice up their love life with threesomes, then he's gotten what he wanted. He wouldn't still be asking for more. Maybe all he wants is to live out his heat fantasies. Betas don't understand how bad a heat gets until they have to service a needy omega through one. The reality doesn't always live up to the porn-fueled fantasy.

Jamie stops talking about his carpenter grandfather and the knife knicks in the kitchen doorway that tracked his and his brother's heights as they grew, and their father's before them. He purrs, and I realize that my pheromones must be tinged with stress. He must be smelling it. I take a deep breath to try to get my roiling insecurities under control.

His purring helps. Not that I'd ever admit it out loud.

"Did I do something wrong?" Jamie asks, his voice hesitant and his expression worried.

"No, you didn't do anything wrong. I'm…" *Nervous.*

Anthony comes up behind me in the kitchen and the crack of his hand on my ass makes me jump and yelp. "Your nest is ready. Come check it out, baby."

I rub the sting out of my butt while my belly flutters with nerves. They made me a nest?

Jamie blushes and ducks his head, then gives me a small

smile before he scoots past us and leads the way to the bedroom. The wooden four-poster bed has been piled high with blankets and pillows in various shades of white, cream, and warm taupe. My soft teal blanket and matching pillow take up the center, and my empty duffel bag has been folded and laid on a chair.

Sheer mosquito netting covers the poles and drapes around the bedposts in generous folds. The entire effect is so dreamy and romantic. It's a far cry from the small, sad nest I make in my room whenever the urge can't be ignored.

My skin itches with the need to strip out of these too tight clothes and climb in and cover it with my scent. *Our* scents.

"Do you like it?" Jamie asks. He steps into the room and reaches out to stroke the canopy fabric, and I wonder if they put it up especially for me. Because omegas like small, tight, safe places during a heat. The netting can be drawn to make the nest cozier.

The idea that they went shopping while thinking about me and what I might like makes my insides feel squishy and frag- ile. Jamie's face is carved with lines of longing as he looks between the nest—what I'm guessing is his courtship offering —and me. I can't bear the thought of him thinking I don't like it or that I don't appreciate it. Appreciate *him*. It's not his fault I'm a shitty omega.

I cross the room and reach for him, cupping his square jaw in my hands. His beard stubble scratches me, and I should hate the sensation against my overly sensitive skin. But all I want is to feel the rough slide of it against my inner thighs. My thumbs stroke over his cheeks as I revel in the prickling.

"I don't like it," I tell him.

His hazel eyes widen and the skin between his brows pinches.

"I love it," I rush to tell him so he can stop looking so worried.

Relief makes him sigh, and then he purrs and turns his face into my hand so he can nuzzle it. He cups my hand with his own, his palm dwarfing mine, and holds it there. Not demandingly. Not to pry my hand off his face and move it lower, to where I know he's desperate for me to touch him. But gently. With reverence, as if something as simple as the touch of my hand on his face brings him such immense pleasure it has to be savored.

Oh, Jamie.

He makes my heart ache. My big, sweet, beautiful alpha. I want to wrap him in bubble wrap and hide him from the world's endless cruelties. I'll probably hurt him—I always do even when I don't mean to—but I'm not strong enough to tell him no. Not when he's begged so prettily. Not when he's put together such a beautiful nest for me.

A cramp twists my insides and I take a deep breath to get through the pain of the agonizing emptiness. Each wave of heat delirium will get harder to control, but for now I'm still me, even with these omega urges riding me.

And I want to do things my way.

"Undress for me, alpha."

Chapter Eighteen

VERONICA

Jamie drags in a shuddering breath and presses a kiss to my palm, then does what I command. I drop my hands to my sides as I watch him disrobe. It's a simple act I've seen a thousand times on stage. But here in this nest inside his house by the beach, it's intimate. Like it was the very first time when he auditioned. He was all fumbling, trembling hands and clumsy footwork. But I saw his potential. All he needed was molding. A strong but gentle hand to shape him.

Mine.

Jamie drags his shirt up over his chiseled stomach, his muscles flexing as he works it over his head. He drops it to the floor, then kicks off his sandals and shucks out of his shorts. Then he's bare for me, exactly as I like him. I put my hands on his shoulders and push, and he lets me move him. I guide him to the floor so he's kneeling. Exactly where I like him.

I run my fingers through his hair and work out a snarl as I pet him. "Undress me, pet."

"Yes, Ma'am." His hands tremble as he works my skirt's zipper down. He shimmies it down my hips and over my ass until it falls to a puddle at my feet. I step out of it and use him for balance when my heels sink into the plush rug that extends from under the bed.

He shoves my shirt up, and I help him. I pull it over my head and shake my hair out, then toss it onto our growing pile. When he gets to my bra, I don't help him. He fumbles at the hooks for a bit, and I let him work it out until he's got it undone. My breasts drop as he pulls the lace down my arms and discards it on the floor.

His eyes darken with lust and he moves to palm a breast until I make a noise in the back of my throat. It's a sound that tells him no. There will be time for him to lavish them with strokes and kisses, and there will be a point where I'll lose all reason and control and I'll let him do what he wants with me, but that time isn't now.

Right now he has only one task, and that's pleasing me by doing what he's told.

Jamie ducks his head, his expression sheepish. He hooks his thumbs in my black heat panties. He rolls them down my ass, then groans as the scent of my thick, wet slick fills the room. His face is inches from my pussy as he drags the soaked fabric down my legs. I lean on him again and step out of them.

He struggles with the metal hooks of my garter belt until I take pity on him and show him how they work. It's that, or risk a rip in my stockings, and the vintage style silk ones are expensive and difficult to find.

Once he's got all eight hooks undone and there's nothing to hold them up anymore, the stockings sag down my thighs. He rolls them down along with the belt, and I kick out of my heels so he can bare me completely.

A tiny shiver of a cramp pinches me from the inside and a burst of wetness makes my cunt slippery. A bead of it rolls down my inner thigh. I cup the back of Jamie's head and bring his face to my juncture. "You know what to do."

"Yes, Ma'am."

When his tongue laps at my wet cleft, then slides through my folds and grazes my clit, I sigh and rub against him. "Good boy."

He licks me until my core clenches and another rush of slick drips down his chin. I've barely begun to really enjoy it when the urge to be filled, the incessant need of it, makes me pull away from him.

"That's good, pet. Now get in the nest."

Jamie scrambles upright and gets into the nest, then sits there as he waits for his next order. I put a knee on the bed and then I crawl over to him where he's waiting in the center. One fingernail digging into his sternum is all he needs to follow the silent command and lie back amongst the pillows.

The idea of having such a large, powerful alpha trembling underneath me as he waits for my orders makes my pussy drip with need. I straddle his hips and wiggle my cunt down over his cock, trapping it to his belly and rubbing my clit against him as I ride him and bite my lip.

"God, that's so good." I drop my hands to his abdomen and dig my nails into him while my hips pump with the heat's frenzied need to come. It would be better with a cock in me, but this is good too. *So fucking good.*

"You're so hard, pet. Does it hurt?" I ask. "Does your cock ache for me?"

"Yes. I need you bad, Miss Vee."

I rub harder, faster, and devour the sight of my red-tipped fingers making divots in his washboard abs as I ride his cock without giving him any relief. This is about my pleasure. My needs. And this alpha is exactly where he belongs. Underneath me, giving me everything I need and want, while demanding nothing I don't offer him in return.

He's perfect.

Jamie's large hands cradle my hips, but he doesn't use them to move me. He doesn't dig his fingers into me and attempt to shift our angle. Force my hips up so he can line his cock up with my hole and sink inside. He waits. He takes it. And he suffers in my cruel denial as I use him for my delicious, swirling pleasure and give him so very little of his own.

His fat alpha cock is as hard as a rock underneath me. His urge to fall into a rut to match my heat must be fierce. Which means his self-control is strong. As strong as my need to control him? Suddenly I want to test that resolve.

"You're being such a good boy," I tell him as I reach down and rub two fingers against his ruddy head. Moisture soaks my fingers, but I can't tell if it's my slick or his pre-cum without tasting it. So that's what I do. I rub my thumb over his wet slit and bring it to my mouth, where I suck it clean and pull it free with a wet pop.

The overwhelming salty musk of pre-cum fades to the creamy coconut of his pheromones. The taste is subtle for now, but when he comes for real, he's going to be so fucking delicious. I could drink him down right from the source. My omega instincts think that's a very good idea. I can't bear the thought of food right now, but I could eat this alpha up and ask for seconds and still be hungry for more.

"Mmm," I hum as I swipe at his leaking head for more.

He groans and throws his head back, the veins in his neck popping as his cock leaks a steady stream of pre-cum against my fingers. I play with it as I rub myself on his length. It pools on his stomach in rivulets, which I scoop up and bring to my mouth.

Noisily, I stick the pre-cum-laden fingers into my mouth. I swipe my tongue over them and lick them clean, then go searching for more. He's so fucking mouthwatering, and I can't get enough of him. I want to catch his cum on my tongue and fill my belly with the flavor of him.

My pussy throbs with aching need. Slick coats him, mixing with his arousal as we make a mess of each other. I ride his trapped cock, sliding up and down his hard length. His dripping cockhead bumps against my clit. I drag it down all the way to his base, where his knot is swelling.

"You're so handsome." Leaning down, I kiss him. "So sweet and gentle. Patient, and good at taking orders." I suck his lower lip into my mouth and bite it gently to hear him groan. "I love giving you orders, pet. My good boy."

"Yes. I want that, Miss Vee."

I groan and swivel my hips over him. His cock's head bumps at my entrance, then slips higher. I lean down and slide my mouth against the shell of his ear as I press my face to his. "What would you give to have that knot inside me?"

"Everything," he groans, his voice breathy and strained. His cock jumps against my pussy, its length trapped between my labia. "Anything."

"Good," I whisper, pressing a tender kiss to the side of his face. I slide my cheek against his, enjoying the prickle of his stubble and the desperate scent of his desire. His pheromones are in overdrive as he tries to woo me, his alpha to my omega. To trap me in his chemical desire.

I nuzzle his neck until I find the source, then lick that knotted ball of tissue under the skin at the base of his neck. He groans, his body tensing under me, as my teeth graze over that sensitive bundle of tissue and nerves. "Because that's what I deserve. Everything. Now beg." I nip his scent gland and he descends into babble.

His words string together in a litany of prayers and pleading. "Please, Miss Vee. I want you so bad. I need you so bad it hurts. Please let me fuck you. Let me knot you. Use my cock. I'll make you so happy, I swear."

Instead of answering his pleas, I look over my shoulder and find Anthony. He's gotten naked while I amused myself at our poor alpha's expense. This is my first good look at him, and the sight of him steals my breath.

He's whipcord lean, with the faint line of muscles that promises a hidden, wiry strength. His tattoos cover him from his hands to his neck to his thighs. In the center of his upper chest is a tattooed rosary, the cross dangling over his heart. Black and gray cover his body with images and swirling script. I can't read the words from here, but at some point, I will. I'll trace each letter with my eyes, and then my fingers, and finally my tongue.

The stark white bandage wrapped around his battered knuckles makes me proud. I wish I'd gotten to see him kick that alpha's ass up close. Smelled the blood flying. I bet it was glorious.

Maybe the thought of watching one man pummel another shouldn't make my cunt squeeze with desire, but it does. In the end, we're animals. During a heat, my dynamic's core needs are simple. Find a pack, fuck them blind, and lock that shit down with a baby and a claiming bite. Civility can't argue with instincts.

A death's head hawkmoth decorates his abdomen and groin. A grim reaper dominates one of his sleeves while an angel stabbing a spear into a serpentine dragon makes up most of the other.

The time and dedication it takes to sit for that many tattoos over so many sessions proves that he's an extremely patient man who doesn't balk at difficult things or pain.

That's promising, because I've been called both by more than one ex.

I cock one brow at him while I grind on Jamie's pinned cock and bulging knot. "Aren't you joining us?"

His lips curve with a creeping smile, and he steps closer until his knees hit the edge of the nest. He stands there and brings a section of my hair to his nose to sniff it. "Oh, I don't know. I like the view from here fine. Besides, it might be a good idea to let him warm you up for me."

"Have something special planned, huh?" I ask. My belly flutters. I'm desperate to know what it is, but I won't be reduced to begging. Not like Jamie is.

He grins instead of answering, but his eyes sparkle with calculating mischief. It doesn't matter that he has a beta's slimmer, knotless cock. If he says Jamie's cock will be a warmup, he means it.

His sheer confidence is impressive, but I know he's not bragging about his plans lightly. He is nothing but sincere, especially in the depths of his depravity.

Whatever he has in store for my heat is probably nefarious. I should run for the door, terrified, not coiled taut with anticipation. My hips roll in a circular motion as I tease myself on Jamie's cock and wonder what Anthony's scheming.

When I can't take the emptiness in my pussy anymore, I reach down and grab Jamie's cock by the base and notch his head at my opening. Jamie's eyes widen and his nostrils flare as I hover there with his cockhead brushing against my hole.

"This cock is mine once I fuck it," I tell Jamie. I cup his jaw with my hand and squeeze. "Other omegas can look. They can want you. But the only omega pussy I'll let you fuck is this one. Is that what you want?"

I don't have to wait long for his answer. Jamie nods. He pleads and begs with his eyes for me to sink down on his cock. But that's not enough for me. I want his pretty words. I need to hear him say them.

"What is it you want, pet?" I ask as I drag one ruby nail over his lower lip.

"To be yours, Miss Vee. Please make me yours."

"Good boy," I tell him as I sink down on his cock. He stretches me wide and the howling need swelling inside me like a hurricane breaks. The stretch is intense, but our recent play has broken my dry spell and made it bearable . The slick from my heat smooths out the rest.

"This is my cock now," I say as I rise, then sink back down, fucking myself on him. I do it again, and again until our bodies make filthy wet sounds that fill the room. I rise until his cock is almost free, and then I sink down on it again until he hits the end of me, his half inflated knot nudging against my swollen pussy. It begs for entry, but I don't work myself over its girth yet.

"Yes," Jamie says. "It's yours. Oh, fuck. It's so good… your pussy feels so good, Ma'am."

His abdominals flex while I ride him and my tits bounce with every slap of my ass against his thighs. I work a hand between my lips and find my clit, rolling the swollen nub in circles until my walls clamp down on his cock. He jerks and mutters a breathy curse each time.

"Please let me come here, Ma'am," Jamie begs. "Please. I want to come inside you."

"Not yet. I haven't decided if you've earned that privilege." I edge us both twice until his hands fist in the sheets and twist. He wants to grab my hips and force me to ride him harder, to let him come, but he won't do it because the urge to please me matters more than his own brief seconds of pleasure.

And I love to reward a good boy for behaving.

I ride him harder. Slick pools between us and leaves us both dripping as I take his big cock and circle my clit until the urge to keep going, to finally let myself come, overwhelms me. My plans to edge us both a third time, to build up his release so it's voluminous, fly out the window. All I can think about is making him knot me.

"If you don't stop I'll come, Ma'am," Jamie warns me, his face turning red and his neck cording from the strain of holding back. He's trying so hard to be good, to play by my unfair rules while I revel in his anguish.

"Good," I sigh, dropping my head back and sinking down again. "I've decided I want to come on your cock. Give me your knot, pet."

His back bows until his head digs into the pillow and he fucks up into me, my hips rising from the forceful way he seats himself deep. He thrusts four times, and then it's done. He shoves his knot up inside me while it's filling, and the stretch turns into a burn that fades into a glorious warmth.

Jamie cries out as he comes, his knot swelling until it locks behind my pubic bone. He pumps me full of alpha cum. I'm so deliciously stuffed, so stretched wide, that it barely takes three swipes of my clit for me to come on his knot.

The tension in my pelvis snaps and ripples move through me, spasms making my pussy clamp down on his cock to suck more seed from his balls. A new tension builds as he fills me to bursting, his load heavy from the edging.

My body strains to contain everything he's giving me. His chest rises and falls with deep breaths under my hands. I lean on him for support and remember how to breathe myself while my aftershocks milk his knot for every drop.

Jamie erupts into a rumbling purr and goes completely limp underneath me.

"You should be good and ready for me now," Anthony says, startling me back to reality as the heat-drunk fog tries to drag me down with contentment.

"What?" I try to sit up straighter, forgetting for a moment

how thoroughly we're tied. Jamie whimpers when the movement tugs at his knot.

The bed dips as Anthony climbs into the nest and positions himself behind me. He strokes his hands over my ass and hips, then grips them. He slips fingers between us, wedges it inside, and pries me off of Jamie's swollen knot. I gasp from the shocking loss of it. Semen and slick splatter over the alpha's groin as the stopper pops free prematurely.

"What are you doing?" I demand. It's unpleasant to pull a knot free early, and dangerous if done wrong.

Anthony cages me with his body, his thighs pressed to mine until we're straddling Jamie together. He bends me forward and reaches around to grab a breast, playing with it and tweaking the nipple until my pussy contracts around Jamie's still-buried cock.

"Making room," Anthony says. He presses a tender kiss to the side of my face and then I feel it. The head of his cock is a blunt intrusion into my already-stuffed hole. He rubs it along my slick opening and puffy lips. It grazes me from pussy to ass while he slicks it in our mess of fluids.

"You can't fuck my ass without prepping," I warn him.

"I wasn't planning on it, baby. I'd never hurt you like that." Anthony's arm brushes against my ass, and then he slides lower. He notches his cockhead against my pussy and presses in, using Jamie's buried cock as a guide. "Never."

The stretch is intense, even more so than Jamie's alpha knot. I suck in a breath, only letting it out when he pulls back out. "Then what do you call *that*?"

"Shh," he whispers against my ear. "You can take it. This is what your pussy was built for."

"My pussy was built for a knot, not two cocks—Jesus Christ, oh my God." I gasp as he inches deeper and bottoms out until I'm so impossibly full it seems like I'll split in two.

Anthony chuckles and pinches my nipple again, twisting it until I moan. "You can call me God, but Daddy's still my favorite. That's it, baby. Let me in this sweet pussy. Relax. You can take it. Trust Daddy to make you feel real good."

He pulls back, only to surge forward again, and I whimper. The mewling sounds he fucks out of me are embarrassing, and every time he pulls back only to thrust in again, I swear that's the time my body is going to cleave in two.

"How does it feel knowing my cock is stuffing her better than your knot did?" Anthony asks Jamie. "Look at her. I've fucked the words right out of her head."

"I love the slide of your cock against mine inside her," Jamie says.

"It's…" *Too much. Agonizing. Glorious.* I can't think long enough to speak.

I squeeze my eyes shut and dig my nails into Jamie's shoulders. I don't know if I'm scratching him up, and I can't bring myself to care. Not while Anthony moves, his hips pushing his cock in deep, then pulling back so he can do it all over again. Unlike Jamie's light, tentative grasp, there's nothing gentle about Anthony's clasping. He digs his fingers into my hips and tugs me back to meet his ruthless thrusts. "Oh, God."

"That's it, baby. Let go. Let Daddy satisfy you real good. I know what you need. A good, deep dicking and a pussy full of cum. Fuck, yeah, squeeze my cock like that again. God, you're so fucking wet. You can pretend you don't like this, but your pussy says you're a liar. You're soaked, baby."

I want to snap and snarl at him that it's slick from my heat and anything would make my pussy a slip-n-slide right now, but I can't talk. I can barely remember how to breathe. He puts a hand between my shoulder blades and pushes. I'm powerless to resist him as he folds me over Jamie's chest and ruts me from behind, his dick going deeper with the change in angle.

He picks up speed, his thrusts coming faster and faster against Jamie's buried cock. The crack of his thighs against my ass is louder than our panting. "Beg me to come, baby. Beg, or I'm gonna edge us twice like you edged Jamie."

The thought of him dragging this out any longer makes me want to cry. I don't know if my frustration is borne from my heat's demand for cum or from my body's aching exhaustion. All I want to do is collapse into the nest and sleep with the sound of purring underneath me.

So I beg. "Please. Please make me come, Daddy."

The begging is embarrassing, and somehow that's enjoyable in a way I don't fully understand. It's like I want him to make me want to shame myself, but I'm too self-conscious to go there without his goading. Maybe Anthony understands my twisted head better than I do.

Now that I've spoken the embarrassing words out loud, they've lost their power. Nothing changed. I'm not afraid of them any longer. Maybe it's okay to be weak and needy during a heat if I'm doing it with the right people.

He grabs my hips and tilts them, tugging my pussy higher and nearly dislodging Jamie's cock, and then he hits something deeper that makes my thoughts go completely blank. Tension coils taut in my belly as a second orgasm rises from the first one's ashes. The heat's gift of multiple orgasms has finally arrived. "Oh, fuck, yes. Fuck me, Daddy. I need to come."

"Not quite right, baby. Try again." He slows his pace and I cry out from the loss of momentum.

"Fuck me, please. Harder." *What did he want again?* I rack my brain, but every snap of his hips drives the thoughts away like scattering clouds. All I can think about is coming. *Cum!* "Come for me."

"Where do you want me to come," he asks. He grips my buttocks and spreads them wide.

The movement stretches my poor, over-stretched pussy even more. I suck in a breath and arch my back, but all this does is drive myself back onto his cock. "My pussy. Come inside my pussy, Daddy." I don't care where he comes so long as he doesn't stop again until I've orgasmed.

Anthony tilts my pelvis with his thrusts, moving me exactly as he pleases. "This is better than an alpha's knot, isn't it, baby? Don't you like being stuffed full of cock? A knot doesn't fuck the air out of your lungs. It just sits there. You needed me, baby, didn't you? Needed my beta cock in this greedy little pussy."

"Yes." My leg threatens to cramp from the tension in my body as I balance on that precipice, desperate for the relief he dangles in front of me like a baited hook. "I need you."

"It was so nice of your alpha to warm you up for me, don't you think?" Anthony prompts.

"Yes." A rough thrust that sets my toes curling makes me close my eyes and drop my forehead to Jamie's rumbling chest. The next pounding movement makes my knee slip in the nest, and then the way Jamie's knot rubs against my entrance and my clit makes my pussy squeeze. I'm so fucking close. Just a bit more.

I spread my legs wider until my groin aches and then I move, thrusting back on Anthony's plunging length. I fuck myself on both their buried cocks as I rub my swollen clit against Jamie's knot.

I moan, and rub, then moan louder. "He's such a good alpha for warming my pussy up for you."

Anthony groans, his movements slowing as he goes deeper while we find a rhythm together. My release swells as I focus on it with single-minded precision. I will come on both their cocks or die trying. My heart hammers against my ribs until it's ready to burst from my chest.

"That's it, baby," Anthony says. "That's a good girl. Come

on my cock so I can fill this pretty pink cunt. I've got what you need, baby. Let me give it to you. I'll make you drip so good."

"Fuck me, Daddy. Come in my pussy. I need it. I need you. I need to… to…"

My pleas turn into whimpers as I'm thrown over the cliff's edge of my release and pleasure drowns me in waves of spasm and warmth. My entire body flushes hot as I come, my poor, stretched walls trying to milk both their cocks in search of a knot to squeeze.

"Fuck, baby, that's good. Your pussy's so tight. Here you go, baby." He grunts and his cock jumps inside me. It kicks with every spurt of his release as he paints my walls white with his cum. Their semen mingles inside me as his thrusts turn shallow while he milks his cock till it's empty. I'm so full that it's leaking all over us without a knot to stop it up.

Anthony fucks me until his cock begins to soften, then he pulls off us. His hand brushes against my thigh as he guides Jamie's knot back inside me. My fluttering walls squeeze down on it, and it's blissfully small compared to the ruthless stretching our beta demanded from my body.

I go completely boneless on top of Jamie, who hasn't stopped purring this entire time. My eyes slide shut, and I breathe a sigh of relief as little aftershocks zip through me.

"Keep her good and plugged, babe," Anthony says. "That's some top-shelf cum for a top-shelf pussy." He slaps my ass until it jiggles. Like he's a satisfied car salesman, slapping the hood of a car he just sold.

"Okay, babe," Jamie answers. His arms come around me as he hugs me against his chest.

I try to open my mouth to call them both dicks, but I'm too damn tired and satisfied. I can't open my eyes. Jamie's purr, combined with a pussy full of cum and a knot to clench around, is a dangerous recipe.

I'm asleep almost instantly. Only the feel of warm limbs and soft blankets rouses me to the point of consciousness as they readjust our positions. I curl against the nearest body and burrow my face into a neck, inhaling their scent.

With the smell of coconut and cherries in my nose, the coziness of a pack scented nest, and the tenderness of a well-used pussy, I finally fall asleep warm and content.

Chapter Nineteen

ANTHONY

VEE STIRS WHEN DAWN BREAKS. GOLDEN LIGHT STREAMS through the curtains. She chirps in her sleep and burrows deeper into my side, her leg thrown over mine as if to keep me from running. Silly omega. I'm not planning on running away. She'll have to move out of state to get rid of me. Probably out of the country.

Her nose glides up and down my throat as she hunts for a scent gland in her sleep. My chest pinches, because I'm a beta so mine isn't developed enough to give it to her, but I can give her something else she needs.

I grab her by the ass and tug her all the way on top of me, then reach between us and guide my morning wood inside her. *Oh, fuck, that's good.* She's so slippery and warm. Her pussy clamps down on my dick as I bottom out inside her and hit her cervix.

She whimpers with every hilt-burying thrust and whines with every withdrawal. Her hips roll as she tries to find a rhythm while she blinks sleepy eyes open. Her pretty brown eyes are dark with lust and unfocused.

"I got you, baby," I tell her as I take her by the hips and

wrestle the control from her. She hesitates, her hip gyrations fighting mine as I work her up and down on my cock and ignore her weak attempts to dominate me. That's a battle she won't win, and I'm all too eager to make her happy to lose. "I've got what you need right here."

I sit up and lean her onto her back, flipping our positions as I get to my knees without pulling my cock from her warm, slick cunt. She whines when the thrusting stops, but sighs when I hook her knees over one shoulder and band them there with one arm. When I thrust, her tits bounce and I revel in my gorgeous view as I work to destroy her pussy and shatter all of her illusions of control.

This is my pussy. My omega. My mate. And I'm going to fuck her until she believes it, then fuck her some more for the hell of it.

Jamie stirs beside us as we get louder. He rolls over and opens an eye. His pupils are blown, too. He sniffs the air, then shoves the blankets aside.

Will he try to take her from me? When he's lost in a rut, I won't be able to stop him unless I'm willing to hurt him, which I'm not. Not unless he's hurting her. We've never shared an omega in heat before. It was a risk. We knew this. We'd talked about it so many times as we strategized how to crack Vee's hard shell. Our omega's one tough nut. Hard and brittle on the outside, but deliciously soft and sweet on the inside. She's worth the effort.

Before Jamie's purr can turn into a jealous growl, I grab a fistful of blond hair and drag his mouth to mine. His lips are stiff from surprise, and then they soften as he melts into my kiss. Vee's ass slaps against my thighs as I fuck her pussy hard and deep and show my big alpha mate how much I love him.

I break our kiss and reach down to stroke his cock. It's already hard and leaking. She hasn't stopped pumping out *fuck me* pheromones since she came so hard she passed out with a cock still inside her. I drag my thumb firmly along the underside and dig it hard into the divot underneath his corona.

"Your omega's hungry, alpha. Feed her."

Jamie looks between me and her, his face blank. He's confused, I think. When we talked about this, he tried to explain what a rut was like. How it fogs his head and makes it hard to think beyond impulse and instinct. But hearing about it and seeing it are two different things. They're about as different as watching a heat porno versus actually tending an omega through one.

I squeeze his hard cock and tug, milking a drop of coconut cream-tinged pre-cum from his tip. "Put your cock in her mouth," I tell him.

Vee finally catches onto the plan and she helps things along by reaching for Jamie. Her hand fights mine for a grip, and I relinquish control as she guide's our alpha's cock to her lips. Her tongue flicks out to lick his dripping tip.

Jamie grunts, his hand moving to pet her hair and then sliding down to play with one of her breasts as she swallows him down. The sight of that thick alpha cock disappearing down the tiny omega's throat makes me groan. I slam my hips up and batter at the mouth of her womb while I watch.

The force of my thrusts make her bob on his length, and I grin when I realize that even like this, I can control them. Me. The beta. While Jamie and Vee are lost to their rut and heat, I orchestrate their blowjob like a damn maestro.

A series of shallow thrusts let her swirl her tongue around his head. Deep, rolling thrusts make her slide up and down his length. Fast, furious plunging makes her gag until last night's mascara smears under her eyes.

Shit. Forgot to take her makeup off her.

We're bad at this—unpracticed—but we'll get better. I'll

bathe her after I get done fucking her brains out and filling her up from both ends with the fresh batch of cum she needs.

I fuck Vee, and by proxy, I fuck Jamie, and then I get lost in my pleasure as I watch her swallow his cock while mine's buried deep in her pussy. When Jamie's half-swollen knot barely fits past her teeth, I wrap my fist around his base and squeeze. I can't let him hurt her by accident.

Jamie's head drops and he groans as he fucks my hand and her face. His expression contorts with a pleasure-fueled agony, and then he comes. His knot blows against my palm, and I squeeze it hard so he's not tempted to shove it deeper down her mouth.

Vee's throat bobs as she swallows and drinks her alpha's cum. It's the most erotic thing I've ever seen in my life. My cock kicks inside her in a desperate bid to continue what we were doing, and when I'm certain that I can pay less attention to the two of them without one of them getting hurt, I refocus on her pussy.

Her wet pink lips stretch thin around my girth as I tilt my hips and bury myself to the root. Her sucking noises mix with her dainty omega purr and the combination makes my balls pull tight. "Fuck, baby, why is this pussy so good? I can't wait to watch it drip."

She laps at Jamie's tip, and then her tongue swipes over her lips as if she's searching for any lingering drops.

"Was that good?" I ask her. "Did you like your breakfast?"

Vee looks up at Jamie, who's still looming over her, his softening dick resting on his thigh, and a smidgeon of jealousy pinches me. I reach down and grab her breast, giving it a good squeeze, and then I slap it. She gasps, her eyes darting to me, and I hold her gaze as I pinch her taut nipple and twist until her cunt squeezes my dick like she wants to break it.

"I asked you a question, baby. Did you like your breakfast?"

Her brows knit together as her eyes roll up while I fuck her through my interrogation. Yeah, she liked it. Her cheeks are flushed a healthy shade of pink and her pussy's so wet she's making a mess of the sheets. Slick beads down her ass and rolls down my thighs before pooling in the blankets.

"Too horny for words?" I tease her. "Okay. I'll let you come on my cock, and then you can thank me later."

I work a thumb between her swollen labia until I find her slick nub and make circles around it. Her hips jerk against me and she mewls as I tighten my grip on her legs with my other arm. I pin her lower half to my chest as I work her clit until her hands make fists in the nest. Jamie watches me wind her up, and then I shove her right over that edge.

It's too early and I'm too fucking horny to deny either of us with more edging. She squeezes her eyes shut and her head digs into the mattress. Her spine bows and her cunt flutters on my cock. Its little squeezes tip me over the edge.

My balls pull taut and my belly cramps as the first rope of cum sprays inside her. My hips sway with long, slow thrusts as I use her orgasm to squeeze out every drop. And when she gets more restless instead of less, I shove three fingers alongside my cock and stuff her full.

Vee goes limp on my cock, and then she purrs. I rock my dick against my hand to wring out every single drop inside her greedy pussy as I fill her up and wait for her to quiet. When I grow too soft to stay buried, I finally pull free. She lets out an annoyed chirp, but otherwise doesn't make a sound until I move to lift her from the bed.

Jamie sits up straighter, the intensity of his attention prickling at the edges of my awareness.

"Just cleaning her, babe."

He watches me carry her into the bathroom. I sit her down on the toilet and leave her to do her thing as I turn the tub's tap on and get the water warm. I don't know how hot she normally likes her showers or how much heat she can handle right now while she's somewhat feverish, so I make it barely warm like you would with a baby. Then I eye the line of omega heat washes we bought and set around the edge of the tub.

We didn't know which scent she might like, so we bought them all. At the time, it felt excessive. Now, with a blissed-out, purring Vee a foot away and waiting, I worry we don't have enough options.

What if she hates them all? There are delivery apps, I guess, but what if the driver's an alpha? And here I thought that we'd planned for everything.

Anxiety makes me fumble as I rip plastic safety seals off. What if I fuck this up? What else did I not think of? Jamie is relying on me to get this right. I can't stand the thought of disappointing either of them. I try so hard to pretend like I don't care what anyone thinks, to dodge their expectations of me, but deep down I still think that no matter what I do, I'll never be good enough. The black sheep of my family. The family business liability. Nonconformist. A disappointing bisexual beta son. Vee, Brendan, and Jamie are different, but will it be enough?

I take a deep breath and let it out slowly. The annoyingly thick plastic finally gives way. I shake it into the trash, the static cling making it difficult. Then I do the same with all the others until I have a row of bottles at the ready.

"Which one do you want, baby?" I ask her as I pick up two of her ten choices, a pink one and a purple one, and bring them to her. I show her the bottles with the different flowers on the labels, but she's more intent on nuzzling my hand than reading the text.

I sigh. "Right. Let's try them all then, hmm?" I set one on the counter and flip the top up on another and hold it to her nose. She rears back like I've slapped her and rubs at her nose until it turns pink.

"Hmm. Not flowers." I put both of the floral options on the counter and grab the yellow one, citrus, and the white one, vanilla. Both seem like fairly neutral options. I flip both their tops up before wafting them under her nose, but she's not interested in them either. Her attention pulls to the doorway and I turn and see that Jamie's standing there watching us.

His eyes are less glassy and unfocused, and his body language is relaxed, so my concern dissipates.

"She doesn't like the floral or food scents," I tell him, unsure how much he understands while in a rut. "Maybe she's an experiences girl, whatever the fuck that means. Let's try the gray one, baby."

The gray one makes her growl, a low sound under her breath, and I flip the lid closed and toss it straight into the trash. I have to admit that the smoky campfire and pine smell don't do much for me either.

Jamie sways on his feet, his movement stealing her attention from the peach colored bottle that is supposed to smell like clean laundry. I snap my fingers at him to make him look at me. "You're distracting her. Sit down."

To my never ending surprise, Jamie only hesitates for a moment before he does it. He sits on the floor and I grab Vee's chin and make her look at me. "How about blue?"

Her face relaxes as she sniffs it. When she tries to steal the bottle from me, I know that we have our winner. "All right. Blue Bahamas it is. Now be a good girl and wait for me to get it ready." I pour a good amount into the tub and swirl it around until it foams, then herd her into the bath. She plays with the bubbles, making a game of popping them while I wet a washcloth with girly face wash and scrub the smeared makeup off her face.

She fights me and soaks me in half of her bathwater until she realizes she can't win, no matter how slippery she gets. When she gives in and lies back and lets me take care of her, I feel a rush of victory.

Okay, we can do this. We're doing the thing. I haven't fucked it all up yet.

I scrub the washcloth over her while being careful not to get her too worked up. She likes the rough slide of the fabric over her breasts and thighs. I thought omegas hated that sort of thing, but she arches into it and purrs, and if I let the cloth linger a bit longer than I need to in order to clean her, nobody is aware enough to call me out on it. When I get the cloth between her legs, she's panting and rubbing against it as I clean her, and Jamie stirs with interest behind me.

Alphas and omegas… They're worse than a pair of dogs.

I grin and work two fingers inside her under the guise of making sure she's nice and clean for round three. When her hips pump in search of relief, the cooled water sloshing, I show her the benefits of dating a guy who used to play guitar. I work her until she's panting, my hand moving so fast for so long that it cramps, and then she cries out as she rides my hand to completion.

With the orgasm and the worst of the pheromones cleaned off her, her eyes clear up and she lets me scoop her out of the tub without much fuss. Now it's Jamie who doesn't want to do what he's told. He stands in the doorway while I towel her off and blocks us in despite me telling him to move.

It's the shrill ringing of a phone that finally snaps through his rut and her heat. I push Jamie back and carry her to the nest, and both of them settle once she's back in its safety. Jamie crawls in after her and tugs her into his arms. He rubs his cheek over her wet hair until it's frizzy, and I sigh.

Fuck.

I don't really know anything about taking care of curly hair, but I know it involves lots of bottles of different kinds of hair goo and wearing special microfiber turbans. And the only reason I know this is because of my sisters. My hair's never been long enough that it needed anything more than some mousse and a comb.

The phone rings again, and I hunt for it until I find it in Vee's purse on a chair. It's an alarm, not a phone call, and it says it's for her meds. I turn the alarm off and see that her phone's nearly dead, so I hunt down her charger and plug it in. I grab a bottle of flavored protein water from the fridge and her packet of birth control pills from her purse.

I stare at the plastic and cardboard pack and follow the arrows and teeny tiny printed directions until I find her next pill and pop it into my palm. *Hope it's the right one.*

When I return to the nest, they're already fucking. Vee's on her hands and knees while Jamie ruts her from behind, and I take a moment to appreciate the view before I crawl into the nest with them and wait for a lull.

When Jamie drops his pace so he can watch his cock as it glides in and out of her, I tap her on the nose until she looks at me, and then I show her the pill. "Open."

Vee's mouth drops open obediently and I place the pill on her tongue, then hold the bottle to her lips and force her to drink the entire thing until the empty plastic crinkles. When it's drained and I'm certain she got the pill down okay, I lie back to enjoy the show. I've never seen Jamie take a dominant position in bed before. It's hot as fuck.

Seeing them switched like this is unbelievable, and I bank this memory for later. I wouldn't want him to dominate me, but seeing Vee let go and enjoy her heat gives me hope. Hope that this will work. That we haven't royally fucked up everything for nothing. That this is the start of something new. Something real. Something really fucking important.

Jamie's breathing changes like it does right before he comes, and I look over her head so I can watch the changes on his face. He grunts and drops his head, his eyes glued to their joining as he shoves his thickening knot in and ties her to him.

She hasn't come yet, and she writhes as much as she can from her position underneath him until he growls when she tugs too hard on his knot. Vee goes still, but whines.

Poor horny omega. Poor unpracticed-at-topping Jamie.

I realize that I've neglected his preparations in a way we completely didn't plan for. We spent all that time exploring his submission fantasies and working on his ability to take a cock that we forgot Vee might want him to top her. That when she's in the thick of her heat, her omega instincts will ride her hard.

She's always shown switchy tendencies, but never with Jamie. It's a surprise, but not an unpleasant one. I reach a hand underneath her and find her clit while I consider our options.

She gasps and wiggles against me, her movements making Jamie's contented purr stutter until it's punctuated with groans. But he doesn't growl or pin her or do any of the things an alpha might do. He simply digs his fingers into her round ass and pants.

By the time she's crying out with relief and a fresh burst of slick coats my hand, I have a new plan.

I wait until the afternoon to set things in motion when they finally have a lull in the heat and rut that lasts longer than half an hour. I'm in the kitchen cooking when Jamie pads over, his big body curling around my back while I flip my food over and set the spatula down.

"That smells good," he says, his voice almost a growl as he presses his face into my neck. "I'm starving."

I smile and lay my hand over his while I watch the omelet

solidify. "I'll bet. You've been doing a lot of cardio. She's sleeping?"

"Yeah." He laughs, his breath stuttering against the side of my face, and then he presses a kiss to the corner of my jaw. "How are you?" Jamie asks. "Is everything…"

"I'm good," I reassure him. I turn in the circle of his arms and tilt up so I can give him a proper kiss. "I'm *very* fucking good. How are *you*? Is it what you hoped it'd be like?"

"No," Jamie says, his forehead pressing to mine. "It's even better. You're sure that things are okay? You don't feel… I don't know, left out?"

A quick laugh escapes me as I test the golden edges with the spatula. "No, babe. I don't feel left out. But I do have an idea."

"Okay." Jamie lets me go so I can tuck the omelet's sides in and roll it. When it's done, I scoop it onto my spatula. "I'll get another plate," he says.

"Why? You're not eating and neither will she." I switch my spatula for tongs as I grab some bacon from the cooling baking tray and add it to my plate.

"I'm not?" Jamie asks, pausing in the middle of pulling a cabinet door open. He lets it go and the door swings shut.

"Nope," I tell him as I turn the stove knob off and flip the last pancake onto my plate. "You get to go prep. You can eat after."

"Oh." He blinks as he processes my meaning, and then he nods. "Ohhhhh. Right. You think we can? Do you really think I'll let you?" His voice is breathy. Hopeful.

I stab a fork into the fluffy omelet, breaking off a bite along with a chunk of bacon and shoveling it all into my mouth. While I chew, I go over it again in my mind. By the time I've swallowed, I've decided.

It could fail spectacularly, ending with one of us in the hospital, but we won't know unless we try. I'm okay taking that risk for the potential reward. They're both worth it. "Yeah."

Jamie gives me a hopeful smile and watches me eat while we both stand in the kitchen. I put the plate and fork in the dishwasher, then put the frying pan and spatula in the sink to deal with later. From the fridge, I grab another protein water for Vee, then think about it and hand a second one to Jamie. He drinks his down while I bring hers into the bedroom.

She's sleeping. Vee stirs from under her mound of blankets when we enter the room, but she doesn't fully wake. I set the cherry flavored drink on the nightstand for her later, then point Jamie to the bathroom and smack him on the ass. He keeps his eyes pinned to the snoozing omega, but he follows orders as he goes into the bathroom to prepare. He knows what to do.

I take advantage of his absence to crawl back into the nest and pull her warm little body against mine. She's a space heater underneath those blankets, and I make a mental note to turn the AC down so it's colder the next time I get up.

The water runs in the bathroom as Jamie gets his ass ready for me. When the water shuts off ten minutes later, my dick twitches with anticipation against my thigh.

Jamie pulls the bathroom door open, and my heart skips a beat as I watch him walk over to us. I eat up the sight of him. His tall, broad frame seems extra defined today. Either it's her heat pheromones making his muscles bulge more than normal, or he needs to drink more of the fancy protein waters we bought. He needs the extra fluids since he's using a lot of his energy stores to make all that cum.

"I hope you're good and ready," I tell him with a grin. "Because your ass is about to be mine."

Chapter Twenty

ANTHONY

A SLEEPY, PURRING VEE CURLS INTO MY SIDE, AND I PALM MY dick and stare at Jamie while I stroke it to life. My cock thickens in my hand as I tug it from root to tip and dip my thumb into my slit. Jamie crawls onto the bed and lies between my legs, his mouth going straight to work as he wraps his lips around my cockhead and sucks with practiced ease.

His tongue laves my underside and traces the veins. I try to keep my moans and sounds contained, but Vee stirs beside me. She throws a leg over mine and her hips twitch, and then I feel her wet pussy soak my thigh as she uses me to rub herself.

God, she smells so fucking good. Her normally sweet, juicy scent is mouthwatering. It's extra thick and sweet, with enough of an acidic tang to keep it from being cloying. It's the difference between something orange flavored and a freshly squeezed orange.

I want to drag her on top of my face and drink her down. If it's this bad for me, a beta, I can't imagine the torture Jamie is going through. Not with his more sensitive nose and the clamoring of his alpha instincts.

"Did you have a good nap, baby?" I ask her as I shove my

face in her soft hair. She smells like her shampoo. Feminine and sweet.

"It hurts," she whimpers, her hips pressing hard against my thigh. "Please. Pleasepleaseplease."

Her heat-drunk begging doesn't satisfy me like I thought it would. I realize that it's because she's not quite herself when she's in her delirium. We could be any alpha, any beta, and she'd be begging us for our cocks. Jamie's knot.

That's not what I want. I want her to beg me for *my* cock. For *Jamie's* knot. Brendan's too, if that pans out like I think it might.

She likes him. I can tell by the way she watches him. How her body angles toward him when he's in the room. The glances she sneaks when he's not looking. How she smiles more when he's around.

Vee's begging won't be a victory for me until it's Vee making breathless demands that we please her, fill her, breed her sweet little pussy after her heat's done.

But while it's not quite the victory I thought it would be, her pleas still make my cock twitch in Jamie's mouth. "I know what you need, baby," I tell her. I claim her mouth in a deep kiss that stops her from begging. Then I pull Jamie's mouth off me by getting a fistful of his hair.

I get up, dislodging them both. When Vee moves to follow me, I put a hand to her breastbone and push her back down into the nest. She drops back, her legs falling open. Her hand goes straight between her legs as she plays with herself.

Jamie is already crawling over to her. He fits his body between splayed legs and his mouth replaces her hand as he laps at her juicy cunt. She bites her lip and buries her fingers in his long hair as he feasts on her cunt.

While they're both occupied, I grab the lube from the nightstand and position myself behind him. I rub my hands over him, lightly, to see how he reacts. When he does nothing more than stiffen briefly before mellowing again, I move lower. I rub teasing circles over his legs. His ass. I spread his cheeks and rub my thumb over the bulge of sensitive skin between his ball sack and his hole.

His big, thick cock leaks pre-cum as it hangs, swollen and ruddy, between his spread thighs. My fingers trail lower, playing with his sack and kneading the testicles inside, and then lower still. The extra skin at his base shifts as I grab his cock and tug, using it like a cock sleeve as I toy with him. I jerk his cock until he pumps into my hand. Vee cries out underneath him from whatever his mouth is doing to her pussy.

While they're both distracted, I flip the lube's top open and tip it upside down, drizzling cold lube right over his hole. I close the bottle and toss it onto the bed, and then I slick my fingers through the puddle and press one digit in.

Jamie tenses, something he hasn't done since the night I took his asshole's virginity after his blushing confession that he'd always wanted to try anal but had never had the courage to ask before. I firm my grip on his cock, one of my fingers sinking into his weeping tip as I jerk him harder, faster, until he forgets what I'm doing behind him.

I press in again while I tug, and this time he lets me. His ass gives a token resistance before relenting to the intrusion of my slicked up finger. He's clean, thoroughly prepped like I showed him, and so warm.

Vee whimpers under him, her hands fisted in his hair as she keeps his face buried between her thighs and his mouth busy. I add a second finger in his ass. He stretches easily. His body knows mine, although his rut makes his head fogged with lust for our omega. He'll fill her and I'll fill him and then I'll be fucking them both.

When two fingers move easily, I scissor them apart, then

slick them through more of the lube and add a third. His ass moves back to meet my hand and I finger him until he's ready. I pull back and slap him hard on the ass. Vee whimpers as he rocks against her.

Oh, yes. This is going to be so much fun.

"Mount her, alpha," I tell him.

Vee whimpers, but whether it's because she expects what's coming next or he's sucked her clit especially well, I can't discern from back here. When Jamie doesn't move to listen, I knock her hands from his hair and pull him off her. He snarls, and she whimpers again, but I'm not budging.

We're going to make this work. It has to.

I tighten my fist in his hair and tug harder. "Mount your omega, alpha," I order. "Put your cock in her pussy."

Jamie's growl dies as he rears back and gets a good look at the omega sprawled underneath him. He grabs her legs and drags her down the mattress. Hooks them on either side of his waist, then lines them up and sinks into her tight, wet heat. I let go of his hair as he thrusts, her breasts bouncing with every jarring movement.

When I put a hand on his shoulders and bend him over her, he goes. While he's busy fucking her, I get into place and fist my cock. Every time he pulls back, he knocks his hole against my cockhead.

When that doesn't trigger his instincts, I grow bolder. I wrap my hands around his hips, ignoring his low warning growl, and move with them both. Slowly Jamie relaxes and we all move in tandem. My thrusts match his, my thighs pressed tight against his ass while my cock brushes against his rim.

I dig my fingers into his hips to take control of his pace. I make him go slow, switch to long, lazy thrusts. Then I shift until my cock lines up properly and I slowly sink inside him.

Jamie drops his head back and inhales as I fill him, my cock knocking against his prostate as I feed it deep. He stills completely as he adjusts, and I hold him like that as I pull back, then cant forward and fuck my length into him. Vee makes an impatient sound and grows restless, only stopping when he growls at her in warning. She whines, a desperate, placating omega sound.

I pull back, then snap forward hard. Jamie grunts, his ass well used to my mercurial moods and sometimes forceful nature. Vee moans as his cock slams into her.

"You like that, baby?" I ask as I do it again.

I pull almost all the way out of him and thrust. I wish I could see her. See the way my thrusts rock him against her and her tits bounce and her eyes go unfocused. We should put in mirrors so I can do exactly that next time.

"It's almost like I'm fucking *you*, baby. Using him and his cock like a toy. Like an alpha cock sleeve."

I press a kiss to the flexing muscles of his back. Nip him with my teeth while I reach around him and stroke a hand up her leg. She lets me lift it and hook her leg on Jamie's shoulder. I squeeze her ankle and thrust, bouncing him on my cock and forcing him deeper inside her. They both groan, and I grin.

Then I move for real. I fuck him hard and fast, claiming his ass while he's buried balls deep inside her. She takes it, her pussy making wet smacking sounds as I fuck him deeper inside her and build a rhythm that makes them both gasp for breath.

It's heady knowing I control them both. That I have both my omega and my alpha underneath me, taking my cock. Because it's my cock that's driving us. Setting the rhythm. It's his cock inside her, but it's mine inside *him*.

And he makes such a delicious conquest. If only everyone could see him now. The biggest, most cut alpha at Rut. The handsomest one who all the omegas come to see. The dancer who sells the most signed photos and merch. And here he is, taking my beta cock like the good cock slut he is.

Jamie's ass pushes back to meet my thrusts, and we're all panting by the time Vee throws her head back and cries out with her orgasm. Her leg trembles on Jamie's shoulder and I tighten my hand around her ankle to keep her from moving too much as I force her to take it. To take all the pleasure we're giving her. The orgasm. The relief from the never-ending demands of her heat.

He groans and tries to pull free from my rhythm, to rut her through her pussy's aftershocks so he can knot her, but my grip on his hip won't let him. Jamie growls until I fuck his ass harder, my balls slapping against his perineum.

And then he surrenders too. It's a beautiful thing seeing him give himself over to me. I cherish it every time he does it.

Jamie takes his pounding like a good boy, and then he comes. I slam my hips against his ass hard and drive his knot deep inside her. I give them a moment to catch their breath. Then I move. I pull back and rut him. Use him. I chase my pleasure and I ignore her whimpers and his warning rumble.

With my front plastered to his sweaty back, I let go of him to reach around and feel where he's tied to her. Her swollen pussy is stretched around his bulging knot. I slide my thumb through her slick-drenched folds and find her clit. Every thrust of my cock in his ass makes his knot shift inside her, but his growls stop when I rub her so she's clenching around him. Milking him.

"That's it, baby," I tell her. "Tame this beast so I can fill his ass with cum. You're both gonna be dripping like good cum sluts, isn't that right, babe?"

Jamie pants as her cunt flutters on his knot while I rub her toward another orgasm. Tension and need coil in my belly as my balls pull tight with anticipation. I want us all to come together. Need it in a way I can't explain. He might be the alpha, but it's my cock and my hand that's making her come right now. I'm in charge.

I rub tugging circles around her clit while I pump until I can barely hold back. She comes right before I lose control. Filling his ass to the sounds of her moaning is heaven. My hips drive home as I shoot my load deep in his gut and work the last shuddering pulse of semen from my cock.

Jamie purrs and I can feel the rumbling where I'm still inside him. No wonder she loves it when he purrs while he's licking her pussy.

"Fuck, that's good, babe." I pull out halfway and reach for my base, massaging one last spurt of seed from my tip until he's taken all of it, and then I pull out and spread his cheeks apart so I can watch it drip down his balls.

"Did you fill her up good, babe?" I reach for his balls to check and roll them in my hands. He stiffens, though I'm being gentle. His cock tugs at her pussy, making her whimper. "Yeah, I bet you did. I bet she's gonna drip cum for days after we're both done with her."

She sags with relief. This is only a lull. A brief respite. In half an hour, she'll need a cock again, but for now, she's sated. We all are.

I play with him until his knot shrinks, and his softened cock pulls free. Vee's pussy is drenched. Slick and cum have made her an absolute mess again. We collapse on the bed in a puddle of tangled limbs and sticky sheets. When Vee and Jamie are both half-asleep, I roll him off her. He's too heavy to stay on top of her for long.

"Time for another bath, baby." I tug her from the nest. He stirs and watches, but doesn't follow when I take her into the bathroom and we repeat the process. This time, while she's playing with the bubbles and napping in the warm water, I watch YouTube videos about curly hair and try not to panic about all the steps.

"What the fuck is a Denman brush?" I didn't know there were different hair brushes. I don't use one. I have a wide-tooth comb or I run my fingers through my hair. Without all the specialty products, I do the best I can with what we've got.

When Vee gets grabby while I'm trying to work conditioner through her hair so I can untangle it, I lose my patience. I sit on the edge of the tub and fist my cock, slapping its tip against her whining mouth. "I'm busy, baby. Entertain yourself."

She holds my gaze while she wraps her lips around my length and sucks my cock into her mouth. *Fuck, she's so good at this. Where'd she learn to suck cock like this?*

I work faster, dragging the conditioner through her hair and picking the snarls free with my comb. I fist her roots while I do it so that it won't tug at her scalp. She has zero qualms about tugging as she buries her nose in my groin and takes me all the way to the back of her throat till I know she can't breathe.

"Fuck, baby, oh my God. That's good. You're such a good cocksucker. I'm gonna make you blow me at work like this. What do you think about that? Should I make you get down on your knees and suck me off while I tend bar? The club's dark, and they're always so drunk. They probably wouldn't notice. But maybe you'd want them to, hmm? I think you'll want them to see you on your knees on a filthy bar floor sucking your bartender's cock while he pours them their drinks. You like the drinks I make you, don't you, baby?"

I grin and remember how we added our special ingredients to her cocktails. I still can't believe it worked, but it did. It kept her craving us. Made her body admit how badly she wanted us. Needed us. Kept her sane too. Made the worst of her preheat symptoms more bearable and bought her more time to work through her audit. She'll be mad if she finds out, but it's for her benefit.

It was an asshole move to feed her Jamie's cum without telling her, but I can't regret it. Not when it gave her what she needed. Put her exactly where she needed to be. In our nest. In our soon-to-be pack. Someplace safe where we can take care of her. She's too busy and stubborn to do it herself. So it's up to us. I'll make the hard choices if it's for *her*.

Vee is ours. We've known it for years, though she was too stubborn to admit it. Now that we've got her, we're gonna take such good fucking care of her. She's our stubborn, driven, skittish omega. She's perfect. And I'm gonna have so much fun spoiling her.

I work the last knot free until the comb glides freely and her hair snaps back into wavy S-shaped curls. She sucks and licks and hums while she does it. And since she's being such a good girl during bath time, I reward her with a load of fresh cum down her throat.

Vee pulls back and licks her lips, staring at me as if she wants seconds. *Fucking insatiable omegas. Damn.*

I understand why betas talk about them with that weird mix of reverence and fear. Why it's practically impossible for a single beta to keep up with one in heat without a pack behind them.

I chuckle and set the comb aside, then unhook the shower hose from the wall. "Patience, baby. You're almost done, and then I swear I'll set you right down on Jamie's cock the minute we get back to the nest."

She lets me wash the conditioner from her hair while I shield her eyes with my hand, and this time she doesn't fight me as I haul her from the draining tub and rub her down with a fluffy towel. I use one of my T-shirts to scrunch the water from her curls without causing frizz, then I slather her in lotion and rub omega salve over her pussy. The label on the jar says it's extra strength for chafing.

True to my word, Jamie's cock gets hard with one look at her freshly bathed and lotioned body. I help her get into the nest and pick her up by the hips, fitting his cock to her needy pussy as I press her shoulders down until she's taken him completely. She sighs once he fills her, her hips moving as she rides him.

While Jamie keeps her busy, I clean up the bathroom then wait for their next lull so I can make them both drink another protein water before they finally fall unconscious in the nest.

The brief respite won't last forever. She's getting hornier. Needier. The time in between her bursts of delirium is getting shorter. Soon, when her heat's at its peak, we're going to have trouble keeping up with her.

Jamie might not be able to manage it. He's used to taking more than giving. He'll do his best to please her, but it's not in his nature. Maybe if I edged him, made him so pent up with need he turned a little feral. But there's no time to experiment. Soon it won't matter if his alpha instincts are muddling his submissiveness in his head. It still won't be enough to turn him into a proper top.

What we need is another person.

I watch them sleep for a while, and then I make the hard decision. Instead of crawling in beside them to take a well-earned nap, I grab a fresh pair of jeans from the dresser and hop into them. Once I'm clothed, I kneel by the bed and press a kiss to Jamie's lips. He stirs against me, his eyes fluttering until they open. He blinks while they focus.

"Be good," I whisper. "I'm stepping out to get something we need. And remember, if you bite her, even if she begs for it, she'll never forgive you. Keep your teeth to yourself while I'm gone, Jamie. Do you understand?"

Jamie nods, his brow knitting together.

I kiss him again. "I love you. Be back soon."

He tracks me as I stand and leave the room. On my way out, I grab the rag we're using to mop up the worst of the spilled fluids. Vee won't let me change the sheets. When I try, she snarls. I shove a corner of the cloth in my back pocket and let it hang like a hankie.

Despite my warning to him, I'm not too worried. For an alpha, Jamie is as submissive as they come. Even when he's topping, it's more about servicing her and giving her what her omega instincts make her want.

I shove my feet into my boots, grab his car keys from the dish by the door, and get into his ridiculous van.

I have a stubborn alpha to track down.

Chapter Twenty-One

BRENDAN

"WHAT THE HELL?" I SAY AS I RUSH DOWN THE HALLWAY FROM my office. The banging starts up again. It sounds like the police are about to knock my door down.

I throw the door open without looking through the peephole. "Can I help y—"

My mind stutters to a grinding halt when I see that it's the beta bartender from Rut. Anthony. The man who blew me last night.

My forehead creases with a frown. *Why is he here? And how the fuck did he get my home address?*

I glance in either direction to see if anyone is out and about. Two of my neighbors, middle-aged married beta women, power walk by in their expensive pastel athleisure outfits. They crane their necks to stare as they walk on. The tatted-up beta on my doorstep looks more at home at a biker bar rather than a sleepy suburb where every cookie cutter house looks like the next one.

"Anthony. Come inside." I step aside and pull the door wider so he can slip in before the entire neighborhood can come out to watch.

Anthony pops upright from where he was leaning on the

doorway. He looks me up and down as he strolls into my home like he owns it. His dirty boots leave marks on my clean tile. I shut the front door and lock it out of habit.

"How did you get my address?" I ask.

He wanders through my house, ignoring me while looking at everything with zero shame about his snooping. I feel suddenly protective of my modest valley home.

"The secretary at your office is a flirt." Anthony folds his arms over his chest as he looks at the family pictures hung up in the hallway.

"What did you tell her?" I ask, worried. Ashley is a sweet girl, but she's a total gossip.

"Relax." Anthony turns to look at me and smirks as he shoves his hands in his jean pockets so they ride lower on his stomach. His black shirt is tight and a strip of inked skin shows in the gap. "I told her I was your cousin, the black sheep recently returned into the flock's folds, but wouldn't you know it? I broke my phone and lost your address and phone number." He pulls a slip of paper from his pocket and shows me her tidy script on the yellow sticky note. "She was happy to help me reconnect."

I resist the urge to take the bait and reach for the note. That's probably what he wants. Instead, I fold my arms over my chest. "Well, you found me. What can I do for you?"

Was this entire thing a ruse? Some weird sort of blackmail to get their audit passed with flying colors? God, I'm so stupid. Of course, that's what this is. It was stupid to think otherwise. What pack would want an old, injured alpha?

"She needs you," Anthony says.

"What?" My crossed arms slip from surprise.

Anthony ignores me and wanders into my sitting room. He flops into a chair and puts his boots on my coffee table. And then he reaches into his back pocket and throws something at me.

I catch it out of the air to keep it from hitting me square in the face, but that doesn't stop the waft of pheromones from punching me in the sinuses. My cock twitches to life in my pants as I get a good whiff of Vee's heat-thick slick and their cum.

"It's not surprising," Anthony drawls with his chin pinched between his fingers, "that Vee's a demanding little thing. We need another top to balance the pack."

My hands clench around the pheromone-soaked towel, and I drop it away from my face so I can think. But no matter what direction my brain keeps spinning, I keep coming back to one thing. "Why me?"

He shrugs. "Why not? She likes the way you smell. I think your personality fits. Jamie thinks you're cute."

I sit in the seat opposite him as all the air goes out of me. "He thinks I'm cute?" The idea is laughable, but Anthony isn't laughing. His eyes sparkle with mischief as he watches me sit there, stupefied. I can't get over the idea of the tall, muscled, handsome alpha thinking I'm attractive. He's everything I used to be back when I was young and my body wasn't wrecked.

"Yeah," Anthony says, his lips curling into a smile. "He likes the hot dad vibe."

Papa bear. That's what Anthony called me last night during our drinking game before all hell broke loose. I guess he really meant it. "Huh."

"I can't stay. I don't wanna leave them alone too long, you know? So… are you in?"

My fingers clench the towel. "I can't. I… Not until the audit is—"

"We need help *now*," Anthony says. "This is our one shot at it.

If we don't make her ecstatic with happiness, she'll get all in her head afterward and talk herself out of something amazing. So I didn't ask if this was a good time or a good idea or if you can put your insecurities aside for a few days… I asked if you were in.

"Tick tock, papa bear. Are you really gonna smell that pussy and walk away? Because I guarantee there won't be a next time. Hell, I'm still a bit surprised she agreed to it at all. It took a lot of planning to get to this stage of our plan. If you don't come with me now, you're gonna regret it for the rest of your life and you know it."

He's right. I know he is. I've never been so drawn to a scent before. And maybe that wouldn't be good enough for a pair of betas, but for alphas and omegas, our scents are everything. Scent matches don't mean the relationship's going to work out, though. And of course, you can have a good relationship without one.

But it's the difference between sparklers and fireworks. Vee makes me want those fireworks. She makes me think they're possible, and I didn't lose my chance at them over twenty years ago.

"I'm not into receiving anal," I warn him. When all he does is shrug, I keep going. "I like guys too, but my preference will always lean more toward women." He hums his acknowledgement. "My knee's fucked up. I take meds for it when it's bad. Sometimes when it's really bad, I use a cane."

"Cool." Anthony threads his fingers together over his abdomen. "My uncle uses a cane. Does yours have a sword in it too?"

My brow knits together. *What the fuck?* "No."

This is a bad idea, and I'm not the sort of guy who makes risky moves anymore, but can I really say no and walk away? We only met a week ago, and I know it'll take time to sort everything else out, but that rare spark is there. Every spark needs tending to catch before it can become a flame. And my gut tells me that Vee's fire is worth burning for.

"I'm in. I can't promise it'll work." Not all alphas will tolerate having another alpha in a pack. "But I'll try. If Jamie fights me, I'm out." There's no way I'd win against him.

Anthony's grin widens, and the look of happiness—or maybe that's smug satisfaction—on his face makes me nervous, but in a good way. Anticipation makes my palms sweat.

"Good choice, papa bear," Anthony says. "But leave your ropes behind for today. We'll have to talk about that, and she's skittish enough already."

His prompting makes me realize that I've got planning and packing to do. I nod and get up to go do exactly that. While I'm throwing clothes and toiletries and my medicine into a suitcase, I call work and tell them I'm taking FMLA for a few days.

When I get back to the living room, Anthony is gone. I find him rummaging around in my kitchen, inspecting my food. If he came here right from the nest, he's probably starving and in desperate need of electrolytes. I remember what heats are like although it's been a long time since I took part in one.

"Try the pickles," I tell him as I shoulder my bag. "They'll perk you up."

"Thanks." He pops the jar off the pickles and grabs a spear with his fingers, then crunches it in his teeth and hums while he chews. "You're right, that's good. I didn't know it'd be so…"

"Exhausting?" I supply, and he nods. "It's not like in the movies or porn," I explain. "By the end of it you're gonna wonder how you're not a dehydrated husk of a person. You're keeping her healthy, right? She needs more than alpha cum. It'll help, but it's not enough."

"Relax, papa bear." He finishes his pickle and snags another, then closes the jar. "I got her those fancy vitamin blended protein waters that are in all those TV and magazine ads for omegas. We're taking care of our girl."

"Good." My tight shoulders unbunch.

"Come on." Anthony slides past me and heads to the door, where he waits for me as I make sure all of my doors are locked before grabbing my keys. He fishes a car key from his pocket and goes to the most memorable vehicle I've ever seen in my life. The mint green vintage VW van is the opposite of nondescript. It's also completely at odds with Anthony's bad boy aesthetic.

I'm glad we're not getting on a motorcycle, though, between my knee and my duffel bag. That wouldn't have been comfortable.

I ignore the way my nosy neighbors watch me climb in after him and settle on the car's long bench seat with my bag in my lap. The van smells like Jamie's tropical scent, plus a hint of Anthony's more subtle cherry and sex. They've hooked up in this car. Or fooled around. I look over my shoulder, halfway expecting to see a mattress in the back, but there's only a second row with a big open space behind it containing nothing but sand and a folded-up blanket.

Anthony backs out of my driveway and heads toward the interstate. "I can't believe you live all the way out here. It must take you forever to drive to Rut."

"I don't mind it. I'm used to driving for work," I tell him. "I do most of my assignments in the field rather than at the office."

He adjusts the car's old radio and settles on a station and we drive the now familiar route toward Rut, but then he keeps going. The sun is well below the horizon and I can't see much outside the window, but I notice the brine of the ocean when he finally pulls the car into a driveway. We wait for the garage door to roll up and he pulls the big van into the tiny one-car space.

Although I can't smell or see or hear her yet, some part of my alpha awareness prickles with Vee's nearness. Her heat is like a satellite dish. It sends her presence out like a broadcast. When the garage door rolls down, adding one more layer of protection between her and the world, I breathe easier.

"Let's go see what they got up to," Anthony says as he gets out of the van. He grabs my bag from me before I can protest and I follow him inside.

Her heat pheromones wash over me like a horny curtain as I enter the house. My dick answers its siren's call as it plumps until my pants strain to contain it. Anthony brings me to where the smells are thickest.

The nest.

The sight of Veronica in heat is everything I ever dreamed of as a teenage alpha. She looks like a goddess as she rides Jamie's cock, her breasts swaying with every rise and thrust. The pillows and blankets are scattered around them in a chaotic mess. There's no rhyme or reason to her nest, and I realize Anthony was right. She's restless. Her basic needs are being met, but she's not fully satisfied.

Veronica lifts her head and sniffs, and then her eyes find mine. I stand still as I wait at the edge of her nest to see how she'll react. She stops bouncing to grind, her body searching for the scratch of a knot she needs to soothe her pussy's ravenous itch.

When she doesn't snarl or get fearful or defensive, I take a step deeper into the room.

Anthony's already undressed, his crumpled clothes in a pile on the floor. His slimmer, smaller cock points toward her as he grips it by the base and tugs. I take a moment to drink in the sight of him undressed. I've seen Jamie nude before from his dancing, but not Anthony. The beta's tattoos almost cover his entire body, and the silver ring through the tip of his penis makes me wince in sympathy. *That had to hurt.*

"I'm gonna fuck his mouth," Anthony says. "Keep him busy. I think you should approach from the side and see if you can get her to suck your cock. Once your scent is in the nest, I think everyone will chill."

I frown and tear my attention away from Anthony's dick piercing. Jamie's scented me by now. He tips his head back and stares, his eyes dark and full of primitive need. His lips peel away from his teeth in a grimace. I go still, a shiver of trepidation making my cock twitch.

My body wants to shed these clothes, to palm my cock until it's dripping and edge my way in. To be his competition. To steal her from him. Fight him for her if I have to. All for the chance to knot her. Breed her. Tie her to me and bite a claim into her throat so nobody else can steal her away.

We've evolved beyond these instinctual urges, but it's hard to fight them. Especially when they're so close to the surface, like they are during heats and ruts. So I do the opposite of what my instincts demand. I force my posture to loosen. My shoulders round. I stop looking them in the eye. I don't need to play dominance games. My therapist's mantra that I'm still an alpha even if I'm dealing with a chronic injury flits through my head.

Veronica whines, and Jamie stops posturing so he can focus on her. He grips her hips and fucks up into her. Neither of them pays any attention to the prowling beta until Anthony edges in and grabs Jamie by the face. He tips the alpha's head to the side and shoves the pierced tip of his cock past those teeth that would likely bite me if I tried to do the same.

Before I can whisper that Anthony's plan is a bad idea, Jamie's head is bobbing as he swallows the beta's cock while their omega rides him. Jamie purrs, and Anthony grunts a curse and drops his head back while he palms one of Vee's tits and squeezes until she whines for more. He pinches her budded nipple and twists. Her sweet heat slick fills the room with an extra burst of perfume.

Well... fuck. Guess we're really doing this.

Without making too much noise, I take my clothes off and fold them neatly. I hesitate for a moment. My body doesn't look like it used to, but the sounds of their sucking and fucking drown out the white noise and negative thoughts in my head. My cock is so hard it aches. It stands out from my body at a near ninety-degree angle, and I squeeze the base and tug as I approach. I stay behind Anthony as I edge my way toward the nest and when nothing horrible happens, I move around to her other side.

Veronica's head turns on a swivel as she tracks me. She whimpers and then she licks her lips. When I'm close enough for her to reach out and touch, that's exactly what she does.

She throws an arm around my neck and drags me closer, her face knocking into my head as she nuzzles me. I stand there and let her scent mark me while my cock drips all down my hand. When she chirps, content, I take her face in my hand and bring her mouth to mine.

Her kiss is clumsy and desperate. There's no room for subtlety in a heat. No romance or sweet seduction. If an omega finds someone compatible, they fuck. As long as she likes my scent, that's all she cares about right now. Scent matches and coming. Her instincts tell her there's time for everything else later when the dust settles.

Anthony drives his cock into Jamie's mouth and keeps him distracted while I stroke Veronica's pretty face, then thread my hand into her damp hair. I fist it and catch her fast, her mouth dropping open against mine in surprise.

Without speaking the order out loud, I force her to bend as I drag her head down. All the way down. She's short. I'm tall. And my grip on her hair doesn't give her any option but to bend.

When her lips graze the slick tip of my cock and she gets a lick of my pre-cum, that's all she needs to motivate her. Veronica's hot mouth envelops me and she sucks on my cockhead like she's trying to pull the cum right from my balls.

Before I can stop myself, my head tips back and I let out a quiet curse. "Fuck."

Anthony chuckles. "Sucks like a pro, right?" He brings his palm down on one of her breasts with a noisy slap, and the sound she makes as she jerks and chokes on my cock shouldn't be as hot as it is.

"That's good, sweetheart," I tell her as she feeds my length into her mouth while Anthony does the same to the alpha under her. "Good girl. Can you take some more?"

My hand at her nape doesn't shove so much as guide her as I make her bob and find a rhythm we both like. I'm too big for her to take all of me at once without choking, so I squeeze my base while she blows me. Saliva runs down my knuckles as she bobs and sucks. The sight of my brown cock filling her mouth, stretching her berry pink lips wide, is almost enough for me to lose it.

She's so pretty. And she smells so fucking good. I don't know what I ever did to deserve her, but I won't question it anymore. If she wants me in her nest, her life, she can have me. I'm hers. Body, mind, and soul. She can own me and I'll say thank you every day she continues to choose me. This woman is a precious fucking gift.

"That's it, baby," Anthony says as he watches us. "Suck that alpha cock. I bet he's got a big load of cum for you. Feel how big his balls are."

She does. Veronica's hand palms my sack, grabbing at them

to stop their swaying as I fuck her pretty face. I can't last much longer. I'm glad that our first time is a blowjob, so I don't embarrass myself by coming too soon. "You want it, sweetheart? You want my cum?"

She tries to talk around my cock, but all that comes out of her mouth is distorted mumbling. My knot swells against my palm, and I squeeze it exactly the way I like as I fuck her mouth harder, faster, until her eyes get wet and glassy. A tear gathers and then leaks from the corner of her eye. *God, she's so pretty when she cries.* I never want to see her cry for real. Only when I'm fucking her face and she can't breathe.

"Here you go, sweetheart," I grunt. "Swallow it all. Every single drop."

My knot pops against my hand as I keep her from trying to swallow my entire cock. My balls empty into her mouth, filling her, and tears run down her face as she listens. Her throat bobs.

What a good girl.

I come so hard that my leg twitches. She swallows every single drop as I fill her belly. My cock jerks against her tongue with a last spasm. Vee tongues my slit for more.

"Fuck, baby. That's hot," Anthony says. "You like that? You like having two alphas? What a greedy omega. You can't get enough cock, huh, baby? Don't worry. I've got plans for that. Now be a good girl and come on Jamie's cock so I can finally fuck his mouth properly."

Anthony is an excellent multitasker. While he thrusts his cock in and out of Jamie's mouth, he leans over her and thumbs her clit while she licks me clean.

Veronica cries out and straightens up, my cock slipping from her lips, as her hips become frantic. Frenzied. And then she comes, her body going completely still as her chest heaves with the force of her breathing.

Anthony makes good on his promise. The minute she's

done, he puts all of his focus on fucking Jamie's mouth. His hips snap with hard thrusts as he shoves his cock down the alpha's throat, with no regard for something as trivial as breathing.

While the other alpha's distracted, I reach down to stroke her wet pussy. He's knotted her, his cries of release drowned out with his face fucking, and I stroke over the hard bulge of his knot and the stretch of her pussy around it. She whimpers and leans forward to bury her face in my chest, her hips rocking as she searches for more. More stimulation. More orgasms.

For an omega in heat, none of it's ever enough. If they're conscious, they want it. And they don't sleep for long.

I'm gentle as I slick my hand through wetness and find her clit. It's swollen and tender, and her cunt is so warm. I rub circles around her clit while her nails scrabble over my back. They scratch, but it's not to push me away. She wants to pull me closer. To keep me there. As if there's any chance of me walking away and leaving her.

"You'll come on his knot again," I lean closer and whisper directly into her ear. "Milk him good, omega."

I can feel her pussy throbbing against my hand as I work her up. It doesn't matter that she already came. I won't give her body the option to refuse me. I'll make her cum all over her other alpha's cock. Show them both that we can share. We can be good together. For her.

While my hand rubs her between her legs, my fingertips brushing over the swollen knot that ties them together. I bend down so I can claim her mouth again. I don't care if she wants to come more than she wants to kiss. I need her sweetness. I have to have her lips against mine. Already, I can feel the hormone spike of an incoming rut. My thoughts are slower. My muscles are taut and bulging under my layer of softness. And all I can think of is plunging my cock in her even though I've already come.

That's the power of a rut. When you're in it, that's all that matters. Pleasing your omega and breeding them.

I plunge my tongue in her mouth and taste myself on her, and she shudders against my hand. Her pussy ripples as she comes a second time. I swallow her cries and don't stop.

She can take another. She's made for it. Even if she thinks she hates it. Veronica wiggles against me, gasping into my mouth, her sensitive pussy trying to come down for a release. But I won't let it. She'll have a third before I'm satisfied.

Once she realizes I have no intention of letting her get away without coming again, her body sags in submission. I catch her and hold her upright as my hand moves faster. I rub her until her thighs tremble where they're stretched over his body. I work hard and fast, turning her aftershocks into a tidal wave. She comes, and she screams, and I swallow all her sounds.

A gush of slick leaks around his stoppering knot. It coats my hand and pools on Jamie's belly, then soaks into the nest. When she sags completely, her eyes fluttering shut, I catch her before she can fall. She's so slight in my arms. So delicate, despite how tough she normally acts.

I press one last kiss to her slack mouth and glance at Anthony and Jamie to check their progress.

"Did you finger fuck her unconscious?" Anthony asks, awed.

I brush a fingertip against her eyelashes to see if they'll open, but they don't. Her chest rises and falls as her breathing steadies. She's fine, merely exhausted. After this, she'll get some good rest. "Yeah."

"God damn," Anthony says. "I knew you were the one."

My stomach flutters with nerves. I'm going to spend this heat showing them exactly what I bring to the table. Prove to them and myself I deserve a place here, regardless of my fucked up knee.

Anthony's hips haven't stopped while we've been talking. He pumps in and out of Jamie's mouth until the blond man's face turns red. Jamie gasps for air around every thrust, his nostrils flaring as he struggles to take it. It's the most brutal face fucking I've ever seen.

I hope he doesn't do that to Veronica or we're gonna have words because I won't tolerate it.

I tilt my head and watch. "I'm not sure he can breathe," I warn Anthony.

Chapter Twenty-Two

BRENDAN

"He can breathe after I come," Anthony says.

Anthony smiles down at the crying, red-faced alpha and gently tucks a strand of blond hair behind an ear. "He likes this, don't you, babe? You like having your face fucked like this. Because that's what you're good at. Taking cock. Sitting in a nest with an omega in heat, I've still got you under me. Suck my cock, alpha. Oh, fuck yeah, I'm gonna come."

Anthony drops his chin to his chest to watch his cock pulse as he buries his root to the alpha's nose and shoots his cum straight down his bulging throat. "Fuck, babe. That's good. Now clean me up." He pulls back, and the alpha purrs as he licks the head clean, most of his focus on that silver cock ring.

I leave them to it while I give Veronica a tug to see if Jamie's knot has shrunk enough to separate them. There's a slight resistance that makes her stir enough to whimper, but he's deflated enough that I can lift her off him.

A flood of semen and slick splatters us and the bed. I lift her and set her on her feet. When she wobbles, I end up holding most of her weight as I steady her.

While Jamie cleans Anthony's cock, I do the same to her. I

swipe my hand through her tender folds and scoop up the mixture from her pussy, then lift it to her mouth and shove those fingers inside. She gives me a token protest about the unexpected intrusion before she gets a taste of the slick and cum, and then she sucks my fingers clean.

"Good girl," I tell her, pressing a kiss to her cheek. I tug my fingers free from her mouth with a wet pop and repeat it. I feed it to her until she's humming and happy, her thighs as clean as they'll get without a bath. Her slim body sways against mine as she leans on me for support until my bad knee aches.

"Let's get you cleaned up, sweetheart," I tell her.

"I'll take her," Anthony says.

He pulls away from Jamie and gathers her in his arms. While I'm grateful to not have to support her weight, I have a brief flicker of hesitation at being left alone with another alpha while we're both in varying stages of rut. But Jamie does nothing more than blink as he lies there, his cock and knot deflated and his rumbly purr filling the room.

To test the boundaries, I sit on the bed, and when he tolerates that, I collapse in it. It's late, and with my cock drained and my knee smarting, I'm ready for bed.

When did you get so old, old man?

The water runs in the bathroom while I burrow under the covers where it's warmer. *Why the fuck is the room so damn cold in here?* The AC licks at my sweaty skin and I can only imagine what Jamie is feeling. He's drenched in a thick sheen of pheromone-laden sweat. His muscles gleam in the harsh overhead lighting as he pants, his chest heaving, and purrs.

I make a list of all the things they got wrong while I lie in the rickety nest. The lighting is too harsh. The room is too cold. There aren't enough good quality nesting materials. She may not care all that much right now when she's in the dicked-down phase, but when her heat breaks and she goes into nesting mode, she'll want them. The room is too big, but they put bed curtains up, which means they did *some* research. But why the fuck are they sheer? The whole point is to close off the nest and make it cozy. It's not cozy if they're sheer.

Anthony and Veronica's return pulls me from my mental shopping list of all the things we'll need to buy. He carries her to the bed and sets her down. She wastes no time burrowing under the blankets for warmth. I pull her to my side and turn so I can spoon her. Her head fits so nicely under my chin. Like she's meant to be there.

Veronica nuzzles her face into my chest, then purrs and my heart nearly weeps from the sound. She's so much more caring and accepting than I think she knows. And I can't wait to prove that I deserve her. Every damn day.

"Babe," Anthony says as he nudges Jamie awake where he's passed out at the foot of the bed. "Get in the nest."

Jamie harrumphs, but crawls up toward the head of the bed. He tugs blankets aside, ignoring her agitated warning chitters as he disturbs her, and then we all settle.

Anthony leaves the room and moves around the house for a few minutes, doing all the normal human things that we idiots forget about when our hind brains get stuck in heat mode and rutting. After he's done locking up, he turns the lights out and slips into the nest with us. It's cramped.

After a few minutes of silence, I whisper, "We're gonna need a bigger bed."

"Yeah," Anthony whispers back. "I'm realizing that right now." There's another beat of silence before Anthony speaks again, "I know a store that's not far. They have everything."

With a lush, content omega curled into my side, I fall asleep before I can think of a reply.

I WAKE UP TO HANDS SCRATCHING THROUGH MY CHEST HAIR. I take a moment to luxuriate in the intimate and pleasant sensation before I open my eyes. I slept like the dead, and if I dreamed, I don't remember them. From the light coming through the window, it's the next morning, but it's still very early.

Veronica's awake, and there's a clarity to her eyes that wasn't there last night. She's hit a lull in her heat before the delirium sweeps her up again. "Hi," she whispers.

"Morning, sweetheart," I say with a sleepy grin.

She smiles, and with her wild, wavy hair tumbling over her shoulder and her breasts curving over the edge of the sheet she's wrapped around herself, she's the prettiest picture I've ever seen.

I'm not a man who has one-night stands. Who falls into bed with strangers. Or who makes big decisions quickly without drafting a pros and cons list first. But last night, I tossed all the rules and every single one of my morals into the wind because I scented her slick. This tiny omega has no idea how much power she holds over me.

"I thought I'd hallucinated last night," she says. "But you're really here, aren't you?"

Before I can answer, she tips her face closer and hovers her lips by mine. It doesn't matter that we both have morning breath. That I let her suck my cock before taking her on a date and buying her dinner. We're doing things backward. But that's how it is with alphas and omegas.

When the chemistry is intense and you're a scent match, the

quiet moments come later. I'm looking forward to a lifetime of quiet moments together with her.

I tip my head and close the tiny gap between us, and she deepens the kiss. Veronica leans over me, her hair brushing over my chest, and then she pushes me back so she can throw a leg over until she's straddling me.

She makes a noise of appreciation in the back of her throat as she drags her nails through the dark hair on my chest and wiggles until her center rubs against my morning stiff cock. It thumps to life when her hot, slick core slides against it. There's a desperate edge to her movements as she moves her hips and twists her tongue around mine. As if she can't wait another moment to have me in her. When she fumbles for my cock, I grab her hips and lift her to help her get a better angle.

Veronica sinks onto me, and I groan. She sighs as her tight, wet heat envelops me. Her hands cover mine as she traps them on her hips and tosses her hair out of her face, her eyes sliding shut and her teeth cutting into her lip again as she rides me.

The others stir awake beside us, but all they do is watch as she gyrates, her hips making circles that do nothing for me but seem to do a whole hell of a lot for her. I don't mind letting her use my cock for her pleasure, not when she makes those whimpers of delight.

"Oh, fuck, you're so big," she says as she drops her hands to my chest for leverage so she can lift herself up only to come back down. Her movements get frantic. Choppy. As if she's racing to a finish line and can't wait to get there.

From the way her brow pinches and she winces, I worry that I'm *too* big. That we didn't spend enough time warming her up. If she's struggling to take my cock, she's not going to handle my knot unless she's all slicked up in a full-blown bout of heat delirium.

"Stop, sweetheart. You're wincing. What's the rush?" I grab

her hips and make her go still, then set her back to her grinding. She liked that.

"I want to remember our first time, and I might not if…"

If she's in the throes of it. So she's trying to take my cock without being fully aroused yet, because her arousal might trigger her heat. The logic is sound, but it's crazy. My cock loses interest at the thought of her not being fully into this. Into me.

I pin her hips so they're still as my softening cock threatens to slip out of her. "I don't fully understand, sweetheart, but I'd like to. Can you walk me through it?"

She frowns and looks away. "It has a way of making me want things I might not normally enjoy."

Me. I'm the thing she might not normally enjoy. *Yeah, that does it.* My cock completely deflates.

We pushed her too hard, too fast. I should never have come. She knows Anthony and Jamie. Me? I'm practically a total stranger. I'm damaged goods, and she's already got an alpha. A younger one who isn't crippled whenever it rains. Of course she changed her mind the first time she surfaced for air. Hormones aren't love, and a scent match doesn't guarantee a happily ever after.

My chest pinches as I wrap my arms around her and roll us onto our sides. And then I do the hardest thing ever—I let her go. My alpha instincts roar at me to flip her onto her belly and make her want us, to prove my worth in the only way it knows how.

But I'm better than that. Being an alpha isn't about strength, or violence, or rutting. It's about family. Providing for them. Sheltering them. And sometimes that means protecting them from yourself.

I won't make her ask me to leave. That's one indignity I can spare her from. "I see." When I pull away from her and roll to slide out of bed, she stops me by grabbing my arm.

"Wait, are you leaving? Because I won't... Really?" She sounds hurt, which makes me frown and glance back at her and search her face for answers.

Anthony groans and throws an arm over his eyes. "Baby, it's too early for all this angst. Brendan, dude, sit the fuck down. She's not telling you to get the fuck out. She's saying she wants to top you until the heat hits her and it makes her want to bottom again. If you don't wanna do it, then roll her over to Jamie."

Anthony sighs like he's weary. "Can I go the fuck back to sleep now? Jesus Christ." He rolls over and buries his face in the pillow and mumbles something insensible.

I look at Veronica for confirmation, but she refuses to look me in the eye and her cheeks are pink. "Really? Is that all?" I ask her.

"I want the first time I remember to be my way," she mutters.

My lips curl as I lie back down and hook my arm around her hips. "Sweetheart, if you want to ride my cock, I won't complain. Come here." Before she can get too awkward and self conscious about it, I pull her into my side and claim her lips.

It doesn't take long for our sweet kisses to turn deeper. Desperate. While her tongue explores my mouth and twists with mine, I run my hands over her. She's curved in all the right places, but she could be softer. Anthony's not making her eat enough. Her nipples are taut nubs and I play with them before sliding lower and teasing her between her legs.

She moans into my mouth when I work a finger between her folds and rub her dampening slit. Her hips and tongue make a matching rhythm as she thrusts her slippery pussy against my hand. I press my middle finger in and find her clit. She moans into my mouth. Her rubbing gets faster. Desperate.

What a way to wake up. If I woke up to her like this every single day, I'd never have a bad day again.

Veronica whimpers against my lips, then breaks our kiss and presses her forehead to mine. She's breathing hard, and her hips jerk as she tries to find what her body craves most. To be filled. Friction.

On her next slide, I push lower until I find her slick hole and press in. She arches against me, her nails digging into my shoulder as she tilts her body to take my finger deeper. Each thrust makes her slicker. Readies her for me. I add a second and pump them deeper in a pantomime of fucking, and then I scissor them apart and stretch her.

"Fuck, that's good," she groans as she rides my hand. "I need you inside me."

A deep, rumbling purr breaks loose in my chest as my heart stutters at her words. She needs me. *Me.* "Then have me, sweetheart."

As if that's all she was waiting for, she crawls over me, her movements knocking my hand away. I cup her thigh to steady her as she mounts me and grabs my cock like she owns it.

After this, she probably does.

I don't think that I could ever move on and forget about someone like her. She defies all the stereotypes of her dynamic, and she gives me hope I haven't felt in a long time.

When she lines my cockhead up with her pussy and sinks down onto it with a single slow thrust, I close my eyes to savor the feeling of bottoming out inside her. She's wetter, looser, but still too fucking tight. But that doesn't stop her. She's not sweet at all as she lifts and slams her cunt back down. Her fingers curl in my chest hair as she uses me for leverage to ride my cock.

Veronica's hips roll as she finds a pace she likes, her pelvis grinding in a circle against me when she's fully seated. I keep hold of her hips in case she loses her balance, but I let her have this moment. Let her have her way. There will be plenty of time later for me to rut her brains out. Right now, she's in charge.

She leans back and drops her head, her hair tumbling down her back. The sight of her bare pale throat is so damn erotic that my knot stiffens against her stretched entrance. Her breasts jiggle as she moves, and all I can think about is licking them, sucking on them, but she's out of reach. She's having her moment, using my cock, enticing me like a damn siren, and I've promised to lie here and take it. I'm a fucking idiot.

"You're so damn beautiful, sweetheart," I groan.

She bites her lip in a barely contained smile, and the sight of her teeth cutting into that plush pink lip makes me nearly feral.

"Your cock feels so good inside me," she moans. "You're so deep it hurts."

I want to grab her and roll us. Get her under me. Knock her legs apart and press her into the mattress while I rut her hard and deep, then knot and breed her. *Fuck, that's the rut talking.* I pry every single one of my fingers off her and twist them in the nest instead. There, that's safer.

The urge to wrestle control from her and thrust, bounce her on my cock, is nearly impossible to ignore, but for her, I try. I lie there. I close my eyes and focus on my breathing. I think about soccer and try to name all the players on my favorite team in alphabetical order. When fingers brush over my halfway swollen knot, I curse.

My eyes crack open and my breath shudders as I realize the fingers don't belong to the hand I thought they did. Jamie's woken up, and he kneels beside us. I didn't notice the bed dip. He teases her mound, his fingers brushing over me too as he toys with her pussy.

"If you turn around, I can eat your pussy while you ride him, Ma'am," Jamie offers.

She stops abruptly and my cock pulses with agony at the sudden loss of sensation. Veronica reaches over and strokes Jamie's hair, then caresses his cheek. The look of pure adoration on her face fills me with longing. I want her to look at me one day like she looks at him right now.

"What a good idea, pet," she says, smiling as she rises until my cock pops free. It slaps against my abdomen, heavy and filled with need.

I groan from the loss of her pussy while she turns around and gets settled again, and then I groan again as she fists my shaft and guides me inside of her.

Her ass has two little dimples above her crack, and I can't help myself. My hands cup her hips and my thumbs slide into the divots like that's what they were made for. Perfect handholds.

While she rides my cock, I stare at the curve of her back and the flare of her hips. The way her rounded buttocks meet my pelvis. The tumble of her hair down her shoulders. Jamie climbs around and settles on his belly between my spread legs. His fingers brush over us both, and while she uses my cock to fuck herself, his wet tongue replaces his hand and I'm lost.

"Mmm. That's good," she says, speaking my thoughts to life. "You're so good with your tongue, pet. Lick me. More."

He laps at her, and occasionally he catches my swelling knot as I stretch her pussy wide while she rides me. Knowing this alpha, this perfect adonis of a man, is lying on his belly for her while he feasts on her cunt and licks my knot is too much. It's more pleasure than I can stand. My pelvis tightens and my balls tingle with the urge to empty.

"I'm gonna come," I warn her.

"Come inside me," she orders.

I don't need to be told twice. My breath hitches as the moment stretches and the world fades until the only thing that matters is the urge to breed this pussy. Fill her and stop it up.

Veronica looks over her shoulder, her eyes meeting mine. Her mouth drops open as if she plans to speak again, but all that comes out is a whining moan as Jamie's tongue strokes over us both.

An alpha's licking my cock while I fuck our omega in her nest and I can't take it anymore.

My control snaps.

My instincts surge.

I have to breed her before I lose my chance.

My fingers dig into her hips, and I pull her down to meet my thrusts as my hips buck her with the force of our slapping. Eleven. That's how many pounding thrusts it takes for my knot to pop. It blows outside of her, some unfortunate mistiming, so I pull her down over it and grind it into her until it pushes in and locks behind her pubic bone. She groans from the brutal stretch, but her pussy's so slick and primed it sinks in without more than a token protest.

Deep inside her, my cock kicks with the first jettison of cum. It lashes at her walls as my groin pulses, pumping her full. She whimpers, so I purr to soothe her, and then her whimpers turn to moans as a broad, wet tongue licks over our tie.

Jamie cups my balls and kneads them while his tongue goes to work and he feasts between her legs. Her pussy tightens on my knot, and I groan as my body gives up another spurt of cum.

"Oh, fuck," I curse. "Again." And then he does it once more.

Her tight pussy clamps down on my cock and knot like she wants to break it and when she finally comes, her walls fluttering and cramping, my heart stutters in my chest like it's about to stop. She's loud through her release as she cries out.

My balls are drained, and all the fight goes out of me as I sag against the bed and catch my breath.

Jamie's licking doesn't stop, not even when my knot finally shrinks and my softening cock slips out. She puts her hands on my thighs and uses me for support as she leans back to give him better access as he cleans her. He purrs while he laps up our sticky mess of cum and slick, and I groan at the absolute perversion of it.

Another alpha's eating my cum right out of our omega's pussy.

It's unheard of.

He purrs while he feasts on her, and then his attention moves to me. He sucks my soft head into his mouth and licks me clean and the rough vibrations of his purr make my cock twitch back to life.

It's so fucking wrong, it's right. Omegas purr. If one likes you enough, they'll purr while giving head. But an omega's dainty purr is nothing compared to an alpha's rolling thunder.

And Jamie knows how to give head.

My cock rallies as he sucks it deeper into his mouth, like he can't get enough of me. He tongues my slit, then teases the sensitive webbing of skin under the flared corona. It doesn't matter that I came, that my balls are spent for a while. Between her heat pheromones and his deep purr, my body answers their call.

"Fuck, that's hot," Anthony says from his vantage point on the sidelines. "You like him, babe?"

Jamie purrs with agreement as his head bobs and he takes me deeper, all the way to the back of his throat where the purring is more intense, the vibrations world-shattering.

"Fuck," I pant. "Oh, God, that's so good."

Veronica moves to get off me, but I band an arm around her waist and pull her back so she has no choice but to lie on top of me. Her weight is comforting, and I'm not ready to let her go.

She angles her head for a kiss, and I'm more than happy to oblige. Her lips are sweet, and I pour all of my happiness, all of my contentment into our kiss until Jamie hollows his cheeks and sucks.

He pulls off my cock, and I groan at the loss of his beautiful mouth. Veronica fists her hand in his hair and shoves his nose into my groin.

"Don't stop," she orders.

Jamie takes one of my balls into his mouth and sucks on it while his tongue moves over the sack, stretching the skin. My hard cock smears a line of pre-cum against his stubble covered cheek. When he slips my head past his lips again, I drop my hand onto hers on his head and nudge him down.

I'm done being teased. If he's going to suck cock, then he's going to do it right.

And he's going to swallow.

Jamie purrs while he takes my cock all the way past the deflated knot. My cockhead hits the back of his mouth and knocks against the tight ring of his throat. But it doesn't stop there. His throat opens, and he takes me deeper still.

"Good boy," I tell him, enjoying the way his purr stutters at the praise. I thought his kink was degradation, but maybe he likes praise too. "You're so good at sucking cock, alpha."

He pulls back and laves the tip, then swallows me again, his throat squeezing around me as he takes me all the way down and holds me there until he needs air. I remember how hard Anthony fucked his face last night. How the alpha took it, his face red and his eyes leaking from the strain. But I'm bigger. Thicker. And I have my knot to worry about. It wouldn't be safe to keep risking it.

Jamie has no such reservations. He swallows me to the root

again, knot and all, and I'm lost in the sheer pleasure of it as his purr rumbles all around me while I drip right down his throat. He pulls back, takes a noisy breath, then does it again. And again. Until my swelling knot barely fits past his teeth and we flirt with the line of danger a bit too hard.

Veronica must sense it too. How close I am. How oblivious to suffocation he is. Because she wraps her hand around my knot on his next resurfacing. I breathe a sigh of relief as I finally let myself go.

My hips snap up as I fuck his mouth and ignore his noisy, wet sounds. His purr falters as I wrest control from him. Veronica bounces on top of me. She's along for the ride as I fuck the alpha's face, my knot swelling in her hand. The bulge knocks against his lips as my cockhead batters at the back of his throat.

I grunt, my pelvis tight and tingling again. My nostrils flare as I bury my face in her throat and inhale her heat-sweetened pheromones deep into my sinuses. Normally I wouldn't be able to come so quickly again, but ruts are magic, even for an old dog like me. I sink into the urges and let them take me as her pheromones wrap me in their spell.

"Swallow it," I growl, my only warning right before I come. My knot strains against her tiny hand as my cock kicks between his lips, my seed flooding his mouth. It's swallow or drown as I pump my release onto his tongue. Her fists tighten, and I grunt again as my balls dredge up one last burst of cum.

Jamie makes noisy licking and sucking sounds and his purr rumbles while he cleans me. He laps up every single drop, then swipes his tongue over my knot and her fingers to be sure he got it all.

"Morning, baby," Anthony says as he crawls closer with his knees on the bed and kisses her.

"Good morning," she says, smiling.

"Morning, babe." Anthony leans over to ruffle Jamie's knotted, blond hair. "Did you enjoy your breakfast?"

Jamie finally lets my soft cock go, then sits up on his haunches. He wipes spit and slick and cum from his jaw, then licks his fingers clean. "I did. He tastes so good." He gives me a shy smile, then looks away and blushes. "I haven't had beer in forever. Too many empty calories."

My purr catches. "Beer?" *That's a new one.*

"He smells like bread to me," Veronica says, saying what I've usually heard.

Bread isn't really the most attractive scent to be saddled with. When I was younger, it used to really bother me. It made me feel like I had to prove myself. Other guys smelled like whiskey or campfires or leather. Me? I smelled like a sack of bread. But I'm fine with it now. I grew up, and I realized the scent didn't make the alpha.

I had wondered how my scent fit in with theirs, though. Coconut, cherry, and orange all make sense together. Bread? No. But beer? My stomach swoops as I let myself wonder. Hope. Maybe this wasn't a crossed wire. We really might be a scent-matched pack.

She wiggles, so I let her go so she can slide off me and lie down beside me, her ass pressed against my hip. I drop a hand to her side and slide it up and down her curves to keep her from going too far. We haven't had enough post-rut cuddles, and she seems like the type to pretend she doesn't need aftercare until she has a mental breakdown three days later and wonders why she feels like shit.

Anthony curls up to her front while Jamie sprawls out sideways in the nest at our feet. We really are going to need a bigger bed. I grab the blanket from the other side of me and throw it over all of us, arranging it so we're all tucked in.

Jamie shrugs. "Smells like beer to me. What do you think, babe?"

"I'm not sure my nose is good enough to tell the difference," Anthony says, but he leans over Veronica to shove his face in my neck and sniffs to check. "Definitely yeasty. I'm not getting any bitter aromatics of hops, though. I guess he could remind me of a German malt or a milk stout. Is that what you meant?" He settles back, but grabs a lock of her hair so he can roll it between his fingers while he looks me up and down like he's appraising me.

A German malt. Huh. "My mom is German. She met my dad in Lüneburg when he was doing a study abroad economics class."

"Well, the Germans do love their beer," Anthony says. "It makes sense. So your mom is…"

I know what he's asking. Being mixed race means people are always trying to figure out where I fit and what my story is. As a teenager and a budding alpha, it bothered me. I always felt like I was never Black enough for Black people and never white enough for white people. Like I could never just be seen for myself. Now that I'm older, it doesn't bother me. I don't worry about what music I should listen to or if I should change how I act depending on who's around me. I'm just myself. I wish I'd found this peace earlier. It would have saved me from a lot of teenage fights.

"My mom is white and my dad's Black," I tell them. "My parents moved back to Germany after they were done raising us. They take care of my grandparents. I think my *oma* has a family beer recipe. I'd have to ask her what it is."

"Oh, I definitely want that recipe now," Anthony says.

Veronica makes a grumpy sound as if she's demanding more pets, her body wiggling against me.

While I was distracted, my fingers stopped making swirls

up and down her side. I smile into her hair and go back to stroking her. Jamie rubs her feet and legs from his spot at the bottom. She sighs, her eyes drifting shut as all three of us worship her like she deserves.

She tolerates it well until her heat drags her under and her sleepy chirps turn to moans. Her hips twitch as Jamie moves higher. I soften my petting until it's teasing, my fingertips barely touching her as I draw patterns in her skin. She shivers and moans, then throws a leg over Anthony to drag him closer against her front.

"Do you need us again, baby?" Anthony asks.

Chapter Twenty-Three

BRENDAN

"You need more?" Anthony asks her. "We've got what you need right here."

Anthony drops kisses in Veronica's hair, then moves lower. When she arches for a kiss, he grabs her face and tilts it back so he can lick his tongue over her throat. She moans as he drags his lips lower until he finds her scent gland and sucks it into his mouth.

Envy makes my teeth ache as the beta does what I can't. He nips her throat with his blunt teeth and digs his fingers into her soft, round thigh.

"Daddy," she moans, her ass rubbing against me as she arches. "I need you. Fuck me, Daddy. Please."

I watch, enraptured, as Anthony grabs her by the back of her neck and tugs her up from the bed. He's rough, dominant, and completely possessive as he manhandles her into place in the center. He turns her around and shoves her face into the mattress until she's kneeling with her ass in the air.

"I'm gonna fuck this pussy so good, baby," he growls. His knee slides between her legs and knocks hers wider, the movement spreading her lips apart so I can see the petals of her wet sex. He lines his hard, bobbing cock up with her hole and sinks inside with a rough thrust.

The pace he sets is brutal. Demanding. His fingers make divots in the globes of her ass while he pounds into her. The vulgar smacks of her slick mound are as noisy as her whimpers. His thumbs notch in the Venus dimples of her hips.

Anthony swings his head to look at us as he ruts her into the mattress in a brutal pounding that she seems to love. He smirks. "Her mouth's free. Are you waiting for an invitation?"

Jamie wastes no time getting to his knees. He kneels before her and gently turns her face, then moves her hair aside. He fists his thickening cock and taps it against her lips as he follows orders. She wraps her lips around his cockhead and her cheeks hollow as she takes him into her mouth and sucks.

I take a few minutes to figure out a position that won't aggravate my knee. I end up standing at the edge of the too-small nest with my good one kneeling on the bed and my side flush against Jamie's. Despite being in his rut, he doesn't mind the touch.

A month ago, if you'd told me I'd be tag teaming an omega with another alpha I'd have laughed. But when Veronica pops off his cock to suck mine while she switches between us, I'm not laughing at all.

There's no room for gentle lovemaking right now. No time for slow thrusts and lazy touches. This is rutting like her heat demands. And all three of us are happy to deliver.

My cock bumps against his as we compete for her mouth. A line of saliva connects us, the strand sagging, then breaking, as she moves from one cock to the other. I don't mind the way his perfect body brushes against me. His purr as she sucks him to his growing knot. Because when she's done with him, she moves to me, and our omega needs all the sweet, nutritive alpha cum she can get. So that's exactly what she'll get.

Anthony looks on at us with a smirk as he fucks her pussy from behind. He tugs her back on his cock, more dominant with her than either of us alphas have been allowed to be. Daddy, she calls him. Her beta. It would be amusing if Veronica's nose weren't buried in my groin while Jamie's cock smears a line of pre-cum across her cheek.

"Good girl," Anthony sighs. "Sucking those alpha cocks. What a good little cum slut you are. I bet you can't wait to swallow two fat loads while I creampie this pussy."

She hums with pleasure as she sucks me to the back of her throat and I can't hold back. I can't stop. I stare at her ass and the way it claps against Anthony's inked stomach as he tugs her back with every thrust, his cock buried deep inside her.

"Here you go, sweetheart," I warn her. I fist my hand in her hair until she looks at me. Her hand reaches up to squeeze my knot as it knocks against her lips. It makes a tight vice, not as good as a pussy but close enough, and I pump one creamy load after another until it fills her mouth and drips from the corners of her lips as she struggles to swallow it all.

She's not as good of a cocksucker as Jamie is, but we'll teach her. Train her.

I purr, my hips canting to work the last spurt of seed out so she can drink it down. Her throat bobs and then her lips drop open to show her mouth is empty. She lets me go so she can move onto the next cock. The next batch of filling alpha cum. She wraps her lips around Jamie's head and swallows him down.

Before she can get her hot little fist around his growing knot, I beat her to it. I lean against him and fist one hand in his hair and the other around his cock. I curl myself around him to put my lips to his ear and squeeze until he grunts.

"You haven't been feeding her enough. She needs more than what you've been giving her. If you come on her tits or face, you've gotta swipe it up and feed it to her. If you load up her sweet pussy, you've gotta scoop it out and feed it to her. She needs you, boy. Your cock. Your cum. And you don't wanna disappoint your omega, do you?" I squeeze his knot for emphasis and he grunts, his hips jerking as he fucks her face.

"No," Jamie answers, his voice breathy.

"No, what?" I ask. I need to hear him say it. Say that he'll do right by her. Take care of her the way she needs it, but is too stubborn or embarrassed to ask for it.

"No, Sir," Jamie moans.

I blink, stunned, then growl. Because I like it. I enjoy knowing that this perfect golden boy is looking to me for orders. That he wants my respect. My approval. My dominance over him? I squeeze his knot like it's a pussy milking him and feel a burst of pure pleasure when he groans and purrs while I stroke him. My fist bumps against Veronica's slick mouth.

"Good boy," I tell him, and then I nip his ear lobe. "Now feed your omega."

"I'm gonna…" Jamie doesn't get to finish his sentence before he comes.

His knot inflates in my hand, but I keep my fingers wrapped around it like a vise. The harder I squeeze, the more he'll come and the happier our omega will be. While she sucks on his head, I milk him until his purr grows shaky. It's only when I'm certain his cock's completely drained that I let him go and clap him on the back. He sways and pants, his chest heaving as if he finished a run.

I smirk, because he might be in better shape than me, but experience counts, and if he's not used to fucking omegas, then he's used to being a lazy alpha.

We'll work on that.

With her mouth free, Veronica buries her face in the mattress and groans. Anthony slaps into her, the smacking of their skin as loud as their breathing and her moaning.

"Fuck, baby, you're so damn wet. Did you like having all of us like that? You need all these cocks to satisfy you?"

"Yes," she whines. "I need you."

I forget how to breathe as he fucks her confession out of her. She'll probably pretend she didn't mean the words later, but we know the visceral truth of them. She needs us as much as we all need her.

"Which greedy little hole needs us, baby?" Anthony demands. "This pussy?"

"Yes!"

"What does this pretty pussy need?" he asks, refusing to let it go. To let her off easy.

"Cock!" she moans. "I need your cock in my pussy. Please, Daddy, I need to come." Her moan turns into a sob. "It hurts. Please let me cum."

"Okay, baby. Since you begged so nicely, I'll let you come on my cock." Anthony tilts her hips and shifts their angle. He hits a spot inside her that makes her whine and her thighs tremble. He's relentless as he pounds that spot, over and over.

She comes with a gush of slick that soaks the nest as he fucks her brutally through her orgasm until she's twitching, her body trying to get away from the sensation he's drowning her in. But he won't let her go. He has her, his hands firm on her hips as he tugs her back on his cock. He stares at the spot where his cock sinks into her slick pink pussy and his black inked hands keep her ass cheeks spread wide.

When he comes, she sags into the mattress with a deep sigh as his cock shuttles in and out of her while he works his load inside. "Hmm, that was good, baby."

She purrs and lies there while he pumps one last spurt of

seed out. I don't like that she's still awake. That was a good, long session, and she earned her rest, but she probably needs the stretch of a knot to get there. No wonder she has dark circles under her eyes. They're only getting half the job done.

Jamie moves to lie down next to her, but he stops when I squeeze my hand on the back of his neck. Anthony looks up at me in surprise.

"Fist her," I tell him.

"Huh?" Anthony arches a brow.

Veronica moves like she's going to sit up. That she's not babbling heat nonsense or passed out in her nest means she's not deep enough in the right headspace for actual relief. No wonder she's always so cranky. When was the last time she had a satisfying heat?

"Show me your nails," I order.

Anthony holds a hand up and I'm pleased to see they're neatly trimmed and short. I give him a nod, then sweep a hand toward her to tell him to proceed. "She needs the stretch." I shrug. "Your hand will work. She's got enough slick."

"Hmm," he says as he slides two fingers through the mess he's made of her. He slicks his hand up, then works two fingers in. "I've added a couple of fingers before, but never a whole fist."

"Like this." I show him how to fold his hand so his fingers pinch together and make a taper. "Get all of that slick on you. Start with three fingers before you add the others."

Veronica shifts. "Do I get a say—oh, God. Fuck. Fuck! It's too much, it's..." She pants, her eyes squeezing shut tightly, but her protests turn into whimpers and then moans.

"Shh, sweetheart." I stroke her hair, ignoring the snarls and smoothing it out of her pretty face. "You're made for this. It's okay. Let go and enjoy it. Don't tense up, it makes it worse."

"F-fuck you," she whimpers.

But the way her hips move with Anthony's thrusting hand makes her protests a lie. The sight of his hand disappearing to the wrist inside her and the wet sounds her pussy makes leaves me breathless.

She's perfect.

The inked hand thrusting in and out of her slick pink folds is obscene.

"Whoa," Jamie says under his breath. "She's taking his whole hand."

"Fuck yeah she is. You like that, baby?" Anthony asks. "You like Daddy's hand as much as a fat knot?" But he doesn't give her a second to catch her breath. His hand works in and out of her stretched pussy, sinking deeper until she takes him to the wrist. "You're such a good girl taking all of it. Are you going to come on my hand? I'm so damn deep inside you."

Her answer is a series of unintelligible moans, and when she comes, it's with a scream and a another gush of slick. Seconds later, Veronica's snoring. She's passed out with her ass in the air and Anthony's fist buried in her satisfied cunt.

When Anthony moves to pull free, I put a hand on his shoulder and stop him. "Give her a minute. She needs this."

Anthony nods, his eyes searching mine as he gets comfortable. "You know a lot about this stuff."

I nod. "In high school, when they split us up by dynamic for health class, this is the stuff we learned about."

"Really?" Anthony says. "Your health class sounds a lot more interesting than mine. All we learned about was how to roll a condom on a banana and how beta women have periods instead of heats." Anthony looks at Jamie for confirmation.

Jamie ducks his head, his cheeks turning pink as he gives a sheepish grin. "I don't know. I fell asleep a lot."

Anthony snorts.

"What?" Jamie looks between us. "It was right after lunch,

and they liked to make us watch videos in the dark. I always get sleepy after I eat carbs." He frowns. "But I'm pretty sure I would have remembered learning about this." He sweeps his hand out to gesture at the sleeping omega, then scratches his head. "I think."

"It wasn't this specific scenario," I say, getting comfortable. "But I've learned how to apply the basics. She needs the stretching to feel completely satisfied. It makes her feel safe enough to actually rest. Once an alpha's tied and bred her, he's forced to protect her from his competitors."

"Good to know." Anthony strokes his free hand over the line of her back and we all listen to her dainty snores.

After a few minutes, Jamie's stomach growls and we both glance at him. He gives us another bashful look. "I'm starving. Anyone want to eat?"

"Sure. I'd appreciate it," I say. We're going to need all the energy we can get to keep up with her.

"I could eat. Thanks, babe."

Jamie gets up and stretches, putting every dip and curve of his Adonis body on full display while he yawns, then heads for the kitchen without getting dressed. His ass is so muscled his cheeks have divots. Handholds, exactly like our omega.

When I turn my attention back to Anthony and the still sleeping Veronica, he's staring at me with a calculating look. My eyebrows rise toward my hairline. "What?"

His lips curl into a Cheshire grin. Between the dark scruff on his jaw, his messy bedhead hair, the leanly muscled body covered in tattoos, and his blue eyes framed with thick, dark lashes, he looks dangerous. Sinful.

Anthony leans over until his face is next to mine, our breaths mingling as his lips hover as close as they can get without touching. "I'm glad you're here," he whispers, his voice low and deep.

"Oh." My stomach swoops with sudden nerves. He means it. I have a feeling Anthony doesn't say things he doesn't mean. "Thank you, I—"

He silences me with a kiss, his lips firm and dry against the corner of my mouth. I could turn my head and give him my cheek or pull away. For a panicked second, all I do is go still. But he doesn't push or press. All he does is offer himself with a kiss that's quite chaste for a guy who looks like he does.

The sounds of metallic banging are faint through the open doorway as Jamie cooks for us, oblivious to his boyfriend kissing me. But if this is a pack trial… My heart thumps in my chest while I process what's happening and consider all the outcomes.

Anthony pulls away when I don't return his kiss while I'm thinking. "I'm sorry. I know you said you preferred women. I thought—"

I thread my fingers into his hair, get a good handful, and squeeze. Anthony stops talking, then sucks in a breath. With my grip on his hair, I drag his face back down to mine and kiss him for real. His lips part for me, for the intrusion of my tongue. I don't kiss him so much as I fuck his mouth with my tongue, my hand in his hair keeping him where I want him and angling his head perfectly so.

I claim his mouth. Conquer it. There are benefits to being an old man, and having experience is one of them. Anthony moans into my mouth and I swallow the sound before pulling back and nipping his lower lip between my teeth. I drop a kiss to the stinging flesh and stare into his eyes. It's a challenge. I don't mind if he wants to dominate the others, but he won't do that with me. In the bedroom, I'm the alpha.

"If you want me to fuck you, I suggest you get on your knees," I growl, my voice thick with a held back purr.

Anthony's pink tongue darts out to lick across his kiss-swollen lips.

"Food's ready," Jamie calls from the kitchen. Cutlery clinks as he sets places.

My held breath huffs out, and I chuckle. Saved by the bell. I slide off the bed and stretch the kinks from my body, joints popping. I go to my bag and pull out a pair of old gray sweatpants and pull them on, then drag a soft, faded shirt over my head. Once I'm dressed, I'm more comfortable again.

There's a wet sucking sound when Anthony finally pulls his hand free from Veronica. She whines in her sleep, but doesn't stir. Not even when Anthony prods her into a more comfortable position. She's adorable, with her hands curled under her chin and her knees tucked to her chest. Her hair is a tangled mess. We'll need to attack it with a wide-tooth comb and lots of conditioner, but she chirps while she sleeps. She's happy, for now. And sleeping. That's the most important part.

I go into the bathroom and wet a washcloth with warm water, then hand it to Anthony. He cleans her up, but when he goes to toss it into the growing pile of filthy clothing in the corner, I stop him. She needs the pheromones. They've let her keep the nest too clean, and that could be part of why she's so fatigued.

I take the used washcloth from him and leave it near her face, then tug a blanket from the nest and cover her so she doesn't get cold. Veronica's nostrils flare, and she stirs long enough to snag the pheromone-soaked washcloth and curl herself around it. Chuckling, I stroke a hand gently over her hair and lean down to press a kiss to her cheek. I purr for her until she settles again.

"You're good at this," he says in a low voice.

I don't want to admit that most of my knowledge comes from reading. That I read every book I could find on pack dynamics and bonding and nesting. On the off chance I ever found one—though the odds seemed low—I wanted to be prepared.

This is the strangest pack I've ever seen, but somehow everyone seems to fit. I think I might have a place here.

Anthony slides from the nest and stretches. Every inch of his inked, toned skin is on display. He has no such qualms about his nudity outside of the bedroom. Instead of dressing, he walks out of the room naked.

I follow the mouthwatering smell of breakfast, and when I join them in the kitchen, I get to watch Anthony have Jamie clean slick-covered fingers with his tongue. Jamie purrs while Anthony slides two fingers over his tongue, and his soft alpha cock plumps with arousal.

Smiling and shaking my head at the horniness of youth, I take my seat and dig into my food. The size of the omelet is enormous. It takes up nearly the entire dinner plate, and it's loaded with chopped vegetables and bite-size pieces of ham and cheese that turn into strings I have to twirl with my fork. I shove the bite into my mouth and chew, sighing around it. The eggs are fluffy without being dry. It's perfect.

Anthony and Jamie both look at me with varying expressions of amusement.

"What?" I ask, cutting off a larger bite. "It's good. You're a wonderful cook."

Jamie's cheeks turn pink from the praise. "Thanks."

"So when did you start cooking?" I ask, wondering how long he's been doing it to get this good. Maybe if I start now, I'll be able to make something passable in a few months. With an omega to take care of, it's a good skill to have. I could kick myself for not thinking of it earlier.

He glances at the clock over the stove. "About ten minutes ago?"

"Ah…" That wasn't exactly what I meant. I clear my throat and ignore Anthony's ducked smirk. "I meant when did you first show an interest in cooking?"

"Oh! My mom was always cooking, and I used to help her. She taught me a lot," Jamie says.

"Yeah?" I chew my bite and wash it down with coffee.

I want to get to know them. There's a lot more to a pack than rutting. "Do you like it? I've never been much of a cook. I'm more of a take it from the freezer and heat it up kind of guy. With how much I'm away from home, there's always a lot of takeout, fast food, and food trucks in my rotation."

They stop messing around and join me at the table, taking their seats and digging into their own food as if their nudity doesn't bother them one bit. Jamie pats his rock hard stomach. "I do all of my cooking. I have to watch my macros when I'm dancing. The customers tip better when I'm cut."

"I bet they do," I say, looking him over.

Jamie's body is perfect. He even has the coveted eight pack some guys can't achieve, no matter how many crunches they do. Looking at him should fill me with envy—he's everything I used to be—but I'm no longer jealous.

Maybe it's because he's been submissive with me. Or it's because I know, deep down, that by the end of this heat I'm probably going to fuck him. It's an obscene thought. Nearly a taboo. An alpha fucking another alpha? I can't fucking wait.

He's a beautiful man. I might prefer women, but there's an energy about him that sparks my interest. I wonder what he'd look like covered in rope. With rope marks dug into his skin, their impressions left behind even when he's freed. The idea of all that powerful male bound up and helpless for the taking makes me wish I didn't have to leave my rope behind.

Next time, I tell myself. *God, I hope there's a next time.* I think I'll put him in pink. Veronica in black. And Anthony… I want to see all that black and gray inked skin bound in pure white. *I have some rope I haven't dyed yet.*

The idea of a next time and later fills me with a hope I haven't known for years. We chat while we eat, getting to know one another, until our plates are clean and Veronica stirs in the nest.

Time to get back to work.

Chapter Twenty-Four

JAMIE

omega. Us.

Packing up is better than I ever imagined. So much better than I've heard it is from other alphas. All they talk about is rutting and knotting. Draining their cocks. They don't talk about how warm it is. How limbs tangle as we pile close. How mouths kiss and tongues lick, heedless of where one person ends, and another begins. There is no I in the pack, only us.

When Anthony's grip on my hair drags me from the soft press of bodies, I whine at the loss of the warmth and the scents. He ushers me into the bathroom and gives me orders to prep. Anticipation curls in my stomach.

Even with the heat and the rut, we're still ourselves. I wasn't sure if we would be. It was a risk. A gamble that's paid off so far.

The toilet's bidet attachment helps me get ready, and when I'm all clean, I wash my hands and return to the nest.

Veronica is spread out in the center, her legs splayed wide and bent. Anthony is behind her. He curls over her and fingers her until she's wiggling and whining. Her head is in his lap as she uses him like a pillow while he traps her exactly where he wants her, with a hand around her throat.

She's laid out like a feast.

For me.

My heart stutters in my chest at the sight of her and my knees hit the edge of the bed. I glance at Anthony for permission, and he rewards me with a smile. After a brief hesitation, he nods. It's a magnanimous gesture. Like a dark god granting his faithful servant the right to worship.

And oh, how I plan to worship at their feet.

I climb into the nest and position myself between her thighs, basking in the sight of her. She's gorgeous. Her eyes are half-lidded and her fingers twist the bedding while her hips rise to meet Anthony's rapid fingering. And then they stop. A whimper rips from her throat as she mourns the loss of sensation.

He won't let her come until I'm inside her. Until she's squeezing my knot. The one she craves but is too tough and self reliant to ask for. With us, she'll never have to ask.

Doesn't she know all we want to do is satisfy her? Make her happy?

I settle between her thighs and take a moment to stroke her thighs and belly. A part of me still can't believe we're here. That all of Anthony's scheming paid off. But I shouldn't have doubted him. He's so smart. Always thinking ahead and planning.

Veronica whimpers, her eyes trained on me, and I smile while I drag my cock over her wet pussy to get it slick.

Anthony's grip on her is the only thing keeping her somewhat in place as Vee tries to wiggle herself onto my cock. "Shh, baby, he's gonna give you what you want. What you need. Be a good girl."

Hearing those words from his lips makes my cock drip with pre-cum. As I slide into her tight, wet heat, my fears about whether I'm any good at this fade. It only takes three thrusts to get slicked up enough to bottom out inside of her. To hit the end of her and watch her pussy swallow up every inch of my thick, veiny cock.

Once I hit her cervix, she settles. The tension drains from her body. Vee goes limp. Pliant.

Anthony grants her one last stroke of her clit, a move that makes her walls squeeze me, and then he slides out of the nest. I want to track his movements, to watch him get the lube, but the way she squeezes me steals all of my focus. It muddles my thoughts.

It fogs them so all I can focus on is her. The slick heat of her center. Her heady perfume of sweet, juicy pheromones. The bare expanse of her perfect throat. The way she looks at me with lust hazed eyes and pouty lips strips me raw and leaves me exposed.

Please her. Rut her raw. Breed her. Bite.

The instincts are overwhelming and I'm lost to them. I slam into her, giving Vee what she craves. What she needs. The wet slap of our thighs and grunts fill the otherwise quiet room. I'm so focused on maintaining a rhythm to satisfy her I forget what's coming next.

Callused fingers stroke across my back and butt, and in a moment of insanity, in instinctual fear that my omega's being taken from me, I growl. The sharp pinch of two slick fingers pushing inside my hole makes me stiffen and suck in a breath.

"Relax, babe," Anthony orders.

A moment of clarity breaks through the fog of a rut. My body knows what to do before my mind comes back online. It relaxes. Anthony strokes deeper, working the lube inside me and scissoring his fingers apart to get me ready. He teases my prostate, and the sensation interrupts the movement of my hips.

Veronica whines, and I focus on her as I go back to thrusting. Each surge forward drives me deep inside her, and every pull back drives me deeper onto Anthony's fingers. The same fingers that were buried wrist deep in her cunt not that long ago.

My eyelids flutter as I remember it. The memory is burned into my brain for later. I'm going to come to that mental image the next time she allows me to jerk off.

Anthony adds a third finger and fucks me, then withdraws completely. I have barely enough focus to hold still for this next part. We ignore Vee's desperate, nonverbal pleading as his cock probes between my cheeks. He slides over that sensitive ring of muscle. Hot cock and a cool metal ring tease me. When he gently pushes in, I moan.

"That's it, babe. So good." Anthony babbles a string of praises while I hold still so he can seat himself completely. "I'll help you fuck her. We'll do it together."

Anthony thrusts, his cock filling me completely. With nowhere to go, his movement pushes me even deeper inside her. Way deeper than I've dared to go for fear of hurting her. Her belly pouches as the head of my cock fucks her deep. Vee moans, her hips rocking with us. I love how he uses me. That my cock has become an extension for him. That he's driving us, now.

It's so easy to surrender control to him. To let go and let him take the reins. Anthony sets our pace, our rhythm getting faster and harder. Using me, he fucks her more roughly than I ever would have dared. And she loves it. Vee goes boneless, her eyes unfocused. Her pretty breasts bounce and sway with every thrust. My teeth ache to latch onto one taut peak and suck.

Vee's whines roll into an omega purr that makes my cock kick inside her and my balls tighten. She wants this. My cock. My knot. My cum. *Me.* And it's all because of him. Because he listened to me when I confessed my attraction to her one night and he promised me he'd make it happen. That he'd make her ours.

Now here I am, buried balls deep inside our omega while he fucks my ass and uses me like his alpha cock sleeve.

His hips slam hard against me and his fingers tighten on my hips. He pleases her with my cock in a way I haven't been able to on my own yet. She moans, her pussy fluttering and clamping down, strangling my dripping head.

Man, he's so good at this.

He should have been the alpha. Not me. He's so much better at it. At knowing what we need and getting it for us before I think to ask. The things I've struggled with the most all my life come so naturally to him.

When Anthony abruptly pulls out of my ass, my rhythm falters. Vee and I both cry out together at the loss of it. He slides over my puffy, well-fucked hole again.

And if I weren't so lost in a rut, so drunk on Vee's mind numbing pheromones, I might notice there's no cool kiss of metal on heated flesh. No cock ring. But I'm so lost to it, I don't.

He slips inside, only an inch, and works his way deeper with careful thrusts. I thought I was readied, but the stretch is unreal. It's like the very first time he fucked me all over again. It took a week of training for me to take him.

"Relax, babe. Let go. Enjoy it," Anthony coaxes as he sits on the bed.

He sits.

On the bed.

Then…

I take a second to process what I'm seeing. What I'm feeling. Who's behind me?

The cock inside me surges deeper, gaining another inch. "Halfway there," Brendan says, cupping the back of my neck with his large hand. His grip is firm, but not punishing. It keeps me from turning, keeps me there on his cock, but doesn't squeeze. There's no need. Among all of us, we both know who's in charge. And it's not me.

"Good job, boy. Think you can take more?" he asks.

"H-half?" I whimper. He's already so deep. I can't imagine how much further he has to go till I've taken all of him.

Brendan chuckles, his cock jumping inside my ass with the movements. Vee mewls her displeasure and takes matters into her own hands, her hips gyrating as she works herself deeper onto my buried cock.

Trapped between the two of them, I can't move. His grip slides down to my shoulder, to the place where a bite would go, as he uses me for leverage. He tugs me back, working me deeper on his length. If I weren't already slick and warmed up, this would be too painful to bear.

I moan as his large alpha cock rubs across my prostate as he methodically strokes in and out of me. "You're so big," I pant.

How did Vee take it? She's so tiny. I'm not tiny, and I'm still struggling.

"Just wait," Anthony says, smirking. He gets to his knees and comes closer, pinching my chin between his fingers and stretching until we're nearly kissing. His breath fans my face as he hovers. "His knot's even bigger."

A groan rattles in the back of my throat. Brendan uses my distraction to gain another inch. How many more inches are left?

"He's going to knot your ass," Anthony says. His nose slides against mine. "Make you his bitch." His tongue flicks out and licks my lips, making me gasp. "Because that's what you are. Our beautiful cock slut."

Brendan thrusts the last of his cock deep, his thighs smacking against the back of mine as he buries all of his cock inside me. "That's good, Jamie. You're doing so well taking all of me."

Between Anthony's degradation and Brendan's praise, I'm a mess. My head swims as Brendan moves for real. He slides out and slams home, the slap of his hips driving me deeper inside of Vee. Again, he does it. If I thought Anthony fucked hard before, I was wrong. Brendan sets a brutal pace. He drives his cock deep and gives me no time to catch my breath before he does it again.

It's obscene for him to be inside me like this. It's not something that's done, or talked about if it is. An alpha fucking another alpha. Our instincts don't allow it.

But as Brendan moves, hips flexing in a less brutal cadence at my back, I don't have the urge to fight him. Why would I fight it when it feels this good? And if his cock is inside me, then it's not inside her. My instincts send me two different, conflicting thoughts.

His big alpha cock stretches me wide and fucks me deep, rearranging my guts with every steady, ball-deep thrust. Together, we find our rhythm. When his balls slap against my inner thigh, I bury my cock deep inside her. When he pulls back, I follow. He leads.

Anthony fists his cock and taps his head against the corner of her mouth. A dribble of pre-cum smears across her face. She turns her head and opens, sucking him inside as he thrusts and fills her. Her reward is the working of his fingers between us. He strokes between her slippery folds and brushes across my dick as he finds her clit.

She clenches and cries out, her sounds muffled because she's stuffed with cock. I shouldn't be enjoying this. I shouldn't want to be fucked by another alpha. Have my ass knotted. Not when we have the sweetest smelling omega in our nest.

But I can't help it. I can't fight my real nature. My urges.

Giving up the fight, I lean my shoulders back against Brendan. I let go of the idea that I have to be big and tough because I'm an alpha. He's taller than me. Older. Wiser. And he catches me.

My head lolls on his shoulder, my long hair slipping and baring my throat for him. He lets out a surprised sound that morphs into a throaty moan.

Strong arms wrap around me and keep me upright. It feels so good to let go. To lean on someone stronger. I've always had to hold back with Anthony. He's smaller. Strong, but in a wiry way rather than bulky. I love him, and don't want to hurt him, especially not by accident.

With Brendan here, I can fully let go. I can give up the pretense that I've ever had control. That I wanted it.

Because I don't want it.

And I never have.

Being an alpha is hard. Everyone has expectations because of my dynamic. Something that can't be controlled. I don't want that responsibility. Making decisions and bossing others around and always being in charge. I'm not super smart. Not good at giving orders. I've never wanted any of that.

Anthony is the first person who made me think that was okay. He speaks my fears into existence, and they lose all power over me. He says all of my deep, dark thoughts, and stays. I don't have to hide them. Be ashamed of them any longer. He frees me by saying the quiet parts out loud, and proving they don't matter.

Vee doesn't want my power. My command. She craves my submission. And now Brendan too. His rough claiming of my body allows me to let my mind go blank. To exist as myself, as I truly am, and not the Jamie the world wants me to be.

If that makes me a bad alpha, then so be it.

I'd rather be bad than something I'm not. I don't want to go back to pretending to be anything other than me.

"Feels so good," I moan, catching my breath again.

Brendan fucks me, and our movements fuck Vee. Anthony strums her clit until she's writhing on my cock. His fingers satisfy her more than my cock ever has. She squeezes and moans, her pussy clamping down so hard it's like it's trying to push me out. But Brendan's fucking the both of us. There's nowhere to go. His fingers make divots in my thighs as he grips me tight. He drives my cock forward, burying me deep inside her.

"That's a good cock slut," Anthony says.

It's unclear who he's talking to—Vee, whose mouth and pussy are both stuffed with cock, or me, whose ass is stretched with a real alpha's cock. Maybe both of us.

"Yes."

My balls tingle with the first inkling of my pending orgasm. It's a powerful one. The kind that wrecks you after it passes. And I don't know if that's because I'm buried in our omega who's in full heat or because my alpha's stuffing me full, or because now that I've been forced to submit completely, I don't have any fear left. Only a pleasure so deep I'm drowning in it.

They've seen me brought to the lowest an alpha can get, and they're all still here. They want me. I'm good enough. Desired.

"He's close," Anthony says. "See the change in his breathing?"

My lover knows me so well. He knows my secret desires and urges before I do. Under his perfect control, I'm more free than I've ever been.

"Good," Brendan answers. The alpha gets a fistful of my hair and drags my head to the side. He exposes my throat, my hair sliding free to give him a better view.

"Don't," Anthony orders, steel in his voice. "No biting."

Fear tinges the edges of my rut drunk bliss, but my head's too foggy to keep up with the abrupt change in tone or mood. Everything is perfect. Why is Anthony upset?

"Trust me." Brendan dips his head to my scent gland and licks a wet stripe over the pheromone rich skin. "Make our omega come, boy," he orders, his voice deep and commanding. "I want her milking you when I knot your ass."

I shiver against him, but I don't tense or pull away. I'm balanced on the edge. One slight push and I'll career off it. My chest heaves with the effort needed to drag it out, to hover on that precipice.

The graze of his sharp alpha teeth along my neck makes my thighs tense. I inhale sharply, the sound turning into a moan. He sucks my scent gland into his mouth and bites it lightly. Not enough to break skin or create a bond, but enough to let me know he has me.

Right now, I'm his. It's his cock in my ass. His teeth at my throat. I might be the one buried in our omega's sweet pussy, but I'm not in control. I'm only between her legs because he's allowing it.

The unspoken permission to let go is all I need to stop my fight against coming. He growls, the sound vibrating my sensitive scent gland, and I fly apart. With a series of grunts that turn into a purr, I come. Cock jerking inside Vee, my pelvis tightens. My knot swells.

Brendan's hips snap forward and he buries me deep inside of Vee, my swelling knot locking us together as it fully expands. He's letting me knot her.

She pulls herself off Anthony's cock and lets out a long, ragged moan. Her pussy spasms on my knot as she comes against Anthony's fingers. My balls empty with one jerking thump at a time. Hot rope after rope lashes her walls. Fills her. She'd be dripping if she weren't stoppered.

Her channel squeezes, milking me. Demanding more. For an omega in heat, it's never enough. More, more, more, her greedy pussy says. That's why our omega needs her pack. She needs *us*.

Anthony fucks her slack mouth. He reclaims her attention and shoves his cock between her lips. Focuses on his pleasure as she works to take him.

Brendan ruts me. He slams deep, fast, and hard. His teeth bruise my neck where they pinch, and then his thrusts slow. He growls, a low rumble, the sound traveling straight through me. It startles a bigger purr from my chest. We purr together as his cock pulses inside me. It jerks, buried deep in my gut, as he comes.

A dull, slow pressure grows in my ass. Stretches me wider than I've ever been stretched before until I worry that it's too big. Too much. That I'm too unprepared. His knot makes his huge cock double in size. It's a pleasure that borders on pain. Only his complete stillness and the residual aftershocks of Vee's pussy on my knot keep it manageable. Bearable.

Brendan lets my unmarked neck go, but laps the pheromone-laden sweat from my skin. "Good boy," he murmurs. "You take a knot as well as any omega."

He sounds proud. Bliss keeps my thoughts mellow and sated. I like being a good boy. I love how they want me even though I'm not dominant.

"Fuck, I want to see," Anthony says. "Hold that thought, baby." He pulls his cock from Vee's mouth and gets off the bed. He kneels behind us.

When Brendan spreads his legs wider to give Anthony a view, it tugs at me. At my ass where we're tied. I whimper. *How does she stand it?*

"Fuck, babe. That's so hot. Does that feel good?" Anthony asks.

Tentative fingers probe at our tie. He teases my puffy, lube-slicked hole and the bulge under my balls where the knot's buried deep. "It feels good," I gasp, holding still. "I'm so full." The alpha's knot is wider than any cock, toy, or plug I've taken.

"What a good cock slut you are." Anthony palms my balls and I twitch, groaning with Brendan and Vee when the movement pulls at all three of us. "Oh, that's promising. You're giving me ideas."

"Don't," I beg, keeping still. "Please." If he fucks with us, I'll fall apart. I'm barely holding it together right now. All I want to do is collapse in the nest and nap.

Anthony chuckles, but the sound isn't reassuring. He gets back onto the bed and cuddles Vee. The look he gives us is full of dark promises. I can see the wheels turning in his beautiful blue eyes.

Fear and anticipation war with each other within me.

Whatever he's thinking, planning, I know I'm going to love it. He knows me too well.

Anthony reaches slowly down Vee's body. He plays with her breast, pinching her light brown nipple until it's a stiff point. He skims it down her hip. Over the short brown curls that cover her mound. Between her swollen pink labia and stretched thin lips. Anthony teases her until she stirs, gasping and moving.

Her twitching pulls at our tie and I groan. My hips surge deeper on instinct, and my ass aches around Brendan's knot.

Omega needs more.

My body aches to give her more. To find the dredges of seed in my balls and stuff her full. Brendan said if an omega's still moving after being knotted, they haven't been properly dicked down.

Anthony plays with her clit, his grin widening with every twitch of her hips. I can't help it. I move. I fuck my knot deeper into her, pulling back enough to savor the tightness of our tie.

I'm too swollen to pop free. And the more I tease her opening, the more Brendan's knot rubs against my prostate.

"Oh, fuck," Brendan groans. He presses his face against mine and holds me tight. Keeps me close. His big, heavy balls smack against my ass. His purr stutters.

With his hand working faster and faster, Anthony brings Vee to a screaming orgasm. Her walls clamp down on my knot and a gush of slick and cum seeps from our seal while she squeezes me tight. My balls draw up, the internal movement tugging at my perineum and the knot stuffed deep in my gut. All I can do is whimper and take it, sandwiched between them.

Brendan moves with me, our hips working in tandem as he fucks his knot deeper. We come again together, his cock's pulsing triggering mine. It's a ghost of an orgasm. A tiny jerking of seed. When we're done, I can barely keep my eyes open. I'm sated and exhausted.

No wonder she passes out after.

It's Brendan who keeps me from toppling onto her. His fingers dig into my chest, where he hugs me tight. When Anthony goes back to fucking her mouth, it's a relief for all of us.

"That's it, baby. God, you're so good at sucking cock. I can't wait to teach you how to deep throat." Anthony fucks her mouth, but he's careful not to choke her. He doesn't use her as badly as he uses me when he's fucking my face.

He's right, though. We need to teach her how to take him properly. It's not in his nature to hold himself back. Although, knowing Vee, if he tries to throat fuck her outside of a heat he'll probably end up meeting the pinch of her teeth.

"Here you go, baby. Enjoy your breakfast."

He throws his head back and groans as he comes, and Vee laps it up. She swallows every drop and sucks his cock as if she's looking for more, until Anthony pulls his cock free. He slaps his softening cock against her lips, then laughs when her tongue darts out as if to ask for more.

"Still hungry?" Anthony asks. His eyes slide to me.

Brendan grunts and pulls away, his softened knot tugging at me painfully before popping out. He pulls out. A gush of cum and cherry-flavored lube slides down my leg.

When he's free, they both look at me expectantly. My legs tremble like it's the end of leg day when I press a thumb to the bulge of her pussy and ease my knot out of her with a more gentle tug. It pops free, white cream welling at her entrance. I put a hand underneath and wait, gathering my cum from her pussy before it can drip down and soak into the nest.

Leaning over her, I feed my cum-slicked fingers to her. She sucks them into her mouth, humming with happiness as her tongue licks my hand clean. Two more times I repeat this until she's gotten it all. We watch her tongue curl around them in search of more. She purrs while she sucks. Not a single drop is wasted. By the end, her eyes are closed more often than open and her purr stutters. She's half-asleep already.

"Time for a bath, baby." Anthony drops a kiss into her hair and slides off the bed to start the tub.

I use a blanket to wipe the mess off my legs till I'm reasonably clean. On either side of her, Brendan and I both flop down into the nest. Until her bath's ready, we cuddle her close and keep her warm. The first time that Brendan's hand brushes against mine, I assume it's an accident. We're both petting her. The second time he does it, I realize it's on purpose.

My eyes find his, and I see that it's me he's staring at. Slowly, to give me time to pull away, he leans his face toward mine. When I don't retreat, he presses his lips to mine. I'm hesitant from the surprise of it, but when he pulls away, I surge forward to deepen the kiss. Anthony said to not get my hopes up, just in case. That Brendan likes girls more than men and was mostly here for Vee. That we'd need to feel everything else out slowly and give it time. Fucking isn't intimacy. It's sex. But this… this is sweet.

For some, a hole's a hole and a mouth's a mouth. He's not straight, but I didn't assume he was really into us. I don't like everyone I meet just because I'm bi. Neither does Anthony.

The kiss is tender and sweet. It's so different from the brutal pounding he gave me that it leaves my head reeling. When we break apart, it's to see Anthony looking down at us. He smiles, and I'm relieved that he's pleased, and then he turns his attention to Vee.

He drags the sleepy, sticky omega from the nest and cradles her like a groom carrying a bride, then brings her into the bathroom.

Things are a little awkward without her there between Brendan and me as a buffer. It's not common for packs to have more than one alpha unless they grew up together. What if I say the wrong thing? Sometimes when I talk, people laugh and I don't know why. I end up laughing with them, although I'm confused.

After a few minutes of tense silence, Brendan is the first to break it. "Does it hurt?"

"No." My ass is sore, but it's a good pain. A reminder of how much pleasure he brought me. I might have trouble sitting for a day, but he was surprisingly gentle for how big he is. And Anthony prepping me first really helped. "Well, maybe a little. Nothing I haven't dealt with before, though."

Without Vee's clouding pheromones perfuming the air, my head clears so it's easier to think.

His eyebrows climb toward his hairline. "You've been with another alpha before?"

"What? No." *Wait, are there more alphas like us out there?* "Have you?"

"Once."

I sit up on one elbow and wait for him to continue. This is a story I have to hear.

Brendan laces his fingers together over his stomach. There's a hint of his alpha physique under a layer of softness. I remember how powerful he was when he held me upright. He reminds me of those Highlander strongmen who toss entire trees instead of lifting weights in a gym. The ones that are strong, but not showy. Their muscle and strength are hidden under bulk. Staying cut is a lot of work. It means a lot of food restrictions. Before a photoshoot, I'm not even allowed to drink water. If I didn't have to look like this for my job, I wouldn't. It's hard to maintain.

"In high school," Brendan starts, "I messed around with one guy on my soccer team. We were both trying to figure out what we were doing. What we liked. I'd only dated girls before, mostly betas, and I was confused by my attraction to him.

"It was clumsy teenage fumbling. Something we did when we were both between girlfriends. The summer before senior year, he quit the team and left the school. His parents had gotten divorced, and he had to move out of town.

"The next time I saw him was at our first game of the season. He was on the other team. I didn't recognize him at first. He'd presented as an alpha over the summer and gained fifty pounds of muscle and grew four inches. I guess he was a late bloomer. Their team beat us zero-to-three that night. After the game, we both snuck under the bleachers where we used to meet. He was eager to show me his body's changes.

"Two games later, I took a kick that ruined my knee and ended my pro career before it really got started. I never saw him again."

"Man," I sigh. "I can't imagine not being able to surf anymore. That sucks."

Brendan pointedly glances at my neck. "Did I take it too far?"

I reach up and brush my fingers over my scent gland. It's tender, maybe bruised, but it'll take a day to know that for certain. The skin's not broken, though. He was careful. Although, in the moment, I don't think I would have tried to stop him. "No. But I might need to put makeup on it when we go back to Rut."

"Sorry," Brendan says, looking guilty.

"Don't be. I liked it."

The bathroom door opens and Anthony carries Vee, depositing her in the nest. She turns onto her side and lets out a sleepy grunt.

Brendan smiles and pulls a blanket over her. "She needs cuddles."

None of us have to be told twice to take care of our omega.

Chapter Twenty-Five

JAMIE

Two days later, Vee's heat breaks in the middle of the night. I'm the first one to wake and the first to notice. The syrupy scent of her pheromones has died down to its normal sweet citrus. My head is clearer than it has been since this started. And the siren call of the ocean sings to me through the open window.

A quick swim out won't hurt. It's so early, they probably won't notice I'm gone. We were up late, and they're exhausted from keeping up with her.

Before I'm lured back to sleep, I drag myself out of bed and rake a hand through my hair to pull it back from my face. Anthony doesn't stir as I grab my wetsuit from the drawer and struggle into it. He's used to me sneaking out and back before he gets up.

Careful of the noise, I slide the glass door open slowly, then grab a board from my quiver and head outside. The sand is cold, but the sunrise is breathtaking. There's only a few people on the beach. They're walking and looking for the shells that washed in overnight.

Waves splash up my ankles and I'm about to paddle out

when I see them. "Oh. Oh, she needs to see this." I bury my board in the sand and head back to the house, heedless of the sand I track inside. I'm too excited.

"Vee," I whisper.

Anthony rolls over and Brendan cracks his eyes open. Vee only grumbles. There's no time to wake her gently. The moment will pass if we're not fast.

"Vee," I repeat louder.

When she still doesn't stir, I pull the covers off her and lift her from the nest. She flails before she realizes it's me. "Whatthefuck?" she mumbles.

I set her down, then dig around in my drawer until I find what I'm looking for. I unzip my old spare wetsuit and kneel at her feet. "Step into it. Hurry."

Vee rubs the sleep from her eyes and lets me get the suit on her. It's way too big and it won't do much to keep her warm with all that room, but it's better than nothing and she doesn't have a swimsuit here.

"Come on," I say. "I need to show you something."

She stumbles behind me, slowly waking up when the wind lashes at her. "Where's the fire? God, I feel like I got hit by a truck. Between my thighs. Repeatedly."

"You can swim, right?" I probably should have asked her that before dragging her out of bed at dawn. I grab my board from where I wedged it into the sand and lead her toward the shore.

Good, they're still there.

"Yeah. Why?" The waves lap over her toes. "Jesus Christ, that's fucking cold. Nope. No. I'm going back to bed. Wake me in a month."

"You'll like this," I tell her, threading her fingers with mine and squeezing her hand. I lock eyes with her and refuse to budge. "Please. Trust me."

She's so grumpy it's cute. It reminds me of Anthony. He's not a morning person either. I've learned not to ask him too many questions before he's had his first cigarette.

Vee glares at me, then huffs and nods. "Fine. But it better be amazing or you're making it up to me. With your tongue. For a month."

I grin. "Deal." I squeeze her hand and drag her into the water until we're deep enough that I can put her on the board. I get on behind her and paddle us out beyond the swell of waves.

"What's so amazing?" she asks, squinting while she looks around. "I mean, the sunrise is pretty and all, but I could have watched that from the shore and—holy fucking shit." She flinches and tries to lift her legs out of the water, nearly toppling us into the ocean. "There's something moving down there. Did you see that?"

I lock my arms around her middle and keep us steady. "Wait for it."

I hold my breath, smiling when she whimpers, and then the first dark fin breaks the surface. The dolphin breaches, blows out its breath with a spray of salt water, sucks in another breath, then dives back down. A second joins it, and then a third. We're in the middle of their pod. A brave one sees us and swims close, its eye swiveling to keep us in sight as it jumps higher on its next surfacing. It's showing off.

"Oh my God," she croaks. "Those are dolphins."

I grin and hold her tighter, even though she's no longer struggling. "They like an early breakfast. They're most active at dawn."

"You do this every day?" she asks, her voice breathless.

"Every day I can. Dawn patrol's my favorite time to surf."

We sit there in silence and watch the pod swim past us. There's a mother and her baby, which makes Vee squeal with such omega delight that my insides feel as soft as cotton candy.

I prop my chin on the top of her head and grin. She's not as cold and tough as she pretends. When the pod swims on, their fins only visible in the distance, I turn us back toward shore. She's shivering by the time we get through the surf and back onto the beach.

"Thank you," Vee says, throwing her arms around me.

"You're welcome." I rest my chin on the top of her head and savor the moment. "I'm glad you saw it, and that you liked it. I like seeing you happy." And I really like knowing that I'm the one who put that smile there on her pretty face. I pull away so I can see it again.

The wind blows her hair into her eyes, and I drag the strands back before she can. I tuck the wayward lock behind her ear and cup her jaw in my hand, stroking her cheek with my thumb. "I like making you smile, Vee."

"Oh," she whispers. Her cheeks pinken.

"I'd like to make you smile every day. We all would. If you'll let us."

Her mouth opens and closes while her eyes search mine. "I… I'd like to watch you surf. If that's okay."

"Of course." The winds are picking up, but the waves are still small. They're barely more than ankle slappers. "This isn't the best board for these little waves, but I'll try to catch a few."

I leave her on the sand and crash into the surf, pushing my board out until I can barely reach the bottom. I climb onto my stomach and paddle out there. After a few minutes of waiting, I catch one in the pocket, getting up on my board and rolling in until I have to dig the fins into it and turn around to get enough force from an airy jump off the white to keep going before it loses all of its power and height. Two more times, I find a decent wave and pull out every trick I know to make it look good, and then I ride back toward shore.

I'm panting and pleasantly sore—some of it from surfing

and some of it from her heat—when I grab my board and hike up the beach to where I left Vee. She's sitting there with her toes buried in the sand and a smile on her face. Her hands are clasped around her knees.

With her beach waved hair and the wetsuit, she's a surfer's wet dream. Plus I know she's not wearing anything underneath it. I need to get her a suit that fits her. One that'll show off all her amazing curves while keeping her warm.

"You're really good," she says while I lay my board down in the sand and sit beside her so our hips and thighs touch. She leans into me, laying her head on my shoulder, and my heartbeat kicks up. "Do you miss doing it professionally?"

"Sometimes. I miss traveling and doing competitions. Seeing new places. But the waves are so crowded with kooks now and the big falls rattle me a lot more than they used to. Ten footers make me feel my age." I laugh and watch the waves turn into foam while birds search the receding surf for their next meal. "I'm happy with cruising my little slice of heaven here."

"I'm happy too. Rut's doing well enough to think about opening a second location. Or maybe doing a traveling show. I haven't decided yet. We have to get through this audit first."

"Do you like Brendan?" I ask.

She's quiet for a bit before she answers. "I like him. I know that sounds crazy because we just met and we're barely more than strangers, but…"

"He fits." I think of all the ways he fit so well during her heat. From the burst of her perfume, she's thinking about it too.

She hums in agreement.

"He smells good." *Tastes good too.*

"I know, right?" She sighs and glances at the house. "We should head back." Vee stands and I miss her warmth already. She brushes the sand from her butt and legs.

"You missed a spot," I tell her, patting her ass to wipe it clean.

Vee gives me a squinty look I can't decipher. "You only wanted an excuse to touch my butt."

I take my hand off her, confused, and tilt my head. "Do you not want me to touch your butt anymore?"

She snorts. That's laughter adjacent, right? She doesn't seem mad. "It's fine. I was teasing you."

"Good." I smile and go back to brushing her off. I wipe her butt as clean as it's going to get until she rinses off with my outdoor shower. "It's a nice butt."

Vee rolls her eyes, but extends a hand to help me up. I let her think she pulls me up from the sand, then I grab my board.

"Are you hungry?" I ask her. She hasn't eaten food in a couple days. Nothing but her special omega waters and cum. I know how hungry I am after a fast. I can't imagine how she feels after this many days of no food.

"My stomach is trying to gnaw its way through to my spine."

The sand shifts underneath our feet, warmer now than it was when we first came out here, and we walk up the dune until we reach the weathered planks of my path. When we reach the fence, I cut ahead to open the gate for her.

"I'll cook something," I tell her. "What do you want?"

"What kind of stuff do you make?"

I shrug. "Anything you want."

I turn the outdoor shower on and rinse the sand from my board, then stick it back in its spot in the quiver. I step under the spray and unzip my wetsuit, peeling my arms out of it and letting it hang down my legs.

Vee watches me scrub the worst of the sand off my chest and abs, her tongue flicking out to dampen her bottom lip. I watch the movement, my scrubbing slowing. When I reach up to rake my wet hair out of my face, she follows the movement with hungry eyes. She likes this.

"What do you want, Vee?" I ask her again.

"What?" She rips her focus away from my abs.

"For breakfast," I gently remind her.

"Oh." Her cheeks turn pinker.

I zip the wetsuit all the way down and peel myself out of it, letting the shower rinse the sand off my legs.

"Jesus," she mutters under her breath, glancing around. "Aren't you worried someone will see you?" Vee stares pointedly at my dick, her blush a darker shade of pink.

She sees me naked all the time. Why is she blushing? "No. There's a fence."

Her eyes dart to the houses on either side of mine. "Yeah, but they could see you from up on the dune or from their balconies."

I follow her line of sight to the bedroom balconies of my neighbors. "Huh. I didn't think of that." I shrug. "They've never complained."

"Are they women?" she asks.

"They are!" The neighbor in the peach house is a retiree with a tight white perm and big purple-rimmed glasses. She always smiles when she tells me how much she loves bird-watching. The one in the blue house is younger and divorced, but she's almost never home. I think she works for the movie studios as an artist because sometimes she asks me to come over and model for her so she can sketch me. "How'd you know?"

"Lucky guess." Vee braves the spray and puts her hands on my wet body, turning me around and pointing me toward the sliding glass door. "Get inside."

"Yes, Ma'am." I pick up my wet suit and hang it on a peg to dry, then go inside and shiver from the blast of air conditioning on my damp skin. I really need to remember to put a towel by the door.

Vee follows me inside without showering the worst of the sand off first, but it's fine. I need to sweep and mop anyway since I ran in so quickly earlier and tracked sand throughout the house.

Anthony and Brendan are still in bed, and they've gravitated to one another in their sleep. They're complete opposites, but they look good together. Brendan is big and clean cut, his hair graying at the temples. Anthony is lean and tattooed, his face unlined and young.

Vee passes me, looks at them for a bit before smiling and shaking her head, and then she walks into the bathroom. A moment later, the shower starts. I hesitate, unsure if I should follow her or if she wants her space. She still never told me what she wants to eat.

From the pile of dirty laundry in the corner, I grab a towel that's mostly clean and dry off, then pull on a pair of pajama pants. I sit on the edge of the bed and put a hand on Anthony's shoulder to shake him awake.

"Anthony."

"Hmmpf." He rolls onto his stomach and buries his face in the pillow.

"Anthony," I repeat, a little louder. Sometimes it takes a few tries.

"Ergh."

"What's wrong?" Brendan asks, rolling onto his side. He glances around the nest, then looks at the bathroom. "Her heat broke?"

"Yeah," I say. "She didn't tell me what she wants to eat. Should I give her more omega water?"

"Waffles or pancakes," Brendan answers, pushing the covers aside and sliding from the bed. He stands, and a joint pops. Wincing, he stretches his arms above his head and pops another. "She needs carbs."

Carbs. Crap. The one thing I don't keep on hand. "I don't have either. Should we run to the store?" I glance at the bathroom door and try to remember how long she's been in there. Girls take a while, right?

"You have fruit?" Brendan asks. He dresses in his gray sweatpants, then claps a hand on my shoulder. "Let's start there."

"Fruit. Right. I have fruit. I make smoothies. What kind of fruit?" Most of my smoothie fruit is frozen, but I think I have a few bananas left and those are fresh.

He squeezes my shoulder. "Let's see what you've got to work with."

Chapter Twenty-Six

VERONICA

My phone is charged, and I wonder which one of them plopped it on a charger when I was out of my mind from my heat. The thoughtful gesture makes me feel things I can't describe. It's… nice.

And it's not only about waking up blissfully well fucked and satisfied. It's also about being coddled and pampered. When I insisted I was fine to eat at the table, they bundled me onto the plush sofa instead. Brendan tosses a cozy comforter around me, then Jamie brings me food and lots of fluids to rehydrate. Anthony sits down beside me, his fingers untangling my hair. He plays with it while I drink my smoothie.

It's pleasant. Domestic. Completely foreign.

I'm used to waking up sore between the legs, crusty, in desperate need of a shower, and parched like I'd spent a year in the desert. But this time, I'm good. Fantastic. Still sore, but pleasantly so.

My eyes don't feel bruised from a restless sleep. I'm still tired from post-heat, but not exhausted. I'm not wrung out and depleted with a thousand things to rush to catch up on. I can sit here and drink my smoothie and simply exist.

When I finish my smoothie and the straw sucks air more than liquid, Anthony pries it from my hands and settles it on the coffee table, then he pulls me against his chest so he can play with the other side of my hair. His fingers rake, gently detangling any snarl he meets until they card freely. My eyes drift shut in contentment.

This is nice, but I should really get up. Get dressed. Get back to work. This has been an enjoyable couple of days, but now it's time to get back to work.

I tell myself all of this, but my limbs won't listen. My feet tuck up beside me instead and my eyes slide closed. His fingers untangle the last knot in my hair and massage my scalp. I sigh, releasing the last bit of tension from my body.

"We should get back to work," I mumble against Anthony's chest. My limbs are so heavy. Like they'd require way too much energy to move. It's easier to stay cuddled against him under this blanket and take a nap.

"Or, and hear me out, we play hooky today. Nobody knows your heat broke. Take one more day off with us. You've more than earned it. When was the last time you had a day for yourself?" Anthony doesn't wait for my answer. "Besides, Rut's still closed. There's nothing for you to do anyway."

"It is?" Tension bleeds all of my satisfaction and laziness out of me. "Fuck, I need to check on the repairs." It shouldn't have taken this long to get a window fixed and some glass swept up. I probably have ten emails from the insurance company sitting in my inbox.

"Darlene's niece is a painter," Anthony says, confusing me with the sudden switch in topics. "She's hand-lettering the new window. It'll be done tomorrow. Dan ordered new stools and chairs to replace the ones that were broken. Everyone already cleaned everything up and restocked the bar. Relax, Vee. It'll be as good as new when you get back." His hand drifts down to my shoulder and tightens as he keeps me from getting up.

His tight grip on me should make me anxious—I hate being held down—but the panic never comes. I feel secure, not smothered. My scalp tugs as he goes back to playing with my hair. "You have a team full of people who love Rut, who love *you*, so let them help. Take a day off. You can go back to being the boss tomorrow."

I should get up on principle alone. I've never enjoyed being told what to do. Years of being told I was too young, too female, too omega to run a business—especially a business like Rut—has made me obstinate. When I'm told I can't do something, I'll do the opposite to prove them all wrong. Instead, I sink deeper into Anthony's grip.

I'm exhausted. I've been running on fumes for far too long, and all it took was one good heat full of pampering to make me realize how depleted I've been for a while now. And he's right. We have a good team of people at Rut. Sure, there are a few who are only in it for a short time for the money and then they move onto something else, but the core group is dedicated. They believe in what we're doing. I can trust them.

What's one day?

Besides, some omegas have heats that last a week. At three days, mine is shorter than average. One more day won't make a difference. And Brendan can't audit me if he's here helping clean the splattered smoothie off the kitchen ceiling from when Jamie forgot to put the lid on before blending.

"Fine," I sigh. "But we're going in early tomorrow. We'll have to do inventory, and I'm sure the insurance company has more forms for me to fill out."

"Deal."

I should probably be concerned that I've made a deal with a devil, but the way Anthony's fingers knead the back of my neck makes my eyes slide shut. If this heat was a dream, it's one I don't want to wake up from.

By the time he's done massaging my shoulders, my limbs are boneless and I've collapsed in a puddle on the couch. My phone alarm goes off in the bedroom, but before I can get up, he puts a hand on my thigh and squeezes, then goes to get it.

He comes back with my birth control packet and a bottle of water, but when I reach for them, he holds them out of my reach. "Uh-uh. Open for Daddy."

It's easier to comply than fight. Resisting Anthony when he's set his mind to something is like arguing with a brick wall. I give him an unamused look, ignoring his smirk, but let my mouth fall open. Anthony pops a pill out of the foil and holds it out to me, his eyes locking on my mouth as he places the pill on my tongue. The sweet coating that masks the underlying bitter medicine dissolves as soon as it touches. He uncaps the water and feeds that to me too, instead of letting me do it myself.

"Swallow."

I gulp down half the bottle. Somehow, after drinking everything liquid they've thrown at me, I'm still thirsty.

"Good girl," he says once I've swallowed it down.

My belly squirms at the praise. I hate that I like it so much. I hate being needy. It makes it too hard when they leave. And they always leave. They always want more from me than I can give them. More time, more attention, more omega-ness. I'm a terrible omega. I'm married to my job, I'm bossy, and I don't have any plans of popping out babies anytime soon.

His knees bump into mine as he stands between my legs. The fingers at my nape squeeze as he tilts my head back and leans down, claiming my mouth in a gentle kiss.

His hand tightens, creating a dull ache at the back of my head, and my mouth softens with surprise. He wastes no time slipping his tongue inside, as if he's making sure I did what I was told rather than self-sabotaging for the sake of being defiant. As if I'd fuck with my birth control. *No thanks.*

Anthony ends the kiss with a nip of my lower lip that makes me squeak and my pussy clamp down on nothing. Soreness radiates from my pelvis as I take a deep breath and groan. He chuckles, his fist releasing my hair so he can palm the nape of my neck instead. His thumb strokes along the corner of my jaw. A meager bit of slick dampens my fresh panties and makes them stick to me.

"You good, baby?" Anthony rakes a hand through his tousled hair and grins at me, as if he knows my traitorously horny omega pussy wants to boot and rally for another round. As if I didn't spend the last three days getting dicked down and knotted.

I'd squeeze my thighs together to stem those thoughts, except he's still standing between them. "My pussy is closed for business. Maybe permanently. It's like someone rammed a car between my legs." Muscles I didn't know I had are sore.

"That's not what I asked, baby. I asked if you were good. I know your pussy's feeling well taken care of right now. But what about the rest of you? How are *you*?"

"I…" I've never had a heat hookup ask before. And most alphas cut and run after the heat's over. Usually, once the pheromone levels drop, they can't get out of my place fast enough. They certainly don't stick around to make me smoothies or knead tense muscles or finger comb my hair. "I'm good."

"Only good?" Anthony sucks his teeth, his expression thoughtful.

Jamie pads into the room, holding up a white plastic bag from the grocery store. "Who wants pancakes?"

My stomach rumbles at the thought, and the rest of me is glad for the interruption too. "Me. I'm starving." The smoothie helped, but it won't tide me over for long. I have three days' worth of calories to eat my way through.

Anthony pulls me off the couch, his hand never straying far as it dips to the small of my back. It's like he doesn't want to let me out of his reach. As if he thinks I'll disappear the moment he steps away.

The clinginess should bother me. I'm not used to it. But I don't mind. Not even when he takes the seat next to me and reaches over, dragging my chair closer so he can cut up pancakes and feed them to me. The fork twirls slowly so syrup doesn't drip everywhere.

"I can feed myself now, you know," I tell him, frustrated that he won't let me take the fork. It's not like I'm in heat and clumsy or unfocused anymore.

"Where's the fun in that?" he asks. "Open. Jamie and I made these coconut cream pancakes especially for you and I want you to eat all of them."

When a drop of syrup lands on my chin, Anthony gathers it up with his thumb and sucks it into his mouth. "Every. Single. Bite. You'll feel better once you're fed properly."

I hate to admit it, but he's right. By the time I'm finished with the plate, I'm refreshed. The magic of carbs for hangovers and post heat is inexplicable.

The sweet, creamy coconut flavor sticks to my tongue for hours after. I end up craving them all day.

"ARE YOU SURE THIS IS OKAY?" BRENDAN ASKS AS JAMIE stacks wood together in a pit he dug out of the sand with his hands. "We won't get in trouble with the fire department?"

"We're above the high tide line, so this part of the beach is still my property." Jamie piles the split logs together, then stuffs twists of newspaper into the cracks. When he's done, he wipes the sand from his hands and pats down his pants. "Oh, I forgot the lighter in the house."

"Here." Anthony fishes his lighter from his low-slung jeans and hands it over.

Jamie takes it, saying thanks, then leans forward on his knees and flicks the silver wheel until it catches on the third try. He touches the flame to a newspaper twist and we all watch patiently as one of the smaller logs catches.

After a few minutes, the fire grows. I tuck my windblown hair behind my ear and inch my toes closer to the bonfire's heat. Despite being summer, the beach is cold at night. I borrowed one of Jamie's warm oversized hoodies, but the cold sand is chilly against my ass.

Anthony sits down beside me and pulls out a new pack of cigarettes, smacking the bottom against his palm before unwrapping it and shoving the trash into his pocket. He pulls a cigarette free and lights it, or tries to. The wind makes it a struggle.

I cup my palms together and he leans over, using them as a shield until he finally gets his cigarette to light. He sucks in a drag and holds it, then lets out his breath with a puff of smoke, angling his head away from me so the wind doesn't blow it in my face.

"Thanks, baby," he says, his voice deep and rough from the smoke.

My stomach squirms, and I hate how much I love pleasing him. I'm unsettled by how much I enjoy it. What are they doing to me? This isn't me. I'm not submissive. I'm not the omega who happily follows orders or does cute things like helping her boyfriend light his cigarette when it's windy.

Wait… Boyfriend?

I swallow past the lump in my throat and hide my unease at the intrusive thought with brattiness. "I was tired of watching you struggle."

"Hmm. Do you need more attention, baby?" Anthony asks. He flicks ash off the red end of his cigarette. "We were gonna have ourselves a nice, quiet night on the beach with wine and conversation. I thought you'd like to get to know Brendan more before we go back to Rut tomorrow, but if your needy pussy wants a pounding in the sand, then ass up, baby girl. We'll be happy to oblige. I'll spank that bratty bottom while I'm at it."

Anthony grabs the open bottle of wine from its well in the cool sand and puts the lip to his mouth, slinging it back. I watch his throat bob as he swallows, the firelight flickering dark shadows across his face. The dark scruff of hair on his jaw and the way his hair hangs over his eyes lend him a dangerous air.

He'd do it too. I don't know if he has an exhibitionist kink or if it's a healthy disregard for the law, but I believe him when he says he'd fuck me into the ground regardless of who might walk by and see. My clit throbs, throwing in its two cents that it doesn't quite hate that idea. I ignore it because I hit my sex quota for the month with three days of being spit roasted by these three men.

"I'd rather not get arrested for public indecency, thanks," I tell him as I pry the wine bottle from his grip and bring the lip to my mouth. I take a smaller drink than he did, then pass it on to Jamie.

"You wouldn't," Jamie says between sips. "We've done it and we got caught once and nothing happened. Anthony's family is connected."

I frown and glance between them. "What does *that* mean?"

Anthony's silent as he smokes, his focus on his cigarette. He flicks it, knocking a bit of ash free to flutter down over the crackling fire.

"Oh, uh… I'm not sure, actually." Jamie scratches his head. "That's what the officer said when he let us go and apologized for the misunderstanding."

"You don't know?" Brendan asks. All of our attention swivels to him, and his shoulders square from the extra scrutiny.

"You do?" I ask, one brow raised. We met Brendan a little more than a week ago. How does he know more about my bartender, who I've known for years, than me?

"I'm sure Anthony would rather be the one to explain it," Brendan says.

Anthony sighs and takes a deep drag, then flicks the butt of his cigarette into the fire. "My extended family is well connected."

"Connected how?" I ask, still not understanding.

"The unsavory way. The kind I don't get too involved in. The family business wasn't for me, not after my dad died when I was eight and his death left my mom to raise five kids alone on one salary. I didn't want to end up in prison or dead by forty. The cops know my family name, but they don't know I'm not in the family business and I'm not exactly going to volunteer that information when it gets me out of speeding tickets."

"They're mafia," I say, putting two and two together. His Italian ancestry. His uncle Tony. The fact that he's worked for me for years and he's never talked about them once before.

Anthony shrugs. "Like I said, I'm not really involved, but I have a lot of uncles and cousins. I saw how hard it was on my mom for my father to be in the family business. The long out-of-town trips. The two a.m. phone calls. Coming home bleed-ing. The drinking to deal with it all. The prison stints some of my uncles and cousins have done. That wasn't the sort of life I wanted."

I tug the too-long sleeves down to cover my hands and wrap my arms around my legs, then lean against his side. He's tense for a minute until he shifts and his arm comes around my shoulders, hugging me closer. The fire snaps and pops from a log breaking. Smoke and embers fly up with a whoosh.

"We're not responsible for what our families do," I say, thinking about my own family. The bottle slowly makes its way back around and I drain the last of it, running my thumbnail along the edge where the label is peeling off the glass. "You're not your dad."

"Thanks, baby." He sighs, his fingers squeezing me as if he's scared I'll get up and walk away although that's the furthest thing from my mind right now. There's nowhere I'd rather be.

"It's hard to talk about him, you know?" Anthony says. "I loved him and I miss him, but… I'm also glad he's gone. He put my mom through hell. Sometimes I'd hear them fighting in the night. My mom started drinking a lot when she found out about his mistress. That's how it is for them, you know? Live hard and party harder because you never know when there's a bullet with your name on it."

I dig my nail into the adhesive label and scratch, lost in thoughts I've never been able to outrun. "It's not easy. You never stop loving them, no matter how shitty they are."

"Sounds like you know that from experience," Anthony says. It's a statement, not a question. But the question is there. He wants to know more, but he's not pushing. He respects the boundary I set when we were playing truth or dare.

We sit like that, nobody saying anything, for a while. Only the sound of the waves breaking on the surf and the bonfire surrounding us. Here, on this empty, dark beach, it's easy to pretend that we're the only ones in the world right now.

A lump of emotion and swallowed words lodge in my throat and I almost stop there, but the words want to be said. I'm tired of carrying so much emotional baggage with me all the time. If these men want me, really want me and not just the omega side of me, then they need to know me. They can't do that if I keep them at arm's reach.

Speaking up is scary, though. It takes me a moment to gather the courage and find the words. I stop and start three times, but none of them rush me. Instead, they wait.

"When I was a kid, my mom got sick. Ovarian cancer. It was so fast… It's not like she was sick for long before they finally figured it out. A few weeks of abdominal pain and no appetite and a general sense that something was very wrong. The doctors kept telling her she was fine. It was anxiety. She was in her late forties and fit and healthy. Then she started having issues with her cycle. She was bleeding, and we had to buy the pads and special underwear that betas use. They said it could be the start of early menopause, because she only had one kid and she had me later in life. Omegas have a higher risk for cancer if they don't have a lot of kids or if they wait too long, did you know that? It's fucked up is what it is. As if we're only good for breeding and if we don't do that, then we get sick like it's some sort of cosmic punishment."

I scoff and take a minute before continuing. "When she finally got diagnosed, it had already spread. She had surgery and did chemo, but within a year she was gone. I was eight. My dad couldn't handle losing her. He tried, but… he didn't know how to be an alpha without his omega and they'd never found any other packmates, I guess. If he'd had more support, he'd still be here. He hanged himself. A social worker picked me up from school and then my grandparents came down from their place in the mountains and took me home with them the next day."

Talking about my grandparents brings up bittersweet memories. I was angry and confused, but they were patient. Things settled, and then it was good for a while, though my whole life had been turned upside down. New guardians, new school, new house, new friends. But my grandpa taught me how to gut worms on the fishing hook and my grandma taught me how to make pie crust from scratch. They fed me, clothed me, loved me, and made everything seem like it was going to be okay.

And it was. Until it wasn't.

"They were old," I continue. "My grandparents were betas, and they didn't think they could have kids until they had my dad by accident and he'd had me later in life. My grandma got Alzheimer's and had to go live in a special home, so then it was me and grandpa for a bit. She got pneumonia that winter and passed. He died a month after her, same as my parents. His body just... gave out without her to keep him there. I was fourteen by then." The strangeness of being orphaned not only once, but twice, isn't lost on me.

"What happened after they died?" Jamie asks, his voice soft.

"My parent's life insurance had been put into a trust for me. My mom's brother took me in for a while. He lives in LA with his partner. But they went away a lot on business trips. I told them I was old enough to stay home alone as long as they left me money for pizza and food. I went wild with no adults around to supervise me. I was fourteen and angry. I started getting into trouble. Partying with older kids. Not doing homework. Failing tests. Skipping school and getting into fights."

"I bet you were a spitfire," Anthony says, chuckling. "I wish I'd known you then. We could have been bad together. I used to skip my afternoon classes to smoke behind the dumpsters or hang out with the other kids. We liked to ditch after lunch to hang out in the woods behind the school. Took them forever to put up a fence, not that it stopped us from hopping it."

The image of a young, less tattooed Anthony hopping a fence to smoke and shoot the shit in the woods behind his high school makes me smile. If I'd known him when we were teenagers, we would have absolutely gotten into the worst kind of trouble together.

"There was this asshole named Kurt who sat behind me in my homeroom class," I tell them. "He'd tease me every single day. The sort of elementary school bullshit that a ninth grader should have left behind a long time ago. I don't remember what it was he said, but one day I'd had enough. I was walking to first period, and he was behind me and bothering me again. In the middle of the crowded hallway, I turned around and backhanded him. You should have seen his face. He was so shocked. Like he'd thought he could do whatever he wanted to me and because I was a girl and an omega, I'd take it."

I draw shapes in the sand as I think of the day that changed everything. "I wish I'd waited until we were alone and there weren't any witnesses because somebody told on me. When the office yanked me out of second period and called my uncle, they couldn't get a hold of him. He was in Tokyo closing some big merger. I'd been alone for two weeks at that point. That's when they put me in foster care."

My bittersweet reminiscence fades, leaving me feeling nothing at all. There was nothing sweet about foster care. The overcrowded three-bedroom house, the couple who treated us like breathing paychecks and got annoyed whenever we were too loud or hungry or needed anything at all. Having to throw all of your clothes in a trash bag when it was time to move. They don't give you a suitcase. Only a thin, white plastic trash bag that you can't stuff too full or it'll break and spill all of your clothes in the dirty street. We were the kids who didn't fit anywhere. The ones nobody wanted.

"Foster care was horrible." There are no words to adequately describe it. If I wasn't dodging the leers and wandering hands of my foster mother's current boyfriend of the month, I was avoiding the other kids. Nobody adopts teenagers. Unless your parent gets out of prison or sobers up and comes to get you, you're aging out of the program.

"Being a teenage girl in foster care was hard enough, but being an omega too? Being an omega in foster care was hell. Alphas think you're fair game." More than one alpha thought he could get me alone and take whatever he wanted. Pin me down. Make me too scared to scream. They quickly learned that my elbows are sharp and I'm not afraid to knee them in the groin and run. I'm small but fast.

"Names," Anthony growls.

"Hmm?" I ask, distracted by all of my dark memories and bitter thoughts.

"Give me a list of names. I have connections, remember? I want the names of everyone who ever hurt you."

I twist my neck to look up at him, my chin perched on his shoulder. He's deadly serious. Anthony scowls at the fire as if it's personally offended him. The sight makes me smile. "Are you going to kill my enemies for me?"

The idea shouldn't amuse me. Shouldn't make me smile. Make my stomach flutter. But it does. And I decide at that moment that I refuse to feel guilty for it. Stretching, I press a kiss to his cheek and enjoy the way he squeezes me tighter to keep me from pulling away.

"The next alpha who hurts you is going to get a lot more than a broken face," he promises darkly.

"What makes you think I didn't already handle it?" I ask, teasing him. "I've found that alphas are a lot less interested in sticking their cock in you after you stick a taser in their balls."

Anthony palms the back of my head and shifts in the sand, pulling me into his lap until I'm cradled against him with my head tucked under his chin. His arms are comforting instead of caging. A tightness in my chest eases.

"My little spitfire," he murmurs against my hair, his breath fanning the baby hairs along my forehead. "I love how strong you are. So fucking tough. I'll throw your bleeding enemies at your feet so you can stomp them into the dirt."

I grin, my face pressed to his chest. His heartbeat is slow and steady under my ear. "Fine, but I'm keeping the taser."

Anthony huffs out a laugh. "I don't know how you got your hands on one. They're illegal here."

"You're not the only one with connections."

"You can tase them first, then crush their balls with your stilettos," Anthony continues.

"I want to hear how the story ends," Jamie says.

"Me too," Brendan adds. "What happened after you got out of foster care?"

"I was lucky. I realized that if I kept doing what had put me in the system, it wouldn't take me long to end up on the streets where I'd get grabbed up by some alphahole. I was always good at school. I just didn't care to try hard after my grandparents died.

"Well, now I had a reason to care because I was getting out soon and I would not end up homeless and pregnant and turning to sex work or drugs to survive. So that's what I did. I turned my grades around and put in the work. When I turned eighteen, I finally got access to my trust. It was enough for me to go to college with the scholarships they give us for aging out of the system. I could get my own place so long as I worked part time while going to school.

"After I graduated, I still didn't know what I wanted to do with my life. I worked different jobs, not staying in any place for very long, and finally moved away from student housing. I got a job as a receptionist in an office. One day, some of the girls got together for a coworker's birthday. We barhopped and ended the evening in some gross rut bar. I was standing in the middle of the tiny dance floor of that bar, getting hit on by creepy alphas who wouldn't stop rubbing against me and growling, and I thought to myself, *I wish omegas had somewhere safe to go to party.*

"And that's when it hit me. The idea for Rut. A haven for omegas to let their hair down and have the same fun that alphas have. Somewhere designed especially for us. There are thousands of strip clubs and scent bars for alphas. As if omegas aren't equally as horny."

I roll my eyes at the thought. A completely untapped market. One that's made me millions with no signs of stopping. Our gross rises every year. And once I open up a second location? There won't be any stopping us.

"Yeah, they are," Anthony agrees with me. He jostles me on his lap. "Horny cum sluts that need a good dicking down."

Irritated with him, I grab whatever I can reach and pinch him through his shirt. I think I got armpit skin.

"Ouch! Get your pinchy little claws away from me, kitten!" Anthony shrugs my grip off him. "I'm not into the rough stuff like Jamie."

"Hey!" Jamie protests while Brendan chuckles. "I don't like pinching." Jamie is silent for a moment. "I don't *think* I like pinching."

"How will you know if you don't try it?" Anthony asks him, feigning sincerity.

Jamie frowns, as if he's really considering it.

"Don't listen to him, Jamie," Brendan says. "Don't let him talk you into doing something you don't like."

"I'd never do anything to him he wouldn't thoroughly enjoy," Anthony says. "You too, Vee. You can't deny it. We took good care of you and your sweet little pussy, didn't we?"

They did, and I'm not thinking only about the sex. They kept me hydrated and clean. Calmed me. Made sure I took my birth control. Kept in touch with Rut and the staff and made sure the repairs were being done right. For the first time in years, I've been able to take a break without all the balls I've been juggling crashing down around me.

"You did," I admit, stroking him through his shirt as I watch the fire flicker. Another log collapses as it's consumed. Beyond it, Jamie and Brendan study me. "Thank you for taking good care of me during my heat." Jamie smiles, and Brendan nods, looking thoughtful.

"We need more wine," Anthony announces, rising suddenly and taking me with him.

I let out a brief shriek at going from sitting to being lifted so abruptly. Anthony cradles me in his arms in a bridal carry and walks around the fire. "Your turn. Watch out for her pinchy fingers. She has the grip strength of a gorilla." Then he bends, depositing me into Brendan's lap.

Anthony taps Jamie on the shoulder. "Help me carry everything?"

The comforting scent of fresh baked bread envelops me. Brendan's grip is more gentlemanly, his hands not wandering so much. Jamie stands and brushes sand off his backside and follows Anthony up the beach to the house. Then Brendan and I are alone. It's the first time we've been alone in days. Now that his cock's been inside me, it's a bit more awkward than it was before when I was only lusting after his scent.

His thumb strokes over my knee. *My knee. Shit.* "Am I

hurting you?" I ask him. "I can get off your lap if I'm too heavy."

"Not at all," Brendan says. "You're not hurting my knee." His voice is deep, but gentle. Soothing. There's a confident air about him that sets me at ease.

"Good," I say, giving him a small smile.

"I like having you in my arms. It feels right. Like I could get used to this."

He's right, and I sense it too. I always thought that *when you find them, you'll know* stuff was nonsense, but there might be something to all those movies and romance novels after all. It's cheesy to put it down to fate, but chemistry… Scent matches. Opposites attract. Those things I understand.

Brendan's energy is quiet and calm. Like the heavy comforter you wrap yourself in when there's a nip in the air and you're comfy on your sofa. He's not loud, vibrant parties or ocean dips at six in the morning. He's coming home to your own bed after traveling. A cozy nest. Home.

Despite his calm vibes and soothing scent, nerves make my pulse jump. I'm not good at being vulnerable, and I've stripped myself raw tonight. All I can do is hope that letting them in won't be a mistake. I've been burned before. "I think I could get used to it too."

But I'm not ready to tie myself to a relative stranger. We have a lot of getting to know one another to do. Anthony and Jamie have an advantage. I've known them for years. Brendan is the wild card I never could have seen coming.

And packs are a whole different ball game. One that I don't think any of us are truly prepared for. Unless…"I don't really know much about packing up. Have you ever been involved with one before?" I ask him.

"No. I didn't think one would ever want me, to be honest. Not after I injured my knee. Some days are worse than others, and I can always tell when it's going to rain. Maybe if I had a more attractive scent…"

He sighs and his arms tighten around me. "I fooled around in college, but nothing that stuck. Most people don't want to settle down into partnerships or packs until they're in their mid or late twenties at the earliest. They want rut bars and Heat Buddy matches, not matings. So I focused on work. Then when I hit thirty and I was still mostly single, I did the usual rounds that single alphas do. Matching centers, heat clinics, and all the dating apps. I tried a few scent bars too. I had one long-term relationship over the years. She was a beta and we had a scent match. Or at least I did. Her name was Jenna."

"What happened?" I ask.

"She was a beta working as an admin assistant for a tech startup and she thought her boss was a better match for her. I'd known things were off and not great for a while. A year in, I bought a ring, but I could never seem to find the perfect time to give it to her. She started working late. Going on business trips with him. She got weird about her phone, never leaving it anywhere, not even when she was showering and it needed to charge."

Oh, no. I know where this is going.

"I found out about their affair one night," he says. "She forgot to lock her computer. All of their messages were in the texting app linked to her phone."

"Fuck, that's awful." I set my hand on his chest. I've never been cheated on. I've never been with someone long enough to get to where exclusivity is expected. I can't imagine how that sort of betrayal hits. "I'm sorry."

"She was right," he says, surprising me. "He was a better match for her than I was. They've been married for years and they have two kids now. She was probably always going to be better off with another beta, anyway. A lot of betas like the fantasy of dating an alpha better than the reality of it. Ruts are all fun and games until the chafing starts."

My laugh turns into a snort. He's right. I can't imagine dealing with an alpha in rut without the benefit of slick and heat delirium. "Well, her loss is my gain."

"And mine." He grins, the movement making a dimple appear in his cheek. It makes him look younger than he is. He's late thirties or early forties, I'd guess. There's a bit of gray at his temples. I slide my hand up to his face and let my thumb dip into that dimple. Rough beard stubble scratches my hand. No wonder my inner thighs are chafed red.

"I'd like to court you, Veronica," Brendan says.

I arch one brow. "I thought that's what we were already doing."

"That was a start, but I want to do things properly. I want to do this right. I'm going to get you a courting gift that's perfect. Something you need. Something nobody's ever given you before. A present you don't know you want yet."

"That's a tall order." Especially considering that he doesn't know me that well yet. "What's the timeline of this mysterious perfect courting gift?"

"Oh, don't worry." He grins, and another dimple forms on the other side of his smile. I get a glimpse of the heartbreaker he was when he was a young alpha coming out of his first rut. "I already have an idea or two. I'll deliver it by your next heat. It'll be perfect, or you can send me packing."

His confidence is attractive, and I have to remind my pussy that we've hit our sex quota for the month. What the fuck are these three men doing to me? And why the hell do I like it so damn much?

Chapter Twenty-Seven

BRENDAN

"Got everything?" Anthony asks the next morning while he tosses my duffel bag into the back of the van.

"I think so." Mentally, I run through a list of everything I brought. I've got my dirty laundry in a plastic bag. I only brought one pair of shoes. I barely had time to unpack my toiletries, so all of that's still in its special bag. But something is nagging at me. I've definitely forgotten something, but I don't remember what it is.

Well, whatever it is, they can always bring it to me at Rut tomorrow.

"Okay, let's go," Anthony orders. He backs the van out of the garage and puts sunglasses on.

"Wait!" I yell, finally remembering what's been bothering me.

Anthony slams on the brake and the old van jerks to a stop.

"I left my medication in the kitchen. I'll just be a minute." I unlock my door and get out, then close it and run back inside through the still open garage.

Jamie and Veronica are still at the kitchen table, but they're not where we left them. She's sitting on the glass table, her borrowed shirt shoved up her belly while Jamie kneels between her spread thighs and laps at her pussy. Her hand fists in his long blond hair while she grinds herself against his face.

I stand there and watch, unable to look away. Veronica stares me down as she rides his face and comes, her mouth dropping open with her whimpers and moans. She's beautiful.

Jamie surfaces for air and turns to see what's distracting her. He raises a hand to wipe her fluids from his mouth and chin and licks his fingers clean. "Did you change your mind about going home?"

His question spurs me into motion while I study the lined up bottles of pills and vitamins on the counter and pull mine from the row. "No, I forgot my meds." I meet Veronica's gaze and hold it. "I'll see you tomorrow."

"See you tomorrow."

Before I'm tempted to say *fuck it* and spend the night again, then end up with absolutely nothing to wear when I go back to work tomorrow. Will anyone at Rut notice or care? Hesitating, I deliberate in my head before deciding to do the adult thing. I shove the pill bottle into my pocket and force my feet to walk through the garage.

Veronica follows and stops me at the van door before I can grab the handle.

"Did you need somet—" I start to ask.

In the driveway, she grabs my face and pulls me down for a kiss that steals the rest of my sentence and leaves my head spinning. I kiss her back, wrapping my arms around her waist, and then I lift her so I can get a deeper angle. She's tiny, and this is a good day for my knee, so it's doable.

Her tongue slides against mine like she's invading my mouth. Conquering it. And I'm happy to let her because she's so perfect in my arms.

When my cock strains against my pants, a damp spot darkening the gray sweats material, I realize that I have to let her go unless I want to carry her inside and fuck her instead.

Setting her down is the hardest decision I've ever had to make. But one of us has to be the responsible adult here. Otherwise we'll all end up fucking all day and then it'll be two in the morning and far too late for them to drive me home. All of my clothes smell like sex and pheromones. It's not an unpleasant scent at all. The heady blend of Jamie, Anthony, and Veronica is unlike anything I've ever smelled before. But it's not a combination I want to broadcast to the entire world.

It's our little secret. For now, anyway.

I set Veronica on her feet and break the kiss. Part of me still can't accept this is real. That this isn't the best dream I've ever had, and tomorrow I'll wake up and go back to my quiet, boring life. The concept is unfathomable. My entire life is now separated into before and after Veronica.

"I'm really glad you came," she says, her voice breathy and her expression unguarded. She looks younger, more vulnerable, and I'm happy she's letting us in. I love her strength and confidence, but she doesn't need to be alone to be strong. Not when we're all happy to be there and support her.

"Me too." My heart beats faster. *Should I ask what we all want to know?* I'm not sure that I have the right to speak for all of us. I joined them last. But with Veronica, if we give her an inch of space, she'll talk herself out of a good thing.

Before I lose my nerve, I ask what we all want to know. "You never really answered me last night. Can we officially court you, Veronica?"

Her eyes widen. "I…" She takes a deep breath, then drops her eyes. "I wasn't sure if you'd still want to after this was… you know… over."

I give her waist a squeeze. "I'm all in."

She nibbles on her lower lip, still not meeting my eyes.

"You hardly know me. This was all so sudden. I can be a real bitch sometimes."

I shrug. "I'm really difficult to ruffle. And if you need it, I'm sure Anthony will volunteer to spank you." When she blushes, then shoots me an unamused expression, I can't help but grin. "I like you, Veronica. I like how passionate you are. How much you care about your people. How hard you work. Not only for Rut, but for the other stuff too. The good work you're doing for your dynamic. The community. You can pretend to have a hard shell, but I know your secret."

"My secret?" Her eyebrows rise.

I lay one hand flat against her chest. Find her heartbeat. "You're soft on the inside for the people you care about, and I'd like to be one of them."

"Oh." Her lips round with an exhale.

Drawing up straighter, I pull my hands back to my sides. "You didn't say no, so I'll take that as a yes and start working on your present."

She cocks her head. "What is it?"

"That would ruin the surprise, sweetheart. I have to go," I tell her.

"Do you?"

I close my eyes and pray for self-control. *No. This is the responsible, mature thing to do.* An intrusive thought whispers I could order a set of clothes for same day delivery or borrow something from Jamie and make it fit.

No. As the elder alpha, it's my job to put the pack's needs before my own personal interests.

"I'll see you tomorrow," I tell her. And I'll only think of her for every single minute until then. All—I glance at my watch and quickly do the math—all seven hundred and seventy-four minutes of it. I steal one last kiss to tide me over until then.

A car rolls by, then slows to a stop, its brakes squealing. A woman leans out of the window and slides sunglasses down her nose. "Brendan? I knew that was you. Are you having a beach day too? See, Bill? I was right. It *is* him."

Are you kidding me? This is really shitty timing.

I close my eyes and take a fortifying breath while I wish I had a reset button. If I'd said *fuck it* to my meds, or I hadn't remembered, we'd be heading to the highway. If I'd taken Jamie's offer to stay, I'd be in the house. Instead, I'm standing in Jamie's driveway with a half-mast chub straining my sweatpants and a half-naked Veronica leaning around me to look.

"Are those friends of yours?" Veronica asks.

"Ashley, how are you?" I try to keep from giving her a good view of my half-hard dick. From the way her eyes flick over me, then study Veronica, I'm not sure I'm being all that discreet.

"Good," she answers, a bit hesitant. "We're having a beach day. This is my husband, Bill. You met at the Christmas party. Remember, Bill? Anyway, we're having a beach day and we wanted to see all the cute little houses. Is that a, uh, friend of yours? It's nice to meet you. I'm Ashley. Brendan and I work together."

Veronica gives her a strained but polite smile. "Nice to meet you too."

"I found more pancake mix!" Jamie yells from the open garage door. He holds a yellow plastic jug over his head like a trophy. "But it says it's expired. It was buried in the back of the pantry. Do you think we can still use it?"

Jamie sees us talking to someone and palms the dusty bottle of pancake mix as he walks over. He didn't bother to throw on a shirt before coming outside. But then again, his work uniform is a thong. He's not body shy.

"Oh. H-hello." Ashley's cheeks pinken and she glances quickly at her husband.

Fuck. Ashley might not know who Veronica is aside from being a half dressed woman who was kissing me, but she probably recognizes Jamie. It doesn't help that the handsome alpha's face and rock hard eight-pack abs are plastered all over the city with hundreds of flyers. There's even a billboard along the highway.

"Well… have a nice day! I'll see you tomorrow," Ashley says, then sits back in her seat and rolls her car window up.

Idiotically, I wave while she drives away.

"She works with you," Veronica summarizes.

"Hmm."

"She recognized Jamie. She'll put two and two together."

"Mmhmm."

"Put what together?" Jamie asks.

Veronica puts a hand on my arm and leans into me. "Are you okay?"

"I'll be fine," I insist. But anxiety eats me up inside. *This isn't good.* Ashley is the biggest gossip in the office. She's probably on the phone with someone right now, telling them what she saw.

Fuck.

"Are you sure?" Veronica squints at me.

But this isn't something she needs to worry about. It's not her responsibility. As our omega, it's our job to worry about her. Not the other way around. Whether she's used to it or likes it or not.

"Yes," I say.

She opens her mouth to argue, but I lean down and press a kiss to her lips to silence her.

Veronica breaks it, then huffs and gives me a wry look like she doesn't believe me. "Is this going to mess up my audit?"

"They might assign you a new field agent," I admit. "But your books are solid. You shouldn't be worried even if they do."

She throws her head back and groans dramatically. "It's going to take longer?"

One corner of my mouth curls up. She's so cute. Some of my anxiety takes a back seat, because I realize that she's worth it. No matter what happens. No matter what price I have to pay. I can't regret anything we did. Anthony was right. I would have hated myself forever if I said no and missed out on helping her through this heat. If I'd lost the chance to court her.

"Jamie, throw that old pancake mix out," I order. "I'll order more groceries and have them delivered again. Don't let her tell you she's fine and she can eat whatever she wants. Her stomach's going to be sensitive for a day or two. I'll research recipes to send you."

"I'm standing *right here*," Veronica complains.

I drop a kiss onto the top of her hair, taking a deep whiff of her faint orange scent underneath the bland null wash she showered with. "I'll see you later, sweetheart. Don't ignore the urge to cuddle. You need it more than normal during post-heat. Don't look at me like that, you know I'm right."

"Okay, Dad," she says, rolling her eyes. "You know I've done this before, right?"

I grope behind me for the car's door handle. If I don't get my hands on something solid, I'm liable to reach for her again and then we'll get nothing done. My instincts surge and tell me that's not a bad thing. It wants post-heat cuddles too. But I have a courting gift to plan and damage control to do.

"Mmhmm." I tug the car door open and pull myself inside, shutting the door. I click my seatbelt into place, then roll the vintage window down. It takes forever. "Are you gonna be a good girl and give your body the rest it needs today?"

Her cheeks turn pink. "I can take care of myself, you know. I've been doing it for a long time."

"But you don't have to do it alone anymore," I tell her, giving her permission to be soft. To need people.

Anthony leans over me and jerks his chin toward Jamie. "Jamie needs it too. He's a touchy feely guy, but he won't ask for it."

Veronica gives Jamie an assessing once over, the wheels in her head no doubt turning.

I give Anthony the same look. *That was smooth. Not subtle, but smooth.* And it seems to work.

Jamie scratches the back of his neck and smiles sheepishly. "I like cuddles."

"Fine!" she sighs, giving in now that she's been given an out. If it's for Jamie, then it's not an omega weakness if she does it. It's for her alpha.

"Inside, bedroom, now," she orders the blond alpha.

Waving goodbye, Jamie chucks the expired pancake mix into the trashcan on the side of his house, then goes inside. Veronica follows, and Anthony backs the van out of the driveway. He fiddles with the radio at a stoplight until he settles on an alternative rock station. Once we're on the road and the breeze picks up, I crank the window back up.

"So how fucked are you?" Anthony asks.

I pull my phone out and open up a grocery app that has delivery and start adding things to the cart. "Completely. But it's fine. I'll be all right."

Even if they fire me, I'll be okay. I have savings. A fully vested 401k thanks to how long I've been working there. And the accounting chains are always hiring, or I could branch out on my own. It's work that's easy to do freelance from home. Having a contingency plan or two in place eases the worst of my anxiety.

Once the groceries are purchased, I read through a few omega blogs until I find some post-heat recipes that sound good. They're too complicated for me, but Jamie can probably manage. Anthony says he's good at following directions as long as they're laid out clearly. "They'll get the groceries in about two hours."

Anthony taps his fingers on the wheel and nods. "Sounds good. You're great at this, man. I appreciate it. I wouldn't have thought about the food she needs to eat after it was over."

Absently, I watch the scenery pass. "You got the protein water, and you handled her birth control. Neither Jamie nor I would have been capable of carrying that thought from one rutting to the next."

He chuckles. "Yeah. You guys really turn into knots for brains when a pretty omega's in heat."

I run a finger over the rough stubble along my jaw. I'm in desperate need of a shave. "There's a reason betas rule the world and get everything done."

He merges onto the highway and weaves the old van around a slow sedan. "What are you gonna do for your courting gift?" Anthony asks.

"I have a few ideas. But I'll need to talk to Jamie first. Would he let me tie him up?"

"Probably. We've done it a few times with cuffs and bondage tape. But you'll have to ask him."

I turn in my seat to stare at him. "What about you?"

"Me?" He side-eyes me. "No way, man. I'm not into it like that."

I shake my head. "Good to know, but that's not what I meant. I was asking what you're going to do for your courting gift."

"Oh." He frowns. "I'm not sure yet, but it'll come to me."

"I assume since we spent the heat at Jamie's that his house will be the home base for the pack."

"Yeah, probably," Anthony answers. "Vee and I both have tiny apartments."

"And my house is big enough but it's pretty far from Rut." It's also not beach front property. I'm not sure how Jamie afforded it. How much does exotic dancing pay? Clearly I picked the wrong profession.

I think about all the things we need to accomplish and make a mental to-do list. "At some point we'll need to take her to Nested and get her a proper nest that's big enough for everyone."

Anthony nods. "I've already got an aesthetic board going."

"There's something else we need to talk about," I say, licking my lips and hoping I word this correctly. I've just been invited in and while I don't want to rock the boat, I can't stand by and say nothing either.

"Yeah?"

"I know you've both known her longer and you know her better than me, but dial it back a bit with Veronica."

His grip on the steering wheel tightens, and for a moment I wonder if he's gonna pull over and kick me out of the car. But things can't stay as they are—with Anthony goading Vee at every turn. Getting a reaction out of her. He's young. Probably still in his twenties, which means he's not thinking long-term. Not really. He'll learn, but we don't need the drama till he gets there.

Before he gets defensive, I throw him a bone, "I know you care about her. It's clear that you've been taking care of her a long time. And you've done a great job." As good of a job as she let him, anyway. "You make sure she eats. You protected the bar. Your coworkers like you, and it seems like you do a great job managing the bar."

"Thanks." His voice is tense, but his blanched knuckles regain their color.

"And this isn't me trying to take her away from you or cause problems. That's not what pack does. But it seems to me like you enjoy pushing her buttons to get a reaction out of her, and I'm telling you now that she's not going to think it's amusing forever. Eventually, at some point, it comes across as asshole behavior."

At a red light, he glances at me. His expression is unreadable, his face carefully blank. Knowing who his family is, it'd be easy to get intimidated. To back off and see how it plays out. But I can't do that—not if I'm going to be this pack's alpha. It's my job to protect them, and that includes from themselves.

"You think I don't know what I'm doing?" Anthony asks softly. Dangerously.

I return his stare. I refuse to back down. This is too important. "I realize it got you this far. So maybe you're thinking it needs to keep escalating, to get more and more from her, but that's the way to play this. That's not how healthy long-term relationships work. She needs to trust you."

The light turns green, and the cars behind us honk as he sits there. Slowly, he puts his attention back on the road and resumes driving. "You think she doesn't trust me?"

"I think she has a lot to lose if she's wrong. If she makes a bad decision. You have an apartment and some furniture. Clothes. A car. She's got a business and a charity. People who rely on her for their living."

I turn in my seat to face him. "Do you know how many people she employs? Fifty-seven. If she makes a mistake and Rut fails, that's a lot of people filing for unemployment. Not to mention what it'd do for the charity. She has everything to lose. We need to be taking her burdens off her, not adding to her stress."

He's silent as we merge onto the highway and slip into thicker traffic. "I did what I had to do to get her attention. It's not like I can sit there and let some magical scent make her look at me. I had to work for it. It's not easy being a boring beta in a world designed for a sense I don't have."

I want to say I understand it, but I don't. I can't. He's right. This is why most betas end up together in monogamous pairings. Being an alpha or an omega certainly isn't easy, but I can see why he felt like he had to try so hard to not be invisible.

I clasp him on the shoulder and squeeze before letting him go. "Okay. But you've already got her attention. So now you can focus on making her happy instead. We all can. Playtime is whatever, I'm not trying to kink shame someone, but Veronica's a serious person. She's gonna want to get her work done first and keep work and play separate."

"You're right. I know." He sighs, then cranks his window down. "Mind if I smoke?"

"No." I roll mine down too as he fishes his cigarettes and lighter from his pocket and lights up. He blows the smoke and flicks the ash out the window. I think he enjoys the routine of smoking more than the cigarette itself.

We spend the rest of the drive to my home in silence, but it's comfortable.

Chapter Twenty-Eight

BRENDAN

I WAKE UP THE NEXT DAY TO MY SHRILL ALARM CLOCK GOING off and a voicemail from my manager asking me to come into the office today. There's also a text from Anthony with a photo that shows Veronica and Jamie cuddling while they sleep.

Both sides of my life tug at me like I'm the handkerchief tied to the rope in a game of tug of war.

Fuck. Here we go.

My feet hit the floor, and I'm strangely resolved. I should be nervous as hell. A sweaty mess. But my stomach is hollow and somehow I'm calm. My morning routine passes in a blur of muscle memory. I don't remember the drive in until I blink and I'm there.

I greet everyone like normal, set my briefcase in my office without unpacking it except for my mug. Chatter around the break room stops as I walk in and pour myself coffee. I blow on it to cool it and take my first sip. "Morning." They offer weak, polite conversation, and when I make excuses and bow out, they let me.

My manager's office door is open, and she's working on her

computer. I knock two knuckles against her open door and wait. "Morning. You wanted to talk?"

"Brendan, good morning. Please shut the door and have a seat."

Well, fuck.

A closed door is never a good thing. I do as she says, and sit. "Good morning, Barbara."

Barbara gives me a tight-lipped, polite smile. "Brendan, I wanted to talk to you about an allegation of misconduct that's been made, but first, I'd like to hear what you have to say. What happened?"

That's a trap if I've ever heard one, but what can I do? Lie and deny what happened? Even if I thought it would save my hide, I don't want to. I want the entire world to know that I found my pack—as unconventional as we might be—and we have the brightest, fiercest omega anyone's ever seen.

"I found my scent matched pack," I tell her, my voice calm as I sip my cooled coffee.

"I see." She doesn't look pleased. But then again, she's a beta. Scent stuff and heats and ruts are an annoying hindrance to her as a manager. Nobody says the quiet part out loud, but if corporations could get away with not hiring alphas or omegas, they probably would. "So I take it the allegations are…"

"They're true."

She leans back in her office chair and it squeaks. "When did you discover this connection? Was there a sudden, unplanned *heat*, perhaps?"

She whispers the word heat, like it's dirty. To a beta who's never experienced one, maybe it seems like it is. For the rest of us, it's beautiful. Natural. The stuff of dreams when you find your scent matches.

"I saw the signs from the beginning," I admit.

She gives me an annoyed look, as if she's throwing me lifelines and I'm batting them away. And then she sighs and sits up straight, pulling a disciplinary form from a manilla folder.

"The Omegas and Alphas Protection in the Workforce Act requires that you fill out a declaration within twenty-four hours of discovering a scent match or recovering from a triggered heat or rut that interrupts your professional duties. The OAPWA won't protect you from disciplinary action if you fail to file or notify management in a timely manner.

"Personal involvement brings your entire audit into question," she says. "We'll need to disrupt everyone's assignments and start the audit over from scratch, wasting taxpayer dollars."

I nod. "I understand."

She slides the paper forward, then takes a pen from her cup. "So I want to clarify. Was there an unplanned heat or rut that puts you within twenty-four hours of the law's obligations?"

I could lie and say yes. But I'll have to listen to the office talk about it for months until bigger, juicier gossip-worthy news happens. They'll pull all of my recent audits and question the integrity of my work. There could be an entire investigation. They might want to transfer my desk to another office. One that's farther from Rut.

And I can't bring myself to care. There's no panic. Inside, I'm hollow. This career has become a slow death by a thousand paper cuts.

I fucking hate my job.

I hate scouring through people's lives and livelihoods to find a mistake and fine the shit out of them. It's not the big corporations that get shafted. Not with their fancy ivy-league educated legal teams and accountants. It's the doctors. Tradesmen. Small businesses and family restaurants. The ones who are just trying to make a decent living.

Good people like Veronica, who bring happiness to the world. Yes, the happiness she provides is covered in glitter and body oil, but it's real. I think about her work with her underground omega rescue network. *It's meaningful.*

I don't want to be here in this office. I don't want to do twenty more years of this. The commute. Mind numbing office gossip and small talk. Annoying cubicle mates. Being gone from town for days or weeks. Missed heats and cuddles. I work sixty hours a week during tax season.

She wiggles the pen in the air, as if I need prompting. I lean forward and read the top of the OAPWA declaration form, then shake my head and sit up straight. "I had over twenty-four hours of notice. Do what you have to do."

Barbara sighs and drops the pen with a clatter onto her desk. "I'm sorry to see you go like this. You're one of my best agents."

Where was that attitude when I asked her to not dump Amy's assignments all on me? To let me move desks so I didn't have to sit next to Sharon? I keep these comments to myself. It's pointless to voice them. Management doesn't actually care.

"I'll have security escort you so you can gather your things."

The floor hushes while I'm packing everything I care about into a cardboard box. There isn't much. It barely covers the bottom. I carefully set the framed photo of my family inside, then scan the drawers to make sure I'm not forgetting anything. I leave all the office clutter behind. The stress ball with the cracked IRS logo printed on it, the sticky notes and correction fluid and half-dead pens. I shut the drawer and leave the trash behind.

That's their problem now.

I drain the last of my coffee and set the mug down, then follow the security guard to the door. He holds his hand out and

I give him my badge with the key card. Nobody stops me to say goodbye. I've worked with these people for years. The door swings shut behind me and I suck in a deep breath of fresh air.

And like that, I'm gone. Free. It's a surreal thing. Like the world tilted on its axis and there's a new magnetic north. I wait to feel a sense of loss or grief, but there's nothing. Only a numb sense of *huh*.

What now?

I don't stand there and think about it for long. I go where I want to go. To Rut. To my pack.

I unlock my car and set the box of my things and my briefcase on the passenger seat, and then I drive.

Anthony

WHEN BRENDAN WALKS IN THROUGH THE PROPPED-OPEN BACK door, no jacket or briefcase or company badge clipped to his pocket and the top button of his shirt undone, I can guess what happened. He sees me and nods, and I return it, then jerk my chin to indicate the stool where he should sit.

He pulls it out, the metal legs scraping along the floor, and settles himself. Then he unbuttons his cuffs and rolls up his sleeves. "Anything I can do to help? I have a lot of free time on my hands now."

"Got fired, huh? That sucks. I've been there."

When I was first out on my own and struggling to land on my feet, I bounced from job to job and worked under the table a lot. That sort of employment isn't stable.

I set my juice-covered cutting board on top of the bar and pull some oranges from their netting. I slap a knife down. "Cut those into wedges."

Without bothering to ask him if he wants a drink, I make him one. Everyone deserves a stiff cocktail after getting fired. Grabbing a bottle of wine and the mixers, I catch the popped cork in a bar towel and whip up today's new signature drink. I take an orange from his pile and another knife and cut the rind off as a single curl, then balance it on the rim so it's dipping into the drink. It's a pink masterpiece. I give him a napkin, then set it in front of him.

He's only on his second orange, but each edge has been cut with precision. Every single section is exactly the same size. I frown at his tidy pile and almost say something about how drunk people don't care if their fruit wedges are perfect, then I think better of it. I don't want to kick a man while he's down.

Brendan accepts the drink and takes a sip while I wait for his verdict. "Wow, that's good. It's bubbly, but not too sweet. What's it called?"

"A Pink Slip." *Okay, I guess some good-natured kicking is acceptable. We're pack, after all. Isn't that what families do?* "It's prosecco, pink grapefruit juice, and a dash of red bitters." I grin at him.

He gives me a wry look, then hides his smile behind the lip of his glass while he takes a longer sip.

I lean against the bar top and smirk, enjoying the way his eyes linger over the tattoos on my arms. "You know, my uncle could probably use a tax guy."

He snorts mid-sip, then grimaces, the bridge of his nose wrinkling.

Fuck. It sucks getting bubbly up your nose.

Brendan sets his glass down. "Are you trying to get my

other knee broken? No offense, but I'll probably live longer if I go work at a cubicle in a big box store."

I roll my eyes at his dramatics. "I meant my uncle Tony, the one who owns the restaurant. There's work and then there's *work*, you know? They know how to separate the two." *For the most part.* Although now that I think about it, I suppose it could be a front. *Hmm.*

"Don't worry about me. I'll figure it out," Brendan says, drinking the rest of his drink.

I take his empty glass and wash and sanitize it, then set it upside down to dry. I feel for him because I was the one who made Brendan put his neck on the chopping block, and then the idiot got himself chopped. Talk about bad timing.

Now that I *really* think about it, he's probably right to refuse my tentative job offer. I can't tell if the dude is lucky or unlucky. He matched with us, which makes him lucky, but then the dude got fired for getting laid. Pretty damn unfortunate.

"I have wondered," he says before pausing. "If you don't mind me asking…"

I slap my bar towel over my shoulder and lean on folded forearms. "Shoot."

"How'd you end up working at Rut instead of being forced into the family business?"

He's seen too many gangster movies. I smirk and level him with the panty melter, tipping my chin so the overhead lights catch my eyes just right. I arch one eyebrow. "How do you know I'm not? What if I was lying, so I didn't freak Vee out?"

I can't help but tease him. He's cute when his eyes widen. "I'm kidding. Untwist your panties, fed."

He snorts. "I'm not a fed anymore, remember?"

I grin and stand upright, then focus on wiping down the bar. "My family is an offshoot of the main family. This is California, not New York. Do you get what I'm saying?"

He nods, so I continue, "When I turned twenty-one, they introduced me to my bride. A pretty little beta from a good family. She was eighteen, but still in high school. It was an arranged thing. We didn't know or love each other, but I still took her to church and canna and held her hand at family dinners. I was more interested in her older brother. Her family caught him and me fooling around and the wedding got called off."

Phantom pain makes my ribs ache with the memory of it. I took quite the ass kicking from her other brothers for it. "So my family decided it was time I saw what life was like out in the real world without them and their money. Guess they didn't think I'd like it. Jokes on them because I liked it fine. I see them on Easter Sunday and Christmas, I kiss my mama and nonna on the cheek, drink a beer with my siblings and the cousins and watch a game on the TV while the omegas cook. Then I go back to my life. Everyone's happy. Or they will be once I finally give my mama a grandbaby to spoil rotten."

"Does Veronica want kids?" Brendan asks, perking up. "After hearing the story about her parents, I wasn't sure."

Typical alpha. They've all got a massive breeding kink.

"Not now, but in the future. Do you?"

We probably should have asked him that first before bringing him into her nest.

He picks up the knife and an orange and goes back to chopping while he thinks. The sound of his knife thumping into the cutting board is rhythmic. "If she wanted them, yeah. But I think I could be happy without them, too, if she didn't."

"Good. Because I'm definitely gonna knock that omega up the minute she lets me." I stare at him and wait for any sign of jealousy. Of alpha posturing.

Brendan nods, his knife coming down on the cutting board with a heavy thunk as he makes more perfect orange wedges.

"Until then, I don't mind practicing," I say. "I want to go first."

"What does Jamie think about that?" Brendan asks.

My grin widens. "He's into it. He's got a cuckold fetish."

Brendan laughs under his breath and reaches for another orange. "Got it. Well, I can think of a few ties to put him in that'll keep him controllable when he's in a rut."

"Excellent." *Look at us being all agreeable and shit. This pack dynamic thing's not as hard as most people make it out to be.*

Movement in the corner of my eye catches my attention. It's Vee stretching her arms above her head to work out the kinks in her neck from bending over her computer. Her body blots out the blinding glow of the computer screen through the floor to ceiling windows that make up her office in the loft. She always does this when she needs a break. She's too stubborn to take one without prompting.

I grab the carbonated wine from the chiller and set out everything I need to make another Pink Slip, then get to work mixing. "Let's go see Vee and Jamie."

He leaves his orange wedges and follows me up the stairs, where we barge in on her with only a cursory knock. Her hair is already frizzy from how many times she's run her fingers through it.

Jamie smiles at us without getting up from his chair. He's on his phone and I glance at his screen and see he's shopping for women's wetsuits. The mental image of Vee in a tight neoprene suit that hugs all of her glorious curves is a delight.

"Today's drink," I announce, handing it to her. Our fingers brush and I enjoy the slide of her skin against mine.

Vee drains half the glass before the bubbles finally make her stop. *Stubborn omega.* "It's decent. A little bitter underneath the sweetness. What's it called?"

"The Pink Slip. Thought it was appropriate for today, all things considered." I give Brendan the side-eye.

Her face scrunches in confusion before she gets it, her attention sliding to him. "Oh, Brendan. I'm so sorry."

"It's okay," he says before she can get too upset. "I'm fine. To be honest, I hated that job. I only took it because of the benefits. But it was miserable. I never quit because of inertia, I guess."

"Who's that?" Jamie asks, looking up from his phone.

The room goes silent for a beat. "What?" I ask, swiveling to face him.

"Who's inertia?" Jamie asks.

We're all silent for a long stretch. "Inertia isn't a person," Brendan explains. "It's when you get so used to something that you don't do anything differently."

"Oh, right on," Jamie says, his head bobbing. "Going with the flow."

"Right." Brendan says, then turns back to Vee. "Anyway, your case will be reassigned, but I'm not sure which agent will take over. I can help you put the files they'll need in boxes if you'd like. They'll likely be taking the records back to the office instead of working here like I did."

So my hunch was right. "I *knew* you were hanging out here because you had a thing for her," I say.

"More like I have the world's most annoying cubicle neighbor, but coming into Rut every day has its perks." Brendan shrugs and gives Vee a soft smile. "I'm happy to help if you'll have me. I'm sure I can come up with a few deductions you haven't thought of already."

Vee pushes her chair away from her desk and stands, leaning her weight on her palms. "That could actually solve one of my problems. My old accountant, Harvey, wants to quit. Or he needs to, anyway. Or… he sort of already did?"

"What?" I stare at Vee to see if she's kidding. She's not. How long has she known this, and why would she keep something so big to herself? "Harvey quit and you didn't tell us?"

Her cheeks pinken as if she's embarrassed. Veronica's attention flickers from Brendan to me. "His wife is sick and they want to move out of state to be closer to family. He was going to see us through this audit remotely and refer me to someone, but… I hate to bother him while they're dealing with her chemo appointments."

She tucks her hair behind her ear. "You offered to help, but I don't know if you'd ever be interested in actually working here —working for me—and I don't want you to feel you have to say yes, but—"

"I'll do it," Brendan interrupts her. "Of course I'll do it, Vee. I'll do anything for you. You don't have to ask. What you're doing here… It's important. I'd like to be a part of it."

He scrubs a hand along the back of his neck. "I spent my entire career working for an agency that mostly punishes people and small businesses for making stupid mistakes or trusting the wrong accountant. The huge billion-dollar titan industries with hordes of lawyers? They almost never get held accountable. I'm tired of being a part of something that I'm not sure is good. So whatever I can do to help… Wherever you need me, I'm there for you, Veronica. Put me to work."

"Okay. You're hired."

He glances at the pile of cardboard file boxes and shoves his falling sleeve up higher. "All right. I should get to work before the new agent comes over. I'll start by reorganizing the boxes I haven't gotten to yet. We can fill out the new hire paperwork later. I found a few minor errors and missing receipts while I was working. If you let me use your computer, I can work on pulling those together before they get the case reassigned."

I watch in awe as Brendan gives Vee gentle commands, and

she listens for once in her stubborn life without a single argument. He's a miracle worker. It usually takes me at least thirty minutes of arguing to get her to this point. I'm slightly jealous. But then again, maneuvering her is half the fun for me.

Would I like it if she didn't fight me? *Probably not.*

Jamie scoots over on the couch so Brendan can pull certain boxes aside, and then every horizontal surface is covered with paperwork as he lays out the records he wants to tackle first.

Voices sound from the floor below, breaking through the murmurings of the talk radio playing over the speaker system. *Sounds like the other staff are here.* I dip out, motioning for Jamie to follow me. We leave them to it with the understanding that he's got it handled.

I never thought I'd be grateful to have an alpha one day, let alone two. My experience is that most of them aren't worth the trouble they bring, but here we are. A pack with two of them. It's nice. I enjoy knowing I can leave her in his hands and know he's got her. Whatever happens, he'll handle it and keep her safe. This pack thing is working out better than I ever could have planned.

I wave in greeting to the other bartenders showing up for their prep work and chop the rest of Brendan's stack of oranges. My wedges aren't nearly as symmetrical as his, but they'll do.

While the dancers cluster and Nate changes the music for rehearsal, I pop an orange wedge into my mouth and look up at Vee's office. Veronica and Brendan are looking at her computer together. He towers over her at twice her size. She leans in closer to him, her body instinctively seeking the protection of his alpha presence.

She's not a bad omega like she thinks. She only needed the permission to be soft and the security of a pack to let her guard down.

Orange juice runs down my throat as I smile and toss the

rind into the trash under the bar. Yeah, this worked out perfectly. But now that we have her, we need to figure out how to keep her. Stop her from getting spooked and closing off now that she's opened up to us and finally let us in.

Now all we have to do is figure out how to lock her stubborn ass down before she can panic and get in her head and self-sabotage our pack.

Chapter Twenty-Nine

VERONICA

I CAN'T BELIEVE IT'S ALREADY TIME FOR PAYROLL AGAIN. HOW has it already been two weeks since the last time? I swear I just did this yesterday.

Fuck. I need an assistant or something.

Especially if I'm going to be focusing on this presentation on franchise opportunities, I have to give in New York to those investors in ten weeks. I still can't believe I let Anthony talk me into setting up meetings. It's too early. I'm not ready, yet.

Sighing, I pore over Jamie's time card. Eleven times. That's how many times he's forgotten to punch in or out in the last two weeks. Even for him, that's a record. I thread my fingers through my hair and cradle my head.

Hands clap down on my tense shoulders and rub, thumbs digging into the ever-present knots there. "What's wrong, sweetheart?" Brendan asks. "I can help. I've been told I make an excellent sounding board."

The offer is tempting. Brendan's presence makes me feel safe. Taken care of. There's something about the warm comfort of his scent and his large, cozy body that makes me want to snuggle with him under a mound of blankets and shut the world out forever.

"I don't need a sounding board, I need a clone," I whine. "But I'll settle for an assistant. I can't get ahead on my paperwork enough to work on this proposal for the New York investors I found. I realize it's not for another two months, but I really need it to go well and I *really* need this audit to be done by then."

"It will."

His deep purr is a low rumble that makes my body want to melt into a puddle. Brendan's massage hits the focal point of all the pressure in my neck giving me a raging headache. I didn't notice how bad it was until all of his rubbing got it to release. The chair creaks as I settle back so he's not straining over me.

"You don't know that," I sigh.

"I do. Because I know your books are fine. That you've built an amazing business from the ground up. You've flipped the entire rut bar scene on its head. You're also helping the omegas who need it most. And you're going to pass your audit with flying colors. Those New York City alphas are going to be fighting each other for the right to fund your new location."

His gentle, sincere confidence makes me smile. He believes what he's saying. That we can do this. That I'm not making a huge mistake and stretching the club, the finances, and myself too thin.

Setting up the new rut bar will have to come first. Once we've settled in and learned the lay of the land and made the right connections, we'll switch focus to the nonprofit side of things. And one day we'll have a foothold in all fifty states. But one thing at a time. I've got to get through this audit first and not stumble at the finish line.

Brendan's thumbs work their magic on the knots in my

shoulders and the tension melts from my body. My sigh turns into a moan as I turn to putty underneath his hands.

"There you go, sweetheart. That's it. Let that tension go. You're going to do fine. You know what you're doing. You simply need confidence." He brushes my hair over my shoulder and leans down, his nose sliding against my jaw as he drops a kiss onto my neck.

For the first time in a long time, I wonder what it will feel like for teeth to cut me there. Instead of the fear such thoughts used to inspire, now I'm filled with curiosity. Instinct makes me yearn for a bite which does more than bruise. The love marks they suck into my skin are a rough approximation of something my dynamic craves. How can you so thoroughly desire something you've never known?

I have no personal frame of reference for this strange need. It's like dreaming about something you've seen in movies or read about in romance novels, but have never experienced for yourself. You understand the mechanics of it. You know what it looks like, but when it happens in your dream or daydream, there's no feeling. No sensation or emotion behind the act. Only blankness. The mind can't conjure a memory from nothing.

His kisses are tender and his palm cradles my face as Brendan rubs his cheek along my scent gland. Scent marking me. Claiming me. At least until the next time I shower.

Liquid heat pools in my center from the way he nuzzles me. His distraction worked—I'm no longer panicking—but now it's created a worse situation. The death knell of my productivity. I'm horny.

Not that it takes much to get me going right now. My libido's been kicked into overdrive ever since my heat. If we make it quick, I can get back to finishing payroll before a dinner break. If we don't bother with taking our clothes off, we can get it done in about fifteen minutes.

"Ms. Taylor, is this a bad time?" a stranger says from the open doorway.

I startle upright, my eyes flying open and my head clipping Brendan on the nose. He grunts in pain as I gasp. There's a man in a tailored suit standing on the threshold of my office. He holds a brown leather briefcase in one hand and a paper to-go cup of coffee from a chain store in the other.

"I'm a little early," the stranger says. "My previous appointment was canceled, and I was already in the area. I can wait downstairs if you'd like."

What. The. Fuck?

He's not another auditor. There's no IRS badge visible and his hair cut, suit, and shoes are expensive. His suit is custom made or tailored well because it fits his broad shoulders and the taper of his slim waist like a glove. He's a handsome beta.

"Can we help you?" Brendan asks, stretching to his full height.

"I have the papers I was asked to draft."

That explains absolutely nothing. "Someone asked you to draft papers? What papers? Who?"

"Shit, Nicky. You're early," Anthony says as he joins us. He wipes his hands clean on a black bar towel, then shoves the tail back into his pocket. "It was supposed to be a surprise over dinner. Well… surprise! This is my cousin, Nicky. He's a lawyer. Comes in real handy to have him around."

Stunned, all I can do is blink. After a moment, I recover. "Nice to meet you, er… Nicky."

Nicky isn't fazed by the awkward tension or blank staring. He grins, and then I see it. The family resemblance. His eyes are brown, not blue like Anthony's, but there's something familiar about his smile. Nicky sets his briefcase down on Nate's-turned-Brendan's desk and cracks it open, pulling out a paper clipped sheaf of papers.

He hands them to me. "Most of it is a standard boilerplate pre-pack agreement, although I added a nondisclosure agreement as well because of your pack's more sensitive, private matters. I've tabbed and color coded where everyone needs to sign and initial."

Frowning, I take the papers from him and skim through the first few paragraphs before deciding to actually read through it carefully. It's like he said, a pre-pack agreement that protects Rut and its related assets in the event of a pack dissolution. The NDA part covers the nonprofit work we do with the omega safehouses. I read each page, skimming through the thickest of the legalese until I get to the final page.

"If everything's in order, we can start the signing process," Nicky says. "But I'll need to take a photo of everyone's IDs for my records first."

I look at Anthony, who's been observing me while I read. "You asked him to draft this?"

"Of course. Seemed important that you know we want you, not Rut. Rut is yours and it always will be. No matter what."

Nicky shrugs. "It is unusual to be hired by the party who wouldn't get anything if the pack were to dissolve... but my cousin's always done things his own way."

"Can I see that?" Brendan asks. When he reaches for the contract, I let him take it. He spends a few minutes reading through the dense text. "He's right. It's all pretty standard. Do you have a pen? Mine is blue and I know they prefer black ink for contracts."

Nicky takes his fancy gold and black pen from his breast pocket and hands it to Brendan in exchange for the ID from his wallet. When Brendan swivels the tip out and sets it to the first tabbed line, I feel a brief flicker of alarm. This seems permanent. Like a really fucking big deal. Shouldn't we talk about this first?

"Wait." Everyone stops and stares at me. Do they really want me? *Me.* Forever. I'm a workaholic. Stubbornly independent. Bitchy. A poor excuse of an omega who doesn't want the normal omega things. A house in the suburbs. Two point five kids. A fenced yard for the dog. You can't bring a dog to a strip club, let alone a baby. What if they tire of this life? The grind? Late nights and early mornings? Of me? What if I don't suddenly turn into the perfect omega one day?

"Are you… sure?" I ask, scared of their answer.

Brendan's smile is small, but sincere. "I've never been more certain of anything in my life." He ducks his head and scrawls his initials on the line, then flips through all the pages until each one is marked. After he hands the drying document and pen back to Nicky, he grabs me by the nape of my neck and leans down for a kiss. It's brief and chaste, a dry brushing of lips, but it's momentous all the same. Because he signed a contract that says all he wants is me, and he means it.

He breaks the kiss and leans his forehead against mine. "You're everything I've always wanted. You all are. We might be unconventional, but if it works for us, that's all that matters. I couldn't want anything more. Forever."

"I'll text Jamie so he can get his cute little ass up here," Anthony says as he takes the contract. His phone chimes with the sent message alert, and he pockets that before taking the offered pen. "Wow, that's a nice pen."

"Don't you dare think of stealing it," Nicky answers.

Anthony snorts and flips to the next page. "I would never. Pens are sacred in the serving world. Here."

"I'll buy you one for Christmas."

"Do you really need my ID?" Anthony asks.

"Yeah. I'm waiving my fee, but I still have to file the paperwork. Consider this your mating gift." Nicky takes the contract and pen back. "You know your ma's gonna be pissed if you don't have some sort of ceremony."

Ceremony? Uneasiness rolls through me, making me tense again. The thought of having to put on a big white gown and walk down the nave in some church while one half of the pews are conspicuously empty makes me want to throw up. I don't like tons of attention on a good day. I definitely don't want to broadcast how alone I am in this world. "Umm…"

"If Ma wants a big fancy church ceremony, she's gonna have to wait for Sofia to get married," Anthony says. "We're doing things our way."

Nicky shakes his head, but grins. "You always do. Well… is the third guy on the way?"

"Miss Vee? They said you need to see me?" Jamie says from the doorway.

Jamie joins us, and I see he came straight from dress rehearsal. His muscular body is covered in sweat, body oil, and a few flakes of fake snow. His furry brown thong and reindeer horns are for the upcoming Christmas in July set for this weekend. He jingles as he walks thanks to the big brass bell around his neck.

"Oh, this is good." Nicky laughs. "I'm telling *everyone*."

"Shut your fucking mouth or I'll tell your ma about what really happened that summer before senior year with your chorus teacher. What was her name again? Mrs. Esposito?" Anthony threatens his cousin, then turns to Jamie. "Babe… You forgot to put on pants."

"Nate said I only get five minutes," Jamie answers. "I didn't have time to change."

"I don't suppose you have your ID hidden in there some-where," Nicky says with a pointed glance at Jamie's impressive bulge stuffing his thong.

Jamie tilts his head and is silent for a moment, as if he's

taking the question at face value. "No. It's in my locker. Do I need it? Am I in trouble?"

"No, you're not in trouble," I reassure him. "Anthony asked his cousin to draft up a pre-pack contract. This is his cousin, Nicky. He's a lawyer."

"Oh! Family!" Jamie's smile is full of white teeth and absolute sincerity. "It's great to meet you, dude. So are you guys hand shakers or huggers or…"

Nicky holds a hand up to stop him. "No offense, but this is cashmere and you're very shiny right now. And as a general rule, I don't make a habit of hugging naked men I just met. Although I'm sure you're a lovely man if my cousin likes you."

Jamie looks down at himself, his fingertips brushing over his bare abs. "But I'm not naked."

Nicky struggles not to smile. "Here, we're ready for you to sign this. Anthony can text me your ID card later. Front and back," he says, aiming the last bit at his cousin.

Jamie takes the pen and paperwork and tries to sign the papers before realizing he didn't swivel the tip out. He tries again, the pen scratching his initials over the paper this time.

"Wait, you didn't read it," I say.

Jamie pauses his signing to look up at me bashfully. "I have to sign to be with you, right?"

"Well…" I'm at a loss for words. This wasn't my idea, but now that it's been brought up, I can't deny that it's a good one. I've really been thinking with my pussy lately if I didn't stop to consider how forming a pack could affect Rut. I should have had a call out to a lawyer the day after my heat broke.

Jamie bites his lip and shrugs. "I trust you all. You're my pack."

Jamie's sweetness melts my icy heart every single time he says stuff like this. There's something about him that makes me want to wrap him in cotton wool and hide him from the cruelties of the world. Protect his heart. Keep him safe from life's many disappointments.

"You're right," I say, smiling. "We are." If anyone ever tries to hurt him, they're gonna have to get through us first.

After he's finished initialing and signing, he hands the papers and pen back to Nicky, who checks the document before tucking his pen away and latching his briefcase closed. "I'll mail you a copy of the contract. Congratulations, again. I'll show myself out."

Once Nicky's gone, I crook my finger at Jamie. "Come here."

Jamie comes around the desk. Without being told, he goes onto his knees and settles himself between my legs. My hands go to his hair on instinct, playing with it. "Jamie, honey, you should never sign documents without reading them."

Jamie frowns. "But I trust you. We're going to be pack. You'd never hurt me."

"Someone less scrupulous and kind might take advantage of that."

"I wouldn't love someone who wasn't kind." He says it so off the cuff that I know it's nothing but complete honesty. He genuinely believes it. That I'm kind. That I'd never take advantage of him or his submissive nature.

Fuck. He loves me. I do too.

"Still," I tell him, sighing as I think of how to phrase it. "Even if it's me telling you to sign something, you should always read it first. You don't understand what you agreed to." I tuck his hair behind his ear, ignoring the way his ridiculous reindeer's antlers jingle. The tips of his antlers have bells, too. Tiny gold ones sewn onto the branching tips.

"I'm not smart, though," he says. "I wouldn't understand it."

"Don't say that," I order.

"But it's true." He shrugs. "People have been calling me dumb my whole life. I don't mind. It's like how some people are prettier than others. And I'd rather be dumb and pretty and happy than smart and ugly and miserable. You… don't mind that I'm not smart, right?"

The hopeful look in his eye makes my chest pinch. I want to find every school ground bully who ever made him feel stupid and stomp them into the dirt. "I think you're smart in a lot of ways. You're smart when it comes to people. Way smarter than me. You know how to get them to like you. I'm not good at that and I never have been. So that's something that you're smarter about than me."

"People like it when you agree with them. You like to argue," he says.

I open my mouth to argue that I don't enjoy arguing, then snap it shut. "Huh."

Jamie smiles and rests his chin on my knee, his nostrils flaring and his pupils dilating. "Your pussy is wet. Do you want me to lick it?"

I lick my lips and get ready to tell him no, that he needs to get back to rehearsals. But I'm still horny from before Brendan and I were interrupted. Instead I say, "sure."

His smile widens as he grips my skirt and rucks it up my thighs. I lift and help him tug it higher, laughing when he dives right in to lick me through my panties and it knocks his antlers off his head. They fall to the floor, jingling, and my giggle turns into a moan as he sucks my cloth covered mound into his mouth.

"I'll tell Nate that Jamie's in a meeting with the boss and to start rehearsals without him," Anthony says as he heads to the stairs. "Want to help me restock bottles?"

"Sure," Brendan answers.

The boss. Fuck. That shouldn't be so hot, but it is. I'm

letting my stripper eat my pussy while he's supposed to be dancing on stage. It's so wrong. But he's so great at it. He deserves a raise for how well he eats pussy. A huge one.

My clit throbs from the pressure of Jamie's mouth, and I scoot lower in my seat to angle my pelvis and give him better access. My panties are soaked by the time Jamie works the fabric to the side and thrusts his tongue inside me. I clench around it, my fingers tangled in his hair and squeezing.

"Fuck, pet. That's good. You're so fucking good at that. Suck my clit more. Mmm."

He mumbles something, his words stifled against my mound. I put my hand on the back of his head and tug him harder against me. "No talking, more licking. Make me come on your face. I want you to smell like me all night while you're dancing for those omegas."

Jamie slicks two fingers through my wetness and pushes them in deep, fingering me as he works my clit until my thighs are trembling. Not smart, my ass. This man is a goddamn cunnilingus genius. He worships cunt like he's an acolyte praying to his goddess at her temple.

My legs tense with the threat of a muscle spasm. I throw one over his back, hoping that the change in angle stops it from ruining my impending orgasm. It's going to be a good one. The kind of orgasm that leaves you limp and breathless, your legs achy. He's so perfect, my Jamie. My sweet, submissive alpha. I wouldn't have him any other way.

I'm careless of my heels as they dig into his back, too far gone with tightening bliss in my core to care about any marks I'm digging into his pristine flesh. His fingers curl inside me, brushing over my sweet spot with every stroke as he circles my swollen clit with his tongue. "That's it. Right there. I'm gonna come, pet. Don't stop. Don't…"

"Jesus fucking Christ," Nate says from the doorway just as

my orgasm rips through me. I moan, muscles clenching and releasing around his fingers. It's not as good as coming around a cock, but it's better than coming empty.

Jamie laps up my arousal as I crack my eyes open and I'm greeted with the furious, red-faced glare of my angry choreographer. I take a moment to catch my breath and longer to think of something to say other than *oops*.

"What's the one rule, Vee? THE ONE RULE?" he yells, reaching for the door to pull it shut so the entire club doesn't hear everything.

Fuck. Probably should have shut the door before Jamie started eating me out. To be fair, I'd assumed that Anthony and Brendan shut it behind them when they left.

"Don't fuck the dancers," I pant, putting my leg down and nudging Jamie away from lapping up all the arousal smeared on my inner thighs. He doesn't seem to mind getting caught fooling around at work. Doesn't seem inclined to stop while we have an audience either.

Jamie sits back on his heels and tugs my skirt down so I'm covered, but he doesn't get up from his place at my feet.

"You gave me so much shit for this when you caught me with Matt and now I find out you're dipping your pen in the Rut Bar ink? Fuck, Vee. Goddamn it. How long has this been going on? How many of my dancers are you fucking?"

"Don't talk to her like that," Jamie says, moving to get up as if he plans to defend my honor.

I put my hand on his arm and pull him back down so he doesn't become a target for Nate's wrath. I don't need Jamie to defend me, not when it'll sour his relationship with Nate. And Nate isn't saying anything I don't deserve to hear. We should have been honest with everyone from the start instead of sneaking around and hiding things. It wasn't fair to my pack or to the rest of the staff. Or to myself, if I'm finally being honest.

Fear held me back from accepting what I was too scared to admit was true. But I don't want to be broken and alone anymore. I want the family—the life—they're offering. Because… because I deserve to have a family and be happy, dammit.

"I'm not fucking all of your dancers, Nate. Jamie is special."

"Oh, I heard exactly how special he is," Nate sneers as he crosses his arms over his chest.

"He's pack. Jamie is pack, and I… I love him."

All the color drains from Nate's face and his arms slip down to his side. "Oh, fuck. That's worse. If you were only fucking him… You're taking my best dancer from me, Vee."

"No, I'm not," I tell him.

Now that Nate's calming down, I pat Jamie on the shoulder to tell him he can rise. He stands, his hand reaching for his bulge to reposition his raging erection that's straining the brown fake fur to its manufactured non-stretch material limits. "Jamie doesn't want to stop dancing, and neither do I. We're… figuring things out. That's why we haven't told everyone."

Nate stares at Jamie like he's grown a second head. "I thought you were gay."

"I'm bi," Jamie says with a shrug.

"Yeah, but aren't you and that bartender… Wait." Nate turns to me. "You said we. Are there more people involved in this we? Who else are you involved with?"

Well, shit. Of all the days for Nate to not be strung out on a coke binge… "Anthony and Brendan are part of my pack too. Once we've sorted through some things, we'll be making it official."

Nate hesitates for a moment, then chuckles. "I *knew* it was weird when you hired him and all of a sudden we had a new IRS agent poking around. Wait, is that why you gave him my desk? Because I thought you were mad about… Never mind, that's not important right now. What's important right now is that you're fucking three employees. That's two more than I ever did. I want my desk back. You and your boy toy can share."

Nate is wearing my patience thin and ruining my post-orgasm buzz. I pinch the bridge of my nose where a headache is forming between my eyes. "You don't need your desk, Nate, because you won't be in it for much longer. That's why I gave it to Brendan."

"Are you fucking firing me?" Nate gasps. "I'm the reason Rut is the success that it is. My shows, my choreography, my eye for detail and storytelling. You can't do this without me."

"I'm promoting you, you stupid asshole!" I yell at him with rapid hand waving. "Because you're good at your job and I respect the work you do here. I'm meeting with investors in New York City soon. If we get the funding and find a suitable location, we're opening a second location, and I want you to run it."

Nate looks at me with suspicion. "New York?"

"Yeah. You're always going on and on about Broadway. You still have your connections there from Julliard. You know the city. And I trust you to run Rut. You understand what Rut is supposed to be, and while your set design dreams and spending are out of fucking control sometimes, I trust that you'll make it the best experience possible for customers. Also, I can't be in two places at once."

"Well." He sniffs, then rubs his nose. "That sounds like a lot of responsibility, which I'm willing to accept, but more responsibility needs to come with the right pay. And the cost of living is high in New York City, so… Listen, about earlier… I jumped to conclusions. I'm so glad to hear that you found your pack. You deserve to be happy, and it seems like…" His gaze slides to

Jamie and his erection. "It seems like he makes you *very* happy. We'll keep this between us, okay?"

No. No fucking way. I will not give Nate leverage over me. I will never let a man have power over me like that.

I trust him to run Rut. The man is obsessed with giving our customers the grandest, sparkliest alpha stripper show known to mankind, but I am not letting him use my pack as a negotiation tactic to extort me. "Your salary will be adjusted to reflect the cost of living and your new job title. Let me get the financing and location secured first before you go buy a flashy new car, though."

Nate's face scrunches up. "Why would I buy a new car if I'm moving to New York? A car service is better. Do you have any idea how much a parking space is? See, this is why you need to put me in the New York location. I know these things. We should look for something in the West Village. They'll love us there. Ooh, I can picture it now. We should get leather thrones, three of them, and rope them off as VIP seats. Charge a ridiculous amount for the privilege of sitting front and center."

Standing up, I smooth my skirt down my thighs. It's a wrinkled mess and there's no helping it. Fresh panties wouldn't hurt too. I need to keep a stash here at work. I shoo Jamie out of my office and nudge Nate along with me.

"I'll take your advice into consideration," I say. "Now, let's keep this expansion under wraps. Nothing is a done deal yet, and we have to get through this audit first."

We take the stairs as a group, and I ignore Anthony and Brendan's curious stares. Did neither of them notice Nate coming up to the office? I can't find it in me to actually be mad, though. The thought of coming clean, of telling everyone, makes my palms sweaty, but I'm nervous in a good way. I don't want to hide this beautiful thing we have anymore. I don't want to treat it like it's a dirty secret.

"Everyone, if I can have your attention for a minute, I have an announcement," I say loud enough to be heard over the music. Someone turns the volume down. I put my hand on Jamie's shoulder, forgetting how sweaty and oily he is, and slip. I hold his hand instead, our fingers threading together like they were meant to be. It's funny how something as simple as holding hands in public can be so intimate.

"I want to let everyone know that I've found my pack, and… well, you've met them already. Jamie, Anthony, and Brendan, who recently joined us to replace Harvey. We're going to be together. All of us."

There's a collective groaning except for Darlene, who cackles. She takes straight pins out of her mouth and stops fixing Margot's Mrs. Claus costume, stabbing them into the pincushion on her wrist and standing.

"Pay up," Darlene orders.

I watch as money changes hands, eleven people handing crumpled and folded bills to my costumer.

"How the fuck did she guess all of them right?" Darren asks.

"If we guessed one right, does that mean we get part of the pot?" Amy, our newest bartender, asks.

"No," a dancer says. "It's all or none. She won all of it."

"I didn't know we could pick more than one option," Amy argues.

"That's not how packs work, sweetheart," Dan adds.

"What the actual fuck? Were you betting on me?" I ask them.

"Yeah," a few of them say in unison.

I swivel to Anthony, who holds his hands up in the air, his bar towel forgotten. "Did you know about this?"

"I was sworn to secrecy, boss." Anthony fishes a twenty

from his pocket and hands it to Amy, who passes it forward until it ends up in Darlene's hands.

"Did you bet on us?" I ask him, my hands fisted on my hips.

Anthony shrugs. "I had to keep up appearances." He grins.

I want to ask him who he bet on me hooking up with, but I bite my tongue. This isn't the time or the place. A blush heats my face. Fuck this. I have payroll to focus on. "Get back to work! I'm not paying you all to gamble and bet on my love life."

Ignoring their laughter and chatter, I head up the stairs and hide in my office.

Well, all things considered, that could have gone a lot worse. Finding out your own club has a secret betting pool about your sex life is bad, but knowing that none of them seem to care beyond being mad they lost some cash makes me feel better. They're not pissed. They didn't quit and storm out, leaving me with no staff to open tonight. They know that I'm packing up with not one employee but three, and nobody's about to report me to the state labor board.

Of all the nightmare scenarios I had running in the back of my mind about how this would go down, a workplace betting pool wasn't on my radar at all.

Shaking my head, I unlock my computer and stare at the payroll application while I try to remember what I was doing.

Chapter Thirty

ANTHONY

"You've gotta be fucking kidding me!" Veronica yells at her phone while she sits up on the couch.

"What's wrong?" Brendan asks, pausing the movie none of us were really watching.

"Darlene just sent me this. A friend of hers saw it off the highway heading into LA." Vee hands her phone to Brendan.

I look over his shoulder to see the screen. It's a slightly blurry photo of a billboard lit up at night. Three handsome shirtless alphas post suggestively together while the ad announces the opening of a new burlesque club called Hung. It opens in two weeks.

"Oof." I grimace and take the phone from Brendan to show it to Jamie.

"They say imitation is the sincerest form of flattery," Brendan says.

I roll my eyes and Vee shoots him a murderous look, and that shuts him up. This isn't good. Vee won't tolerate such flagrant copying.

"Oh! I know him," Jamie says, pointing to a model. "He

danced at Rut for a few months last year. He looks good. What was his name again?"

Vee gets off the couch and starts pacing, her hands going into her hair and fluffing it up. "I don't care what his name is. And all three of them used to dance at Rut. They can't do this. This can not be happening."

Brendan scratches a hand through his short hair. "I mean… They can, though. As long as they don't use the Rut name, it's perfectly legal for them to open a club with the same idea. Nobody owns an idea, only the unique expression of it. You've never had competition before?"

Vee folds her arms across her chest and stands in front of the TV. "Of course I've had competition before. And none of those clubs made it. I'm not worried about some generic knockoff of my business. That's not the problem."

Brendan glances at us for guidance or help. I get why she's concerned. The other clubs rebranded themselves for a themed night a few times a month. They weren't dedicated to the concept. Those owners saw Vee raking in money hand over fist and thought they could cash in on the idea for a quick buck. But since they'd made their reputation by serving alpha customers with omega entertainment, they flopped. The omegas didn't turn out in droves because those clubs didn't have a reputation of being a safe space for them. It's been a while since a club tried to copy her.

"It's the name," I tell him. "It's too close to Rut."

"Exactly!" She throws her hands in the air and goes back to pacing. "They're gonna get confused," Vee mutters to herself. "They're gonna go to the wrong bar and ask the wrong people for help. Fuck. I've gotta warn Rob and Moira and the others. Where's my phone? Thanks."

Vee takes her phone back and starts typing furiously, her nails clacking against the screen.

"It's late," Brendan says. "Let's get some sleep and we'll talk to a lawyer tomorrow and see what the options are."

Lawyers? Lawyers are going to tell her there's nothing she can do. Brendan was right the first time. She owns Rut, she doesn't own the concept of an all alpha strip club. She's going to pay a lot of money to be told there's nothing she can do.

"When does it open?" Jamie asks.

"Two weeks," Vee mutters.

Two weeks is nothing in the realm of legal business dealings. They'll be open and running by the time she gets an answer. But if I learned anything from my family, it's that good business isn't always legal.

Brendan distracts and soothes Vee enough that he convinces her to deal with it tomorrow and go to bed. And while we're all settling into the nest, I lie there and think.

Three days later, I haven't made much progress. Vee's probably not going to go for any of the things my cousins recommended. To be fair, kidnapping the owner and convincing him it would be better for his health to rebrand is likely a step too far for most people.

I'll do whatever it takes to protect her. While I don't have any ideas about how to permanently fix this, I know exactly how we can delay their grand opening. And if we irritate and delay them enough, they'll get the hint and make better life choices. I might feel bad about ruining some poor asshole's life, but he fucked with my girl. And that can't be tolerated.

I finish mixing up today's drink special, a pretty drink called In Cold Blood Orange, and bring it up to her office. She's at her desk and Brendan's not. There couldn't be a more perfect time. It's like a sign from God.

"Hey," I greet her and hand her the drink.

She smiles, but it's strained. There are dark circles under her eyes. Her hair is twice as frizzy as it should be at this hour. I hate that she's so upset. It kills me to see her worried. I need to fix this. To prove I'll always take care of her, no matter what.

"It's good," Vee says after sipping it. She puts it down without finishing it. "What's it called?"

My mind is made up now. This can't go on. I hate how Vee shoulders everything alone. If she looks like this after three days, she's gonna be a wreck in two weeks. And that's unacceptable for the love of my life and the future mother of my baby.

I know what we have to do.

"Meet me out back at eleven," I tell her, "but be discreet while you slip away. Don't let anyone see you leave, and don't tell the others."

Vee frowns. "That's way too long of a name to fit on the menu."

"I'm serious. Trust me, Vee. We're fixing this tonight."

After a brief hesitation, she nods. "Okay."

I leave her in her office and head downstairs to teach the other bartender's the drink special and update the board. Once the club is open and packed with customers, I feign a stomach bug and dump my work on the others. They're happy to absorb my tips even though they're mad they have to cover my slack.

My cousins gave me some of the stuff we need, but I still have to grab some things from the store. I throw on a baseball cap I stole from costuming and pay in cash. Vee's standing out back in the shadows when I pull into Rut's parking lot and idle.

She opens the passenger door and slides in, and I haul the duffel bag from the back and hand it to her. "Here. Change your clothes and shoes. They'll be big on you, but you can stuff the toes of the boots with the extra socks." I pull out of the lot and merge into traffic while she inspects everything.

"What are we doing?" Vee asks while she rummages through the bag and pulls out the navy sweatsuit I bought her and another baseball cap I swiped from Darlene's costume cubbies at Rut. "And why am I dressing like an old man?"

"We tried things Brendan's way," I answer. "Now we're trying mine."

"Should I be scared?" she asks.

"Never." Reaching over, I take her hand and squeeze it. "I'll never let anything hurt you."

"Well, that's not ominous at all," she says sarcastically. Vee unbuckles her seatbelt and wiggles into her sweatsuit. She kicks out of her heels and tugs on the socks, then stuffs the extra pair into the oversized boots.

"Don't forget to tuck all of your hair up in that hat," I remind her.

She struggles to contain it all but eventually twists it up enough to shove the hat onto her head. "What, no balaclava to complete the look?" she asks, teasing me. Once she's dressed, she buckles up again. "And what's with the navy? Were they fresh out of black robber chic outfits?"

I shake my head and grin. Trust Vee to be more worried about her outfit than the illegal things we're about to do. I love this girl. She's perfect. "Black stands out too much in the dark. Dark blue or gray or olive green blend into the shadows better. A ski mask would attract way too much attention. Keep the hat on and your face tilted down. We won't have to worry about the cameras for long."

"I don't know if it makes me a bad person that I'm more excited than scared right now," she says while she stares out the window.

"I think sometimes you have to do the wrong thing to make something right."

"So the ends justify the means?"

"If you're doing it for the right reasons, yeah." I've never been very concerned with society's inflexible views of behavior.

What's so wrong with doing what it takes to get what you want? I didn't want my father's life, but I understand why he did the things he did. Because he did them for us. His family.

Vee sighs and fiddles with the temperature controls, cranking the air conditioning higher to keep her cool in the warmer outfit. "So what exactly are we doing? Are you going to tell me now?"

"They can't open on time if their building's a wreck."

I wait for a protest that never comes. Vee is like me. She helps the people she cares about. She does what it takes to take care of her family. I remember how it was in the early days while she was still finding her footing. When the club was struggling to find its niche. The people who fucked with her quickly found out she wouldn't take it. It takes a lot of nerve for a young woman, an omega, to stand up to alphas. That's half the reason I fell in love with her. She's brave. Fearless.

I reach for her hand again and squeeze it, dragging it over so it's resting on my thigh. We make our way to Hung. It's on the opposite side of town, only a half-hour drive with moderate traffic.

Hung's location isn't as good as Rut's. Terrible is putting it mildly. They're too close to Skid Row and too far from West Hollywood. The building is a sad little standalone beige cube with tall windows that have posters blocking the view and affording the club privacy while advertising the services that will be found inside. A vinyl banner on the side says coming soon. Its parking lot is enclosed with a chain-link fence, and the highway overpass hovers over it at the corner. At first glance, you wouldn't know it was a strip club. It could easily be a tax preparer's office or a liquor store. It has none of the charm of Rut.

"Yikes," Veronica says when she sees it.

I can't imagine any omega feeling comfortable enough to

drag their friends here. But an omega desperate to get out of an abusive relationship might brave it from thinking they have no other choice. "Are we still doing this?"

"I don't even know what you have planned."

That's not a no, so I take it as a yes. "Look in the backpack in the back." I circle the block and find somewhere to park further down while Vee drags the heavy backpack up front and rummages through it. She pulls out a can and shakes it.

"Spray paint? You think that'll really shut them down?"

I shrug and park. "Would you want to go to a club covered with a bunch of spray painted dicks?" I ask her.

Vee snorts and shakes the can of hot pink spray paint. "Point taken. I've never done this before."

"Used spray paint?" I ask her, feigning misunderstanding.

Vee gives me an unamused look. "Vandalized a building. Of course I've used spray paint."

"Shake, point, and press," I tell her. "We'll take out their security cameras first. Keep your chin down until we get past the other buildings."

I check for traffic, then throw my door open and climb out. Vee does the same. I meet her on the other side and zip the heavy backpack closed, slinging it over my shoulder. The coast is fairly clear. Only a few people are around in a sketchy area of town like this at this time of night.

Once we're closer, I angle my head and scan for cameras. There's one on each corner of the front aimed at the door and a dome in the back by the parking lot. I shake a can of black paint so it mixes and take the cameras out of working order one by one.

Vee checks our surroundings while I draw the first dick on the side of the building. Paint drips and splatters until I get the hang of it. Sort of. Graffiti artists make it seem so easy. When I add hair to the balls and an arc of jizz with droplets, Vee laughs.

"I want to try," she says, pulling me back so she can rummage through the backpack. She pulls out a can and zips it closed again.

"Go for it." I grin and watch as she gets into it, painting her own graffitied revenge on the building. She draws a bigger purple dick whose stream of cum crosses mine, then she draws a bunch of smaller dicks all shooting their load into one big puddle like they're a jizz factory.

When her can runs out of paint, I take her empty one from her and hand her a hot pink can while I switch out my black one for metallic gold. We make our way around the building, making sure nobody's coming. The empties go back in the backpack as we pick up after ourselves as we work. Can't leave evidence around while committing felonies.

Some cans don't have much paint left in them. I swiped them from my cousin's garage because you need to show ID to buy them new and I didn't want a cashier to remember me in case we ever get questioned about this. I can't be there for my girl from prison.

Vee finishes tagging the front, which we've covered heavily. There's not an inch of bland beige paint left. Dicks overlap dicks. She also scrawled the words *fuck off* directly above the door in thick red letters. Red paint drips down the door like blood.

"You have no idea how cathartic this is," Vee says as she puts the finishing touches on her work. She paints mustaches on the dancers on the window posters.

I keep an eye on the street to make sure we're still good, then snag her around the waist and pull her against me. The top of her sweatshirt rides up, and my thumb makes swirls over her stomach. "It's gonna take them fifty coats of beige to cover all of this. They'll be painting and scraping glass for days."

She turns in my arms and goes up on her tiptoes to kiss me.

When she wobbles in her awkwardly too big boots, I steady her and try not to smile as I kiss her back. "Thank you," she murmurs. "It might not be enough to stop them for good, but it's a start. I was going crazy because the lawyer said there was probably nothing we could really do."

"That's because you're asking the wrong lawyer." I give her one last peck and rub at the paint splatters that dot her cheeks like freckles. "Told you that you should've used my cousin."

"I thought you didn't want to involve your family with this stuff," she says, reaching up to rub my nose. Her finger comes away smeared with black. We're gonna need to stop somewhere and clean up before we go back to Rut. I'm not sure the baby wipes I brought will cut it.

"If it's for you, baby, I don't mind. You're gonna be family. We take care of our own. Now, are you done?"

"Yeah." Vee sighs and looks at her handiwork.

"Good. Let's get out of here." God damn, it's a fucking wreck. I've never been prouder of her. I spot one of our spray paint cans on the ground and go over to grab it and add it to the backpack.

After this, I need a smoke. Every good or bad moment in life is better with a cigarette. While Vee is admiring her handiwork, I pull out my cigarettes and lighter and flick the metal wheel until it sparks.

"Maybe one more," Vee mutters.

I hear the hissing of her can just as the orange flame flickers to life on my lighter. Before I can stop her or shout a warning, the aerosol spray catches fire.

"Oh, fuck!" Vee yells, jumping back.

I stare in horror as the fire spreads quickly. All of the dripping paint and fumes feed it. "Oh, shit. Fuck! Fucking shit, man!"

I shove my lighter and unlit cigarette into my pocket and

pull off my dark gray sweatshirt, using it to beat at the flames. All that does is make the flames spread more and my shirt catch on fire too.

"Oww! Son of a bitch!" I drop the sweatshirt and stomp on it to put out the flames.

When the fire hits the coming soon banner and rope and moves to the roof and wooden front door, smoke rises. That's when I know it's over. It's gone way too far for us to put it out. There's too much paint and too many fumes and too many posters all over the windows. This club's a tinderbox.

"Why the fuck don't they have a fire door? This shit hole's not up to code," Vee bitches as she steps back from the heat and flames.

"I don't know, baby, but we gotta get out of here. Come on." I grab the backpack and my charred shirt and her hand, and together we run into the night.

We make it to the car without incident, and I unlock it, shoving everything into the back. I stick the key in the ignition and turn the engine over. It sputters because I'm cranking it too hard.

"Why isn't it starting?" Vee asks, her voice panicked.

I force myself to take a breath and try again. My hands are trembling. I try again, careful not to flood the old engine, and it purrs to life. I pull out of my parking space and drive past the club to get onto the highway. Glass shatters as the strip club's windows explode. The smoke rising from the building is thick now.

Once we're on the highway and I verify there aren't any police lights in the mirror, my nerves settle. We drive in silence and I go the speed limit and obey all traffic laws. As my uncles say, don't attract attention by breaking two laws at the same time. Driving recklessly is the worst thing you can do after committing arson.

"We burned it down," Vee says, dazed.

"No, we didn't."

She frowns and turns in her seat and studies me. "Yes, we did. I doubt he put in a sprinkler system if he doesn't have a fire door. Seriously, who skimps on fire safety?"

"No, we didn't burn down any buildings tonight. How could we? We weren't even down this way. We were beachside, playing card games at my cousin Nicky's all night. You wanted to get to know my family more before mating."

"Wait, where are we going?" Vee asks when we pass the exit that would take us to Rut.

"I told you. My cousin Nicky's house. It's easier to lie if you sprinkle in the truth. So we're gonna go hang out at his house for a few hours."

Her stare burns a hole in the side of my face while I drive us to my cousin's house. His neighborhood is nice and quiet, and my rusty paint-chipped beater is out of place next to his Mercedes.

When I shut the engine off, she finally speaks. "Are we really not going to talk about how we accidentally burned down a rival strip club? What do we tell Brendan and Jamie?"

I undo my seatbelt and rub at my chest where it chafed against my bare skin. "Nothing. We're going to tell them absolutely nothing. You know why we can't tell them."

We can't tell Brendan, because he's probably never broken a law in his life. He doesn't even jaywalk. And we can't tell Jamie, because Jamie might say the wrong thing to the wrong person by accident. Neither of them can know.

"I know," she finally admits. "So what do we do now?"

"Now we get cleaned up. Then we annoy my cousin and crash on his couch." I grab the baby wipes from the bag and hand them to her. We both clean up the best we can without soap and water. After she peels herself out of her vandalism outfit, I steal her sweatshirt and shove my burnt one into the backpack. I throw the bag of evidence into the trunk, and together we walk to my cousin's door.

The doorbell echoes loudly through the silent house, and we wait about five minutes until my bleary-eyed and confused cousin answers the door.

"Anthony? What the fuck, man? It's two in the morning. What's wrong? Oh, God. Why do you two smell like paint and smoke? Never mind, get in here."

We step into his chrome and marble foyer in our paint-splattered and smoky clothes. Nicky looks around outside, then shuts the door and locks it.

"Thanks, man." I rake my hair out of my face and tug Vee into my side. "And the less you know, the better. We came over to play cards and have a drink while Vee spends more time with the family before our mating."

"Fine." He looks us both over. "You can use my shower and washer and dryer. There's a throw blanket on the couch."

I grimace. "Oh, sorry. No, we've gotta actually have that drink and play at least one round."

"Are you serious?" He pulls his satin robe tighter around his pajamas. "I have a deposition in six hours."

"Yeah, sorry." I clap him on the back and pull Vee deeper into the house. He won't say no. We're family. "I don't know how well Vee will hold up under interrogation."

"Fuck," Vee curses softly under her breath.

Nicky sighs like he's put out, but he goes to the bar cart in his living room and pulls the stopper off a crystal bottle. Amber liquid splashes into a matching cup. He sips it. "Fine, but you're showering and changing clothes before you sit on my couch. It's down that hall and on the left." He points the way.

"Thanks. Come on, baby. Let's get you cleaned up." We find the bathroom and I turn the shower on so the water gets warm as we undress. I throw the smoky clothes and our shoes out into the hallway. Nicky will probably throw everything that's fabric into the wash.

Vee stands there nude as she waits for me to finish. She's got a little streak of purple on her neck that she missed under her jaw. I pull her in close and rub at it with my thumb. "You okay?"

"Yeah. In shock a little, maybe. That was my first arson."

My lips twitch into a smile. "Your first? Not your only one? Who else are we burning down?" I tease her. It's an interesting choice of words. I love that she's holding up. She's brave. Fearless.

Vee pushes at my chest playfully, but I don't let go. I'm never letting her go. She's perfect. It takes a strong person to survive my family.

"That's not funny," she says. "I didn't mean to... I wouldn't..."

I silence her with a kiss. She doesn't need to make excuses with me. It's a building. It's not like she murdered someone. They'll file with their insurance company and get a fat check. That club probably would have failed anyway. If anything, we made them more money tonight than they would have seen if they'd actually opened. Rut is safe. The omega community is safe. Everyone wins. I kiss her while I walk her toward the glass shower stall until the water from the rainfall shower head soaks the both of us.

"How are you so calm?" she asks as I work the shampoo into her hair.

"Because I know what really matters to me and it's not that shithole club that was stealing your idea." I cup my hand over her forehead to shield her eyes as I rinse the suds from her hair.

"It went up so fast," she says, dazed.

I squish the conditioner into her hair and use the excuse of soaping her body up to run my hands over her curves. "It did. You're surprisingly good at arson."

"That's not funny," she moans. "I didn't mean to do it. I didn't know you were lighting a cigarette."

"It was an accident. Accidents happen. Nobody was hurt. It'll be fine. They'll get a check from the insurance company. That's what insurance is for. You know what you should do… You should have the next dance routine be about firefighters."

Vee gasps and smacks a hand against my wet chest. "That's not funny!"

But she smiles, and that's all that matters to me. "What? You don't want to capitalize on the news?"

"And draw more attention and get arrested?" She snorts. "No thanks."

"As if I'd ever let you go to prison," I tell her, paying special attention to her boobs while I coat her in suds. Does she really think I'd ever let her take the fall for something?

"What do you mean?" she asks. Water droplets gather on her eyelashes when she blinks up at me.

"It means I love you and you don't have to worry about it." Before she can argue further, I silence her with a kiss, and then I finish washing her clean of paint splatter.

She's my girl. We only have to make things official. I know that day is coming. All I have to do is to be patient and not push her too far, too fast, like Brendan said. We're perfect as a pack.

AND MY FAMILY PROTECTS THEIR OWN, AND SOMEDAY SOON she'll be a part of it. I'll destroy the evidence in the morning and make sure the car doesn't smell like smoke. The only thing she needs to worry about is acting surprised when she hears the news and picking out a bigger nest.

Chapter Thirty-One

VERONICA

"Explain to me why we're here again?" I ask, looking up at the store's enormous sign. Nested.

I do most of my shopping online, so I've never actually been inside a brick and mortar one before. It's a forty-five minute long two-point-four mile drive during the most infuriating traffic I've ever seen. Why would I bother when I can click a button and have it delivered within a few business days instead?

"Because we've dicked around for eight weeks and your heat is next month. You need a real nest," Anthony says. "So that's what we're getting you."

"What's wrong with the nest?" I ask. Now that I've all but moved into Jamie's house, I've slowly taken over his bed, one blanket and pillow at a time. Sure, it's cramped with the four of us, but we manage. I enjoy sleeping in a puppy pile of limbs more than I thought I would.

"It's sad. Trust me, I've seen what it's supposed to be like and that's *not it*," Anthony says, ignoring my unamused glare in response.

"This is the first day off we've all had together in weeks and you deserve nice things," Brendan says, trying to smooth things over. He does that a lot—plays middleman or mediator.

The Omega Rights Act Day thirty percent off sale means the store is packed. Through the window, I watch two omegas nearly come to blows over a stuffed pillow shaped like a blushing cactus. Everyone always worries about alphas going into rut and fighting, but they've clearly never watched two nesting omegas brawl over the last discount plushie.

"This is pretty," Jamie says, pointing to a blanket in the display window. It's textured, but still soft looking, and the color is a blue ombre that reminds me of ocean waves. "Can we get this one?"

Anthony lays a hand on the small of Jamie's back. "Let's let Vee pick, okay?"

"Oh, right. Sorry." Jamie appears sheepish as he tucks his long hair behind an ear.

"It's okay." I reach for his other hand and give it a squeeze so he knows I'm not mad. "I think it's pretty. We can get that one."

"Shall we?" Brendan asks, getting the door and holding it open.

Walking into Nested during a holiday sale is what I imagine going into battle is like. The four of us have to jostle our way inside. You'd think that having two huge alphas with me would help clear us a path, but it does the opposite. Omegas stop to stare, especially at Jamie. A few give my men very obvious once overs, pointedly searching for bite marks around the necklines of their shirts. A pretty blonde practically eye fucks Anthony.

The urge to bare my teeth and hiss at her like an angry cat bubbles up inside me. It's hard to shove the instinct down. *They're mine*, I want to snarl. I settle for giving the worst one, the blonde, the stink eye until she fucks off toward the register with her armful of pink throw blankets.

I run my hand through my hair and shove it out of my face. "Let's grab the blanket and go. I'll shop online." I need to get out of this store before someone uses the crowd as an excuse to brush up against Jamie and fondle his pecs or something. The last thing I need right now is to get arrested for getting into a fight. Brendan and Anthony cage me into the throw pillow section and prevent my retreat.

"No," Brendan says, his voice deep and as full of alpha command as it can be without being a bark. "Anthony is right. You need a proper nest, Veronica. You *deserve* a proper nest."

My insides melt despite my scowling, and I know arguing won't get me what I want. Not when he takes that tone. Anthony might be Daddy, but Brendan is papa bear. He doesn't pull rank very often, so the fact that he's doing it now means he actually cares about this and they've all talked about it behind my back.

The thought should make me bristle, except it's hard to be mad at someone for wanting to take care of you. And if I'm honest about it, I like the pampering more than I care to admit.

I blow out my breath in an aggravated sigh. "Fine. I'll take that and that and… those." I point indiscriminately, my finger landing on a stuffed flamingo plushie, a burgundy comforter set with black gothic trim, and a box of white paper lanterns. It's a bizarre combination.

Anthony claps a heavy hand on my shoulder and bends down, pressing his lips to my ear. "Do I need to find an empty corner of the store and finger you? You're always in a better mood after you've come all over my hand."

The hair on the back of my nape stands up, and my nipples tighten against my padded bra. My eyes dart around the store because I know that none of his threats are idle. "There aren't any empty corners."

"Then I guess there's gonna be a show today." He smirks, then turns serious. "Or you can behave. Let us spoil you. Be a good girl or Daddy's gonna make you remember your manners."

Glancing around, I look to see if anyone is overhearing us. His voice is low and Nested is playing instrumental versions of pop songs over their speakers, but the store is awfully crowded. A frazzled employee pushes past us with her arms loaded with boxes of string lights.

"I don't see what's wrong with buying online," I argue. "It's easier and then we wouldn't have to deal with all of *this*."

"The hard way it is," Anthony mutters. He bends down and bands me around the thighs and picks me up, pressing me to his chest.

My yelp draws the attention of the entire store as he carries me deeper where the display beds line the back wall. No. Oh, no. He can't be serious. There's no way he's going to throw me down on a bed and actually fuck me here in front of everyone. We'll be banned from every Nested store in the country for life. Arrested.

Moisture gathers, making my panties stick to me. My face heats in a blush. I hate how much I like it.

Anthony sits me down on one of the test beds and stands between my legs, his arms crossed over his chest. He quirks one brow. "Well?"

My heart stutters. It's beating so fast in my chest. "You can't. We can't," I croak. We both know he could. He would. And I'd like it.

Brendan and Jamie step up behind him, one on either side. "Don't tease her," Brendan orders.

"But she makes it so fun," Anthony says, grinning.

"Is this our new bed?" Jamie asks, picking up the tag and reading it.

"Well, baby?" Anthony asks. "Is this the bed we all get to fuck you in?"

A male omega startles and looks up from a display of mattress cores, the kind that shows what the inside of the different types of mattresses for sale are like. He looks at all of us, then at my burning face, and smirks before going back to what he was doing.

"Anthony," I hiss. "Stop. You're going to get us kicked out."

Anthony looks over his shoulder. "We should test it out. Jamie, get in the center. Let's see if it's springy enough. Some of these memory foam mattresses are the absolute worst for sex."

"Don't you dare," I order Jamie to stop.

Jamie stops, one knee on the mattress, and looks between me and Anthony as if he's not sure who to obey. "Are you going to help or stand there?" I ask Brendan, who's being useless and letting this happen.

Brendan takes his hand off his mouth where he was hiding his smile. "We do need a new bed. Something bigger that fits all of us. And springiness is a valid concern."

My annoyed look makes him duck his head to hide his smile from me as he busies himself with looking at the mattress's information tag and price breakdown. Oh, the price. I don't want to think about how much a huge mattress this nice is going to cost.

Anthony puts one knee on the bed and bounces me. I ignore his antics because he treats any attention as good attention. Begrudgingly, I admit—even if it's only to myself—that it's a nice mattress. It's cushioned and bouncy but with a good amount of support. "How much is this one?"

I reach for the card to see the price, but Brendan flips it over so I can't. "We can afford it," he says.

Well, now I *have* to know. "No, really. We should talk about it. I know we need a bigger bed, but this is a big purchase."

"No," Brendan says gently. "We can afford it. Anthony and I set a budget for this trip. Spoiling you will make us happy, so you'd really be doing it for us. Don't worry about the price of anything today. We can afford it. All that matters is if you like it."

"If *we* like it," I say, stressing the *we* part. No matter how much they insist that my opinion on the nest is the most important one, it's not true. It's theirs too, and I wouldn't want to pick out a bed they hate. "You guys should try it too."

"Am I getting on the bed now?" Jamie asks, looking at me for guidance.

When I nod, he sits down beside me and flops on his back, folding his hands together on his stomach. I mimic him, lying beside him so our shoulders brush. It feels right.

Anthony joins us, cuddling up on my other side. He drops a hand on my thigh and strokes. "This is nice."

"I like it," Jamie says. "Is this the one we're getting?"

"Brendan? You have to try it too," I say.

Anthony squeezes my thigh, then gets up off the small mattress. "I'm gonna go find someone who works here. They can tell us what size we'll need."

Brendan takes the vacated spot, and after a few moments of lying there, he sighs. "Oh, that's good. He did a good job picking this one."

"He has weirdly good instincts," I say. "I don't know how he does it every single time."

Some people are lucky like that. Me, I've had nothing come easy to me. I've always had to work twice as hard as anyone else to get where I am. Omega. Female. Orphaned. But I don't resent Anthony for making everything seem so effortless all the time. It's like the minute he wants something, the universe makes it happen.

"Luck?" Brendan asks. "No. He spent weeks researching brands and models and reading reviews. Then he called here the other day to see which models they had on the floor. Then he made us study the store's layout from the photos people left in their reviews."

"He did?" My stomach flutters at the thoughtfulness of it.

"Yeah," Jamie says. "He also made mood boards on that site, Pin It, and had us study them so we'd know what we were looking at before coming here. This means a lot to him. To all of us. Planning today's outing and putting the money aside and helping you put your nest together is his courting gift. We all want your nest to be perfect."

I reach for their hands and grasp them, threading my fingers through theirs. "It will be." Because they'll be in it with me and because I don't need to do this alone anymore. If I'm weak, they'll be strong. If I need a soft place to land, they'll hand me the blankets and down pillows. And when they need me, I'll be there. Because that's what pack—what family— does.

"Good news," Anthony says, returning. "They have one Wyoming King in stock in their warehouse, and if we pay a rush delivery fee, we can have it delivered in two days."

Sitting up, I pull him to me and make him curl down so I can place a chaste kiss on his lips. "Thank you."

His surprised expression melts into something tender. "You're welcome, baby. Now, do you still want that stuffed flamingo and vampire bedding or..."

Pretending to be irritated with him, I roll my eyes. "Have I told you what a pain in my ass you are sometimes?"

"Not today, but if you want to sneak into that dressing room together, I can show you what a pain in your ass I can be," he grins, flashing me his panty melter smile.

Standing up, I force him to spin and point him toward the display window where the blanket that Jamie picked is. All the items on the display are stocked nearby. I trust him to find it while I browse. "Be useful and go get me that blanket Jamie liked. I see the display for it over there."

Anthony tugs me to his side. "So bossy." His hand drags down from my back to my ass, and then he swats me lightly. "Say please."

Blushing, I'm glad that nobody is close enough to hear him or see this. Right now, there's a spat brewing over a diminishing table display of some spinning light up globe that throws colors on the ceiling and walls. There's a small crowd gathered and squabbling right by the end cap where Jamie's blankets are displayed. I don't want to wade into the fray to get one, but I'm not playing his games in the middle of a crowded store.

So I bargain with him. "Get me that blanket and I promise you won't regret it."

"Oh yeah? What are you going to do for me, baby?"

"I'll make it worth your while. What do you want?" I know better than to give him carte blanche. I want to know what sort of payment he wants in advance.

He thinks for a moment. "I want to have you in the car on the drive home."

"Hmm." That's still pretty public, although if we're careful and nobody is in a huge lifted truck…

"You'll like my next idea even less."

I sigh. "Fine." I'm surprised he didn't insist on sneaking into a changing room near the back

He squeezes his handful of my ass, then lets me go. "Deal."

A few minutes later, he returns triumphantly with the ocean blanket and a shopping cart. We browse every aisle, spending way too long in the crowded store. There aren't as many options in person as there are online, but I enjoy being able to feel all the textures of things. Some items I think I'll love, I hate. A beautiful chunky knitted throw causes instant revulsion when I stroke it. I make a face and wipe the memory of the texture off my hand.

We pile the cart high with way more bedding than I think we need, but the boys insist it's necessary. I pick stuff that I think will complement Jamie's beach house. Muted turquoise and cream, pale yellow and warm wood tones.

Brendan insists on double-layer bed curtains to go with our new four-poster orgy size bed. There are sheer inside curtains for everyday use and a thicker light-blocking outer layer to make the nest more cozy. I'm not sold on the idea of a dark, enclosed space until he looks through the string lights with me. A set shaped like tiny seashells makes me pause, and he throws four of them into the cart before I can protest. It might not be so claustrophobic since the bed is bigger.

When the smiling cashier rings us up, the total makes me want to throw up. I haven't spent that much money on something that wasn't for Rut in… Probably ever. I don't think I've ever spent that much money on myself before. Anthony hands over his card without balking.

After the delivery details have been finalized, Brendan and Jamie load up the car and I sit on the back bench seat. Anthony climbs in and sits next to me, his lips curling into a smirk as he pulls the van's double doors shut with a bang.

"Thank you for today," I say. It was nice to be spoiled. Odd, slightly uncomfortable, but nice.

Anthony's hand settles on my thigh, his thumb making circles where my shorts end. His fingers dig into the skin as he pulls my thighs apart so he can stroke higher along my inner thigh.

"You're welcome, baby," he says. "We enjoyed spoiling you. Happy is a good look on you. Now, are you going to be a good girl for me and let me unwrap my present?"

He's waiting for me to protest, but I'm well aware of Anthony's exhibitionism kink by now. Still, I wish I'd worn a dress. After spending nearly every day at Rut in a skirt, I threw on a pair of shorts today. Shifting on the bench seat, I let my legs fall open and meet the challenge in his eyes.

"Unwrap me, Daddy."

Chapter Thirty-Two

VERONICA

Anthony doesn't waste any time. He gets the button on my shorts undone with one hand. I shouldn't be impressed by that, yet I am. He slides the zipper down and shoves his hand inside, his fingers petting me through my panties.

"Fuck, you're so wet, baby. Tell me the truth. Did you imagine us bending you over that bed and christening it right there in the store?"

My teeth pinch my bottom lip as I bite it and nod, my breath stuttering as he fingers me through my panties. As he makes me want forbidden things. He slides them up and down my damp, clothed slit.

"Mmhmm," I moan.

Jamie fiddles with the radio, changing the station until he settles on one he likes. He cranks the air and rolls up the cracked windows. Once Jamie pulls out into traffic, Anthony ramps up the teasing.

He works his hand underneath my slick panties, spreading my wetness and grazing my clit until it swells. He rubs me, working me until my breaths turn into pants and I can't help but moan. Two fingers tease my entrance, pushing in and out until the wet sounds of my body are louder than the radio.

"Do you hear how fucking wet you are, baby? You like the idea of me fucking you, claiming this sweet little hole in front of a bunch of strangers, don't you?"

"Yes. I thought about it. Oh, God. Right there." I've never acted out an exhibitionist fantasy before Anthony. Never dared.

His palm rubs against my clit and his fingers pump faster. The wet sucking sounds my pussy makes are filthy and I'm still picturing Anthony bending me over every flat surface in that store and ripping my shorts and panties down. His cock sliding between my lips. Slicking himself up in my arousal. Sinking inside with no resistance. Need coils in my pelvis until the familiar edge of a growing release tightens inside me.

"You're a dirty girl, aren't you, baby? My perfect little slut. You want my cock in this greedy hole, don't you?" Anthony asks.

"Mm, fuck. Yes." His movements speed up, his fingers curling and hitting a spot that makes my toes scrunch in my shoes. "I want you inside me. Need you."

"Are you gonna come, baby?"

"Yes. Oh, fuck, I'm gonna come."

Anthony stops, and when I moan from frustration, he grins. "Not yet, baby. Not until that greedy hole of yours is squeezing my cock. Take these clothes off." He pulls the waistband of my panties away from my body and lets them snap against my skin. "Now."

With fumbling fingers, I lift my hips and work my shorts and panties down until my bare bottom sticks to the warm vinyl seat. I can't take them all the way off with my shoes on, so I kick my sandals off. My face heats with embarrassment at being completely bare from the waist down. The windows aren't tinted. Anyone who looks in from a car that's higher than ours is going to get a show. But I'm so desperate to come that I don't care.

"Did I tell you to stop?" Anthony asks. He grabs the hem of my shirt and rucks it until my lace bra is visible. And then he yanks that down. My breasts spill free of the cups, my nipples hardening.

"Anthony," I protest. I want to come, but this is a bit much. Stripping naked wasn't part of our deal. He can fuck me with my shirt on. I reach for the fabric to cover myself until his hand shoots out to stop me.

"Take it off, baby."

Glancing out the window, I see that traffic has come to a complete stop. His smirk turns into a Cheshire grin as a full understanding of the depths of his depravity hits me. I never should have agreed to this.

"Only the bra," I bargain. "I'm not taking my shirt off. That wasn't part of the deal."

"What are you gonna give me if I say yes?"

"What do you want?" It's always give and take with him. Like he's some naughty fae who has to strike a deal.

"I want to practice your deep throating some more when we get home. Sound good, baby?"

"Fine."

He grins, his hands roaming. They trip up my back and undo my bra through my shirt. "Deal."

He gets my bra unhooked one-handed through my shirt and —dammit—that's so fucking hot. I let him pull the straps down my arms. It's tossed aside and his hands are on me the second I'm braless.

"You're the worst," I mutter without any real heat. My face is uncomfortably hot.

"But you love me anyway," Anthony says, his tone blithe.

He palms my tits through my shirt, pinching the nipples until they ache.

My heart flutters. He's right. I love him. All three of them. I never thought it would happen to me. But this is right. It's good. Real. The last eight weeks have been the medicine I didn't know I needed. With them, I'm not some deranged, damaged, broken omega. I'm exactly who I'm supposed to be so I can be with them, and all of that pain was worth it because it brought us here to this.

"So beautiful," Anthony says as his rough hands knead. "So fucking perfect." As he tweaks my stiff nipples. "And mine." The sensation zips straight to my throbbing clit. He rucks my shirt up and leans, his mouth leaving a trail of kisses along my collarbone. My breasts. He sucks a nipple into his mouth and lightly bites until I'm breathless.

All of my concerns about being watched by the people in the surrounding cars disappear. Anthony works me up to a fervor. His lips kiss and his teeth nip along the side of my neck. When he sucks my scent gland into his mouth, the dull pressure makes me moan.

Each hollow-cheeked pull of his mouth makes my channel clench. I'm eager to be filled. Desperate. Brendan and Jamie turn in their seats and watch as much as they can while we inch along in nearly standstill traffic.

"Fuck, I need you. Stop teasing me," I pant. "Anthony, please."

He lets my neck go with a wet pop and ignores how I cover myself, pushing my rucked shirt down.

"I love the way you moan my name like that," he sighs. "I love when you tell me you need me. Love it when you touch me exactly where I need you too."

Anthony takes my hand, putting it exactly where he wants it. His jeans are tight over his bulge. I stroke him through the denim, enjoying the hard length of him. Tracing his shape. Loving the way he fills my hand. There's a damp spot where his head is leaking, his arousal soaking into the fabric. I drag my thumb over the flare of his head, scraping the denim with my nail and savoring the way he moans.

"That's good, baby," he praises me. "Take me out. Stroke me. Make my cock hard for you. It's yours."

I'm not as talented at one-handed clothing removal as he is. It takes both of my fumbling hands to get his button undone and his zipper down. I pull the metal tab down, careful not to catch him in the path of its teeth. It's not surprising that he's bare underneath them. Anthony wouldn't want any extra layers between us to slow him down when the mood to take me strikes him.

His cock fills my hand. It's warm and heavy. I grip him firmly and stroke, letting my fingers bump over his flared head and smear his pre-cum over my knuckles. His veins bulge and I squeeze him harder, work him faster. His hips rise to thrust and meet my tugs.

And then he stops me by grabbing my wrist and prying my hand off his ruddy length. "That's enough, baby. I'm nice and ready for you now. Now be a good girl and come ride this cock."

I hold on to his shoulder and throw one leg over him. "I had to be half-naked, but all you have to do is fish your cock out?" I ask, goading him. "How is that fair?"

Anthony's hand lands on my ass with a sharp crack that's quickly followed by a rush of warmth. A burst of slick gathers along my folds.

"What's not fair is how bad I need that pretty pussy on my cock. Now, get settled on Daddy's lap where you belong or I swear to God I'll tug you outside by your hair and bend you over that hood so everyone can watch me fuck your needy cunt."

His threat makes my clit throb, but I don't actually want to end up in jail. "You wouldn't dare," I whisper in his ear, my lips brushing against him. I wrap my arms around his neck and get into place.

"Don't test me, baby. I'm at my fucking limit here with your pussy sliding over my cock like that. Don't make me do something Brendan's gonna make me regret."

Brendan chuckles from the front row, and I bite my lip to subdue my smile.

Getting positioned in such a cramped space is a challenge. Thankfully Jamie's vintage van is roomy. It has to be to fit his surfboards inside where the third row's been removed. Our bench seat in the second row is basically a loveseat without arms. I don't know if this is quite what Volkswagen thought people would do on it when they designed it in the seventies, but who knows? Those were wild times.

Anthony braces me as I straddle his lap. I tighten my arms around his neck so I don't fall off. He reaches between us and fits his cockhead at my entrance. I'm drenched for him.

"So impatient," I tease, taking a moment to rub my slit over his hard length. His head bumps over my clit, and I grind myself on him until my pelvis tightens with need.

"If you understood what sinking into this top-shelf pussy was like you'd understand," he says.

When my pelvis tilts, his head rubs against my hole, and this time I press down. His crown pushes inside and the way Anthony groans, so ragged and desperate, makes me feel powerful even though I'm the one taking commands right now.

"Oh, fuck. That's good, baby. You're so damn warm and wet for me. I bet Jamie and Brendan are jealous that all they get to do is watch right now while I fuck this beautiful pussy."

"The view is nice," Brendan says.

"I like watching," Jamie agrees.

His jeans rub against my inner thighs, the metal button cold against my skin. Knowing that I'm half-naked and vulnerable while he's clothed pushes some kinky button I didn't know I had before I met him.

He doesn't help at first. Anthony lets me work my pussy onto his cock until he's fully sheathed. I ride him, hips rolling and tits shoved into his face as he wraps his arms around my waist to keep me where he wants me. On his cock. In the van. While Brendan and Jamie and who knows how many other motorists are watching. The forbiddenness of what we're doing adds a sense of urgency and danger as my hips rock while he keeps me so full.

He grips me by the hips and works me down his length in a single smooth thrust that bottoms out while demanding I make more room for him. And then he takes over. I stop helping as he bounces me on his cock, using me to chase our mutual pleasure.

My wet pussy makes sucking noises as he fucks me faster. Harder. Mercilessly. My hands grab fistfuls of his hair while I focus on hanging onto him.

"Fuck! Oh my God," I cry before devolving into a whimpering mess on his lap.

"That's it, baby. You take me so well. Be a good girl and come for Daddy. I want to feel that pussy squeeze my cock."

His hips surge so hard that the only reason I'm not bashing my head in on the car's roof is because the old van is roomy. Fingers carve divots into my skin, and I don't care if they bruise. If he fucks his handprints into my flesh. As long as he doesn't stop until I've come.

The flared head of his cock hits the same delicious spot inside me repeatedly, and I need it. I need him. Need to come. Need my pack. The only thing that would make this better is if we were in my new nest. Suddenly, I can't wait to put it all together and fuck all of them in it until they can't remember how to walk.

My need tightens, coiling taut in my pelvis, and I hold my breath as my world narrows to the battering of his cockhead inside me. The rough scrape of his denim against my thighs and ass. The cool blast of air conditioning over my heated skin. His warmth and the way his cock heats my core.

"That's it," he says, letting out a deep groan. "Good girl. Come for Daddy."

"Oh, fuck, I'm gonna come. I'm gonna…" My words trail off to breathless noises as all of that coiled tension snaps. Everything is still for a second or two, but it seems like an eternity, and then my walls flutter. They clamp down on his sliding cock and squeeze so damn hard that he has to force his way back inside me to stay buried.

I collapse against him, letting him take all of my weight as my limbs go boneless. My eyes close halfway. Anything more than a moan is beyond me as aftershocks zip through my body. All concerns over voyeurs and the police disappear, leaving behind nothing but bone deep satisfaction.

"Fuck, this pussy is so good," Anthony groans. "You're perfect."

He's still guiding my hips. Lifting me off his cock and grinding me back down. And I let him use me, use my pussy, until his breath quickens. Sweat gathers on his skin, the fragrant notes of cherries, musk, and male saturating the van. I'm not in heat, yet I want to gather up those scents and rub them into my skin. Let his claim coat me so everyone knows he's mine and I'm his.

Why shouldn't I?

Instead of second guessing the instinct to death, I give into it. I'm tired of fighting who and what I am. They're right. Being an omega doesn't mean I'm weak. Look at everything I've accomplished despite all the hurdles of my dynamic.

So I give in. I slide my palm over his jaw and neck. Slip it into the neck of his faded band tee. I find his underdeveloped scent glands. It's a faint bump over the muscle that connects his shoulder to his neck. When my nails scratch over it, rubbing his faint pheromones into my fingertips, his groan deepens. Our eyes lock.

Once they're coated, I bring them up to my neck and rub them into my skin like they're perfume. His neck cords with strain and his face flushes with his efforts. Inside me, his cock jumps. He's nearly there.

"Come for me," I tell him. "Come inside me."

I want his cum soaking my walls. Saturating my skin. I want everyone who smells me to know how fucking happy my beta makes me. He takes care of me, and I don't always make that easy. Anthony's been there for me since the beginning. He sees the breadth of my ambitions and doesn't tell me I can't do it. Instead, he keeps me hydrated and fed and makes sure I'm rested so I can keep changing the world for omegas one victim at a time.

I want the world to know that this man is mine. Completely. Permanently.

"You're mine," I tell him, not asking. I don't need to. We're beyond that. I was too afraid to admit what I knew to be true before. Doubt made us lose so much time together. What if I loved them? What if they left, as all the others had before? But I can't let the fear of heartbreak keep me from living and loving at all. I can't write our future off before giving us a chance.

"I'm yours. Every… single… inch," he answers, thrusts punctuating his pauses. "I always have been, Vee. And you're mine, baby. Mine." He growls the last word. "Mark me. I want everyone to know I'm claimed."

He doesn't need to tell me twice. He's been telling me for years, one takeout box at a time. I wrench his tee shirt aside, baring skin. A thread in the stitching pops from the force. My jaws opened wide. I lean forward and find his small gland again with my mouth. The taste of him coats my tongue. Floods my senses. My tiny canines scrape his skin, and the way he sucks in a breath makes me flush with feminine satisfaction. I grip him tight to keep his shoulders still while his hips still thrust.

"Do it," he hisses through clenched teeth.

I bite, pinching his gland between my teeth. Not hard enough to break the skin, but more than enough to leave him with a bruise. It'll be the talk of Rut—our best bartender, the only one who's never taken a customer home, showing up with a claiming mark. It'll fuel the gossip mill for weeks. And I don't care. Let them see it.

His thrusting jars me, making the bruise deeper. More painful. If Anthony cares how close my teeth are to puncturing skin, he doesn't show it.

Something primal inside of me hates all of his movement. It wants him still underneath me. Tense and waiting. Doesn't he know my teeth are in his throat? That I could rip a more permanent claim into him if he isn't careful? But it's Anthony. He's reckless and scheming, and he doesn't have a submissive bone in his body. Not even when he's sucking cock.

"Harder," he groans, the pace of his hips equal parts furious and careless. "Do it."

Any harder and my dainty yet sharp canines will break the skin and—oh. Is that what he wants? A bite mark from me? The thought wipes my mind blank for a moment. Most packs don't have omega bites. Omegas are generally too submissive to have that urge. A bite from me, though, would cement him in the pack without him having to submit to one of our alphas.

This isn't the most romantic setting for something as

momentous as a claiming bite… but it's Anthony. He loves to watch and be watched. He likes it rough and dirty. And as I'm learning more about myself, so do I.

I bite harder, a fresh burst of cherries making my mouth water. I moan around my mouthful and my pussy squeezes him tight. His cock pulses inside me and his thrusts slow, deepening. He moans, his breath hissing through his teeth, as he comes inside me.

Each kick of his cock lashes another shot of cum against my walls. Each thrust he makes as he uses my pussy to milk his cock squelches.

On his next pulse, I bite him so hard my jaw aches.

"Oh, fuck," Anthony groans. "That's it, baby. Harder—I can take it."

The metallic taste of blood mixes with his cherry pheromones. An awareness snaps between us like a plucked string as the bond kicks in. Aftershocks of pleasure—his, not mine—leave me sleepy. Content. There's an edge of elation underneath the fog of bliss. It takes me a minute to parse his mood from mine and re-establish the boundaries of my personhood.

Anthony lets out a ragged groan and a string of mumbled profanities. "Fuck, Vee. I can sense you, like… inside me? God, that's good. Weird, but good. Mmm. Yeah, you like this, baby?"

He strokes me, his hands rubbing up and down my back. Between the sore stretch of a well-used pussy and the intense satisfaction of finally claiming a packmate, I'm the most mellow I've been since that one time my college roommate convinced me to smoke pot.

The urge to lick his bite mark, to tend it, can't be ignored. Purring, I lick his bite until I'm sure it's clean. Neither of us is aware of the traffic jam clearing or the rest of our journey across town.

"What's it like?" Brendan asks.

"I don't know how to describe it," Anthony says. "Words aren't good enough."

"You good, babe?" Jamie asks.

"So good. So fucking good. It's like... impressions. They're faint, but maybe that's 'cause I'm a beta. But when I do this—"

Anthony's hands drift lower, cupping my ass, before reeling back and giving me a squeeze that makes my pussy tighten. His softening cock slips free and the mess he made between my legs drips a puddle in his lap.

His grin promises me a lifetime of shenanigans. "Oh, fuck yeah. This bond thing is great."

I move to slide off him, but his arm locks around the small of my back and keeps me on his lap.

"Don't go, baby. I want cuddles too."

Anthony holds me close. After a minute or two, my limbs loosen and I lay my cheek on his shoulder. It's the perfect position to breathe in his faint cherry scent. The effect this man has on me is unreal.

After a while of holding and stroking me, he says, "I love you, Vee."

I can sense the truth of those words. The breadth of emotions that make up their foundation. It's hard for me to say the words. I don't think I've ever said them to him before, but I find the thread that connects us and push those feelings toward it.

When his breathing hitches, I know he received it. When he sniffs, the sound thick with congestion, I know the effect it has on him. Pulling back, I see his eyes are red and glassy from unshed tears. I push his unruly hair out of his face and give him a soft smile.

"I never thought... Never thought I'd be the first, you

know?" His arms squeeze me tight. "Thank you. For making me the first."

There's a vulnerability in him I've never witnessed before. I cup his face in my palms and stare into his eyes, a wealth of information shared in our connection. He's enough simply because he's Anthony. He's pack. And he's not some beta consolation prize.

"I love you," I tell him, my heart hammering in my chest and the words whispered. I kiss him.

A tear rolls down his cheek, wetting my face. I brush his hair out of his eyes, then tuck his head under my chin and card my fingers through the strands until he calms.

Somehow we make it home without being pulled over and arrested for public indecency. Jamie and Brendan work on unloading everything while Anthony and I go clean up. We shower together, and I smile when his soapy hands wander over my body and start grabbing handfuls of tits and ass.

Anthony threads his fingers into the wet hair at my nape and squeezes, pressing me up against the cold tile wall. He fucks me there, my legs wrapped around his hips. My arms locked around his neck.

The first few thrusts remind me that my pussy's sore until slick gathers, easing his movements. Water droplets gather on our skin and steam fills the shower, and his pleasure becomes mine through our new bond. Mine becomes his until neither one of us knows where the other ends or begins.

"I fucking love you, baby," he groans, hips pistoning.

One of us comes and the other one follows, and I bury my face in his throat, my nose searching for the faint scent that's him. Anthony. My first official packmate.

But not my last.

Once we're dry and dressed, we cuddle in bed in a jumble of limbs, and everything is perfect.

Two days later, when the delivery guys haul the old mattress and the unboxing trash away, I have to admit that they were right. The new bed is enormous and perfect. Nobody has to worry about falling off the edge when they turn over in their sleep. Although we still cuddle in a pile in the middle.

Anthony helps me hang up the bed curtains and string lights, and I talk him out of repainting the room when he finds out my favorite color is turquoise. His concern that the nest isn't perfect is cute. He takes it way more seriously than I do.

When he pulls up the Pin It boards and makes me look at crown molding options, I distract him with sex. And that's how Brendan walks in on us and I end up taking both of them while Jamie wanders in from the kitchen to watch until we pull him down too.

Chapter Thirty-Three

JAMIE

IT'S HERE. IT'S HERE, IT'S HERE, IT'S FINALLY HERE. SHOULD I open it? Make sure it turned out right? Or should I bring it to her first and let her open it?

Indecision roots me on the spot. Thankfully Anthony shuts the sliding glass door and tosses his cigarette pack and lighter onto the side table I put there for his smoke breaks.

Good. I'm glad he's home. Anthony can tell me what I should do. He always knows these things.

"Babe," I say, snagging his attention. "I don't know what to do."

He glances at the box. "Is that the wetsuit?"

A wetsuit? Why would he think it's a... "Huh?"

"Didn't you order a wetsuit for Vee that ended up being on backorder or something?" he asks, scratching the five o'clock shadow on his jaw.

"Oh, right. The wetsuit. The wetsuit for Vee. *That* wetsuit."

Anthony grins like he does sometimes when he says I'm being funny, though I wasn't trying to tell a joke. But as long as he's happy and laughing, I don't mind it. I like when he smiles. He's too serious all the time.

"Yeah, babe," Anthony says. "*That* wetsuit. So is that it?"

I look at the box and read the discreet label again to make sure it's not. "No."

Anthony shakes his head and grins. "The suspense is killing me. What'd you order?"

"It's my courting present for Vee. It had to be custom made, so it took a while to get it. I wasn't sure if I should open it or let her do it."

I can't say the words without blushing. It doesn't matter that it's Anthony I'm talking to. That he knows all my secrets. My hidden desires. These unnatural urges.

Alphas take. Claim. They don't beg to have their cocks locked up. To have their omega own their chastity. Despite my embarrassment, I'm excited. My cock is already thickening with anticipation.

His eyes widen, and then his grin does too. "Well now, I definitely have to see it if it's got you blushing like that. Plus, if it was custom made, we should check it and make sure the order turned out okay. Then we can wrap it in a pretty package for her. What exactly did you order?"

I only hesitate for a moment before I agree with him. He's right. Anthony usually is. What if they'd sent me the wrong thing and I didn't know until she opened it?

"It's a cage. For my... For me."

He raises his eyebrows, and motions for me to hurry. I curl two fingers under the flap and rip through the paper shipping tape. My hands tremble as I pull the sealed plastic wrapped contents from the box.

It's lighter than I thought it would be, and I'm glad that I listened to the crafter when he said to pick titanium over steel, especially since I go in the ocean a lot. Anthony takes the empty box and sets it aside while I open the plastic bag and touch my chastity cage for the first time.

It's cool and smooth against my hand. I turn it over and inspect the design. The head is shaped like a cock with a hole in the center, so I can still go to the bathroom no matter how long it stays on. The body is made of a sequence of rings, and where my knot would grow is a thick band of unforgiving metal. The whole thing connects to a ring that will go around my balls with a lock at the top to secure the base to the cage. A triple set of keys hang from the cage with a ribbon.

"Nice," Anthony says, taking it from me when I offer it to him to look over. "Good job, babe. I think she'll love it. But we can definitely spice up the presentation a bit for her. Do you want help, or do you want to do it yourself?"

I love that he asks. That he doesn't simply put up with my fetish, but he understands and encourages it. How did I get so lucky? Finding one person who understood me was uncommon enough, but three? A part of me still can't believe it. Sometimes I wake up thinking this pack thing was a dream.

After my first girlfriend looked uncomfortable when we were confessing our secret fantasies to one another, I never thought this was something I'd ever get to try for real.

"I want to do it myself," I decide. And right now is the perfect time. Vee is out on a brunch date with Brendan.

"Okay, babe." Anthony pulls me down for a quick kiss and then lets me go. "She's going to love it. Don't be nervous." He heads to the kitchen and pulls the fridge open to grab a drink. I put the cock cage in my pocket and grab my car keys from their bowl.

Hesitation makes me pause while slipping into my flip-flops. What if I mess it up? This is important. It's the gift that decides whether she officially takes me into her pack. Forever. I don't want to disappoint her or mess it up. "You know… it wouldn't hurt if you kept me company for the ride to the store."

Anthony pops the top of his soda and smiles. "Sure, babe. I need to pick up some things from the store anyway."

"Yeah, good." I blow out a relieved breath, because now it feels more legit. Like we're running errands together instead of him helping me because I'm afraid of messing this up. "Sounds good."

THE NEXT DAY, I CUT MY MORNING SURF SHORT AND WE ALL get to Rut early. Anthony heads to the bar to do his usual pre-opening duties. When Vee and Brendan go to head upstairs, I stop them.

"Vee, do you, uh… Could we…" I clutch the box in my hands and glance at Brendan, silently begging him to help a brother out.

Brendan doubles back down the stairs. "I'll catch up with you. I forgot to ask Anthony for the receipts from his last beer order." He claps me on the shoulder on his way past me. "You've got this," he whispers, "I know you can do it."

"Thanks, man."

"Did you need me?" Vee asks.

"Always," I answer.

Vee's expression softens. She holds a hand out and waves me over. "Then come, pet."

I follow her up the stairs, my eyes trained on her butt. I can't help it when it's right there. She looks so good in those tight skirts. The flash of the red bottoms on her black heels and the clip clop sound they make on the stairs has my groin tightening.

Dammit. No, that's bad. I can't get hard or she won't be able to put the cage on my cock. I force myself to look away from her butt. I try to. I can't. It's too perfect. The tight skirt emphasizes the upside down heart shape of her backside.

Think about surfing. The cold of the ocean. The smell of salt and brine. Catching a sweet ten-footer and flying through the spray. The way the rest of the world falls away when you're inside a barrel, the water all around you, then you come out the other side with a surge of adrenaline that makes your body soar.

When she shuts the office door behind us and looks at me, one eyebrow raised, I swallow hard.

"What do you have there, pet?" she asks, glancing at the box with curiosity.

"Anthony helped me pick it." When I realize how badly that came out, I panic that I've already messed up. That she won't understand it's my courting gift. "The box. He helped me pick the box. I picked the present. It's your courting gift. I hope… I hope you like it."

Vee leans against her desk and reaches toward me. "I'm sure I will. Should I open it now?"

My gulp is audible as I hand the box to her. I breathe a sigh of relief when she takes it. It's done. It's out of my hands. Now I'll know if this was the right decision and I did a good job.

"It's pretty," she says, stroking the lacquered wood and the ornate latch that keeps it closed.

"It's for jewelry. That's what the lady said." Although I'm not sure this is the sort of metal accessory the little old lady at the shop imagined would go inside the box. "The present is inside. Not the box. But the box is a present too, I guess."

Vee smiles and I stare at her, stupefied, like I always am whenever she smiles at me. She flicks the latch open with a red polished nail and the hinges creak as she opens the lid. Her smile slips off her face.

Oh no. I messed up. I knew I would, and I did. It's not what she wanted. Does this mean she's rejecting me? Do I not get to be in the pack now? Maybe she'll give me a second chance to get it right. I can do better.

I should tell her that if it's not right, I can try again and I'll have Anthony help me next time, so I know it'll be right. "I can send it back," I blurt out instead.

Vee's head whips up, and she stares at me. "You changed your mind?" she asks, her voice neutral. It's the fake voice she uses when she's on the phone. I hate that voice.

"No, I..." I'm frustrated because sometimes the words just don't come out right when I speak. "If you don't like it, I can try again."

"I like it. And if you like it, then I love it." There are three small keys attached to necklaces inside. Two on thicker, masculine chains and one that's dainty. It's the one meant for her. She picks up the small silver-colored key that we attached to a real silver chain so she can wear it next to her heart. "Is this one for me?"

"Yes. It's yours, Vee. To do what you want with. I'm yours… If you'll have me." My heart is beating so fast in my chest. My palms are damp. I'd wipe them off on my pants, but I'm too nervous to move.

"Then I suppose you'd better get undressed." She picks the cock cage up and sets the box aside on her desk. "Oh, it's lighter than it looks, but is this going to be comfortable and safe to wear long term?"

The sight of her holding the cage excites me. My cock kicks in my pants as it swells. "People say the weight feels nice. That you get used to it. It's titanium, and the man who made it said I can wear it in the ocean without it rusting."

"You planned for everything," Vee says, smiling. "Very smart. Good job, pet."

Her praise makes my cock leak as my erection swells more. She thinks I did a good job. That I planned this well. I read a lot about it online but actually doing it is different. It's better. And doing it with Vee? With the omega who doesn't simply put up with my unusual interests but seems to enjoy them as much as I do? She's perfect. I can't imagine serving a better omega. A lifetime with her won't be enough.

"Well? Shall we see if we can fit all that alpha cock in this tiny cage?"

I undress in a hurry, and my hands tremble the entire time. Once the last of my clothes are off, I sink to my knees on the cold, hard floor. My cock rises with anticipation and a bead of pre-cum drips onto my thigh.

Vee's red lips curl in a smile that makes her cheek dimple. "It's gonna be hard for me to put a cage on that pretty cock if you're kneeling, pet."

"Oh, right. Sorry." I stand again, my face heating with a blush as she chuckles. I laugh too, because I'm nervous and all of that bundled energy needs an outlet. I want to touch her all the time. Hold her close. But she hasn't given me permission yet. So I stand before her instead, my hands loose at my sides.

"This is going to be a problem," she says, reaching out and tapping her nail against my dripping head. My cock bobs in the air, my groin tightening from that brief amount of stimulation. "I think we need to drain those balls before we can stuff your cock in that cage. Would you like that, pet?"

"Yes, Ma'am. Thank you." She's so generous. Vee could have made me stick my hard cock in a bucket of ice. Instead, she's going to let me come. This is how I know she's perfect.

Vee reaches for me, her small hand circling only half of my cock but her touch is heavenly. I can't stop the guttural groan that rips from my throat as her fist tightens and she strokes me from root to sensitive tip. Her thumb brushes over my leaking slit and spreads my pre-cum along the flare of my head. Gently, she teases me until I'm fully hard.

My hips want to buck, to pump into her tight fist, but I leash the impulse. I won't take what I'm not given, no matter how much I want it. I want to please her more. Want to please her forever if only she'll let me.

"So full," Vee murmurs, her hand pausing its stroking to fondle my balls. "Look at the mess you're making all over my hand. Let's see if we can get this ring on with all of this alpha slick to help us."

The cold kiss of the metal ring against my sensitive gland makes me groan. She slicks the ring with pre-cum, then slides it down to my sack. She pulls one testicle inside. When she gets to the second ball, that's where it becomes a struggle.

"Hold your cock out of the way, pet."

I tug it to the side while Vee pinches the skin of my sack. She's so careful as she pulls the ring to the side to make a gap and pulls my other ball through until both are finally inside the ring. It's already a tight fit and my cock isn't in yet. That would be a lot easier if I weren't semi-hard, but that's impossible with her touching me. Smelling the sweet arousal in her scent alone is enough to get me stiff.

Feeding my cock through the ring is a challenge. She tugs the ring to the side to make a small gap, and I grunt when she tries to force my cock through. It crushes against my balls and the ring, and a deep ache blooms in my pelvis. My entire gut tightens. It's painful in the best of ways.

"Am I hurting you, pet?" Vee asks, pausing.

"I like it, Ma'am. Please don't stop." Not when we're almost there. When it's almost fully hard. The mix of pleasure and pain is only going to make the task impossible. If we don't do it now, we may not get it all until I've gone soft again.

She grips me again, her touch more confident. She gathers

the leaking fluid from my head and slicks my shaft. "You'll tell me if it becomes too much."

Because she says it as an order, it's easy to obey. I nod, and Vee pushes harder.

"Almost there, pet. A bit more…" She tugs. There's an almost unbearable ache that causes me to hold my breath, and then instant relief.

"Good boy," Vee croons, her touch gentle as she reaches for my cock again.

She takes over, checking the fit of the snug ring around my cock and balls and stroking me until I'm fully hard and it's a secure fit. The urge to thrust, to fuck her hand, is difficult to ignore. Her thumb rubs along the webbed bit of skin where my shaft attaches to the head. She presses it into my leaking hole and smears the drop of pre-cum welling there.

"Touch yourself," Vee commands. "I want you to stroke your cock and know that it's the last time you'll ever have that privilege. That if you want relief, you'll need to beg one of us to unlock you. That your cock is ours now. We own it. Don't we, pet?"

"Yes, Ma'am." A shudder rolls through me as I replace her hand with mine, stroking myself the way I enjoy until my breathing gets faster. Tension coils taut in my pelvis and my balls ache. The cock ring makes them throb. It makes me want to beg for release. For the satisfaction of emptying them. "My cock is yours."

"Good." Vee watches the rapid movement of my fist with a hungry gaze. Her red lips part and her pink tongue darts out to wet them. "I like knowing that it'll be locked up for safekeeping when we're not using it. That you'll need to beg us if you want it removed."

The thought of being owned so intimately, so completely, of giving up all control over my cock, brings me right to the edge.

I love knowing she desires me, even with my cock caged. That it can be locked up and she'll still want me in her pack. That I'm more than just a big cock and knot to her.

I want Vee to own me so profoundly and permanently that it can't be undone. I want her teeth in my skin and her bond in my soul. The thought of her biting me, of her dainty omega fangs cutting her claim into my flesh, nearly pushes me over the edge.

Not yet, I think as I let the moment drag on. "I'm going to come, Ma'am." My ass cheeks clench from having to hold off. To wait for permission.

And Vee makes me wait. She watches my hand stroke my cock, watches the pre-cum drip and fling off, striking her desk. And I wait. I pinch my head harder with each tug to keep from tipping over. My breathing stutters into rapid pants. I can't hold back much longer. I'll need to slow my pace if she won't let me come yet.

"Not yet," Vee says.

My hand slows, and the pending orgasm fades.

"I haven't told you where to come yet." She shifts in place where she's leaning against her desk. Vee reaches down and grabs the edge of her tight skirt. She shimmies it until the fabric bunches around her waist, and then she shoves the papers and things on her desk to the side and sits on the edge, her legs splayed wide.

One painted nail taps against her inner thigh. "Here. Come here, pet. Now."

Chapter Thirty-Four

JAMIE

Miss Vee smiles. "I want you to come on my thigh because you haven't earned the right to come inside my pussy yet."

Stroking harder and faster, a goal in mind now, I finally let my hips move. I thrust, fucking my fist, and I'm right back there on the edge. My eyes lock on her panties. They're pink mesh with a black bow and there's a wet spot above the seam of her gusset. The dark thatch of her trimmed hair is visible through the fabric.

Seeing her pussy without being allowed to touch or lick it is a torment. Her pheromones are thick and heady. My mouth waters with the need to taste her. To lap up all that slick until she comes on my face.

The need to come overwhelms me, blanking all the other thoughts from my mind. I tug slower and more firmly, the tight ring snug around my cock and balls. My cockhead smacks against the soft skin of her inner thigh, pre-cum dripping and smearing. Strings of it connect us after my head lifts away with every stroke. I'm so close. I can't hold it back any longer.

"I'm going to come," I warn her.

"Now."

The permission—an order, really—is all that I need. The orgasm rolls through me as waves of heat. My cock jumps, and my balls ache as I pulsate. It's ruddy and throbbing, the veins bulging from the ring.

Cum splashes over her skin in spurts and dribbles. It paints white splatters over the curve of her rounded thigh. It drips to the floor and runs in rivulets, drenching the edge of her panties.

"See the mess you've made?" Vee tsks. She leans back on her hands. "Good boys clean up their messes."

I don't need to be told twice. I sink to my knees and touch her leg, nudging them apart. She spreads her thighs wide, and I settle between them. Leaning down, I stick my tongue out and lick. I scoop my cum up with my tongue and clean every inch of her. Nails rake through my long hair, carding it out of my face as I work to make her spotless again.

"Hmm. That's good, pet. But you made another mess you need to clean up." She taps a fingertip over the wet spot on her underwear.

"May I undress you, Ma'am?"

"I think you'd better." When Vee nods, I hook my fingers on either side of her panties and tug, rolling them down her hips. She lifts her butt off her desk and helps me take them off her. Once they're folded neatly, I set them aside.

My eyes stay trained on her as I lean forward and set my face between her thighs. I lick her wet seam, lapping up her sweet orange slick. My tongue slicks deeper in between her lips, finding and teasing her clit until it swells. Sucking it makes her grind against my face, her body telling me she's eager for more. For everything I want to give her.

"Oh, fuck. You're so good at that. Mmm. How'd you get so good at eating pussy?"

I pull away to answer her, but her fingers tighten in my hair. She tugs back into place.

"Don't stop," she commands.

Never. Her praise makes me eager. Makes my cock twitch though it's spent and soft against my thigh. I want to be her good boy. Her pet. Her alpha in name only. Whatever title or name she wants to give me is fine, as long as it means I'm hers.

"More," she demands. "Don't stop until I've come all over your handsome face."

I won't. When her wetness runs down my chin, I reach up and probe her hole with two fingers. Her grip tightens in my hair until it's tugging, but she's not pulling me away. She's keeping me between her legs while I feast.

Her pussy squelches as I finger her. Harder. Faster. Curling to brush against the spot that makes her thighs tighten around my head. She moans with every caress and lick and suck.

"Fuck, pet, I'm going to…" Vee's words trail off into heavy breathing. Something falls off her desk and clatters to the ground from her fidgeting. Her pussy tightens around my hand, her body squeezing my fingers like a vise and nearly pushing me out. But she told me not to stop. To give her more.

I'll give her everything.

I shove them in harder, deeper, faster, forcing my way back inside while her body tries its best to keep me out while her pleasure is spiraling. I suck her clit into my mouth and then it happens. She sucks in a breath and holds it. Her pussy spasms on my hand, clenching and unclenching. And the whole time while she's coming, I keep her clit warm with my mouth.

When she makes a satisfied throaty sound and her tense legs soften from their clenching around my head, I know that she's done. That I've done a good job and pleased her. I clean her slick off my face and lick my hand clean while she watches, her eyes hooded with pleasure and her lips curved in a smile.

"Mmm. Very good, pet. Stand up. Now, let's get that naughty cock caged before it gets greedy and wants another round."

"Yes, Ma'am." I stand and try to ignore the vision she makes with her legs spread wide and her panties on the desk. My cock twitches. I try to shut the scent of her out of my nose by breathing through my mouth. Try to not think about her hands putting cool metal on my cock as she locks me away for her pleasure later. Anything to get my unruly cock under control again.

"You'll tell me if this hurts or needs adjusting," she says while she picks up the cock cage and studies it. She takes her key from the box and checks the lock to make sure it's functioning.

I breathe through my mouth and think about things that won't keep me hard. Kooks dropping in on your sick wave and making you bail or, worse, wipe out. Learning a new dance routine. Getting yelled at by Nate when I mess up in rehearsals. Customers who take the groping too far while tipping.

Once I'm soft enough, it doesn't take her long to figure out how to attach it. She's a natural. One of those people who accomplishes whatever she sets out to do. She's so pretty and smart and perfect.

The cage squeezes around my cock, the base tight against my knot so it can't pop. She hooks the two pieces together and clicks the lock into place. Then she puts the necklace on and pulls her hair through so it settles around her shoulders.

It's done. The pressure is intense, like a tight hug that makes my groin ache. The euphoria that washes over me at finally doing something I've wanted to do for a long time is unlike anything I've felt before. And knowing that I'm doing it with Vee? With my pack?

"There, that's a good boy. You're so pretty with that cage on."

She palms me, plays with me, her hand tugging at the metal cage, which turns the ache into a tugging sensation that shoots straight to my spine. It morphs into a dull pressure.

"This cock is mine now," she says. "I own it. I'll play with it whenever I want, then put my toy away when I'm done."

My eyes grow hot and my vision blurs. There's a lump in my throat that's hard to swallow around.

Vee's expression becomes worried. "Is it pinching? Does it hurt? I'm taking it off." She reaches for her key, fishing it out from under her shirt.

"No! No, please." I sink to my knees again and lay my head on her thigh, looping my arms around her waist to keep her close. "It doesn't hurt, I promise. I'm happy. I want you to own me. I want to be yours forever."

A hand comes down to cup my head. Vee strokes me gently and pulls my long hair out of my face. She brushes the tear track from my cheek. It's nice. I enjoy being petted. We could stay like this for hours and I'd be so happy, my head in her lap and her fingers working the knots from my hair.

We're both silent for a while until she breaks it with whispered words, "I want that too. I love you, Jamie. I think I've loved you for a long time. You make it so easy. You're sweet and gentle. Genuinely kind. You never say a mean thing about anyone, not even when they deserve it. You're easy to love."

Hope makes my chest tight. I tilt my head so I can see her. "Really?"

"I don't know why it's so hard for me to use my words and say the things I feel," she says. "I'm such a coward. I'll try to say these things more often because I think you need to hear them. That's a promise."

How can she say that she's not brave? That isn't true. It's

not true at all. So that's what I tell her. "You're the bravest person I know. You survived, and you never gave up. You have plans and you know what you want to do. You're so smart. You run a business and you take care of all of us. I couldn't do what you've done. You made a place that makes people happy, and you help people. And you do it as an omega with alphas telling you that you can't. If that's not brave, then I don't know what is. You're so brave, and kind, and caring, and that's why I love you."

Her mouth rounds in surprise, and then her eyes soften, and she smiles. "I'm proud of you for telling me about something you wanted."

"So you'll keep me? You'll mark me as yours? We did a good job with your heat, right?" I ask, then hold my breath as I wait for her answer.

"You did a *very* good job. It was perfect." She sighs. "But I can't mark you right now."

"Oh." My heart cracks in my chest and the lump in my throat is back. It was stupid to push, to hope that because she marked Anthony, I could ask and she'd do it. He's perfect. Of course she wants him in her pack.

Just because he and I are dating doesn't mean I get an automatic in. I thought she liked me the way I was, but maybe she wants her pack alphas to be more like Brendan. Calm, confident, and in charge.

After her rough childhood, she probably wants that stability. Craves it. Maybe if I ask him… I know he'd help me. He's nice. I like Brendan. Having a plan makes me feel better. Looking at the floor, I nod so she won't see the tears in my eyes. "Okay."

She still wants to own me, I remind myself. *But I haven't earned my mark yet. I'll have to try harder. Be more like a real alpha.*

"I'm glad you understand. You're part of the group number

tonight and you have a solo. It would be too short notice to replace you."

I nod, but then I frown. "Why would you need to replace me?" Will I really not be allowed to dance if she marks me? I love dancing at Rut. It's easy money, and I get to see Vee every day, and the cardio keeps me fit. But if she wants me to quit… Well, I've offered before.

She runs her fingers through my hair, and I clutch her leg to my chest like a lifeline. "None of the dancers have claiming marks."

I blink and the silence stretches as I try to figure out if that's true or not and why it would matter. "Are you sure?"

"Yes. Most omegas don't mark their alpha anyway, but not having a visible claiming bite is part of Rut's contract for the dancers. A mating bite ruins the illusion that you're attainable to the customers."

"Oh. Is that the only reason you won't bite me?" I ask, hopeful again. I brush the tears from my eyelashes and prop my chin on her leg so I can gaze up at her.

"I'm a coward, remember? I'm not looking forward to breaking that news to Nate. You're the crowd favorite. He's gonna strangle me with one of Darlene's feather boas. I'm working up the courage."

Suddenly everything's okay again. She wants me. Wants me badly enough that she's going to risk making Nate angry. He's so loud when he yells. I hate it when people are angry. Why can't they chill? It all works out in the end.

I think about what she said. How she'd mark me, but everyone will see it and Nate will get mad and yell. I don't want Vee to get yelled at. Sometimes they scream at each other in the office and you can hear them from downstairs, even with the door closed. I always plug my ears when that happens.

"What if they couldn't see it?" I ask.

Vee raises her eyebrows. "When you're on stage, there's not a lot of you they can't see, remember? You'd be able to get away with it if I bit you where the waiter uniform could hide it, but then you wouldn't be able to dance. Most of the money is in dance solos and the customers will see the scars when they get up close and personal to tip you. It's okay. We just need more time to hire a new dancer to replace you."

"But I don't want to stop dancing."

"Oh," Vee says in an exhale. Her face goes blank in a way that makes me uneasy, although I can't quite explain why. "I should have asked instead of assuming."

"I want you to claim me, but I don't want to stop dancing."

"Jamie, there's only one place I'd be able to bite you that…" Vee hesitates. "That they couldn't see when you dance."

"Yes." I'll do it. I don't care where my mark is, so long as it triggers the bond. There isn't anything I wouldn't do for Vee. "I want it there."

The skin between her brows knits together, and she stares off into the room like she does when she's thinking hard. "I don't know if it would work. I'd have to research it. Make sure it's safe."

"I trust you," I say. And I mean it. Vee takes care of the things and people she claims as hers. I want to be one of those, and I'll do whatever it takes to make sure that happens.

Vee pats me on the head and smiles, then drags in a deep breath, sighs, and nods. "I know you do. Okay, I have work to do and everyone else will be here soon. You should go get cleaned up while I straighten out the mess we made of this desk." When I stand, her eyes drop to the cage on my cock. "Do you need that off tonight to dance?" Her fingers skim over the key that rests against her breastbone.

"I'd like to keep it on." The weight of it is comforting. It's a reminder that I'm good enough. I'm wanted. Owned. Soon I'll be fully claimed.

Vee reaches for me and taps a nail against the metal, then teases me with light strokes through the gaps until pre-cum drips through the hole in the cage. "I love my present. Thank you. I'll give Anthony and Brendan their keys." She pulls me down for a kiss, then releases me. "Now be a good boy and go get cleaned up before everyone smells how naughty we were."

Her orders excite me. My cock swells to the confines of its cage and the pressure changes from a hug to a denial. I can't get hard, no matter how much my body is trying. I'm powerless against a basic bodily function—and I like it. I love the simplicity of taking orders. Of obeying and doing a good job. Of not having to think. Of knowing I'm pleasing her.

"Yes, Ma'am." I gather up my clothes and dress while Vee tidies up her desk, and then, by the time I get downstairs, a few of the new dancers have shown up for extra practice time in front of the mirror wall. I wave and decline their invite to hang, then rush to the bathroom to deal with the problem of my constantly dripping cock. The task isn't simple when I can't touch a lot of my skin. I use the sink and a fistful of paper towels to wash the scent of her delicious pheromones off me, then spray myself down with the nullifier we keep there for anyone to use.

The rest of the night is a sweet form of torture. Getting used to the weight of the cage and how it makes things shift while I'm dancing won't happen overnight.

After practice, I take a break and accept water from Anthony at the bar while the other dancers head out back for smokes and tacos from the truck two blocks down. He hands me the towel he keeps aside for me and I use it to mop up the worst of the sweat while I suck down half of the water.

"How'd it go?" Anthony asks.

"Good. She liked it." A blush heats my face and I glance around to make sure we're alone. "I'm wearing it now."

Anthony grins and sets the glass he was wiping aside, then leans on his forearms across the bar. "I know. She gave us our keys while you were rehearsing. We talked because she had questions. Sounds like tonight's your big night. Excited?"

My belly feels fluttery and my palms are sweaty. Excited. Nervous. Frustratingly horny from the newness of the cage's constant pressure around my cock and balls. "Yes."

"Jamie!" Nate yells. "Are you planning to join us sometime this century?"

I look over my shoulder and see that the dancers have come back in and everyone is headed to the changing room for dress rehearsals.

The changing room. The room where we change. Where I'll have to get naked. Oh. Well... That's going to be awkward.

"Oh, and Jamie?" Anthony calls out, stopping me from getting far. His grin widens, and he rakes his dark hair out of his face as he comes around the bar and steps close. He claps me on the shoulder and leans in like he's telling me a secret.

With his body blocking the movement, he reaches down and grabs the cage, pulling it away from my body. But there's nowhere for it to go. It tugs at something deep inside me, and the air wheezes from my lungs right before a burst of pleasure from the dull, throbbing pain radiates through me.

Anthony's voice is so low it's almost a growl. "I'm telling you now that during her next heat, this stays on until we're good and ready to unlock you. I'm going to take my time with her. Brendan is too. You're going to have to take a lot of cock to earn the privilege of knotting her. Understood?"

I groan and nod, too overwhelmed to form words. It's my deepest, most closely guarded fantasy. Being forced to endure an omega's heat while caged. I love how Anthony doesn't simply accept my quirks—he thrives in them. I've never trusted anyone else with these secrets. He makes it easy to be honest. Nothing's too dark or rough or twisted for Anthony.

"Understood," I answer.

Anthony squeezes me one last time. "Good," he says. When he releases me, I bite back a whimper of relief.

"Do you need a formal invitation, Jamie?" Nate yells.

"Coming!" I say, forcing my voice into something that I hope sounds normal.

Anthony chuckles and mutters something under his breath like, *no, you're not.*

I hurry through the curtain into the back and take my new costume from Darlene, giving the sweet beta woman my thanks. It's a tight police uniform with navy sequins running up the side seam where the breakaway snaps go from hip to hem. There's a sparkly navy thong with a silver star to match.

I'm the only one left in the changing room, but I know that my luck won't hold forever. At some point, someone will see my cock cage. They'll know that I'm locked, my chastity secured. Thoughts of the future embarrassment waiting for me shouldn't get me hot, but I'm strangely looking forward to it and dreading it at the same time.

When I pull the thong on and check the fit in the mirror, I'm grateful for the dark colors of the costume. It hides the bumps of the cage. It'll be fine for today, but when I wear the angel's tight white pants, it's going to be a problem. One of my mates will have to unlock me so I can dance.

Darlene meets me at the curtain and hands me the policeman's hat that I forgot. I fix it on my head, then join the others. I pay extra attention to Nate's commands and the music. Tonight needs to be perfect. After all, it's a special night.

I only bump into Ryan twice this time.

Chapter Thirty-Five

VERONICA

JAMIE PULLS AN ENORMOUS WAD OF CRUMPLED CASH OUT OF HIS money bag and sets it on the dining table for smoothing and sorting.

"Wow, that's more than normal, right? It seems like a lot," Brendan says. He grabs two bottles of beer from the fridge and twists the tops off with his hand, then gives one to Anthony.

Anthony lifts the dark green glass to his lips and takes a swig before speaking. "Yeah, that's a lot for a Tuesday."

"It's because he smells horny," I say with a grin.

Jamie's scent has been torturing me all night. There's only one air return in the office, so the filtration system takes longer to do a full cycle than it does on the main floor. He also forgot to clean a splatter of cum off the floor, and I missed it until Brendan pointed it out. I've never been more grateful that Nate's a beta than I was tonight. He's also back on coke so his sense of smell is shit right now.

"I can't help it," Jamie says with a blush. "My cock won't stop dripping. Every tiny thing sets me off. It's sensitive."

"Is it?" I ask, laying my trap. I stand right next to him and bury my nose in his neck as I pet his chest, then run my hand down his washboard abs. They tense and tighten, then relax under my palm. Lower. I brush over the bulge in his pants and enjoy the hitch in his breath. "How sensitive is your poor cock?"

"Very," he answers.

I trace the outline of his cage through the cloth. Learn the shape of it with my fingertips. The scent of his coconut pheromones tickles my nose and makes my nipples tighten. It's the edging. He smells like sex and need. Like he's on the verge of a rut. And the crowd could tell. The omegas were ravenous for him tonight.

He's ours. They can't have him. Every inch of him is ours, including this delicious alpha cock they all crave.

The more I tease him, the heavier his breathing gets and the more his wet spot of arousal grows. Only his sack hangs free. I fondle him, palming his balls and enjoying how heavy and swollen they are in my hand.

"Poor pet," I croon. "Do you already need to come again?"

"If it… if it pleases you, Ma'am." Jamie sucks in a breath when I pull his sack away from his body, the movement tugging on the root of his cock.

"Strip and lie down on the bed," I order, letting him go.

Jamie nods, his long blond hair sliding over his shoulders with the movement. He strips right there in the kitchen, a quick removal of clothing with none of the teasing he puts into his dancing. This isn't a show. A fantasy. Things are about to get very real. Very real and official.

When he's nude, Jamie walks to the bedroom and lies down on the bed. It's a glorious sight. He's big and broad shouldered with sculpted muscles. An Adonis. I stand at the foot of the bed and strip too, leaving my clothes and shoes in a forgotten pile on the ground. Brendan and Anthony join us and watch, sticking to the periphery.

I put a knee on the bed, and Jamie's eyes slide to mine, his lips curling into a tentative smile. He's nervous. His gaze drops to the key dangling between my breasts before flicking up to meet my stare. Lips parting, his tongue darts out to wet them.

I'm silent as I straddle his legs. I trail a finger down his pecs, his abs, let it dip inside his navel, then go lower. His body hair is golden and sparse, but there's a faint dusting of a happy trail that leads straight to his groin where the hair is cropped short. It needs to be so it's manageable under those tiny thongs the dancers wear.

"If I unlock this cock right now, this will be the last pussy you ever fuck," I say.

"Yes, Miss Vee."

I grab the key and slide my thumb over the notches of its teeth. "Is that what you want, pet? You want me to own you? Body, heart, and soul? Forever?"

"Yes."

A drop of pre-cum gathers at the hole in his cage and drips onto his thigh. I gather it up and bring it to my mouth, savoring its taste. Decadent coconut and alpha musk. His cum is as sweet as he is. My big, beautiful, strong Jamie. God, he's perfect. Like a marble statue brought to life. Yet he looks at me like I'm the goddess. I want him to see me like that always. Forever. I want him to be mine completely.

I grab the key and pull the necklace over my head, then shake to settle my hair. It takes me three tries to fit the small key in the tiny lock and turn it. The moment I slide the locking tumbler from the hinges, his cock swells. The force of his thickening erection pries the cage apart from the base.

Jamie sucks in a breath and holds still without being ordered as I pull it off him. It sticks over the flare of his crown for a moment before finally coming free. I set the cage aside and palm his dick, inspecting it with my eyes and fingers for any signs of damage. It's perfect.

I leave the ring around his shaft and balls because there's no getting it off with how swollen and needy he is. Poor pet.

"You're not allowed to come until I say so," I order as I climb onto his body and straddle his lap. I'm already wet and ready when I sit, his cock under me as I rub my slit along his trapped length. God, that feels good. And he isn't inside me yet.

"Yes, Ma'am." Jamie holds perfectly still while I use him. Despite his outward calmness, his eyes tighten with restrained need.

Both of our arousals mix as I grind myself on him until my pussy aches to be filled. I'm so empty. Leaning forward, I reach behind me and fit him to my entrance. I sink down slowly, taking him to the hilt in a single smooth movement. "Fuck, that's good. Your cock makes a good toy for me, pet."

"Th-thank you, Ma'am." His nostrils flare and his lips part with his breathing. But he holds still like the good boy he is.

My nails dig into his pecs while I ride him, rocking and enjoying the stretching fullness and the way my clit grazes his pelvis if I lean the right way. "Fuck, I've been thinking about this all night." I bite my lip and grind faster. Using him. My personal fuck toy. My alpha cock on command. Sweet Jamie.

"Me... me too," Jamie says. His eyes lose focus and the veins on his neck stand out as he tenses. His muscles bunch under my hands. "Thank you for using my cock as your toy, Ma'am."

Slowing my pace to stretch things out, I smile as he frowns. "Did you like knowing your cock was locked up? That all those omegas who saw you on that stage wanted you? None of them knew how worthless your pretty alpha cock was to them because they'll never have your key."

"I liked being on stage and having a secret with you. I thought about you the entire time."

I lean forward, licking his pec before taking his small nipple into my mouth, and he groans. I bite it and Jamie groans again, deeper and longer. His masochism streak draws out the inner sadist I didn't know I had. I move to the other nipple and squeeze my pussy around his cock in tandem as I pinch it between my teeth.

His hips stutter with an aborted thrust. The flicker of his self-control wavering fills me with a rush of pleasure. His cock does too. It hits the perfect spot inside me. I give into the impulse to fuck myself on his cock. It surges deep as I bounce, and I let go, savoring the feelings his big dick unlocks. The thrill of knowing I'm the only omega on this planet who will ever know what Jamie's cock feels like inside them is heady.

"I'm going to come, Ma'am." Jamie pants, his hands twisting in the bedding as he fidgets, trying so hard to be still for me. To obey. To be my good boy.

"No, you're not." I don't stop right away. I edge him to the brink, force him to hold back his orgasm through sheer willpower and determination. When he lets out a whimper, then holds his breath, that's when I finally stop.

I scratch my nails over his chest, enjoying the faint streaks of pink that form on his sun-tanned golden skin. They'll be gone by the morning, but for right now, he wears my marks. Inside of me, his cock jumps. I do it again. Scrape him harder. Not enough to leave permanent marks, but enough to know he really feels it.

"You haven't earned the right to come yet, pet."

"I'm sorry, Ma'am."

"Don't be sorry. You're exactly the way I want you. Hard and inside me and desperate for permission to come." Leaning down, I lick my nail marks, then return to his small male nipples.

The peaks are hard and tiny, but they're large enough to bite. I suck the whole thing into my mouth and let my teeth scrape over it. His cock kicks again inside me. I let his nipple go with a wet pop and move to the other. I squeeze my walls around him too.

"Please. Please, Ma'am."

"No. I have plans for this cock and I'm only getting started." Has it been long enough? I rise and sink back down, fucking myself on his cock slowly. When he doesn't come or warn me it's imminent, I do it again. Harder. Faster. It doesn't matter that he's been edged all day. I'll make him take it a while longer.

So he knows exactly who's in charge. And because I know how much he loves it. He doesn't get to come until I tell him to.

I use him. Like he's my living human dildo. I use his cock to fuck myself, stopping every single time he warns me he's about to come. Five. That's how many times I bring him to the brink of release and deny him that gratification. It's not until his face is delightfully pink and tears wet his blond eyelashes into spiked clumps that I decide to have mercy.

"Make me come on that pretty cock, pet, and I'll give you what you want. But don't you dare come too or I'll lock you for an entire week. The only release you'll get is from having one of their cocks massage your prostate. Isn't that right, guys?"

"Sounds good to me," Anthony says, grinning.

"Sure," Brendan agrees.

"Yes, Ma'am. I understand. I won't come." Jamie nods, his expression one of determination. Or maybe it's desperation. I cede control to him to see what he'll do.

His large hands grip me by the hips and gently lift me off

him. He tugs me down, his hips thrusting upward. It's a tentative thrust. Nice. Not the deep dicking I'm craving right now.

"Harder, pet. Make me remember the stretch from that big cock tomorrow, so I'm tempted to unlock you and use this pretty cock again."

Jamie thrusts harder. Deeper. He pulls me onto his cock and thrusts. Our skin smacks together, the sounds wet and loud. His cockhead knocks against the end of me and demands more room. My belly bulges. I'm stuffed full and stretched. Slick spreads between us as he obeys and fucks me hard.

"Mmm, that's good. Good boy," I praise him. "Faster. I want to come on my new toy."

His hips rise off the bed, taking me with him, and my tits bounce as Jamie fucks me. He's awkward and clumsy at first, but then he gains momentum and confidence.

"There you go," I say. "That's it. You're doing such a good job. Keep going."

His thick brows knit together and his face reddens, sweat sticking his hair to his temples as he bucks underneath me.

"Fuck, that feels good." My eyes flutter as a pooling sensation drowns me. "I love the way you fill me."

He can't speak. All he can manage are grunts and groans as he focuses on pleasing me. On fucking me without finding his own pleasure. Twice he has to stop and start again, his eyes squeezed shut as he waits. Twice my pending orgasm stutters and stalls. It's karma, and payback is a bitch. Desperation wells within me. I need to come. Need it more than anything.

"Make me come on this cock, pet. I need you." I splay both hands on his sweat-damp skin and memorize the contours of his body. Each dip and swell and divot while his muscles bunch underneath me and strain.

"I can't," he whines. "Not without coming. I'm not good at this. Can I use my mouth, Ma'am?"

"No. I know you can eat pussy. You're so good at it. You can learn how to be good at this, too. I know you can, pet. I believe in you. Try again."

Jamie nods and goes still for a moment. I watch him think. And then he seems to decide. He cradles me in his arms and flips our positions. Lays me down on my back, his cock slipping out, and then he settles himself between my splayed legs. He nudges them wider until I'm spread wide for him. His cock is ruddy and engorged, his knot in the beginning stages of swelling, as he fits it to my hole and presses the tip in.

I'm so slick he slides right in and we both sigh together as he seats himself. His hips rock, and the change in angle means that the flared rim of his cockhead rubs over my g-spot.

"Smart boy," I groan, encouraging him.

Jamie smiles, soaking up the praise he deserves, and thrusts faster. "It's good?"

"So good." I squeeze his hips between my knees and rock with him, my heels digging into his ass to urge him on. He readjusts his hands on the bed, his arms bulging while he holds himself over me. When his pelvis grinds against my clit, I let out a throaty groan and raise my hips to meet him.

"That's good, pet. I can come like this. More. I need more."

"You feel so good, Miss Vee."

"It's the only pussy you'll ever fuck. Your cock is mine. Say it."

"It's yours." His gaze drifts down to where our bodies meet. Where his cock is buried in my cunt. "My cock is yours. My heart. Me."

My labia are so swollen they're puffy. My clit is engorged and flushed. Slick makes us both glisten. The sight of his enormous cock shuttling in and out of me is almost enough to make me come. His knot catches at my entrance, not swollen enough to lodge behind my pubic bone yet, but getting there. My walls clamp down on his cock and his abdomen tenses. His cock jumps inside me.

I've had enough. Enough teasing. Enough near orgasms. I reach up and grab a fistful of Jamie's hair at his nape, squeezing tight and dragging him more firmly on top of me. His weight is heavy, but comforting. I'm not scared of him. Not my sweet Jamie. Not when I'm so clearly in charge.

"I'm not made of glass," I growl. "Now hurry and fuck me properly or I'll make it two weeks instead of one."

Jamie groans, his eyes sliding closed. His hips slam up, driving his cock home. The flare scrapes over my g-spot. The crushing weight of his pelvis means each thrust tugs at my swollen clit. I watch his eyes glaze over as he loses himself in the pleasure of my wet pussy.

The tension coils taut and my breath hitches as I get close. So close. Almost there. I squeeze tighter at his nape, pulling. His back arches and somehow his cock sinks deeper. His knot pushes and tugs at my pubic bone with every thrust. We're flirting with danger here.

Jamie whimpers—he knows it too. And knowing he's so close, that his balls are desperate to drain themselves inside me and his knot wants to stopper all that mess in deep, is enough to push me over the edge.

"Don't come," I remind him as the tension snaps inside me. I forget how to speak for a moment as he fucks me, oblivious to the fact that I've spiraled. My pussy flutters a few seconds later, my walls clamping down on his cock. I cry out with my orgasm, then go limp.

We're so entwined I feel him shudder with the effort of not following me into his own orgasm. His strokes turn languid and sweet while my spasms fade into aftershocks.

"Mmm." I lie there, spent, as my pussy gives one last contraction around his girth. My grip slackens in his hair, and I stroke his neck while I bask in the glow of aftershocks and satisfaction. "Good job, pet. You were so good for me. You made me come on your cock. I'm so proud of you. I knew you could do it. You can do anything you set your mind to." I brush a tender kiss across his lips.

His arms tremble from strain, and I urge him closer until he's lying flush on top of me, his cock still lodged deep inside me, keeping warm and ready for what comes next. He pants as he struggles to catch his breath while he fights his body's urge to thrust. To claim and knot and spend his release inside a willing omega cunt.

No. I won't let him. We have other plans.

Once I've caught my breath, I urge him off me. All it takes is two fingers in the divot between his pecs to move his bulk. He flops onto his back, his swollen, needy cock slapping against his stomach with a heavy thud. *Poor baby.* I smile and crawl over him again, sliding down his body until I'm settled between his legs.

"You did such a good job, pet. I think it's time for your reward. Would you like that?" I ask, already knowing the answer.

"Yes, Ma'am."

"Hmm." I arch one brow at him.

"Please," he adds.

I smile. Oh, how I love it when he begs.

I start with his sack. I press his cock firmly to his stomach and lick his balls, taking time to suck them into my mouth one by one. I slide my tongue under the ring around his cock and balls, enjoying how his cock jumps under my hand. Once his balls are clean of slick and pre-cum, I move to his shaft. Inch by inch, I lick him until nothing but velvety skin remains. He babbles nonsense, his pleas mixed with grunts and groans and moans while I suck his head into my mouth and hold him there. His taste fills my mouth as pre-cum drips from his tip.

But this isn't a blowjob. It's more than that. And he doesn't get to come yet.

Pulling away, I smile as he lets out a dissatisfied moan. "Are you ready to be mine, Jamie?"

"Always. I want you to make me yours."

"This is going to hurt," I warn him. It's why I've been edging him. I need him close to orgasm so that he can bear what comes next. Pain mixed with pleasure can be tolerated in ways that pain alone cannot.

"I'd walk through fire if you asked, Vee. I'd do anything. I love you. Please mark me."

His words make me smile, and I can't believe how lucky I am to have found these three men. I look up at Anthony and Brendan. Anthony grimaces, a hand rising to cover his mouth, and Brendan gives me a curt nod, his expression inscrutable.

"I love you too, Jamie. Now, remember to breathe." I study his cock while I play with the tip, sliding the skin of his shaft over his head to distract him and tighten things. The veins of his cock are thick and bulging. I map them, taking care to avoid each one as I plan where to bite. Where my teeth will pierce.

Pre-cum drips down my fingers as I slide my thumb over his leaking slit while I open my jaw. I feed the side of his cock into my mouth, pinching him slowly between my teeth as I add more pressure.

I wait for him to cry out or beg me to stop.

He doesn't.

My teeth pinch harder. His cock jerks in my grip, in the trap of my teeth, but he bears it. Gently, so gently, I add more force until my thumb slides, too slippery, over his cockhead and my sharp omega canines puncture skin. The metallic tinge of blood seeps into my mouth.

We wait. There's a moment of panic that this won't work, that the research was bad and I've hurt him for nothing. Claiming bites have a higher chance of taking when placed over scent glands. The largest one is in the fleshy bit of skin between the base of the neck and the shoulder, but there are smaller glands all over the body. The one in the groin is in the pubis, not the cock itself.

How long will it take the pheromones in my saliva to invade his system?

We wait. My jaw aches from holding position, but I don't let go. We've come too far to stop now.

We wait some more. Supposedly it takes longer for a bond to form without a gland. That's why claiming bites don't always work right away with betas.

Am I not biting deep enough? I don't want to harm him. But I don't want this to have been for nothing either. He's still hard in my mouth. Still leaking pre-cum all over my hand. I bite harder. Blood and musk coat my teeth.

After what seems like an eternity, the trickle of awareness of another person deep inside me seeps in. The bond snaps into place, and I release my bite so I can lick his wounds. It's barely bleeding. I inspect the mark, studying the pale indentations of my flat teeth and the four tiny punctures from my canines. They're shallow, but the mating bite is there. It worked.

"I sense you," Jamie says. "Inside me."

I stroke his cock from ring to tip, avoiding the mark. His hips rise and he grunts as I work him at a steady pace, using his pre-cum to slick my fingers so they glide. The sight of his dripping cock with my bite mark on the shaft triggers some feral instinct inside me. I like it. I enjoy knowing we're connected now. Everyone who sees his cock will notice my teeth mark on it and know it's claimed. He's mine.

"How are you?" I ask him.

"Green. Greengreengreen. Can I come now? Please?"

Leaning down, I lap at his tip. The flavor of his pre-cum chases the lingering traces of his blood from my mouth. "Yes, pet. Come for me."

"Okay," he whimpers, his hips rising to push deeper past the ring of my lips.

I let him. He's been such a good boy. Such a good pet. I swallow his cock down to the flare of his swelling knot and hold him there.

All mating bites need licking to be cleaned. Nobody said you can't give head while you're doing it.

Keeping my throat relaxed, I bob up and down. His head brushes the tight ring of my throat and I relax, letting it open, and take him deeper. He groans, and his swelling knot brushes against the tip of my nose. There's no air. Not while he's this deep. But I can take it. And he's more than earned it.

When I purr with his cock still in my mouth, Jamie loses his mind. His hips thrust, pressing deeper until his knot stretches my lips. He babbles nonsense, desperate pleas. I grab his knot and squeeze to keep it from lodging behind my teeth so he won't hurt me. Then I take him to pieces with my purring.

He doesn't last long. On the third purring deep throat, his cock pulses in my throat and he goes limp. I pull back so I can catch his spending on my tongue and massage his knot. My hard work rewards me with another spurt of creamy cum. I savor it.

I swallow and lick him clean, laving his bite mark until my instincts are satisfied and he's limp underneath me. The enzymes in my saliva will keep it from getting infected. When I finally come up for air, Jamie is a puddle of floppy limbs on the bed. His eyes can barely stay open. I crawl up his body and take his face in my hands, pulling him in for a kiss. His eyes flutter open, his gaze unfocused.

"I love you, Jamie," I tell him, stroking his hair out of his face.

"Mmm. Love you too, Vee."

He's already half-asleep again and I'm not far behind him. It's been a long day.

I cuddle into his side and become the big spoon as I possessively throw a leg over his. Anthony and Brendan are still watching from the sidelines. Once we're settled, I motion for them to join us. They undress and get ready for bed. Anthony slips in on Jamie's other side and Brendan throws one of my enormous fluffy blankets over all of us, then scoots into the bed at my back.

"Looks like it went well," Brendan whispers.

With a sleepy yawn, I nod. "It's faint, but it's there. I might need to deepen it. Thanks for helping me plan it."

"You're welcome," Brendan says.

"Oww. My dick hurts just thinking about being bitten like that," Anthony complains.

I shush him. "You're ruining the moment."

I hug Jamie tighter and purr.

Two down, one to go.

Chapter Thirty-Six

BRENDAN

GETTING VERONICA OUT OF THE OFFICE AND KEEPING HER OUT for over an hour is next to impossible, but somehow Anthony managed it. God bless that deviant beta. "How is that?" I ask Jamie. "Is anything pinching or numb?"

"No. It feels good," Jamie admits, his cheeks turning pink.

A glance down at the mess of pre-cum dripping from the hole in his silver cock cage. It pools on his belly, showing me he's telling the truth. He enjoys being bound. "I can tell. Good."

The sight of his broad, perfect body tied up in hot pink rope makes my cock twitch in my pants. Nothing beats a good rigging. The sight of twisted rope digging into flesh, of restrained limbs leaving my poor little bunny helpless... Nothing makes me harder.

"I enjoy seeing you in my rope," I say.

"Thank you, Sir."

I trail two fingers over the loops that bind his arms behind his back. I reach around and make sure they're secure. He's caught. Helpless. Only his legs are free.

The rope makes a pattern of diamonds over his abs and chest. It wraps around his pelvis and upper thighs. Instead of obscuring his masculinity, his beauty, the rope enhances it. Each line draws the eye to the planes of his muscular body. Each crisscrossing holds it taut. Keeps him captive and still. Dependent on my mercy.

The blindfold I made of rope, the one I tied carefully so it wouldn't catch his hair, keeps him in the dark. His head swings, tracking my movements through only his hearing, as I move around him where he's seated in his chair.

I inspect Jamie once more, then I grab something from my bag and press the brass jingle bell into his hand. I reach around him like a hug and work my way to one of his bound hands.

"Hold this. If anything pinches or goes numb or tingles, drop it and I'll hear the noise it makes. Now, open your mouth."

Once he's taken the bell from me and opened his mouth, I pull the rope gag I made earlier from around my neck and fit it between his teeth. I'm careful not to snag his hair as I pull it taut and tie it into place.

Under the pretense of checking each line and pinch point, I tease him. I touch everywhere but his aching cock. Stuffed in that tiny cage, the strain of his erection has to be unbearable right now.

"Time to take that off," I tell him as I reach for the key around my neck. "Not that you're going to be using it tonight. But your erection completes the look, and I want to see how hard my rope makes you." I pull the necklace over my head and slot the key into the lock on his cage. Once the lock cylinder is out, the two pieces come apart quickly. Jamie's cock swells instantly. His heavy penis flops against the seat of his chair.

I wrap my hand around his base and tug him until he's at full mast. I jerk him enough to tease but not satisfy. His arousal leaks against his thigh, the chair, my hand.

"How badly do you want to come?" I ask him.

He nods, desperate, and makes a rough sound in the back of

his throat. A line of drool drips around the hemp rope in his mouth.

"You'll do anything I ask, won't you? What a good toy you are, letting me play with you. Getting you warmed up and ready."

Jamie pants around his gag, his hips twitching with the urge to thrust his cock harder into the ring of my fingers. But every thrust of his hips pulls at the bindings on his arms, putting a strain on his shoulders. After a few halfhearted surges, he gives up and goes still. Surrenders. It's a beautiful thing to witness. That moment when a sub realizes they're truly helpless without my gentle mercy.

Pre-cum leaks down my knuckles and his abdomen clenches as I bring him to the point of orgasm, then stop. "No. Not yet. I haven't said you could come."

He groans around his gag when I let him go. "Now your cock is nice and hard for your Mistress to appreciate."

The scuff of footsteps on the stairs makes my heart race in my chest. It's time.

"What sort of surprise is waiting in my office?" Veronica asks, her words and footsteps echoing up to us. The club is empty after a long night, and the music's off. Everyone else has gone home to their beds. "Your surprises make me nervous. Did you do something to my office? How mad am I going to be?"

"Hush, baby. This one is Brendan's doing and you'll like it. Trust me."

"That's the problem because your last surprise involved a hollowed out pineapple and… oh. Oh my God."

"Beautiful, isn't he?" I ask her. My hand strokes over Jamie's pectorals, which bulge around the rope winched around them. He was handsome before the rope highlighted his anatomy. Now, he's perfect. A glorious specimen of young, cut alpha.

Bound. Blinded. Gagged. Utterly at our mercy. Seeing him reduced to this state, a helpless toy waiting to be used, is breathtaking. From Veronica's reaction, she agrees.

"Yes," she says with a breathy exhale. Her eyes are fixed on my work. They skim over him from head to toe. Double back to his magnificent cock where it's ruddy and swollen between his legs.

"He'd look better on his knees." That's the only warning I give Jamie as I grab him by the handle I wove into his chest harness and haul him from his chair. He scrambles to his feet, his big body swaying until I steady him, then pull him a few feet away from his chair. "Down."

Jamie goes to his knees while I help him. I ease him down and keep my grip on his handle until I know he's safely on the floor and isn't about to tip sideways or fall on his face. His posture is bad. Untrained. Nothing I can't fix with a firm, guiding hand and my wealth of experience.

"Shoulders back," I bark.

He's rounded them to ease the strain of the tie. But that's not what I want. This isn't a punishment tie that binds tighter and tighter the more you struggle, but it still demands good posture. I don't want anything going numb. I want him to feel every inch of my rope. To know another alpha has tied him up. Hobbled him. Bettered him.

With him bound in my rope, it doesn't matter that I'm older. That my knee is fucked, and it hurts every single day. I'm in charge.

I tap him on the shoulders and a thrill runs through me as he pulls his shoulders back and thrusts his chest out. What a good boy. So eager to please. So delightfully submissive when his every alpha instinct must be screaming at his hind brain to escape. To dominate. Challenge me and fight.

His attention wavers as I circle him and inspect my work,

adjusting any rope that's slipped. He tries to track me, though he can't see me. When I'm in front of him, I raise my bad leg and set the heel of my shoe against his knee, nudging it to the side. "Wider. Spread those thighs. Sit on your heels."

Jamie spreads his thighs apart on the cold, hard floor and waits for his next order.

"Good boy." I lay my hand on his hair and stroke what's not bound by his blindfold and gag. Veronica stands there, mute, her mouth hanging open and her gaze hungry as she devours the sight of him. Of my work.

"That's very good," I tell him. And then I give Veronica a pointed look. "Your turn, sweetheart. Strip for me."

She startles, her attention ripped from him to me. Exactly where I want it. She frowns. Her shoulders square.

Before she can argue, I hold one finger up to stifle her budding protest. I close the gap between us and caress her arms. "I'm asking you to trust me. To trust that I would do nothing to harm you. Physically or mentally. I gave Anthony my backup pair of shears. The minute he wants to, he can cut you free. So can I. You know we'd never hurt you, right?"

Veronica looks from Anthony to me, her expression wary. I get it. With her history, it's difficult for her to give up power or control. Even though she so desperately craves it. Needs the release of trusting that someone else will take over so she can rest. Protect her. Guard her. Keep her safe. Because whether or not she wants to admit it, she's precious. She's ours.

Her hesitation to submit right now makes the total submission of her heats all that much sweeter. As long as she eventually does what she's told, I don't mind being patient. Slowly, she nods. But the skin between her brows is pinched. This isn't easy for her, though she has nothing to fear from me.

"I'm asking you to trust me and accept my courting gift," I say, softening my words some more. She doesn't need my bark, not like Jamie does. She needs the nurturing side of an alpha so she can blossom. So she can feel like an omega when being in charge gets to be too much and she needs an escape from that authority.

And I need this too. More than anything. I need to know she accepts this facet of me. That she trusts me. That she'll fully submit, knowing that I'd never order her to do something that would hurt her. Because I don't want to hurt her. Never. She's mine. My omega to shelter. Protect. Guard.

When she still hesitates, I show her the shears hanging from my belt. They're designed for medical staff, but the blunted tip guard and thick serrated blades mean they'll cut through my hemp rope with a few snips.

"If at any point you don't like what I'm doing, I'll free you. All you have to do is tell me to stop. We won't use a safe word today." Not until I know she won't forget it in a moment of panic. I hook the shears onto my belt.

"Will you accept my courting gift and strip?" I ask her again.

She swallows, her throat bobbing, and lets out a shaky breath. Veronica reaches for her shirt, tugging it from the waistband of her skirt. "Don't forget that my taser's in one of those drawers. If you make me regret this…"

I know she won't. Neither will I. This moment is everything. "Sweetheart, if that happens, I'll hand you the taser myself because nothing could feel worse than the knowledge I hurt my omega. Take off the underwear too. I want you nude. You can keep the heels, though. You'll probably need them for the height."

Once she's wearing nothing but her heels and her clothes are a pile on the floor, I take a moment to savor the sight of her. It never gets old. Her tits are perfect for rope. Soft and full, but not too perky. Perky, firm breasts are the worst to tie. Mentally,

I run through the colors I have in my bag and decide what I want to see her in. Black.

"So beautiful," I tell her, enjoying the way her cheeks flush. It never fails. A bit of praise makes her so pleased. Almost like she's got a serious praise kink. *Oh. Oh, yes.*

I know a way to make this better. I'm going to turn it into a game, because she's eager to please even if she's nervous. I think I still have some from that session I had with that model last year. Sometimes it pays to be lazy and not do a thorough clean out of your toy bag.

I walk over to my bag and rummage through it until I find what I'm looking for. A coiled bunch of ink black hemp, softened with use, and a sheet of gold star stickers. I undo the rope, find the marked center and cast off the excess behind me, then drape it over my shoulder for easy access.

Veronica watches me like a hawk as I rejoin her.

"That's a good girl for following orders. I know how difficult this is for you. You're being very brave."

She frowns as I peel a gold star sticker off the sheet and stick it to her chest, then snorts. "You can't be serious."

Tsking, I tap the end of my rope against her sticker. "Careful, sweetheart. Or I'll take your star away and you've only just earned it. Now be a good girl and hold still for me."

To start, I bring my rope across the top of her chest and around so it's running from the side of her neck to her other armpit. Her lungs expand as the rope slides across her skin. I come around to her back and tie a quick-release knot, then bring the tail around her rib cage and cross it over the other side of her neck, hitching the two together and weaving them between her shoulder blades until the first part of the tie is taut and symmetrical.

I run my fingers along her neck, checking her. When I notice that her nipples are hard peaks, I pause to stroke them and palm her breast. Either she's cold, or she's enjoying this more than she thought she would. "Not so bad, is it?"

"No." She fingers the rope, inspecting it. "It's kind of like a hug."

"A hug. Yes, that's the perfect way to describe it, sweetheart. My rope is an extension of me when I'm tying you. It's my will made tangible. It's my arms wrapping you in a hug."

I bring the two strands of rope back to the front of her chest harness, tying a half hitch on one side and framing her breasts as I cross it over from the top of one to the bottom of the other. I hug her for real, dipping my nose into the hollow of her throat as I bring the rope around her to the other side again and weave it around and up, hitching them again until the rope makes a diamond above her breasts and everything's symmetrical once more.

"Is that why you like it? The control?" she asks.

Her question makes me think as I come to her back again, securing the tie and bringing the tails of the rope down to the lower strands under her breasts where I tie a clove hitch. There's not enough rope left to make it around to her front again, so I weave the ends into a flower knot on her back. A pretty knot for my pretty girl.

"I enjoy the control," I admit. "As well as the aesthetics. Highlighting all the things that make you so beautiful. Leaving my mark on your skin." Leaning forward, I press a kiss to her bare shoulder and run my hands over the rope digging into her softness. "I could make you come from my rope alone. Put a knot between your pussy lips and pluck the rope so it slides against your clit. I wouldn't have to touch you. Wouldn't have to fuck you. You'd come on my rope, your juices soaking into the fibers and making it softer than before."

Reaching around her, I tug her against me and rub my hand down her front. Over the knots in the rope. The divots they make around her breasts. I slide lower and sink it between her legs. Her core throbs against my hand as arousal makes her pussy plump. Spreading her lips apart, I slick two fingers between her folds and graze her clit.

"Already wet for me." I let her go, leaving her teased. I take the sticker sheet from my back pocket, peel a gold foil star from the backing, and slap it onto her inner thigh. "That's my good girl."

Knowing she's enjoying this, that I'm the first one to tie her, makes me want to hurry, but I force myself to go slow. To savor this. The first time of many more to come. A lifetime of this.

She watches me go to my bag and grab another length of rope, uncoiling it and finding the center. I add it onto the knot at her back and wrap it around her, letting my fingers graze and torment her more as I lift her breast to start the next diamond underneath it. Rather than keeping the pattern going, I stop at two and tie it off, then fetch another length of rope. A thinner, softer one which I've been conditioning for weeks.

Looping it around her waist, I make it snug, then tie two lark's head knots and finish it all with a half hitch and let the excess dangle. At her pussy, I nestle it between her labia and bring it around.

Once I've pulled it snug and winched it at her back, she sucks in a breath, but says nothing. Smirking, I double back and pull the ends through her waistband, splitting the ropes and tucking everything into place where another half hitch knot ties it off.

One after another, I layer half hitch knots until the front of her crotch rope is thick and strong. She'll need it. When it's at the perfect height, I split the lines again to make sure it's forming correctly.

"That'll do. Are you ready for your present, sweetheart?" I ask her.

"Yes?" she answers, confused.

It's Anthony who rifles through my tool bag and brings out the vibrator. It's huge—the alpha models always are—with large, simulated balls that give it a sturdy base.

Anthony holds it up, turning it in the light and measuring its girth with his hand. "It's a knotting one, right?"

"It is." I take it from him and show them both. "The remote control is in the bag. I charged them both yesterday, so it should be good to go. I think he's going to love this."

"Holy shit," Veronica says, looking from the vibrator to Jamie, who's still bound and gagged on the floor. A pretty present for our special girl. She's finally figured out her bonding gift. "Hurry up and put it on me."

"So bossy," I chide her, taking the vibrator and remote control from Anthony. I press the silicone cock against the rope strapped tight between her labia and click the on button.

She gasps, her back straightening, as the vibrations travel down the rope. God, I love rope. Real rope made from actual fibers. Hemp, jute, cotton, and silk. A lot of people use synthetics for genital ties, but I prefer real fibers. Once it's properly conditioned and worn, it's smoother and safer than synthetics. Rope made from plastic feels silky smooth, but it chafes the skin with friction. But hemp? Hemp sings. The only rope that's better for intimate floor work is silk. My omega deserves silk, but today she'll make do with hemp.

"Naughty girl. Be patient. Unless you don't like the rope after all? Do you want me to untie you? We can stop." Because I don't tolerate brats. Anthony likes to play his little game of forcing submission from her, but I like my sweet girl obedient. I hit the function button, so it changes from slow vibrations to pulses. I show her what she'll be missing.

"Fuck! No. I like it. I want it, please. I'm sorry."

Chuckling, I click the remote again and turn the fake cock

off, then pry her pelvis ropes apart and slot the vibrator into place. I tie a few more ties to keep it secure and then I use the remote to test that its knotting function still works with her rope harness holding it in place.

When the silicone knot swells to a girth that's almost double the size of the cock, she touches it reverently. It's not the largest model they sell. It's not even as big as Jamie or me. But on a tiny omega, the thing looks enormous. Obscene. Another push on the remote deflates the knot and I return my attention to Jamie.

"Are you ready, boy?" I ask him. "We'll see if you can come from a prostate massage alone before we put that cage back on your cock."

Jamie nods and his cock bobs uselessly in the air, a drop of pre-cum splattering against his bare thigh.

"On your feet." I grab him by his handle and help him rise, making sure he's steady and his legs didn't fall asleep while he kneeled there. We weren't exactly quick while I was tying Veronica. Shibari is an art form that shouldn't be rushed.

Jamie's cock drips arousal against his thigh, and it flops while I march him over to Veronica's desk. His hip bumps against the edge. My hand between his shoulder blades forces him to bend over the area I cleared earlier. He turns his head so his cheek presses flat against the wood as I check his arms and hands, making sure the blood flow is good and none of the ropes slipped. He's still holding onto his safeword bell. Good.

"That's it. That's a good boy. Spread those thighs so your omega can fuck you." I nudge his bare foot with my shoe and Jamie spreads them. He arches his back more as he leans all of his weight on the desk. Pushes his rump in the air.

When I'm satisfied, I move my attention lower and grip his ass cheeks, spreading them wide so I can see the plug that I asked Anthony to help him insert earlier. Gripping it by the flared end, I pull it free. His ass clenches tightly, as if it doesn't want to release it, until finally it pops free. Jamie whimpers around his gag. His hole is puffy and slick. He's ready.

I hold Veronica's gaze and slap his ass. I rub him, teasing the jut of his perineum and the rope that crosses there. The lines are taut against his delicate flesh. Jamie mumbles against his gag, his hips twitching and grinding his cock against the desk. That's better. He's probably back to full hardness now. Aching and desperate for release. Ah, youth. There's no substitution for its natural vigor.

"He's all yours, sweetheart."

"Lube?" Veronica asks, her hand stroking her fake phallus as if it's real and she's getting it ready.

Safety first. I like it. I smile at her and pull the small bottle of lube and another gold star from my pocket. I hold both in the air so she has to come closer.

Chapter Thirty-Seven

BRENDAN

SHE TAKES THE LUBE FROM ME AND FLIPS THE CAP OPEN, squirting it into her hand and coating the vibrator thoroughly from tip to knot. Jamie was already prepped before he was plugged, but with anal, you can't ever have too much slick. It's not like he's an omega who makes his own supply.

"I shouldn't be surprised that you're prepared. I bet you were a Boy Scout." Her tone is teasing, and her lips twitch with a suppressed smile. Veronica pours a good measure into her palm, sets the bottle aside, and slicks her fake cock.

"Always be prepared," I answer. When you're a rope top, it's important to think of every scenario, plan for each contingency, and mitigate risk. There's a deep level of trust between the top and their bottom. Especially when they're bound, blinded, gagged, and completely helpless.

Veronica searches me with her eyes as her hand strokes up and down the silicone phallus. "What else you got in there for me?"

Grinning, I rub a hand over my half-hard cock tenting my pants. "I've got your grand prize right here. Once you've earned it." I wink at her.

Although he was plugged, Veronica takes her time to make sure Jamie is ready. She pushes a slick finger inside him, pumps it in and out, then adds a second and a third. When I show her how to scissor them apart, she does it.

Jamie is a whining, drooling mess when she finally deems him ready and puts the slick head of the silicone cock to his puffy, lubricated hole.

"Are you ready for my cock, pet?" she asks, wiping the fake slick from her hands on his bare skin. "Ready for me to fuck you?"

He lifts his ass higher in response. That's all the consent that any of us need.

Veronica sets the tip of her black cock to his rim. She presses. With slow thrusts, she works it inside him. Anthony comes around to the side to lean against the desk and watches as Jamie's hole stretches for her.

"Mmm, that's good, pet. You're taking my cock so well. Just a bit more. Be a good boy and let me in. Let me claim you completely."

When he takes the entire head, the flared corona catching on his rim, he whimpers around his gag. She rewards him with gentle strokes over his rope-covered skin. "Shh. That's it. Good boy," she murmurs. "You're doing such a good job taking my cock."

He takes the tip easily, but struggles with the rest of its girth. He must feel every single inch. Once it's fully seated, he meets her pace. His hips rock back to swallow each of her thrusts. In and out. He's stretched wide and filled. An alpha claimed in the most obscene way by his omega. It's taboo.

And it's one of the most erotic things I've ever seen.

While men aren't my preference, watching them fuck while they're both in my rope gives me satisfaction. The way Veronica jolts when I activate the remote gives me pleasure, too. I grin. All of those vibrations are traveling down that rope that's cinched tight against her cunt. She moans, her gentle thrusts changing to deeper, skin-smacking ones.

Even when she's topping, I'm still the one in charge.

"Fuck, that's good. Why is that so fucking good?" Her fingers dig into Jamie's ass. She spreads him wide so we can all watch her fake cock slide deep inside him, his hole stretched wide to take it until her toy is balls deep inside him.

Jamie groans, his words swallowed by his gag. But he's still holding his bell. He's okay. Judging from the way his back arches to push his ass back against Veronica's strap-on, I'd say he's doing great. Good enough to come from penetration alone? I want to find out.

I dial up the intensity, enjoying the way it makes Veronica go feral. She slams into him.

"Oh my fucking God." She slaps her hands against Jamie's ass, spreading his cheeks wider so we can all see how puffy his used hole is getting. "Fuck, that's good. Do you like that, pet? Do you like taking my cock? Like knowing it's *me* fucking *you*?"

He mumbles something against his gag and arches his back. His hips slam back to meet her as their skin smacks together with every thrust. The bow of his spine makes the bindings pull tight. Too tight? I put a hand on his shoulder and push him back down to the desk, then I lay a hand on his head to keep him there. I hold him down for her.

"Shh. Toys don't participate, boy," I warn him, my voice rumbling with a barely contained growl. "They get used and then put away when their owner's done playing with them." To drive the point home, that this is my gift to Veronica, and it's about her pleasure, not his, I hit the function button on the remote with my free hand.

"Fuck, oh my God, oh my God, ohmyfuckinggod."

Veronica stops thrusting and grinds, her toy buried to the hilt in his ass while the toy switches from a constant thrum to a series of shuddering pulses.

She whimpers, her hips stuttering as her aching pussy moves like it wishes it was filled. Stuffed full of cock. My cock. But the rope binds her pussy tight. It keeps the vibrations of her strap-on pulsing against her trapped clit. So I wait. I'm a patient man, no matter how pretty my prize is.

Reaching over, I brush my hand over her harness. Palm the weight of her breast. Pinch her nipple until her closed eyes flutter open. They struggle to focus on me, and I love how undone I've made her. How a bit of rope and vibration makes her look at me with an expression that screams *fuck me now*. Practically begs me for it.

"Do you want to come, sweetheart?" My thumb rubs across the remote. "Want some help?" She nods. Whimpers.

I kick off from leaning against the desk and come behind her, pressing my weight against her back. God, she's so petite. Even with her high heels, her head still easily tucks under my chin. I give Anthony the remote so he can toy with them while I help her fuck Jamie.

Grabbing the rope along her hips, I use them like handles as I thrust. I rub my clothed cock against her butt. She surges forward, pushing against Jamie, whose body moves up and down the desk as I pantomime fucking the both of them. I'm rougher than she's been so far. From Jamie's stifled moans, he's not upset by it. Veronica stiffens against me before finally going limp. Her surrender is all that much sweeter for the struggle. I know it cost her.

She leans her weight on Jamie as I take over and drive things. I make them fuck harder, faster, deeper than she dared. His hips will probably be bruised from the desk when I'm finished. Anthony has fun clicking through the different functions and speeds on the remote. The vibrator's buzz adds to the filthy sounds our bodies make. Together, Anthony and I reduce them into panting, trembling messes of need.

The ropes dig into her soft thighs as I twist them, hold her tight, and make her fuck Jamie like she owns him. Like the toy he is. Possessively. He's not delicate. Not made of glass. He's an alpha. And he's taking her cock so well. Like he was made for this.

Her breath stutters as she holds it, and that's how I know she's close.

"That's it, sweetheart. Make him come with your knot in his ass."

I pull her back against me and bury my nose in her hair. I drag it down the scent gland in her neck. Lick it, cleaning off the perspiration of her efforts until only her sweet orange scent is there. The unique scent that's all her. The one I crave.

"Look at the way he takes you," I tell her. "He's hungry for your cock. Your knot. I know you can make him come without touching his dick."

Curled around her, I grip her by her harness and pull her tight against me. Make her spine arch. The rope pulls taut, digs harder into skin. Sends vibrations deeper. It's time.

"Now, Anthony."

I slam my hips hard and pin her deep inside Jamie. She comes with a cry, her hips going still. My teeth scrape over her gland. They find the ball of firmer tissue right there under the skin. I suck it into my mouth, and then I bite. Veronica gasps, going rigid against me as my teeth puncture.

The taste of metal and oranges floods my mouth. Working my jaw, scissoring deeper, I bite her harder. This isn't an omega's timid nibbling. It's a claiming bite. Brutal. Efficient. I gnaw my claim into her soul. Hold her under me until, after a few tense seconds, the bond snaps into place. And then I let her go so I can tend to it. Clean and savor it.

Purring, I lap my bite marks clean until she sags against me. We stay like that, her leaning on Jamie while I hold her upright against me, until she catches her breath.

"Fuck, that's hot," Anthony says.

In the bond, she's floating from the high of a good orgasm and the mellowing bliss from being claimed. It's nature's cruel failsafe. The bond doesn't care if she wanted this or loved me. If she was fighting me or happy. The flood of chemicals lighting up her brain tells her she's safe with me. She's mine. All of these are true. But it wouldn't have mattered to her if they weren't.

My hindbrain relaxes for the first time in weeks. *Safe. Mine. Mated.* Our pack isn't completed yet, but it will be soon.

From the thickness of her pheromones, her next heat is close. Very close. Maybe two weeks away instead of the three I had marked on the tracking app I downloaded after her last one.

Through our bond, I catch a hint of Jamie and Anthony. An echo. Arousal. Need. Curiosity. Bliss from Jamie. His coconut scent turns her orange pheromones tropical. I'll bet the desk is covered in his cum from her knot rubbing against his prostate. There's no jealousy in me, which is good. I'm the first to mark her. Claim her. As the top alpha, this was my right. Although I'm not stupid enough to say it out loud where she can hear me.

Veronica makes a sleepy sound of contentment and wiggles like she wants me to get off her. Jamie gasps underneath her, his spine going rigid. She's forgotten they're tied.

"Shh," I tell her, stroking a hand down her rope-covered side. "Not yet, sweetheart. Your knot's still inflated inside him."

"Oh, shit. Sorry. God, I hate when it tugs like that. I can't believe I forgot about the knot."

I pick her hair off her face, smoothing it back and pressing a kiss against her temple. "It's okay. You were distracted. And I don't think Jamie minds it so much."

"Were you a good boy for me? Did you come, pet?" she asks him.

Jamie mumbles a string of muffled words against his gag, and I nod to Anthony, who hits the button to deflate the knot. I press a kiss against her cheek. "Let me take care of him and then I'll check on your bite mark."

Once her toy's knot is deflated, I step aside so Veronica can scoot out of the way while I sit Jamie on the floor and start working on his knots. I pull the quick release loop between his shoulders that keeps everything secure and watch the slack move through the rope as everything loosens. It takes a quarter of the time to untie him, as it did to rig it all.

I take his jingle bell from his fist and set it aside, then massage his joints, checking his blood flow and sensation. His blindfold and gag are less important, so I save them for last. Satisfied that he's okay, I finally take them off him. He blinks against the bright lights in the office as his eyes adjust. The rope is a tangled mess around him as he sits there and recovers. This is my least favorite part of rigging.

"How are you?" I ask him.

"Good," Jamie answers. "Sleepy."

I ruffle his hair and grin. "Let's get you cozy. The blanket," I tell Anthony, pointing to my bag. "He needs cuddles."

Anthony pulls the fuzzy blanket from the bag and takes over Jamie's aftercare while I see to Veronica. She's already slipped the vibrator out of its harness and now she's picking at her rope. Not doing a good job of it, either. She's making a complete mess of the knots as she tries to figure out how to get out of her tie.

I tsk, and she startles. "Naughty girl. I'm going to have to dock one of your gold stars," I tease her as I step between her legs and pry her hands off the rope. She opens her mouth to say something sassy, I'm sure, but I silence her with a kiss. I don't want her sassy right now. I want her sweet.

Veronica leans into it, so I deepen it, my tongue tangling with hers. Can she taste herself on me? Blood and sweet oranges? I nip her bottom lip before letting her go so I can tug at her quick-release knot and unwrap her. If I grope her in the process, well, that's just a hazard of the hobby.

"Did you have fun, sweetheart?" I ask her.

She nods and I gently nudge her closer to the desk. My palm encompasses the entire back of her neck as I spin her around and force her to bend. She takes Jamie's place, her cheek pressed to the desk and her rump in the air. She's gorgeous. Rope marks make indents in her skin. My fingertips ghost over them, feeling each divot along her sides and under the delicious curve of her ass.

"You'll stay however I put you, won't you, pretty girl? So I can give you what you're craving right now." I position both of her arms at the small of her back and use my foot to knock her legs further apart. "I don't need my ropes to tie you down and make you sweet for me."

Veronica nods, her head turning to one side so she can watch me. But she doesn't move when I let her go. Her orgasm and the bite have made her compliant and fuzzy. Almost docile.

Between her thighs, she's soaked. I stroke her swollen clit and tease her hole until she fidgets and bites her lips, her breath coming out as a frustrated huff until I ease two fingers inside of her and pump.

"Oh, fuck," she sighs, her hips twitching to push back on my hand while I finger her till she's tensing.

"That's the idea." I chuckle. The sounds of my belt buckle opening and the zipper sliding down are loud. I empty my pockets onto her desk and shove my pants down far enough to free my cock.

I don't need to stroke my cock to bring it to full mast. It's already rock hard from tying up the both of them. Still, I smack the head of my cock against her pussy. Spank her clit with it and watch her groin muscles tighten. Coat it in the slickness of her gathered arousal.

Sinking inside of her is bliss. The gust of her exhale and moan as I bottom out, sublime. Through the bond, I feel her urgency. Her neediness. She likes being filled. I go slow. Tease her. My cock slides in and out, her wetness soaking me. Her cunt is hot, wet bliss.

"That's good, sweetheart. Look at how well this pussy takes my cock. Like it's made for me." I pry her buttocks apart so I can watch the way my cock sinks inside of her pussy. How she swallows me up as I push deep, hit the entrance of her womb, and make her take all eight inches of me. She's so tiny. How she takes this much cock in such a small package is a mystery. Omegas are magical.

Her arms slip as she fidgets in her attempt to push back onto my cock. To make me go faster. Harder. But she's prostrate on the desk. Under me. And she's not in control right now. I am.

I return her arms into place at the small of her back where I want them and wrap my hand lightly around her wrists. Firm enough to keep them where I want them, but not so tight that she couldn't knock me free if she struggled.

Still, there's a brief flicker of alarm through the bond. I lighten my grip so my hand isn't closed, just resting over her crossed wrists. "That's a good girl holding still for me," I reassure her. Let her know she's safe. She's mine. I'll protect her, even from me. Because that's what a good alpha does.

I let her go, my fingers going back to the divots impressed in her skin, and she relaxes. Her reward is a deep, smacking thrust that makes her suck in air. While her back arches to tilt her ass up, her crossed arms never move. She's working so hard to stay where I put her while my cock does its best to make her forget everything but the way she stretches to fit me.

I palm the globes of her ass, spreading her wide until my fingers dig into her skin. I hope they leave bruises in the shape of my hands. A reminder of how thoroughly she got fucked for days until they fade. "That's it, sweetheart. Look at how well this pretty pussy takes all this cock. I bet you want to come all over it. Milk it dry."

"Yes. I want to come again." Her walls flutter around me, but I don't need to feel their movement to know she's close. I can tell through the bond how she's already spiraling. That taking her from behind, mounting her over her desk, slotting her under me in Jamie's place, unseats her and tips her sideways right into subspace. The head of my cock slides over her sweet spot if I angle it right. I fuck her like I made her fuck him. Hard. Deep. Fast.

My knee aches, but I ignore it. I'll ice it later. She's worth a little pain. Worth a lifetime of the misery that came before our meeting. My sweet reward.

This, her submission, our bonding, is worth any amount of pain. I'd endure worse for her.

I fuck her sweet spot. My aim is focused through the way our bond sings and her breathing turns rough. Her cheeks turn pink as she flushes. Not much longer now.

"That's it, sweet girl. Come on my cock. Let me fill that pussy."

When she shatters, her panting turns into moans. I don't stop. Not when the pleasure coursing through her leaks through our bond and almost triggers mine. My nostrils flare as I bite back a grunt and focus on my breathing.

Not yet.

This is a night she'll never forget. The night she accepted me as her alpha. The night I gave her a gift, something she never thought of for herself. The night we got her past one of her hurdles and I rewarded her with the knowledge she can have multiple orgasms outside of a heat.

"Good girl," I growl, my neck cording with the strain to not follow her down. "Another."

"I can't. I..." Veronica fidgets, her arms slipping. She's quick to put them back into position. To submit, though it's her instinct to fight the need she tries so hard to suppress with everyone but us.

"You can. You will. *Now.*" I punctuate each sentence with a thrust. "When I give you an order, your response is *yes, Sir,* or *thank you.* Do you understand?"

She hesitates. And that makes her eventual submission all the sweeter. "Yes, Sir."

"That's my good girl. This pussy was made to come on my cock, so you're going to have another one before I give you what you want. What you've earned."

"Th-thank you," she moans.

I grab one of her wrists and pull her arm from the small of her back, laying it at her side. "Play with your clit, omega. Make yourself come again."

"Thank you, Sir." She works her hand between her thighs. Her pussy tightens around me as she strokes her clit.

Fuck, this omega's gonna be the end of me. I close my eyes to shut out the sight of her rope-marked skin and think of the most boring things I can think of so that I don't come too soon. The alternative minimum tax formula. Capital gains and losses. Rut should buy Moriah and Rob a new work van so they can write it off as a business expense and reduce her tax liability. I'll have to remember to talk to her about it when—

I feel the first clenching pulses of her release before I hear her moans. "Good girl. That's it. Come on my cock." Her pussy squeezes my cock so hard that it's like it's trying to shove me out. I push in deeper so I don't miss a single delicious flutter. She's been such a good girl. She deserves to have a cock to come on. To be stuffed full and satisfied instead of achy and empty.

My fingers trace the deep lines scored into her body as I chase my orgasm. I use her fluttering to find my release. My gut tightens, and I know it's inevitable. There's no stopping it now. It's hers. All hers. Forever and always now. We're tied in more ways than the knot I'm about to pop inside her.

My inflating knot rubs against her opening. It catches, barely popping in and out with each deep thrust. When it's too swollen to slide free without tugging, I push it in deeper and give into the urge to come. Everything tightens, the pressure building, until finally it releases with the first pump of cum. Jets of it fill her as my cock kicks inside her until she's drained me dry, my knot keeping her stoppered. It's the only thing between us and an absolute mess as I pump what feels like a year's worth of cum inside her tight, hot pussy.

So full. But that sensation is hers, not mine. *Oh, fuck.* The feedback through the bond makes coming inside her intense. If this is how good it is now, then her heat will be… It might actually kill me. *But what a way to go.*

I grin, my hips canting one last time so I can savor the sucking way her body struggles to stay latched onto me. She stops panting to groan as I grind my knot inside her, enjoying the way her walls tighten around my knot as a reminder that we're tied.

"Fuck, sweetheart. That was good." A glint of gold in my periphery catches my attention. "You get all the stars." I grab the sheet of stickers from the desk and peel one off. "Your pussy is perfect." I stick it on her ass. "You milk my cock so well." This one goes on her hip. "You're like your scent. Tart to others who can't appreciate you, but you're perfectly sweet for your pack. You care about your people. You work hard. And you don't ask anyone to do something you wouldn't do yourself. You've built an amazing business and showed everyone who said you couldn't do it they were wrong. Your work does good things for omegas, and they're lucky to have you. You are the sweetest, most beautiful, most loyal omega I've ever known. I'm so lucky I found you."

By the time I'm done, she's covered in gold star stickers and she's blushing. Inside the bond, she's incandescent with pleasure.

Once my knot's softened enough, I pull free and help her up. I take her into my arms and hold her tight, my chin resting on the top of her head. I drag in a deep breath and savor the moment. I'll never tire of holding her, smelling her perfume, or knowing she's mine now. And I'm hers.

"I love you," I tell her, enjoying how sweet she is deep down. She's embarrassed, but pleased. My girl's not used to the praise she needs. With me, she'll get it in bucketfuls. Whether she likes it or not. Because I plan to take care of her. Forever. And sometimes that means giving her what she needs even if she doesn't know it.

Her arms tighten as she holds me back. "I love you too." We stay like that for a while, enjoying the easy silence. But then she surprises me by saying, "I want to mark you too."

My heart trips in my chest. "I'd be honored."

"Lean down," she orders. "Please."

I lean down and savor the slide of her hands over my neck. Enjoy the way she tugs my collar aside. The slide of her nose along my skin. Her lips kiss my scent gland, and then she sucks it into her mouth and her teeth notch around it.

The bite of her teeth is a brief flicker of pain followed by the bliss of the bond snapping once more. It echoes, and our connection deepens. Like the ripples of a tranquil water as a stone sinks, forever changing the landscape of the lake below. In the periphery of our connection, I sense Jamie and Anthony, too. My pack mates are patient and calm. I couldn't have asked for better men to do this with. I tug Veronica closer and hug her tight while she tends it, licking it clean.

We stay like that for a while, savoring the newness of this thing I never thought I'd find. After a beat, she drags in a deep breath and then lets it out with a sigh. "Can I clean all this cum off me now? It's drying."

"Hmm. I'll think about it," I say. "I kind of like the idea of you having to get dressed with Jamie's cum all over you and mine dripping down your thighs."

Veronica makes a little indignant snort. "Gross."

But she doesn't mean it. There's a part of her that likes the idea of being claimed so primitively. Covered in our scents. I could get used to this bond thing. It makes reading her so fucking easy.

Grinning, I rub my arms up and down her back, give her one last squeeze, and then release her so I can smack her on her ass. "Yeah, that's exactly what I want to do. Leave the cum and your gold stars. You can put your clothes on over top."

Veronica rolls her eyes, but picks her clothes up and gets dressed. Under her breath, she mumbles something about payback. I pretend I didn't hear her as I gather up all the dirty rope that needs washing and shove it all into a zippered laundry bag.

By the time all of us are clothed and packed up, we're half-asleep on our feet. It was a long day and while this would have been more comfortable to do at home, it would have been a lot harder to keep it a secret. It's not easy to pull one over on

Veronica. She watches her club like a hawk, and we spend more time at Rut than at home.

Not that I'm complaining. The club is her life. Our life now. And I wouldn't trade it for anything. Not even a cushy government job with a pension and great 401k matching and decent health insurance with dental and vision.

I scan the office one last time to make sure we got all the cum cleaned up and left nothing behind for Nate to stumble upon. Something glints on the floor. It's one of her stickers, and it must have fallen off while she was getting dressed.

After a moment of hesitation, I decide to leave it. It'll be a reminder that she's my good girl when she finds it. I flick the lights off and follow them down the stairs. Not even the aching burst of pain in my knee as I hold on to the railing and take them slowly can wipe the smile off my face as we head home.

Chapter Thirty-Eight

VERONICA

ELEVEN WEEKS IN TOTAL. THAT'S HOW LONG IT TAKES FOR THE in-person auditor to decide we're not doing anything illegal or shady at Rut. Brendan assures me it's all very standard. They've chased down every receipt, pored over every line in the budget, and realized that there's nothing to find.

We're finally free. My dark mood lifts the minute I get the news. I throw my arms around Brendan and I laugh when he uses the opportunity to squeeze my ass, which earns him a rare giggle.

"We did it!" I crow, burying my face in his soft, comforting body. In my pack, he's the most huggable.

"You did," Brendan says. He gives my butt one last squeeze before smoothing his hand over my unruly curls. "Good job, sweetheart. Now you can finally relax."

"Relax? No." There's so much to do. I pull away from his arms, and my mind races with everything that comes next. "Now it's time to book that flight. Oh, and I need to send emails to the investors I found. Let them know it's time to set a meeting. I have to research hotels. Fuck, I need to look at venues for the bar itself and find a broker. Oh my God, there's so much to do."

I should have started on all this weeks ago. But I was so worried about the audit that I didn't want to jinx it by setting up the meetings.

"One thing at a time," Brendan says, pulling me back into the cradle of his arms.

A purr rumbles through his chest, deep and rolling. The sound soaks into my bones where we're pressed together, and it's impossible to not relax in response to it. His hand smooths up and down my back until I let out a deep sigh.

"We'll help you every step of the way, whatever you need," he says. "All of us are here for you, remember?"

I do. That's impossible to forget. These men have invaded every corner of my life completely, flipping everything on its head.

Over the weeks, we've fallen into an easy routine. The occasional early morning swim or walk on the beach with Jamie. Sitting at the bar and taste testing Anthony's cocktail experiments while they watch the alphas rehearse. Nest cuddles with Brendan while he massages my aching feet after a long workday.

It's the little things too. The small things that soon take over your life, changing it one bit at a time. The top of the sink is crowded with everyone's toothbrushes. A magnetic shopping list sticks on the fridge so everyone can scribble what they're out of for the next trip to the store. We bought a rack to keep our shoes from becoming a jumbled tripping hazard at the garage door. A plant appeared in the bedroom one day, and then the next day someone set out an old-fashioned glass misting bottle for it.

We all have different profiles on the streaming apps. I haven't been back to my apartment in weeks except to pay the rent and tell the middle-aged office manager, Gayle, I won't be renewing my lease.

Empty boxes take up my cramped apartment living room, waiting to be filled. Other than my clothes, most of it is being donated to the omega shelter. The spare bedroom at the pack house has made an excellent walk-in closet for us with the addition of an extra chest of drawers found on the side of the road and a brass clothes rack Darlene replaced with a bigger one at Rut.

Anthony makes not-so-subtle hints about what a great nursery the impromptu walk-in closet would make one day. I'm still not ready for children. I never thought about it all that much until recently, until I finally accepted that I've found my pack. But right now, with the expansion on the horizon, it isn't the right time.

Weeks go by in a pleasant routine until I'm staring at a suitcase and trying to figure out how to make it all fit. *What is it about going out of town that makes me think I'll need two pairs of underwear each day I'll be gone?* As if New York City doesn't have thousands of shops that sell underwear in case I need more? But anxiety won't let me leave any behind.

When my suitcase is bulging with twelve outfits for a four-day business trip, I finally decide that's enough. Mostly because there's no room left for anything else.

Next to mine, Brendan's suitcase is downright petite. I frown at the side-by-side comparison. He has a neck pillow wrapped around its handle. I don't have a neck pillow. That's how unprepared I am for this. I didn't realize I needed one. The flight is six hours long and I've never been on a plane before. Are we going to be sleeping the whole way? *Shit. Should we make one last run to the store?* We've already gone twice since yesterday.

"Ready for tomorrow?" Brendan asks, coming up behind

me and slipping his arms around my middle. He tugs me against him and lets out a contented sigh when I lace my hands on top of his.

"No. I don't have a neck pillow," I answer, annoyed with myself for not thinking of this sooner. It makes me wonder what else I'm not thinking of.

Running one successful nightclub is one thing. Starting a chain? Building an empire? It's ambitious and scary and exhilarating, but I forgot to buy a neck pillow.

What if I reach too far and mess everything up and let them all down? So many people are depending on me. Fuck, how do alphas deal with this? Do they really never doubt themselves?

Brendan's purr does its best to soothe me before imposter syndrome makes me spiral. "We can buy one at the airport, sweetheart."

"Oh." Such a simple solution for a stupid problem. Some of the weight lifts off my shoulders.

"You're going to do great, and they're going to love you," he rumbles, his nose running along my scent gland where his bite mark has healed into faint pink marks that have yet to turn silvery. "You'll have to beat the investors away with a stick."

"Can I borrow your cane?" I ask him, smiling when he squeezes me tighter. He's been using it more often lately since Jamie talked him into joining him for strength training exercises on the beach. Despite my concern that he doesn't overdo it, he seems happy.

"Sure, but mine doesn't have a sword inside."

"What?" I ask, baffled. *That's a good thing, right? The TSA would never let us bring his cane if it had a sword in it. Is that a real thing? Why?*

"Dinner's ready," Jamie calls from the kitchen before Brendan can answer.

We follow the delicious smell and eat. The rest of the

evening passes in a blur as all three of my men take turns distracting me in their various ways until I'm too tired to stay conscious. My limbs grow heavy as Anthony wipes his sticky mess from my thighs and Jamie and Brendan are too warm on either side of me to not immediately drift into a deep sleep to the sound of their purring.

JAMIE AND ANTHONY SEE US OFF AT THE AIRPORT BEFORE heading back home to catch a few more hours of sleep before they have to open Rut in the afternoon.

The airport is a lot of hurrying up to wait. We wait to get our tickets at the counter, then hurry to get our bags on the scale so the airline can weigh them. I pay my bag overage fee, and we rush to join the line of people waiting to go through security. Bored TSA agents yell at me to take off my shoes, and I grimace when my socks touch the nasty floor. We sit while Brendan puts his shoes back on while other fliers rush to shove their feet back into shoes while balancing on one foot. The security line looks like it's full of frazzled flamingos in stretchy pants.

"Let's go to the bar," he says. "This'll be easier if you're not sober."

It's only seven in the morning, but we're far from the only ones crowded around the airport bar. Brendan joins me and orders himself a mimosa while I peruse their menu and order the strongest drink I know. The bartender isn't fazed as he sets our drinks down and I stir the straw on my Long Island Iced Tea. The mix of different alcohols with a splash of coke and sweet and sour goes down far too easy and by the time I'm sucking more air than drink, my head is fuzzy and I've forgotten why I was nervous.

"Better?" Brendan asks, his smile amused.

"I can't feel my face." I pat my cheeks and the tip of my nose to be sure. Nope. Slightly numb. That's my litmus test for knowing if I'm drunk or not. "Did you used to fly a lot for the IRS?"

"Some. Not very often. Most of the work was local, although I had to fly out sometimes. Let's go find you a neck pillow and some chewing gum."

Gum? I take his hand, enjoying the warmth and comfort of it. He squeezes mine and throws me a smile over his shoulder. It's such a small thing. Innocuous. But somehow more intimate than sex.

We stop at the duty-free shops and browse until it's time to find our gate and wait to be called to our seats, and then we board. By the time our carry-on bags are stowed away in the overhead bin and we're nestled in our assigned seats, I've sobered up a little for takeoff. I learn why Brendan insisted on the gum. The altitude changes hurt my ears until the plane levels out and I get them to pop.

Flying is weird, but cool. I enjoy looking out the tiny airplane window and watching us sail through clouds. A few hours and three rum and cokes later when most of the passengers are busy with their reheated meal, I enjoy dragging Brendan out of his light nap and pushing him into the tiny airplane bathroom even more. I can't help it. Being drunk makes me horny, and I'm bored.

I'm too wound up to sleep, even with my brand new neck pillow, and I'm too drunk to read or focus on a movie. Besides, isn't this a tradition? I've heard people talk about the mile high club.

We kiss and grope each other over our clothes until I'm wet

enough to make this easy. Figuring out a position isn't simple, though. With our height difference and the total lack of space, we're cramped.

Brendan spins me so I'm facing the mirror over the tiny sink. He works my pants and panties down, his fingers slipping through my folds to check how ready I am. They glide easily through my wetness. I've thought about this for the last half-hour. Anthony's obsession with public sex and almost getting caught has rubbed off on me.

Two fingers sink into me up to the palm, but I don't need to be readied. I'm already aching for him. My hips work back to meet his thrusts as he pumps into me. I bite back my sigh when his fingers disappear. The sound of his zipper sliding down and the rustle of his clothes let me know he's ready. He replaces his fingers with the blunt tip of his thick cock and he rocks into me with a single slow, deep thrust. It fills me up and I sigh with relief at the familiar stretch.

And then he moves. His hips snap behind me as he thrusts, burying his cockhead deep. Rough and fast. We can't afford to take our time. Not when we're stealing this forbidden moment while a plane full of passengers waits on the other side of that door. They're eating right now. Busy and distracted. But they'll want the bathrooms soon and I want to come.

The plane shakes with a bit of turbulence and I almost let out a loud moan as the vibrations rumble up through my clit where my mound presses against the edge of the sink I'm bent over. I slap my palm on the mirror to stop from banging my head against the wall as Brendan works deeper still.

The flared edge of his swelling knot drags over my sweet spot, shoving in and almost not popping out before, finally, my body gives. It pops free in time for him to shove it back in again. Stretch me wider. Claim me deeper.

He can't knot me. He can't. It'll take too long for his

swollen knot to shrink and disengage. They'll figure out what we're doing. Knock on the bathroom door and demand we hurry in here.

As if he can hear my thoughts, Brendan's pace increases until I have to bite my lip to hold in my ragged moan. Our breathing and the rustle of our clothing is loud enough. The plane rumbles again and my clit throbs. My pussy clenches around him and Brendan chokes off a grunt, his rhythm changing as he grabs my ass and shifts the angle of my hips. He positions me exactly how he wants me.

In the mirror, I watch our reflection. The flush on my cheeks, the wildness of my bouncing curls as he thrusts harder. Faster. More demanding. His nostrils flare as he drags in a deep gulp of air, and his brown eyes are dark with lust. So are mine. We're a filthy sight and I watch every minute of him fucking me in this tiny airplane bathroom.

His cock throbs inside me, his raging pulse matching mine as my clit throbs from each tugging thrust and every rumble of the plane. His pace slows, pressing deeper although there's nowhere left to go. As if instinct demands that his cockhead lodge right against the entrance of my womb before he's allowed to find his release.

I'm stretched full to my limit and about to be stretched more because his knot bulges behind my pubic bone until I'm taut. He growls, a low sound made on instinct to warn competing alphas away. It's my warning sign he's about to come.

I need to push off his knot, twitch my hips forward and dislodge it, but his fingers tighten into painful divots on the globes of my ass. We're going to be stuck together when we need to hurry.

His hips rock against mine and his grip slides around to my front, fingers curling around my pelvis until his middle one slips between my labia. It strokes over my clit, pulls the hood back, and makes circles. He goes still, everything but his pulsing cock and stroking fingers locking into place.

His knot pops, filling me until it's too much. Too wide and too stuffed. But there's no choice but to take it. To stretch and surrender. His cock kicks and he grunts with every spurt of seed inside me. He lashes my walls with cum, the fluid trapped by his knot, and his fingers don't stop. They toy with me. Make me pant and arch and writhe on his knot.

He winds me until all I can think about is how full I am. Full of cock. Cum. Need.

There's a banging on the bathroom door that matches the pounding of my pulse between my thighs. Someone impatiently tries the door, the flimsy material almost giving as they jiggle it. My cunt tightens on his cock with unhinged delight.

"Occupied," Brendan growls, his voice deep and rough. His fingers never stop petting me. They stroke over our tie and tease my clit. They work me as hard and fast as his cock did until I'm panting and desperate to come.

"It's been a long time, man. Hurry up. There are other people who need the bathroom."

"Find another one," Brendan answers. He rubs circles, adds pressure, gathers up my slick arousal and uses it until the need to come tightens in my belly.

I whimper, biting my lip to stifle the sound before it can grow too loud, and ignore the way his knot tugs at me as I grind my clit against his hand.

He shoves his other hand down my shirt and pulls my breast free of its bra cup. He finds my nipple. Rolls it under his fingers. Pinches it. Twists. The sharp tug goes straight to my groin and I come on his knot.

I'm no longer capable of stopping my noises and gasps. Now when my walls flutter on the bulge of his knot. When his cock gives another kick deep inside me, his head brushing against my cervix as he gives me one last spurt of cum. A reward.

"That's my good girl," he says softly. Brendan strokes my butt and hips, curls a hand possessively over my belly where his cock is lodged deep. He presses, driving the ache of his knot deep in my guts.

Oh, fuck. If he keeps doing that, he's going to get me going again. We'll be banned from this airline for life. "We should probably get out of here before they get desperate and break the door down," I say.

His agreement is a huff and a fondle of the outline of his buried cockhead through my belly. He shivers and gives me a final spurt that makes his chest rumble.

It takes a bit for his knot to soften enough for us to pull apart. Brendan shoves a wad of nearly see through toilet paper between my thighs to catch the bulk of the spill. He helps me clean up. We fix our clothes and take turns washing our hands, shoving the cum-smeared paper down the metal toilet and flushing it away with a whoosh.

There's no hiding as we leave the bathroom. Brendan scoots around me and goes first, enduring the waiting passenger's displeasure, and I follow him as we head back to our seats. Not even the sour looks on the flight attendants' faces or the shock, disgust, and baffled amusement of the surrounding passengers can ruin my buzz.

We take our seats and I fidget in mine, my pussy delightfully sore. After a moment of silence we glance at each other, and I can't stop my giggle. I can't believe we really did that.

For the rest of the flight, I'm not nervous at all. Not when the plane shakes and shudders or my ears pop as we land. Brendan's heavy hand falls on my thigh and squeezes, and I lean against him, breathing in the comfort of his delicious scent.

Chapter Thirty-Nine

VERONICA

BRINGING BRENDAN ALONG TO JOIN ME IN THESE MEETINGS turns out to be the best decision I ever made. Not because I need him there to do my job, but because he serves as a litmus test for the worthiness of the potential investors.

It doesn't matter that he sits behind me and slightly to the side. Or that I shake their hands and do most of the talking, only deferring to him when they have a specific question about quarterly earnings and expenses from the year before that I haven't memorized. Or that I introduced myself as the founder and president of Rut.

They all talk to him. *Him.* As if the sheer fact he's an alpha or a man means somehow he's in charge, even when I've made it very clear that he's not. I am. Still, the investors disappoint me one by one.

"Thank you for your time," I tell this latest group, my fake customer-service smile and high-pitched voice disappearing the moment the door closes behind them. "Fuck. This has been an enormous waste of time." All of that preparation. The agonizing. Was it really all for nothing?

Everyone is going to be so disappointed when we return to

LA without an investor. I can already hear Nate's displeasure ringing in my ears. He'll argue that I should have brought him instead of Brendan. But that was by design, not by accident.

Nate has a habit of stealing the spotlight. He can't help it. It's the Broadway background running through his veins. Every stage is his show. Every room he's in is his stage.

"Don't say that," Brendan says, coming behind me and rubbing my shoulders over my smart black suit.

I'm so annoyed by their subtle bigotry and the way they look down on omega business owners. I can't be mad that Brendan's shoulder rub is going to wrinkle my suit. What's the point? Not like they'll notice. All they can stare at is the tiny centimeter of tasteful cleavage that shows above the neckline of my modest blouse. I even wore pants for this meeting today to avoid them ogling my legs.

"We haven't found the right investor yet. These things take time," he reassures me. "How many are left?"

"One."

One appointment stands between me and failure. But maybe this is a good thing. A gift in disguise. Perhaps it's the universe telling me New York is a mistake and we should go with Las Vegas instead. Some of the top clubs in the country are in Las Vegas. But I wanted to get a foothold on both coasts before working our way inward. And I know Nate won't be nearly as happy about Vegas. It's a city that's already way over-saturated with sparkly thongs. It won't be a salacious splash.

"And one is all we need," Brendan says. "What's this investor's name?"

"Hmm?" His question pulls me out of my quiet panic. "Oh. The Orello pack. The alpha, Marcus, works in the financial district in a well-established international firm his father founded, but his pack is independently wealthy with deep roots in the UK."

That's why I picked them, and also why I saved them for last. While my primary goal is to establish a Rut in at least ten states spread out across the country, I haven't written international expansion off the list either. This pack's connection to Europe won't hurt.

Although those are plans for later. Much later. Still, it's good to have an end goal in mind.

"Planning for global domination?" Brendan chuckles as we find our seats again.

"Exactly."

"If anyone can do it, it's you."

I can't keep my grin off my face. He knows me well. It's not long before the final pack arrives. A lanky beta shoves his way in front of the burly alpha whose bulk is barely contained by his tailored, expensive suit. The beta, Tom, is tall, slim, and handsome. He has dark hair with light eyes and a twinkle in them, which instantly reminds me of Anthony.

My chest pinches with longing. I've only been away from my pack, my nest, for two days, but it's quickly becoming unbearable. Having Brendan come along has helped. His presence is enough to keep me steady. I thought all the hushed talk about bond separation sickness was junk science, but there might be something to it. I've never been a needy, clingy partner before.

"Pleasure to meet you, luv," the beta says as he reaches to take my hand. He doesn't shake it so much as cup it in both of his before finally letting me go. "I'm Tom, and this handsome alpha is my mate, Marcus."

"It's a pleasure to meet you both," I say, nodding at them. "I'm Veronica, the founder and owner of Rut and this is my mate Brendan. He's taken over our accounting division recently. Please join us. Would you like a drink?"

I motion for the waitress to come our way. After taking up

this table in her section all day and tipping her well after every client we've met with, she heads over quickly and takes our drink orders.

The Orellos order a glass of wine and a scotch that are way too fancy for my tastes, and I get a refill of my orange juice in a bar glass that I'm pretending is a cocktail. We've been at this all day. The last thing I need is to get drunk.

My feet pinch in these heels, and the chair squeaks as I adjust in my seat. We make idle chatter about the city and the best places to eat and sights one can't miss until our drinks are delivered.

"My mate tells me you have an investment proposal," Marcus says, flicking the button of his coat open and relaxing into his seat, one hand dropping to rest on his beta's leg. He directs the question to me, his attention focused as he waits for my answer.

My gut tightens in response and my dark mood lifts. This is promising. He's the first investor who didn't immediately start interrogating Brendan.

"Before we get started, I have a standard nondisclosure agreement for you to sign." I pull two packets from my bag and hand them over. They skim the documents briefly before Marcus pulls a pen from his pocket and signs while Tom follows suit. I tuck the signed papers into my bag.

My heart knocks against my ribs with anticipation instead of dread as I launch into my carefully rehearsed presentation. I tell him about our annual returns and quarterly growth, market potential and how we serve an untapped portion of the market. There are thousands of strip clubs for alphas and betas and almost none for omegas.

Brendan adds details about earning projections when I get too excited at finally being taken seriously and ramble. "And that's why New York would be the perfect place for our second location."

Marcus frowns, his thick brows drawing together, and the fragile feeling of hope in my chest cracks a bit. "This is an entertainment venue? I thought it was a social club."

"It's both, darling," Tom chimes in. "There are social hours for members only, then it opens to the public. Have you ever been to a rut bar? I could have sworn I brought you to one in England after my graduation from A-levels. Across the pond we call them stag bars, so maybe that's where the confusion lies."

Marcus shakes his head. "I've been to my share of rut bars, but I don't remember any sort of members-only social club aspect. They're mostly…"

"But this rut bar isn't like one we've ever been to," Tom says. "It's better." His lips curl into a cheshire grin. "I'd love to see it in person. It looks like such delicious fun. You've really flipped it on its head. Alpha dancers performing for omegas. It's cheeky. I like that."

My customer service smile turns into a real one. "If you're ever in LA, we'd love to have you join us. Or if you choose to invest, you'll always be welcome at the club, of course. My chore-ographer is originally from Brooklyn. He went to Julliard and cut his teeth on Broadway and he's eager to be home again. I'll be looking at potential sites in the West Village while I'm here."

"Oh, the West Village," Tom croons. "What a perfect loca-tion for a naughty little club like this. I have a friend who works in real estate. He got me the absolute best building for my gallery. I'll see if he can put any feelers out. Maybe find some-thing that's not on the market yet."

Marcus shifts in his seat, his pointer finger tapping against the side of his tumbler. "I'm not sure that this sort of venture is for us. Nightclubs and bars are risky. Especially since you don't have a location secured yet. It's also not something we've ever invested in before. We're mostly focused on the arts at the moment."

He shifts like he means to stand up and leave. They can't. They're exactly the sort of investors I was looking for. That Rut needs. And it's time to show them I've done my homework. That I'm serious. I'm not some little omega who succeeded by accident. I've put in the work, cried, sweated, and bled for Rut, and I won't stop now when everything I've worked so hard for is right within my grasp.

"Your mate Emily would like my proposal," I say. "If she were here, she'd tell you to invest."

His gaze snaps to mine, and the friendliness disappears from his face. *Ah, here he is.* The alpha underneath the businessman. It's never far, no matter how much they cover it with tailored suits or charming smiles. Brendan leans toward me in his seat, his body language competing with the male that his hindbrain says is a threat.

"She serves on a committee for omega-run businesses, right?" I ask him. "Last year she helped run a charity fund that benefits omega victims of domestic violence and trafficking. Rut isn't just a social club for omegas, or an alpha strip club. It provides a commercial front of the house that funds my nonprofit."

"A front," Marcus says, frowning. He scans the packet of documents I gave them as if he's looking for something he missed, but he won't find a word of my actual business in there.

He's the first investor I've told about this, although all of them signed the NDA.

Brendan sets his hand on my knee and squeezes, telling me without words to be careful. But my gut says I'm right. This pack is different. They're the ones Rut needs.

"Yes, for my nonprofit. Don't get me wrong, Rut works. It's

profitable. The market is thirsty for what it offers. Omegas are a quarter of the population and no other club caters exclusively to them. It's a completely untapped market.

"But the real work is the nonprofit. I have a small collection of safe-houses and a network across four states to relocate omega victims of domestic violence. They come to us for many things. Abuse of every kind, physical, emotional, sexual, financial. Forced claiming bites. Sometimes with children in tow. Sometimes with nothing but the clothes they're wearing.

"We get them out of dangerous situations and keep them separated so the claim can diminish. One in three omegas experiences domestic violence in their lifetimes. Yet our court system is archaic. They haven't made much progress since the nineteen-forties.

"Omegas can file for a petition of separation, but that system takes months or years and if there are children involved, it's nearly impossible. Omegas are most likely to be murdered while trying to leave. Did you know that? Imagine if someone unsavory had found your Emily first. Forced a claiming bite on her and held her captive through pheromones and emotional manipulation. Imagine if they were cruel. If she wanted to leave, but couldn't.

"We provide safe places for them to hide and wait for their bond to fade. We help them with their paperwork and connect them with lawyers and doctors. The children are fed and schooled so they don't fall behind. We help these omegas get established again. Get medical attention and job training. Give them time and space to heal. Get their life back."

Marcus hears me. The stern edge leaks from his expression, and Tom grows serious, his smile slipping into a thoughtful frown. Marcus clears his throat and settles back into his seat. "That sounds like something she'd want us to help with. Our Emily has a soft heart."

"You wouldn't be involved in the nonprofit operations," I tell him. "No alphas are. Not even my mates know the specifics of its operations. I'm sure you understand our need for absolute discretion."

When they both nod in understanding, I feel better. Lighter. "Rut provides the front-facing business we need to operate in the shadows. And it's a lucrative business. The projections speak for themselves. We've estimated your ROI at thirty-six percent. We'll do well here in New York."

Marcus and Tom share a look, and then it's Tom who nods. He grabs a water ringed napkin and scribbles something on it, then lays it face down on the table. When they stand and button their jackets, so do we.

"It was a pleasure to make your acquaintance," Marcus says, shaking my hand with a firm grip.

"I'll reach out to my real estate friend," Tom adds, taking my hand next. He brings it to his lips and presses a dry kiss on the back before letting me go with a wink. "Welcome to the city, luv."

We watch them go.

"That went well," Brendan says after they leave.

"It did," I mutter, distracted as I reach for the napkin. I flip it over and stare at the handwriting, my jaw nearly dropping at the 1.2M figure scrawled there. It's more than double what I was hoping for and way beyond the twenty percent we'll need to secure a location and licenses.

"Holy shit," Brendan says, picking up the napkin to study it. He hands it to me. My fingers tremble as I take it. "You did it, sweetheart!" He scoops me up into a hug, his scent and arms warm. "I knew you could. You're so smart and determined. You did such a good job researching investors."

My cheeks are hot when the waitress returns to hand us our seventh and final check of the day. The sun's set when we head outside onto the street for the first time in over eight hours. Brendan holds my hand as we walk, no particular destination in mind.

"Should we go get dinner, you think?" he asks.

My empty stomach demands food, and this time I want something more substantial than an overpriced food cart kebab. "Yes. Maybe somewhere in the West Village." We need to eat, but there's no reason we can't multitask. Maybe we'll see something perfect while we're looking for food.

Brendan groans, but steers us toward the curb where he looks for a taxi that's empty. "You want to scout for locations, don't you?"

"Too much for one day?" I ask, pressing against him.

He smiles and shakes his head. "Your dedication and drive are some of the things I love most about you. You don't let anyone tell you no. Far be it from me to be the first."

"But is it too much walking for your knee?" I ask, biting my lip.

He turns to face me and leans down to steal a kiss while he's still got one arm raised in the air to hail a cab. "No. Your massage last night really helped. I promise I'll let you know if it gets to be too much."

"You'd better." I grasp the lapels of his new suit and pull him tighter against me. He looks good in it. Maybe we'll find another bathroom to celebrate tonight. We have one-point-two million reasons to be happy right now. "I have plans for you."

"Oh." He grins, the lines around his eyes creasing. "You do, huh? What sort of plans?"

"The fun kind." I press my hand over his broad chest and slide it down his body, grazing his cock through his pants. It fills my hand even though it's not hard yet. I give it a squeeze, enjoying the way it throbs against my palm. "Oh, look, a taxi." I step around him and flag it down.

The yellow cab pulls over, and I smile at the driver as I pull the door open and get inside. "West Village, somewhere with nice restaurants." When Brendan climbs in beside me and tugs the door shut, our driver merges into traffic.

The noise of the driver's Arabic broadcast muffles my stifled gasps and moans and fidgeting as Brendan teases me right back, his hand slung around my shoulders and sliding under my jacket to play with my breast until the nipple is a stiff peak and the ache of his pinching travels straight to my groin.

New York City's lack of public bathrooms and appalling lack of alleys are the only reasons we get a glimpse of the West Village at all. It turns out that Hollywood lies. There aren't any alleys in New York.

After a bit of wandering and getting a feel for the place, we find a cute Moroccan restaurant that smells amazing and tastes even better. And by the time we make it back to the hotel, we're drunk and more than ready to celebrate. All one-point-two million dollars' worth.

ANTHONY THROWS A BAR TOWEL OVER THE TOP OF THE champagne cork, but I still flinch when he pops it. "To Rut NYC!" he yells as he pours the golden bubbly into the top glass of his champagne tower. After the first glass fills, the champagne runs down. The other bartenders feed him more bottles until his pyramid of carefully positioned glasses is filled, and then they're distributed.

The champagne tickles my nose and isn't sweet enough for my personal enjoyment, but it's a must for celebrations, so I indulge alongside everyone else. We have a lot to celebrate. The audit is over. We got our start-up funding. Tom's real estate hook up is scouring for the perfect venue for us. And I found my pack.

"Vee, I have so many ideas," Nate says while sipping his champagne. He gestures wildly in the air with his free hand as he talks. "For the opening show, I'm thinking of Broadway. The classics. Cabaret. Moody, seductive red lighting and tiny black hot pants with glitter suspenders that sparkle in the spotlight. We'll have them do the chair number with their hats, and then…"

Before Nate can get too excited and spend the next hour bouncing ideas off me, I put a hand on his arm and squeeze. "Nate, if you want Cabaret, then we'll do it. I love it. Have Darlene draw some costume ideas for us to look over this week."

His face lights up with a manic gleam, and I leave him to hold court amongst a small pack of his most dedicated dancers. A few have already asked if they can transfer. I hate to lose them, but it's also nice to know that Rut NYC won't be starting from scratch. We have a lot of logistics to figure out. It's a good thing I enjoy being busy.

"Congratulations," Darlene says, sidling up to me. Instead of champagne, she's drinking something light blue and blended in the most enormous margarita glass I've ever seen before. A wedge of pineapple and a tiny paper umbrella decorate the side. "If anyone could pull this off, it'd be you. Told them not to worry." She sips her drink and grins at me.

"Nate's going to be a whirlwind of ideas. You'll be busy with costume design until we can hire another seamstress. Unless… You're not leaving me for New York too, are you?"

"New York?" She gives me a sour look, then shakes her head and drains a fifth of her glass in one go. "And deal with all that cold and snow? No, thank you. I like it here where it's always eighty-five and sunny, and so does the arthritis in my hands."

That's great news, because having to replace both Darlene and Nate would have been terrible. Nate's work can apply to both sites. He can create and record the choreography he creates, and his replacement here can implement it. But Darlene is the one who makes the vision come alive. I'd hate to lose them both. "I'm glad to hear that."

"Your boy is looking for you," she says, using her glass to point.

Jamie moves through the crowd, stopping to talk to people for a bit before turning his attention back to me. Everyone wants to stop and congratulate him, so his progress across the room is slow.

"If I'd been twenty years younger..." Darlene heaves a wistful sigh. "Off with you. Don't waste your night talking to me. It's your party so go enjoy yourself while I live vicariously through you."

Before she can wander away, I put a hand on her arm and lean in so I don't have to shout to be heard over the music. I ask her what's been bothering me for weeks. "How did you know?" It was Darlene who told me Jamie was interested in me. Who prompted me to take the idea seriously. I don't know if I'd have let myself go there if she hadn't planted that idea in my head.

"Girl, you weren't exactly subtle. Everyone could see you two mooning over each other. The pool wasn't if you'd get together, but when. Took you long enough. And everyone knew Anthony wanted you bad. The man can't stop staring at your ass. Didn't think it would be the IRS agent who'd kick things off, though." She laughs. "That was a fun little surprise. Changed the odds from seven to one to forty-one to one. Thanks for that. Did you see my new earrings?"

Instead of her usual chunky costume jewelry, she's wearing

enormous black and gold Chanel button earrings. They make zero sense with her neon pink and leopard print outfit. "Wow." My response is an understatement.

Darlene preens, fluffing her teased hair. "Time for a refill." She downs the rest of her drink and wanders off. I cringe, wondering how she's not getting brain freeze.

"Your glass is way too full," Anthony says as he sneaks up behind me. He takes my glass from me and sets it down, then hands me a new one before curling his arm around my middle and tugging me back against him. "This is a celebration. Drink up. We made this especially for you."

It's a coconut margarita, and my eyes flutter in delight when I take a sip and the flavor bursts along my tongue. "Fuck, that's so good. I don't know how you do it."

Anthony hums and lets his hand wander over my stomach, his fingers teasing the waistband of my skirt. "It uses a special ingredient we save just for you."

"What, love?" I force myself to sip it slowly rather than gulp it down. It's mostly vodka and I haven't eaten today. Tension I didn't know I was holding goes slack and I smile, swaying with the beat of the music.

"Sure. Let's call it that." Anthony chuckles, his breath hot on my ear as he runs his nose up and down the side of my neck. "Brendan says your heat is close. Another day or two. You know what that means."

My pelvis tightens and my nipples scrape against the lace of my bra. I know what it means. My heat is close and we're going to finish what we started. Brendan's the only one who's bitten me because Jamie says it doesn't feel right for him to claim me since he's the submissive. Although we all expect that might change once he's in a rut. I'm planning on it, because I want a bite from all my guys.

Anthony's plans make me nervous, though. He found some

sketchy website that makes custom-fitted tooth caps for betas who don't want to be left out of the biting. I'm concerned that it won't work and he'll end up disappointed, but I won't tell him no. Being an equal in the pack means too much to him.

Anthony sways with me, his hand on my belly, keeping us pressed together. Despite knowing I need to drink slowly, I can't help myself. His drinks are so good. I drain the glass and he takes it from me and sets it aside when Jamie pushes through the crowd and joins us.

"Brendan said to let you know it's almost six," Jamie says.

"What? No, it's only…" Frowning, I glance at the bar where a digital clock mounted on the wall shows that it's nine minutes till opening. "Shit! It's almost six." I put my thumb and middle finger into my mouth and whistle, the conversation dying down around us. "Time to open, people! Dancers, finish your drinks and start getting into costume. Everyone else, let's get this place cleaned up."

Someone flips the music over to the playlist we use for the first hour. Everyone hustles and we manage to get Rut put back into order in time for Dan to pull the door open and let in the first wave of members. It's a group of three female omegas in clubbing attire.

"Hello." I motion for them to sit at a table that's still damp from being wiped down. "Welcome to Rut, where your pleasure is our business."

Chapter Forty

VERONICA

I'M IN THE CROWD, FOR THE FIRST TIME IN A LONG TIME, TO evaluate Nate's new choreography from a customer's perspective. At least that's the excuse I tell myself. Omegas and a handful of betas scream and jostle as they all surge to get closer to the stage.

Margot is in full dominatrix gear as she leads Jamie around as her slave. Her black dress is latex, the tight material showing off her lean, muscled curves. Tall black heels make her ass look amazing, and the tiny silver spikes all over them give her a fuck-off attitude. She leans over Jamie who's bound and kneeling at her feet. As she moves, her long, thick braid swings like a rope.

It was Brendan's idea to incorporate his experience as a fetish top into the show. With the reaction of the crowd, I'd say the omegas agree. They love it. From the way they scream and the cash piles along the border of the stage, they're eating it up with a silver spoon.

Maybe my particular tastes aren't so unusual after all. Perhaps a lot more omegas want to see a big, strong alpha brought to his knees. What would everyone think if they knew his cock was locked up inside his black spiked thong? Caged? That I owned it?

I can't help but grin as Margo takes Brendan's rope training and runs with it like she was born with a whip in one hand and a leash in the other. She's a natural.

Margo pulls on the leash hooked to the black collar around his neck and tugs him up, using the length of it to wrap around him as she comes around to his back. Long artificial nails shaped into sharp points drag up his oiled abdomen and chest. The crimson is striking against his beach tan.

She wraps her hand around his shoulder and shoves him down. Jamie flows with the move, presses his face to the floor as he kneels before her with his ass up in the air. When she balances her heel on his back, the crowd cheers again. More crumpled money rings the stage. This show is going to break the club's tipping record.

Hands settle on my hips in a firm grip, and I whirl around to put my elbow in someone's face and shout for someone to get Tiny until I see it's Anthony. My pounding heart slows as I let out a shaky breath.

This close to my heat, I know it's risky to join the crowd. But I couldn't resist seeing Jamie's new set up close.

Anthony tugs my hips back against him, and I go back to watching the show. We sway together with the packed crowd, and I don't think much of it until I feel him getting hard. His cock rubs against my ass and his face presses against the side of mine as we move together like we're dancing.

On the stage, Margo nudges Jamie onto his back and stands over him, using his leash to make him curl toward her before using her shoe to nudge him back on the floor. Their dance is an erotic show of submission. Ownership. Fake, of course, but the crowd is buying it.

Anthony rucks the back of my skirt until the rough denim of

his jeans rubs against my skin. He traces the seam of my panties along my buttocks. Rubs a hand between my legs and teases across my mound. It doesn't take long before the fabric sticks to me. Gets wet.

My clit throbs, begging for attention, as he touches everything else. He rubs the divot between my lips, makes the damp fabric dip in and cling until I'm desperate for more.

I should stop him. This is way too public. We're going to get caught. But it feels so damn good and naughty. I never knew I had a public sex thing before Anthony. Instead of snapping my legs closed and dragging him upstairs or into the storeroom behind the bar, Anthony finally, *finally*, grazes my clit and my legs slide further apart of their own accord.

He tugs my panties down, too. Not all the way, only enough for his cock to slide between my wet labia and graze my clit as he thrusts.

Oh, fuck. When did he pull his cock out? Has anyone noticed?

I scan the surrounding crowd, but their eyes are glued to the stage. Anthony's cock slides between my slick lips, his head bumping against my clit with each slow thrust. My core clenches, aching and empty.

Fuck it. Nobody's watching us anyway.

They're all watching Jamie crawl around on the floor as Margot rides him, her legs crossed at the ankles like a prim and proper lady. And we're in the thick of the crowd, so the ring of alphas nursing their beers along the periphery can't see how Anthony is using my wet pussy to masturbate.

My pelvis clenches tight, desperate to be filled, as his cockhead gets fully slicked up and bumps against my clit until I'm throbbing. When my hips rock to move with him, his fingers dig in. He holds me still. Anthony doesn't want my participation. He wants to use me.

I can almost hear him in my head. *Be my good little fuck toy, baby. Be a good girl and hold still for Daddy so he can come in these pretty panties.*

And he does. Anthony fucks my pussy. He uses me for his own pleasure. Gives me some in return, but not enough to come. Not even this close to my heat, where sometimes it seems like a stiff breeze is all I need to shatter into a million different fragments.

Anthony rocks against me, his tense grip keeping me still for him as he uses my pussy like a pocket toy in the middle of the crowded club. The loud music covers the wet sounds my body is making. My low moans. His grunts of male pleasure and heavy breathing. With his lips pressed against the shell of my ear, I hear each breathy noise he makes.

Margot pulls Jamie up by his hair, and his eyes flutter open. They find mine and lock on. My clit throbs against the brushing of Anthony's cock. My pussy aches to be filled. Fucked and stretched. Used until it's deliciously sore.

If Anthony bent me forward and pressed inside, I'd let him. But he doesn't. His jeans chafe my ass while he uses me until his cock kicks. The first pulse is a warning. His cock jerks against my mound. His teeth nip at my ear and his fingers bite into my hips as he holds me tight.

He groans, deep and masculine, as he comes in my panties. Semen soaks my folds and drips, soaking into the fabric.

The sound of him finding pleasure, the wet slide of him through my lips, the bump of his cockhead against my clit, is all I need. I come with him and he keeps me from stumbling when my knees wobble as my orgasm rolls through me.

Wetness floods my pussy. His and mine. He chuckles as he pulls his cock free and tugs my panties, wet and sticky, into place. Tucks himself away, his pants rubbing against my ass while he zips up his jeans. He pulls my skirt down my thighs so I look decent again, although I'm anything but.

His teeth nip my ear lobe, harder, and I gasp, wiggling against him. He splays a possessive hand over my belly. Everything squishes when I move. The mix of his semen and my arousal is cooling rapidly, and my pussy is feverish against it.

Still, it's not enough. I want more. Need it. None of this teasing. I need dick.

"Anthony," I whine, complaining. A beta next to us glances our way, but I'm past the point of caring. My need to come again, to be ridden hard and fucked properly, is growing desperate. I shouldn't have come to work today. Should have stayed home for my preheat. But I wanted to see Jamie's special show. He's been excited about it all week. We all have. My heat is coming on early because we've left things unfinished.

"Let's finish Jamie's show," Anthony says. He keeps a firm grip on my hips as he makes me watch the rest of Jamie's set while I rub my thighs together and squirm in search of friction. Cum dribbles down my thigh and my clit throbs, desperate to be touched again.

I'm about ready to bend over the nearest flat surface and flip up my skirt so he has to do something about it when Jamie and Margot finish to a chorus of eardrum shattering screams, collect their tips, and leave the stage. Nate comes out with the mic and announces the name of the following dancer.

Anthony runs a hand down my arm. "Now we can go." He leans in close, his lips bumping against my ear. "You sound like you need a good, deep dicking and you can't be in here smelling up the place with your preheat like this. There are too many alphas around."

Fucking finally.

I'm barely cognizant of being bundled into the car and driven home. My preheat progresses rapidly. Brendan fingers me the whole way there, his fingers squelching through the mess of Anthony's cum. He adds a third and pumps them inside me, but it's not the same. Not when I know genuine relief is waiting for me on the other end of a knot.

"It came on faster this time," Anthony says, twisting in his seat when we stop at a red light. "We barely got her out of there before she started sweating."

I'm sweating?

I reach up and shove my hair out of my face. Damp curls stick to my forehead, but the relief that washes over me when I brush it aside is nice. Not as nice as the fingers stretching me, getting me ready, but nice all the same. Until a cramp twists my belly, my insides pinching.

A gush of wetness makes the work of Brendan's fingers extra noisy. I whimper and wiggle, caught by my seat belt. Brendan pulls his fingers free and slaps his hand down on my pussy. My surprised cry turns into a needy moan, and my hips twitch as I attempt to thrust on something that's not there.

"It's because the bonding's incomplete. Her body's trying to force it. Trying to get her mated and pregnant. This heat'll be worse until she's properly bitten."

Yes. Yes, that's what I want. Their cocks in me. Their teeth. Cum. A river of cum and a knot to grind on. To squeeze.

"Please," I beg, my hips twisting against the restraint. Brendan's big hand palms my cunt, and I sigh in relief as his fingers curl and dip inside of me again.

"Almost there, baby," Anthony says.

Minutes stretch like hours, but eventually we're home. Brendan doesn't growl when I reach for the seatbelt's buckle this time. Unrestrained, I'm free to climb onto Brendan's lap and grind my aching pussy against him.

He lets out a huff of laughter until I grab the edges of his shirt and rip. Buttons pop off, hit the floor of the van with *pings* and roll. I need to feel him. Need to sink my fingers into the smattering of hair on his chest and appreciate how decadently hard he is under all this plush softness that makes him so cuddly. My mouth devours him and his hands palm my ass and knead. Spreads my cheeks apart.

Yes! Touch me. Fuck me. Fill me with your knot and cum.

Hands pull me off him and I growl, unhappy at being disrupted. I'm tossed over a shoulder, my bare ass spanked. Blood rushes to my head and the air whooshes out of my lungs. My skirt was rucked up at some point during the car ride home, or possibly before we left the club. Wherever my panties disappeared to is a mystery. I don't remember taking them off.

"Behave, baby," Anthony says. "We're gonna give you what you need. Gotta get you inside first unless you want to get rutted on the lawn."

I grunt, too breathless from the shoulder digging into my diaphragm to form words. His idea doesn't sound bad at all. We make it into the house without incident.

My world tilts on its axis again as I'm dropped into a mountain of soft bedding and pillows. The comforting smells of home, of pack, envelop me. It dulls the red haze of my heat.

Home. Pack. Safe.

I go limp, luxuriating in the plush bedding as it rubs against my heated, over-sensitive skin. Anthony takes advantage and uses this time to undress me until I'm naked. Lifting my head off the world's most perfect pillow, I stare at my pack and wonder why they aren't naked yet. We should be fucking already.

"God, she's so perfect," Anthony says.

I'd be more perfect with a dick in me.

To entice him, I bend my legs and let my knees fall apart, enjoying the way he devours me with his eyes. My nipples tighten into stiff peaks that ache, begging to be touched. Licked.

Sucked. Pinched and pulled. My clit throbs, wanting equal attention.

"Are we freeing Jamie now?" Brendan asks, coming to stand beside him.

Anthony shakes his head. "Not yet. He has to wait, remember?"

No. I want all of them. Need all of them. Why aren't we fucking yet?

Another belly cramp makes me whimper. Another burst of slick leaks down my inner thighs. It rolls down the crack of my ass and soaks into the nest. Makes it smell more like me, more like pack.

"Keep her busy while I grab what I need," Anthony says. He slaps Brendan on the shoulder like he's tagging him in for a game of football.

Brendan nods and sets about undressing. I watch, my gaze hungry, as my hand creeps between my slick thighs. I play with myself while he shoves his pants and boxer briefs down. His cock bobs free, the tip already beaded with a white pearl of precious fluid. It's big and jutting, nearly perpendicular to his body as he strokes it to full mast until it's heavy.

God, it's perfect. He's perfect.

Although I know he doesn't see himself that way. He sees damaged goods. A broken alpha. Older, weaker, wounded. He doesn't see how smart he is. Calm. How confident he makes us with his gentle words of reassurance and easy to follow orders. Experienced. I love the hint of gray at his temples. He's the safe landing place I've looked for my whole life, and I love him.

"On your belly," he orders.

I pull sticky fingers free and roll onto my belly like he says, and then I wait. He doesn't keep me in anticipation long. His hand wraps around my ankle and he tugs me down the nest until

I'm balanced on the edge. I bend my legs up so they don't fall to the floor and twist my fingers in the mound of blankets.

"Hands," he barks.

Untwisting them, I pull my arms behind my back. Fold them together at the small of my back. Fingers grasping elbows. He loves this pose. A binding pose without rope. With me, he doesn't need it. I'm happy to obey because I crave his touch. His love.

"That's it, sweet girl. Look at how perfect you are for me."

My reward is a skim of his hand over my ass. He plays with me, prying my cheeks apart. His thumbs spread my labia. My channel clenches. I'm aware of how achingly empty it is. How ready I am.

He teases me as if he's testing it for himself. As if he doesn't see how my pussy and thighs glisten with fresh slick and old cum. How I've been ready since Jamie came out on stage with a collar and leash on. Since Anthony used my pussy to masturbate himself among the crowd at Rut.

Even if these things hadn't happened, I'd be ready. I have been for weeks.

"Don't move, sweetheart," he orders as his cockhead grazes my clit. Slides along my pussy. Slicks itself in my wetness. Nudges against my needy hole. He presses the tip in, then retreats. Ignores my disappointed moan and pleas for more.

"Shh," he shushes me. "I'm enjoying taking you slow. We have all the time we need, sweetheart. There's no need to rush something so perfect."

"Please," I moan, wiggling my hips as I attempt to thrust back. To make him surge deeper. Brendan moves against me. He pulls back until only the tip is inside. The wet sounds my body makes are loud, though his thrusts are shallow. Slow.

"What will you give me?" he asks.

"Anything," I sob.

"I want to touch your arms."

It doesn't bother me as much now. We've been working on it. He can touch anything as long as he puts his cock in me for real. "Yes."

Fingers ghost over my crossed arms at the same time his cock sinks deeper. My sigh turns into a moan at the delicious stretching. The fullness. He pulls out and I whimper, but then he sinks balls deep again. His fingers firm around my arm. I'm too distracted by the throbbing in my untouched clit to care about it.

"That's my good girl," he says. "Look at how well you take me. Like your pussy's made for me. You can take more, can't you?"

"Yes."

His grip tightens and he adds some weight to his hold, but I'm too distracted by the slap of his balls against my clit to care. He fucks me harder. Deeper. Until my toes curl and my vision goes fuzzy. I can't focus on anything but the threat of his swelling knot as it catches against my pubic bone with every cervix-deep thrust.

"That's it, sweetheart. Such a good omega, pleasing her alpha. Being so sweet and good for her pack. You can take more." He pushes me down into the mattress, our bodies slapping together as his slow, deliberate thrusting turns into a pounding.

My toes curl and my pelvis tightens as his balls slap against my swollen clit. His knot rubs against my sweet spot as he pulls it out, only to shove it back in again. I'm panting, too lost for words. All I can do is moan and whimper for more.

"Here's your knot, sweetheart. You earned it. Here's your cum."

Yes!

His knot swells against my entrance and he shoves it deep, burying his cock as far as he can go while it kicks inside me. It pulses, lashes my walls with ropes of creamy cum until I'm so full it seems like I'll burst. I can't take another drop.

His large hand tightens around my crossed arms but I'm too caught up in the way his other hand wedges itself between me and the bed. It slides through my slippery folds. Finds my clit. Rubs until I'm panting. Until I'm squirming, though I'm stuck. Trapped under him. Knotted by his dick.

There's no escape once you're knotted. Only surrender.

The orgasm rips through me. Leaves me a shattered, quivering mess. Inside me, his cock gives one last pulse. A final spurt of seed. My reward for being a good omega and coming on his knot.

"That's a good girl," he says as he lets me go.

There's no need to hold me down anymore. We're tied. And I have no desire to run from my mate. In the circle of his strong arms, I'm safe.

He touches the scar his teeth made in the nape of my neck and I sense our bond pulse. How sated and pleased and happy he is. I enjoy making him happy. Like feeling him soft and fuzzy through the bond. I can't wait to have it this strong with the others once we've finally closed our open loops.

Brendan purrs as we lie there until his knot shrinks enough so he can pull free. The mess we make is instantaneous. Fluid slips from my well-fucked hole and soaks into the nest. It'll be wrecked by the end of my heat and we'll have a mountain of laundry to do.

"Thanks for getting her warmed up for me," Anthony says as he edges in.

Two quick taps on my thigh let me know that Brendan's taking his leave while Anthony takes over. My sluggish mind takes a minute to understand what this means. That's more than enough time for Anthony to get a firm grip on my hair as he pulls. My scalp aches as he uses my hair like a handle. He flips me onto my back and tugs, making me swivel until my head's hanging off the bed.

I open my mouth to whimper from the rough handling. He enjoys my heats because they're the only time I'll let him be this rough with me. Anthony presses the tip of his cock against my lips and pushes inside.

The force of him filling my mouth so completely, so quickly, makes me choke. Not that it stops him. He's merciless as he fucks my mouth. As he drives his cock so deep I have to swallow so I don't choke. His taste explodes on my tongue. Cherries and cum. The sweet orange of my slick. He never washed his dick after he used my pussy to masturbate.

"Fuck, that's good, baby. Suck my cock. You like it when we shoot our cum straight down your throat and right into your belly, don't you? My good little cock sucking slut." His hand comes down on my breast in a slap that stings against my pebbled nipple. He pulls his cock back and lets me breathe before deep fucking my throat again. His fingers press over the bulge of his cock in my throat, caress his corona through my neck.

"That's it, baby. Take me deep. We're gonna be so deep inside you all heat long. You'll walk bowlegged after."

He pulls back, then pulls out completely and waits for me to recover. Anthony grins down at me while I catch my breath. Dark hair flops over his face, and the black and gray ink all over his body makes him look like a devil straight from hell.

A string of saliva or pre-cum connects his head and my lips. Anthony fists his cock, stroking once and sliding his skin over the flare of his head, and then he taps his cock and its silver ring against my mouth.

I lick him. Lap up that string that connects us. Swirl my tongue around his head and dip it into his weeping slit. He groans as I lave him, lick our scents off his cock until he only smells like masculine musk and cherry cum. It's addictive, that scent.

Anthony caresses my face, dips his thumb into my mouth until I suck that too, then pinches my jaw until I drop it open once more. His cock presses inside again. Slower this time. Luxuriating in the slide of his velvety shaft as he fills my mouth and hits the back of my throat. I relax like he's shown me. Open for him. But he's done torturing me.

"That's my good girl. Hands and knees. Get your ass up for Daddy, baby."

I scramble onto my belly, get on my hands and knees in the middle of the nest for him. Brendan's cum smears against my thigh, and a fresh dribble of slick makes my inner thighs slippery. I rest my forehead on the backs of my hands and angle my pelvis to lift my pussy higher as Anthony climbs in behind me.

"So fucking pretty when you're full of cum." He spreads my labia apart and watches me drip. "Tsk. You're losing it all. Let's put it back in here, right where it belongs."

His cock slides against the slippery mess they've already made of me. He fits his cock at my hole and shoves inside. He's not as big. Not as thick. But he makes up for it with the brutal pace he sets. There's no gentle, deepening slide of his cock. He surges inside, presses cervix deep, and pulls out so he can slam home again.

The thrusts are so hard, the force of them rock me up the nest. I grunt from the impact as he batters the mouth of my womb. My knees burn as they slide over the silky sheets. My spine arches, hips dropping as I forget to hold the angle he likes.

"Where do you think you're going, baby? Come back here. This pussy is mine."

His grip on my hips keeps me from going far. He tugs me back into position and his dick carves a path through my cunt. All I can do is breathe. Breathe and pant. The angle changes, his head sliding over my sweet spot until my toes curl. And then I'm coming. The orgasm rips through me with no warning. My thighs tremble as my walls spasm around his cock.

"Fuck, you feel so good coming on my cock."

I moan as aftershocks leave me fuzzy headed and compliant while he chases his pleasure. His hand moves to grip my hair along my nape. Anthony squeezes and pulls me up onto my knees. He curls his body around me, his tongue sliding along the side of my throat. Licking me. Lapping the sweat off my skin. Finding the healed depressions where Brendan marked me weeks ago. In this new position, his thrusts aren't as deep, but that doesn't stop me from enjoying it. My body is already searching for its next release.

"This pretty pussy is mine. Forever," he growls.

Although I know it's coming, in the haze of my heat, I still forget. His cock throbs, pulses with his orgasm, and sharp teeth rip through the skin of my scent gland.

He makes a rough, masculine sound of pleasure as his balls empty inside me and blood drips down my chest. Warm droplets cool rapidly once they hit air. I shiver.

Pleasure, his or mine or maybe both, filters through me. Through our weak, one-sided bond. As he laps at the puncture marks his tooth caps made, it strengthens. Thickens inside me. Something snaps and I flinch. The faint sensation of him becomes a deluge of shock and satisfaction. Pleasure hits me. I cry out as my walls flutter around his buried cock and I come again.

"Oh shit, it worked," he exclaims.

And then he bites me again.

I grunt as his teeth scissor as he bites his claim deeper. Overlaps his mark with Brendan's. My pussy spasms around his cock like it's searching for a knot to milk.

Deep satisfaction makes me sleepy. I'm not sure if it's his or mine. Could be both of ours. It's been a long day and I'm delightfully sore and full.

"You're mine, now," he mumbles. He nudges me flat on the bed and pulls my head to the side so he can lap at the bleeding bites while his cock softens inside me. His weight is comforting, protective, as we lie there together while he tends it.

SOMEONE MUMBLES AND SHIFTS, THE JUMBLE OF PILLOWS IN THE nest tipping precariously. I knock one out of my face and roll onto my side, searching for a warm body. I find one. My fingers trace the dips and swells of washboard abs and taut, silky rope. Jamie fidgets against me. He makes unintelligible rutting alpha noises, and when I run my hands up his body, I learn why. He's been bound. Is that what they were doing while they kept me distracted and fucked me unconscious? Early morning light filters in through the window. Enough to see him with.

Jamie's neck cords with jutting veins as he strains toward me, only to give up and lie there, panting, as he recovers. His legs are tied together at the ankles and thighs, and his wrists are secured to his thigh rope. He has enough freedom to move without being truly free.

His cock is still caged, and when I run my hand over it his straining gets more agitated and my fingers come away sticky. Pre-cum stretches between us until the strand breaks and splatters his bare thigh. His hips rock and he groans.

Poor alpha. My poor restrained, denied pet. I bring my sticky fingers to my mouth and lick, humming as I suck them clean and then go searching for more.

It's a necessary cruelty, and it was his idea, but it still pains me to see him so needy and unfulfilled. So wanting. But if we want him to give into his primal urges, sink completely into his alpha urges, we need to drive him to the edge of feral.

Through our one-sided bond, Jamie aches for me. His cock strains against its cage the same way he strains against his ties and me… And I'm powerless to release him. My neck is bare. Someone took my key while I was delirious or sleeping. They likely thought I'd forget and release him too early.

I slide down his bound body and settle my weight on top of his legs, my face lined up with his cock cage. The metal is cool against my hot skin. I nuzzle my face into his groin and inhale the scent of him. Male and mine. It soothes me to have him close like this.

All of those omegas watching him on that stage wanted him, but he's all mine. They can't have him. And we're going to finalize it when he bites me this heat.

My tongue darts out to lick the opening of his metal cock cage. It slips over hot, velvety skin and laps up the bead of fluid leaking there. Jamie moans louder and fidgets harder. Tries to reach for me. To get his hands on the omega in heat, lying so sweetly next to him in the nest for hours as I slept. To rut and breed me. And to be denied. To be forced to wait.

His hips jerk as much as they're able to, and I palm his heavy hanging sack as I tease the opening of his cock cage with the tip of my tongue. Sweet coconut cream smears over my lips as he thrusts his bound cock against my mouth. As if his cage doesn't prevent him from doing the very thing his instincts must be screaming at him to do.

I've never seen his balls so bulging with pent up release before. I roll them in my hand, comparing the weight of each side. Stretching the skin over the firm testicle inside. Pulling them away from his body until he arches off the bed, then letting them go. I take one into my mouth and suck, enjoying the flavor of his musk. It's thicker here.

My pussy clenches around nothing. The ache of last night's fucking is fading from my heat-clouded mind.

Need more. Need cock. Knot. Cum.

But there will be no cock or knot or cum from this one. I swallow the head of his metal cage and groan in frustration. There's no velvety slide of skin under my lips. No swollen length to fill my mouth. No knot to squeeze in my hand. His cage is a puzzle that I'm growing too confused to solve in this state. All I know is my pussy needs attention. Anthony and Brendan are both snoring, and Jamie is very much awake.

Awake with a mouth that's free. His cock and fingers are useless to me. But I can make do with his tongue.

Chapter Forty-One

VERONICA

Abandoning Jamie's uselessly caged cock, I crawl up his body and settle with my knees on either side of his head. I brush my slick pussy against his chin, then lift and drag it higher. His tongue darts out and laps at me. I sigh and settle there, allowing him to eat me out.

He licks me from top to bottom, swirling around my clit and tugging the hood back as it swells and grows. He adds pressure and speed to his swirling. Then tension, as he sucks. My clit throbs and plumps in his mouth.

Whimpering, I reach down and bury my fingers in his beautiful, long blond hair as I ride his face and rock. His tongue pierces me. Drives deep inside me as it slurps up my heat sweetened slick and his pack mate's leftover cum from my hole. He begs me wordlessly for more while he works, diligent and practiced.

It's not a knot. Not a cock. But the thrusting of his tongue still makes me come. My wetness floods his mouth, threatens to drown him as I ride out my orgasm on his face and make him clean me. He licks my arousal-plump pussy clean until there's nothing but fresh slick left behind. It's good, but it's not enough to quench the fire raging inside me.

"Need a knot, sweetheart?" Brendan asks, his voice rough with sleep.

All I can do is whimper and go limp as he pulls me off Jamie and lays me down on my side. He spoons my back, lifts my leg, and slides inside me with a single smooth thrust that makes me sigh with relief.

"There you go, that's it. Feel how well your sweet pussy takes my cock? Let me take care of you the way you need to be taken care of."

The smooth slide of his cock makes my last orgasm seem like nothing more than a warmup. Tension coils, starting in my back before winding tight in my belly. This position is intimate. It's sweet. His entire body curls around me, guarding my back as he fills my aching, empty pussy and slips two fingers between my legs. All it takes is a few swipes of my swollen clit and I'm coming on his cock.

"That's a good girl coming on your alpha's cock. I'm gonna give you a knot to squeeze, sweetheart. And you're going to milk it dry."

Yes. I need it.

He grunts, his dick continuing its easy slide through my soaked folds. Bottoming out inside me. He pulls my leg over his and changes our angle until it's deeper still. Gentle and deep, but no less satisfying as his knot swells until finally it pops. The relief is instant.

He groans with the first release of his cum. Semen fills me until I'm aching. And then his fingers go back between my labia. Brendan rubs circles, teases me, and forces me to have another orgasm.

I come with a cry, walls fluttering on his knot as his cock gives one more pulse of cum, but his fingers don't stop. He ignores my whimpering, my whining. He winds me up for another orgasm, another squeeze of his knot. Two. A third. I'm whimpering. It's too much. Too much pleasure that borders on pain.

I can't... No more.

"Shh, you can do it. Two more and I'll let you sleep," he promises.

My clit aches, sharp and unyielding, until it gives into his demands. I shudder, my walls clamping weak and tired on his lodged knot. Another spurt of cum. Another strum of his fingers as he forces me to dredge one last orgasm from the empty well of my pleasure.

My body obeys, even though it's spent. Exhausted and over-sensitive, all I can do is lie there as he purrs and strokes my arms. My side. My leg and belly. Fatigue drags me under.

I sleep again, and don't wake for hours until Anthony sets me in a warm bath. I ache. Everywhere. Inside. Out. The bite marks on my neck they've been nibbling and sucking. I throb in time with my heartbeat. Anthony ignores my agitated protests at being washed and distracts me with a hand between my legs until I'm calm again. Warm water sluices down my naked body and he scrubs me until I'm pink and languid, then rinses the shampoo and conditioner from my hair.

His rubdown with the fluffy towel turns frisky. I'm horny again now that I'm clean. It doesn't take much convincing for me to let him bend me over the bathroom sink. The counter is cold under my flushed body as he ruts me from behind. My tits sway and I go up on my toes as he fucks into me, making me dirty again as if he didn't just get me clean minutes ago.

Fingers dig into my thighs, my hips, and then he spanks me. Sharp slaps make my ass burn, which turns into a pleasant throbbing.

"Fuck, baby," he groans. "You're so goddamn wet. Gonna fill this cute little pussy up and make Jamie eat it out of you."

My world rips apart into a haze of need and satiation as I lose track of time. It could be hours or days that pass. Anthony makes good on his threat, then after Jamie is fed he bullies me into drinking water. Forces me to swallow something sweet and hard and round, using the promise of his cock and a belly full of cum to get it down when my thoughts grow muddled.

He buries my nose in the thatch of dark hair at his groin and chokes me on his cock until I'm afraid it'll all come right back up again, but it never does. He keeps me full instead.

"That's good," Anthony says. "Let's both take her while he watches. He'll like that."

Someone sticks their fingers inside my sore pussy, gathering slick, and drags it to my ass. The tip of a finger presses beyond the rim of my hole. Pumps in. Wets it until it glides knuckle deep. I moan and writhe, unaccustomed to being filled there.

That's not where it goes.

"Shh, stop fussing, baby. You said you were curious to try it. Now settle down and be a good girl for Daddy and take this cock up your pretty little ass. I spent all that time prepping you to get you nice and ready for me here."

My face is pressed into pillows that are wet and crunchy from splatters of cum and slick. Anthony pumps a finger deeper into my ass until I've swallowed the digit to his palm. He pulls it out, then adds another. Starts this whole thing all over again until I've stretched around both fingers and I'm taking him easily. My hips rock back to meet his thrusts. He adds a third. Scissors them apart. Scoops up more convenient slick.

The head of his pierced cock notches there. He pushes in, murmurs nonsense I barely hear, and sighs as he fucks more of his cock inside the tight pucker of my ass one inch at a time until he's balls deep.

"Fuck, that's tight," Anthony sighs, pleased.

"Just wait." Brendan chuckles. "It's going to get even better. Move onto your back. Let me get in there."

My boneless limbs are rearranged as Anthony flops onto his back and takes me with him. Brendan settles between my thighs. Spreads them wide with large, gentle hands. All he does is kiss me, at first, and let his weight push us all into the mattress.

Slowly, a bit at a time, I relax until I've forgotten that I've already got a cock in me. Until a second notches at my other hole. Brendan rubs his cock up and down my pussy, coating it in my slick, and pushes in.

My hands slap against his skin as I scrabble for purchase. To get away. Push him off me. He bottoms out inside me and I'm stretched fuller than I've ever been. I pull him closer instead.

Oh, God.

He pulls out, then thrusts back in. Does it again. Again. My breathing turns ragged. I'm panting, my eyes squeezed shut as my world narrows to the two cocks stuffing me so fucking full.

"God, you weren't kidding." Anthony lets out a ragged groan. "I can feel your cock rubbing against mine inside her."

"Wait until I knot her," Brendan chuckles, his cock bouncing inside me as he laughs.

I whimper in response, too tired to find the words to protest. Anthony holds still while Brendan fucks me. He finds a position that doesn't aggravate his knee too much as he picks up the pace until sweat beads his brow. My vision goes black around the edges as his knot drags over my sweet spot. Caresses it like a lover's touch from deep inside. Rubs against Anthony's cock buried in my belly.

Jamie groans somewhere on the sidelines. Bound. Helpless to do anything but watch as they fuck me and reduce me to a whimpering mess between them.

"Here you go, sweetheart. Here's what you need. Take it. All of it. It's yours." Brendan babbles as he comes, his pace slowing as he drives his cock deeper. Rearranges my insides to make more room for himself. His knot swells, and swells, and swells until I'm so full I'm ready to burst. He cums, his groans matching the pulsing of his cock as he unloads inside me and catches his breath.

"Can I move now?" Anthony asks.

I whimper. Want to tell him no. Beg him to give me a minute. But when has Anthony ever known mercy? I feel too much to fall asleep despite being knotted. My skin is too sensitive. My poor clit too swollen. My belly too full of cock and cum.

When Brendan doesn't protest, Anthony slides out of my ass until his cock's nearly free. He thrusts back in, his head dragging over the knot lodged deep inside my cunt through a thin wall of tissue.

My whimpers turn into groans until Brendan drops his head down and mouths at my claiming bites. He sucks my tender scent gland into his mouth and teases it with the sharp scrape of his canines. He rocks against me, his pelvis pressed against mine. Grinding.

Anthony claims my ass and takes his own selfish pleasure while Brendan keeps me docile and focused on the throbbing pulse between my legs until I come apart at the seams between them. My walls squeeze down on his buried knot. My ass clenches tight around him.

Anthony comes deep in my gut while cursing in Italian. Once all three of us are spent, we lie there and catch our breath while Brendan purrs. It's a diesel truck sound. Deep and rumbling. The vibrations hit me bone deep. I'm asleep again before they both pull out, only somewhat conscious of the weight and warmth of a fuzzy blanket being draped over me as their cum drips down my ass and soaks into the nest.

I'm woken when someone settles behind me. A hand slips underneath the blanket between my legs to scoop up the mess from my pussy and bring it to my lips. I growl at the disruption to my rest before my nose latches onto the smell of our combined fluids. They shove their fingers past my lips and I lick them clean, my growls turning into purrs as they feed me the only thing I'll gladly eat right now.

"Baby, are you ready?" Anthony asks, dragging me back into consciousness some unknown amount of time later. He sets the empty water bottle aside. I must have dozed off while drinking again.

"Hmm?" I ask. A bead of sweat rolls between my breasts. I roll onto my back and stretch stiffened limbs. The room is dark. Only the gentle amber glow of my string lights keep it from being pitch black.

Anthony holds up a silver chain, a key dangling at the end. It swings like a pendulum. "Are you ready? He's gonna be pretty feral. We've been edging him for three days."

Three days? Has it really been that long?

Memories come back to me, fuzzy and distorted with events out of time from one another. My hair is damp, and underneath the scent of our pack's pheromones and the musk of sex, I smell the curl cream and lotion that Anthony researched and bought me.

The nest creaks as Anthony gets out of bed. I track his movement, my brow furrowed as he crosses the room and kneels on the floor. I roll onto my side and stretch toward the edge of the nest in time to watch him toss something aside. Metal clangs together as it rolls off the rug and hits tile.

"How do you want to do this?" Anthony asks Brendan,

who's sitting in a chair on the opposite side of the room. "Hands or legs first?"

"Aim him, pull the quick-release knot, and get out of the way. He'll free himself. It's better if we don't handle him too much while he's in full rut. Once he's knotted her, he'll be more manageable."

Anthony steps to the side, and I finally get a glimpse of Jamie. His hands are raised above his head, the rope tied through a silver ring that I don't remember being bolted into one of the ceiling beams. His legs are tied apart, each ankle attached to another ring coming out of the wall on each corner.

The look in Jamie's eyes is foreign. Feral. In the bond, he's all hunger and desperation. His patient disguise is an act. Underneath it, he's broiling with lust and desire. Base need and yearning.

Three days. Three days of sleeping in the nest, bound and denied. Being forced to watch. To be so close without being allowed to touch. Participate or claim. His stare and bobbing, ruddy cock both hold a dark promise for my immediate future.

My pussy clenches at the thought. At the idea of being wedged under his powerful body. Of being forced to submit, subdued, so he can finally claim me as deeply as my heart's claimed him as mine.

I whimper, a fresh wash of slick gathering at my entrance to get ready. To keep from being damaged. It's nature's cruel gift to omegas. The more barbaric the alpha is, the more they fight and fuck and hurt us, the more our body submits. Goes limp. Boneless and yielding. Slick and fawning.

Jamie's nostrils flare as he growls, a low and threatening roil that makes my core clench. It's like looking at a swirling storm. The danger is there, but it's too stunning to look away. An act of awe-filled nature that has to be experienced because there is no other option. Something to be endured.

My body tightens with anticipation. I swallow on a throat gone dry and press deeper into the comfort of my nest as if that will save me. Hide me. But there's no hiding from this. Not when his nostrils flare as he scents the room. Not when this is a bedroom, not a forest.

In the ancient days, an alpha in full rut like this would make an omega like me run. Soft prey chased through a dark wood. Run into the ground, then rutted in the dirt like animals. Seeded. Claimed, and carried home to a foreign village to raise the baby we didn't ask for.

"Get ready," Anthony says.

He angles himself behind Jamie, slipping between him and the wall. The three taut lines of rope go slack, and that's all the warning I get.

Jamie rips his bindings free from the hooks that chain him, and then he's on me. He's faster than he looks. A trained athlete who stays limber through dancing. His muscles ripple as he pounces.

I whimper despite knowing it's coming. That we planned for this and talked about it endlessly. But talking about it and doing it are different beasts. Adrenaline surges, making my heart rate spike. I fidget, my mind fighting my body's primal urge to flee. The heel of my palm lands on a pillow and I go down flat, sabotaged by my own fucking nest.

A hand wraps around my ankle and tugs, and I let out a noise as I'm tugged down the bed while he crawls over me, his shoulders bunching as he climbs on top. Large hands spread my legs apart as he climbs between my thighs.

He bends down to sniff between my legs. His breath is hot as he smells me. To my embarrassment, a fresh bead of slick surges between my folds. I go still, too scared even to breathe, as he extends a tongue and licks me from ass to clit. His low, menacing growl turns to a purr that leaches the tension from my muscles.

Jamie bends me, repositioning me underneath him as he climbs my body. His engorged, ruddy cock is hard and leaking as it drags over my thigh. Moves across the thatch of hair at my groin. Dribbles pre-cum on my cleft. His hips buck as he fucks the air, his instincts riding him hard. Demanding things he's not used to doing.

I fidget underneath him and his purr turns back into a growl that makes me whimper. Makes my pussy sopping wet and ready for a rough and brutal claim. I reach out to him through the bond instead. Try to reassure him. Let him know he's mine. I'm not going anywhere. Not running. There's no need to rush this.

Jamie shakes his head and frowns, then snorts. He rises high enough to grab my leg and hitch it higher, to tilt my pelvis and open me wider, and then his hips thrust again.

This time, his cock notches lower. It slides between my labia, drags through the puddle of my heat-sweetened slick, and sinks home. His thrust buries his cock to the hilt without gentle easing, and his blunt intrusion makes me gasp and arch against him. Once he starts, there's no stopping him. Only enduring it until the rapid pace of his humping mellows from a demanding stretch to a feeling of fullness.

He crushes me to the bed, covering me completely and keeping me safe from competitors as he humps me. As he buries his swollen cock and works out three days of tension and denial on my pussy until I'm a wrecked and moaning mess beneath him.

I shouldn't love it. Shouldn't find enjoyment in the flipping of our natures. The brutality of his rough claim. Of being used like an object. A convenient wet hole to fuck and fill. But there's something about knowing it's Jamie who's been driven to this beast-like fury that makes me feel small and soft. Feminine. Desired. Needed and adored.

Sweet Jamie, my prince, turned into a beast instead of the reverse. Tarzan, untamed. My pet turned feral. For me, his mate.

His knot drags against my sweet spot, and I want it. Want it more than anything. He's never gotten this far without help before. Never learned how to properly top.

He doesn't need help or direction now. He's taking what he wants, and what he wants is me.

I shift the smidgeon I can underneath him, ignoring his growls of protest. My heels notch in the divots of his flexing ass. I wrap my arms around his broad back and dig my nails into his skin. Urging him on. I make him think I'm resisting him, fighting this claim so he won't lose steam and stop. Not when we're so close.

He pounds me harder, knocks the air from my lungs until I'm breathless and panting. His knot swells, my pussy tight around him. It catches on my pubic bone. Pulls free, then shoves back in. He grunts from the effort, his rhythm stuttering. I dig my heels in, refusing to let him go.

I fight through the fog of lust clouding my thoughts and dredge up words. It's harder than usual. "Come inside me," I order.

Two more thrusts, that's all he lasts. He surges deep, his knot swelling in place. Tying us together.

His cock shudders inside me, pulses with the lashes of his cum as he paints my walls white and fills me with so much semen that my belly bulges. The pressure builds against his swollen stopper. It massages my clit from the inside, the deep root of that organ much bigger than anyone thinks.

I grind on his knot, whimpering as my orgasm swells. Crests. Hangs there. Devastating and out of reach. I need more, but I don't know what to ask for. I don't know how much he understands right now.

"Bite me," I whimper.

Jamie's head dips to my shoulder. He nuzzles the side of my throat that's bare of any marks. Finds the scent gland there. His canines graze it and his cock jerks inside me as he tongues it. Sucks it into his mouth.

I open my mouth to repeat the order when he bites. All that comes out is a ragged moan that's equal parts pain and pleasure. I jerk against him, his teeth ripping deeper as his jaw clamps tighter to keep me pinned underneath him. His pelvis grinds against my clit and I come, his knot and teeth buried deep in me as my universe shatters. The bond breaks, reforms, and snaps together stronger than before.

Slowly, one lick and rumble of his purr at a time, Jamie reconnects my jagged pieces.

My lungs refill with air and I catch my breath as aftershocks zip through me, my walls clamping down on his knot to squeeze out one last drop of his seed. In the bond, he's calm and content. Sated. His long-buried instinct to rut finally satisfied.

Trapped underneath his colossal bulk, fully bonded and satiated, I am too. My dainty purr layers with his deeper one as my arms tighten around him. Slowly we recover. Sleep and contentment leave me limp as my heavy eyelids shut and refuse to open. It's too much effort to do anything but lie here and breathe while his knot shrinks.

"Think it's fine now?" Anthony whispers as he comes closer. The bed dips as he sets a knee on the other side.

"Should be. He did a good job. I can sense him through her." Brendan joins us in the nest.

When Jamie doesn't growl and guard me while they edge closer, we end up piled together. The warm, comforting weight of a blanket is thrown over us and I fall asleep like that. With his tongue bathing my claiming bite and his cum making a slippery mess of me when he finally pulls free, but doesn't rise and let me go. The deep ache in my pelvis can't dampen these feelings of lightness inside me.

"Good job, pet." I stroke his hair and enjoy the weight of him.

It's done. I'm fully claimed, and so are they. And in the tangled mess of blankets and limbs, there's nowhere I'd rather be.

Chapter Forty-Two

VERONICA

"WE'RE GONNA NEED TO BUY A NEW WASHING MACHINE WHEN we're done," I say as I scrunch my nose at the sight of all the cum and fluids dried onto the sheets. "Might be better to throw these out and buy new ones."

Despite buying so many sets of sheets for this very reason, none of the boys had the courage to change the sheets during our four-day fuck fest. Apparently I growled whenever they tried. I can't see any hope of salvaging these. They're… Wrecked is too light of a word for it.

Brendan takes the crunchy sheets from me and tosses them into the plastic basket, then drops a kiss onto the top of my damp hair. We're all fresh from the shower, and I've been scrubbed pink and lotioned.

"I bought a laundry detergent that has special enzymes in it," he says. "We'll let it soak before we wash them. It'll be fine."

"Breakfast!" Anthony yells from the kitchen.

Brendan takes the mountain of dirty laundry toward the washer and dryer off the garage while I stretch out my sore limbs and head into the kitchen. I expect to see Anthony setting plates of food on the kitchen table while Jamie cooks eggs or something. I don't expect to see Anthony jerking Jamie off.

Jamie grips the edge of the table and moans, his hips bucking as he thrusts into the tight ring of Anthony's fingers. How the alpha has any cum left in his balls, I have no idea.

After being locked in his chastity cage for the first three days of my heat, he spent the last one balls deep inside me every chance he got. His cum dripped all the way to my ankles. If it weren't for the waterproof mattress protector, we'd be driving to Nested right now to buy a new one.

I stand and watch them, equal parts amused and concerned. How is his dick not chafed? My pussy is sore. I'm tempted to see if we have an ice pack in the freezer to sit on while I coax something solid into my queasy stomach.

"Hungry, baby?" Anthony asks me. He glances up, his mouth twisting into a grin that makes his cheek dimple. "Yours will be ready in a minute."

"What…" That's when I see the piece of perfectly golden toast sitting on a plate before Jamie's dripping cock. Droplets of cum splatter over it like white dots of icing. They soak into the piece of toast. Jamie moans, his hips slowing to deep thrusts.

"That's it, babe," Anthony coaxes. "Let's feed our girl what she needs. Give her what she craves."

I stare in mute fascination as Jamie's chin hits his chest. As his fingers squeeze the edge of the table that bangs against his big thighs. As his ass cheeks clench, that divot forming as he bucks.

His first spurt goes wide. It lands on the plate and table more than the toast, before Anthony adjusts the angle of his grip. He grabs that bulging knot with his other hand and squeezes. Jamie's moan deepens. Anthony aims Jamie's cock so the next lashes of cum paint it white.

Semen coats the perfect slice of buttered toast like icing

until it puddles and drips down the side, making a sticky mess on the plate.

Once Jamie's spent, Anthony lets him go and gives him a pat on the ass, then picks the plate up and sets it on my placemat.

Absolutely not. "I'm not eating that."

Anthony quirks one brow, lifting his cum-splattered hand to his mouth to lick it clean. His hair flops into his face as his tongue darts out to lap up an errant streak of cum. "You're not hungry?"

My stomach twists with hunger and I hate how my mouth is watering as I stare at the cum-splattered toast.

No. That's… No fucking way. That's gross. It's a step too far. "I'm not eating that."

"No? Okay, baby." Anthony doesn't seem perturbed by my rejection as he swipes a bit of the cum off the plate and lets it drip onto the center of the toast.

I watch, enraptured, as the long strand stretches. The droplet at the end grows fat. It breaks. Falls. He sticks his finger in his mouth and sucks it clean, then pulls it out with a wet pop.

"I thought toast would be easiest, but we can put it in a smoothie instead," Anthony says. "Give Jamie a few minutes to recover and we'll make you another one of your special drinks."

Jamie drags his chair out and slumps into it with a tired grunt.

"Another one of…" It takes a minute for my post-heat thick head to wrap around his words. My special drinks. The drinks Anthony's been bringing me for weeks. They're all tropical flavored. Pineapple and… coconut. His drink specials used to be varied. Inventive. I thought he was on a beachy themed kick or something.

My teeth click as I snap my open mouth shut. "Don't tell me you're feeding me cum in my food," I growl.

"Hmm? Okay, I won't tell you then." Anthony nudges my plate forward an inch. "Don't tell me you don't want it. That your mouth isn't wet for it. That it won't be the most delicious thing we could make for you all day. A meal you won't immediately go throw up while your stomach is settling back into the rhythm of solid food."

I swallow the excess saliva in my mouth and glare at him. I can't look at that plate of cum covered toast because… because he's right. My instincts want me to pick it up and eat it. To get that extra shot of protein in nutritious alpha cum.

My stomach twists with hunger as the scent of coconut thick with delicious pheromones invades my nose. My lips press together into a thin line as I glare at Anthony's stupid, smug, handsome, smiling face.

I grab a piece of plain toast from the stack on the table and take a huge bite of it, ripping a chunk free and grinding it between my molars. Chewing takes effort. My mouth is dry, like it's stuffed with cotton instead of bread.

"I'm starving," Brendan says as he joins us, oblivious to the tension around the table. "Pass the bacon?"

Anthony hands the plate of bacon to him, then returns his focus to me. I refuse to catch his eye as I swallow the dry lump of plain toast in my mouth and rip off another chunk, chewing slowly as my jaw gets sore. It's too dry and I'm too thirsty. When I reach for my glass of protein water, Anthony grabs it first. He cracks it and hands me the bottle.

"Dry mouth?" he asks with a knowing smile.

I glare at him while I drink and dislodged the dry toast stuck in my throat.

"Something wrong?" Brendan asks, one brow arched as he looks between the three of us.

"Vee doesn't want to eat her high-protein diet," Anthony answers.

"I'm not eating toast covered in cum!" I yell. I shouldn't have to explain this. And he shouldn't have been putting cum in my drinks for... "How long have you been feeding me cum in my food and drinks?"

"Food? Today. Drinks? I don't know..." He scratches his jaw as he thinks about it. He shouldn't have to think about it. Shouldn't have to do calendar math. "A few months. Since your last heat."

Months? As in plural? As in longer than we've officially been together? "You can't do that! That's fucked up, Anthony."

The smile slips off his face into something inscrutable. "But you were fine with sucking our cocks and swallowing. What's the difference?"

"It's not the same thing at all and you know it." I drain the last of my water and set the crinkling plastic bottle on the table. "I didn't know you were doing it, and I didn't agree to that. What you did was fucked up."

"But you liked it, and it made you happier. Healthier." His brow knits. "That's what the care guides said you needed." He fidgets in his seat, his eyes darting from me to Brendan as if he's just now realizing how badly he's messed up.

"You can't put body fluids in someone's food or drink without their knowledge," Brendan says to Anthony in his soft dad voice. "Vee's right, it's a consent issue."

"But—"

Brendan holds up a hand to stop Anthony's interruption. "No. I don't care that it's what the internet forums say. There's a lot of creepy weirdos on the internet. You don't take relationship advice like that from strangers. Half of it's made up of wish fulfillment fantasies and kinks. Understand?"

"I guess you're not gonna be happy to hear that you drank some too," Anthony says.

Brendan pinches the bridge of his nose and sighs. "Okay...

Going forward, you will not put body fluids in anyone's food or drink without consent. And you won't get Jamie to do it either."

"I'm sorry, Vee," Jamie says, looking sad with rounded shoulders and big, shiny eyes. "I thought it was helping. I didn't know it would make you mad."

"No more stunts like that," Brendan says. "We're a pack. You don't make decisions like that for your packmates without discussing it first."

"Fine, I hear what you're saying," Anthony says, deflating in his seat. "But it really did help. You were in a better mood, and why do you think your skin's so clear and your hair is so shiny?"

I level him with a curdling glare. Excuses aren't an apology.

Anthony splays his hands in front of him. "But you're right. I'm sorry. I shouldn't have done it without asking or telling you. I thought I was giving you something you needed but wouldn't ask for. But that doesn't make it okay."

My chest aches from Anthony's side of the bond. He's sad, embarrassed, and underneath that, afraid. So is Jamie, who sits there dejected and worried. The worst of my anger deflates, although I'm still mad at them. At Anthony for orchestrating it and Jamie for going along with it. Anthony's got some groveling to do before I'll fully forgive him.

Brendan studies the cum-splattered toast with a thoughtful frown. "Vee, are you sure you don't want it?" he asks me, his tone gentle.

"Are you serious?" I ask.

Brendan holds his spread hands out in the air to ward me off. "Doing it in secret was wrong, but he's right that it might help. It would ease you into solids so we're not holding your hair back in half an hour. Is it really that weird compared to drinking it straight from Jamie's cock or having it fed to you from your pussy?"

"That's not the same thing at all. Those are completely different situations." Embarrassed, I cross my arms over my chest. I shouldn't have to explain to them why one is hot and the other is weird. I don't want to eat congealing cum toast.

But my mouth waters every time I glance at it and my sore, battered pussy throbs from the pheromones wafting off it. I ignore my post-heat's cravings for alpha pheromones and cum.

"Because you're conscious of it now?" Brendan asks. "Or because you think we'll judge you for enjoying it? You're an omega, Veronica. It's hard wired in your DNA to crave the comfort of your mates' bodies and their pheromones. You'll feel better once it's in your system. But if you'd rather suck our cocks instead, we're not gonna complain, sweetheart. It's your choice."

Brendan kisses my cheek, then piles bacon and scoops some eggs onto his plate. The smell of his food makes my stomach roil with displeasure. Being hungry but food averse is another sucky piece of the shit sandwich that being an omega is sometimes.

It's going to take me a while to forgive Anthony, but I know how he can start. "I don't want to eat it." I level Anthony with the stare that's made grown men shrink during a negotiation. "I want you to do it."

Anthony arches a brow. "Me? You want me to eat it?"

"Yeah." The ceramic plate scrapes over the wood as I nudge it closer to him.

I expect him to argue, to get offended or disgusted, but he shrugs and picks up the cum toast from the plate. "Okay, baby. You know there's nothing I wouldn't do for you."

He stares me down as he brings it to his mouth. His lips part, and he takes a large bite, chewing and swallowing it without complaint. I watch as, bite by bite, the cum-drenched toast disappears. Once he's finished it, he swipes up a droplet of cum from the plate and sucks it clean, then hums around his finger. His eyes shutter, those long dark lashes of his fluttering over his pretty blue eyes.

Am I... am I into this? No. My heart skips a beat and I fidget in my seat. It creaks as I shift my weight. No, I'm annoyed. This was a punishment—it wasn't supposed to be hot. It's not. I don't know if it's Anthony finally being put in his place in this pack or seeing him eat one of his own schemes, but I'm not prepared to unpack how much I enjoyed that.

"Satisfied, baby?" Anthony asks.

I clear my throat and avoid looking anyone in the eye. "Well, it's a start." From the stack of plain toast in the center, I grab another perfectly golden piece and the butter. Crumbs scatter over my plate as I butter it a little too hard.

"Was that not enough?" Anthony asks.

"Should I eat some too?" Jamie asks, confused.

"I'm fine. Everyone eat your breakfast, please." I gesture toward the collection of plates and focus on adding sugar to someone's abandoned coffee while trying not to blush.

"Is the coffee a good idea?" Brendan asks with a frown.

"I haven't had caffeine in four days." I don't like the taste of coffee on a good day, but Jamie doesn't like having energy drinks or soda in the house. He says there's too many chemicals in them. "You can pry this mug out of my cold dead hands."

The first sip is full of regret, but I choke it down. My stomach protests every swallow after nothing but cum and flavored protein water for the past four days, but I ignore that too. I need the caffeine to feel like a human again.

They eat while I nibble on toast and drain my coffee mug until twenty minutes later when I'm throwing everything right back up in the bathroom. It's Anthony who holds my hair back and ties it into a ponytail for me while I'm sick.

"That's it. Get it all out," he says while he rubs circles on my back.

"I don't want to hear it," I tell him once I'm reasonably sure I'm done. The porcelain is cool against my cheek, and I'm grateful that the first thing Brendan and Anthony did this morning after gathering up the laundry was to scrub the bathroom clean.

"I didn't say anything at all," Anthony says in a calm voice, feigning innocence.

He doesn't need to. I can hear him think it. That if I'd sucked up the weirdness and eaten the cum toast I'd be eating a real dinner tonight instead of buttered rice.

"It was the coffee," I mutter. It had to be the acidity, or something.

"Hmm." His soothing shoulder rub disappears and the tap runs at the sink. He presses a glass of water into my hand. "Here."

"Thanks." I use it to rinse my mouth out first and spit, then drain the glass. It's cold in my stomach and refreshing. When it doesn't seem like it'll come right back up, I let him help me off the bathroom floor and settle on the sofa under a fuzzy blanket.

Anthony perches on the arm and tugs the hair tie from my ponytail. He works the snags out of my hair and smoothes it away from my face. "How about this... We bought steak and the stuff to make caesar salad for dinner. Why don't you let Jamie make you one of his special fruit smoothies, and we'll all pretend it's whey protein powder and we never have to talk about it again?"

Internally I debate the pros and cons of being stubborn versus eating real food tonight. He's right that this is the best I've felt in years. I thought it was from finding my pack and getting through the audit, but what if it's more than that? What if it really is a stupid pheromone thing? While I don't like being fed cum without my knowledge or permission, I also hate feeling like crap for three days during post-heat.

"The parmesan cheese is a block of the real stuff I bought from the cheesemonger my uncle gets all his stuff from for the restaurant. No green shakers of that powdered crap for our omega. So it's your call, baby. Do you want a smoothie or a protein water?"

My stomach churns with spine-eating hunger, and the desire to eat real food wins over pride. I tuck the fuzzy blanket up to my chin. "If I say yes, that doesn't mean you're forgiven yet."

"Of course not, baby."

"You still have a lot to do to make it up to me."

He grins. "Just tell me which building to burn down next."

"Oh my God, that's not funny."

Anthony slips off the sofa and kneels on the rug so we're eye to eye. He cups my face in his palms and strokes his thumbs over my cheeks. "I'm kidding… Kind of. You know there's nothing I wouldn't do for my girl."

"I know."

I know he means it. Anthony can be manipulative and juvenile at times, something Brendan says he'll mellow out of with age, but he's loyal. When he cares about someone, he takes care of them. Sometimes in unsavory ways. Sometimes in sweet ones. He beat a man until his knuckles were bloody. He stopped me from probably getting arrested for having a taser. If I'd been downstairs holding it when the police showed up, it could have gotten ugly. His threat to find the alphas who've tried to hurt me isn't idle. If I gave the word, I know some of them might end up in the hospital or underneath a freshly poured foundation.

I cup his hand and rub his knuckles. They healed well, but there's a scar over one. It fucked up his tattoo, but he refuses to see his tattoo artist and get it fixed. He says he earned it fair and square. That he likes the reminder. So do I. I find myself tracing it with my finger. There's something pleasant about knowing he earned it while protecting me.

"But I don't need you to protect me from myself," I tell him. "Not when it means keeping things from me or making decisions that affect me behind my back. That's not what family does."

He opens his mouth, hesitates, then closes it and nods. "Okay. More talking and asking first. I can do that."

Smart man. He's learning. Anthony stands and rakes his unruly hair out of his face. "So what do you want for breakfast, baby?"

My stomach rumbles, demanding more than protein omega water. I'm really tired of being queasy. Maybe they're right. Is it really that weird compared to anything else my body craves during a heat? Rejecting my omeganess leads to puking. I'm really over worshiping at the base of the porcelain throne. Still, that doesn't mean I'll tolerate any teasing about it.

I tuck the fuzzy blanket more around myself like it's armor. "When you said we'd never talk about it, I'm holding you to that."

Anthony tries to suppress his smile, but fails. "You got it, baby. Does pineapple and passionfruit sound good? Okay, coming right up. Hey, Jamie, I need you! Grab the blender, babe."

Twenty minutes later when I've sucked down my smoothie and my stomach's settled enough to finally eat some buttered toast without getting sick, I can't regret agreeing to it. A quick internet search in private mode tells me it's a lot more common than I knew. I always thought those magazine articles that told you to put your man's dick through a donut to spice up your blowjob were for shock value to sell more magazines.

"Laundry's done," Brendan says in the afternoon. He lays a hand on Anthony's shoulder. "Help me make the nest?"

"Sure."

Jamie and I stay cuddled on the couch while an old classic movie plays. I'm barely paying attention to it as I add another tiny braid to Jamie's hair. It's so pretty with all the different blond and brown tones. The sun has made the top strands lighter than the ones underneath. He falls asleep like that, and then so do I, and we only wake from our nap when the smells of cooking from the kitchen stir us.

After dinner, when my stomach settles in record time and I'm able to hold down a proper meal without getting queasy, I can begrudgingly admit that Anthony was right.

Although I'll never give him the satisfaction of saying so out loud. He doesn't need encouragement. None of them do. I'm pampered enough.

Epilogue

VERONICA

A year and a half later

THE FRONT DOOR SQUEAKS ON ITS HINGES AS IT OPENS, THE sound loud in the otherwise quiet room. All eyes turn to watch our resident himbo alpha walk in. Anthony follows quickly behind him with a shit-eating grin on his face.

"You're late," I snap at them both. "It's almost time."

"Sorry," Jamie says, looking sheepish. "Traffic."

I'd believe him—except he blushes. My eyes narrow with suspicion as I stare at him. "It's LA. There's always traffic."

I never should have let them both run to the store to get a new power cord for the projector. The two-hour errand shouldn't have taken almost four hours. I have an inkling about what made them so late, and traffic has nothing to do with it.

I glance at the time on the clock above the bar. It's nearly five. "Let's get that cord switched. It's almost time." My heart knocks against my ribs as Brendan takes the blue and yellow bag from Anthony and swaps out the new power cord for the old broken one. We could have made do with using a laptop or tablet, but I really wanted to use the projector so everyone could see New York's grand opening of Rut on the big screen.

Brendan makes quick work of it, his fingers nimble as he plugs the projector in and gets it to boot up. When the blue standby screen aligns with the sheet we've hung up as our backdrop, everyone crowds around the main stage and cheers.

He gets it hooked up to the wi-fi, and I text Nate to let him know that we're ready. A few minutes later, I accept his call and Brendan helps me stream the video call to the projector so everyone can watch.

"Vee! You made it. Doors open in five minutes," Nate grins.

I smile too. I can't help it. Everything we've all worked so hard for, all our dreams and planning, is about to come true. This is the start of some big plans. New York City first, then Las Vegas, followed by Miami, and finally Chicago. After that, maybe London. We'll see. We'll have a Rut full of handsome alphas in sparkly, sequin thongs in every major party capital of the country. And in a few years, maybe the world.

"I wouldn't miss this for the world," I tell him, grinning back. "How's the line?"

"Packed. The line wraps around the block. We stopped counting at three hundred heads. I have to admit, I'm surprised you didn't fly up for tonight. We'd have loved to have you join us."

Anthony hands me a drink and I take it, taking his hand with my other one. He squeezes mine. "My place is here," I say. "Besides, I trust you. I know how hard you've worked to make Rut what it is."

A year ago, I would have flown up there for the grand opening. I would have stayed for a few days, then extended it to a few weeks, then a few months, and then I'd have probably moved to NYC by accident. I wouldn't have trusted someone else to run Rut with the same vision I have in my head.

But I realized that part of building an excellent team and creating a family is trusting they'll be there when you need them. That they'll have your back. I can't be everywhere all at once, so I have to believe the people I've chosen to stand beside me will do their part.

"It's eight," Nate says, glancing at his watch.

"Make them wait. It builds anticipation. We don't want to seem too eager."

Nate nods and introduces the staff to us while he's killing time as we leave people standing outside in the cold, waiting and wondering when the doors will open and they'll get to be the very first people in Rut NYC. "Oh, Vee, this is Natalia. She's my floor manager."

Natalia is a petite woman with shockingly large red hair. Her wild curls frame her face like a halo of fire. She's either a tiny beta or an omega. I'm hoping for the latter. It's nice to see women, especially omegas, hired into leadership roles. Our dynamic is obnoxiously underestimated.

"Hello, it's so nice to meet you," Natalia says with a Russian accent.

"Oh my God," Anthony mutters under his breath. "It's the Russian version of you."

I elbow him to shut up and widen my smile. "It's lovely to have you on team Rut."

"I'm excited to be here." She nods and goes back to her work, yelling something in Russian at a server who dropped a stack of black cocktail napkins everywhere. The enormous scantily clad alpha shrinks from her as she berates him. She bends down on her shockingly high stilettos to help him pick them up. "*Nyet!* Not like that," she shouts off to the side at someone else, moving out of the frame to handle the next crisis.

"I don't see it," I say, ignoring Anthony's laugh as I glance at the bar clock again. We've killed twenty minutes. That should be enough. I nod at Nate, who gives the order to the bouncers to open the doors.

The stream of customers fill the space and I watch, gauging how much of a success Rut NYC is going to be by every head that walks past, swiveling to take it all in.

"Okay, who wants to get this party started?" Anthony shouts once we've muted our microphone. "I made a pitcher of shots. Grab it from the fridge, Ashley."

While everyone works on getting wasted as quickly as possible although the sun hasn't set yet in LA, I walk around and accept everyone's congratulations. It's done. We're only getting started, but it's done.

"Congratulations, sweetheart," Brendan says, pulling me to his side and planting a kiss on my head. "You worked hard, and it shows. To your first twenty million year," he says, clinking his glass against mine and downing it.

I let out a shaky breath and take a sip. My cheeks hurt from smiling all day. "Twenty million… I don't know about that. It takes a lot of money to start a club." New York's going to be running in the red for a while until they get their footing and we find out how good the location really is. The liquor license cost more than I thought it would. New York taxes *everything*. I thought California was bad.

Starting a club is hard. Keeping a club open after the six-month shine rubs off the penny is even harder. I learned a lot about the difference between good business and great business in my first two years. Learned even faster that gimmicks like celebrity drop-ins end up costing more in comped liquor for the celebrity and their entourage than you make at the door.

"If anyone can do it, sweetheart, it's you." Brendan kisses me on the cheek and takes my empty glass from my limp hand. "Let's get you a refill. You're far too sober for tonight's party."

I smile and bite my lip. "You want to get me drunk so you can have your way with me under the bar."

Brendan's expression is calculating and full of heat as he gives me a once over, his gaze lingering over the curve of my hip, the nip of my waist, and the flare of my cleavage. The dress I'm wearing has a deep v that goes all the way down to my breastbone. I had to buy a special plunge bra for it, but it was worth every penny.

"Under the bar?" He quirks one eyebrow as if he hadn't thought of that, but now he is.

My face heats with a blush, and I shake my head. There's not an inch of Rut that some horny patron hasn't convinced one of the alpha dancers or bartenders to fuck them in. In the bathroom, behind the bar, backstage, in a dark corner, under tables. If a forensic analyst used that special light up spray they use on TV, this place would glow like a crime scene.

"Don't get any ideas," I warn him. Anthony is bad enough. I don't need two of them competing for first place in the most-public fuck spot.

"Never." His grin betrays his lie, but he disappears into the crowd before I can think of a response.

Fifteen minutes later when he comes back and pulls me from my conversation with Darlene—something about doing a vampire routine with a sheer poet shirt, satin cape, and fake blood—I'm not surprised the drink he hands me tastes like coconuts.

"It's funny how we call them assless chaps," Darlene says. "All chaps are assless."

"I never thought about it, but you're right." I pull on my straw and feel my core clench as Jamie's sweet taste blended with alcohol hits my tongue.

"They're only assless because they're not wearing jeans

underneath," she says. "I'll put velcro under the fringe on the sides and make them tearaway pants."

"Mmm. Sounds good," I agree.

"I could order some thicker rope," Brendan offers. "I'd have to learn how, but I'm sure I could teach them how to wave a lasso around on stage. At least enough to make it look good."

Darlene cackles. "I love it. Told her you were a yummy thing under that business suit. You fit right in here, don't you, handsome?"

"There's nowhere I'd rather be." Brendan pulls me tighter against him, his hand drifting down to cup my ass and squeeze.

I suck on my straw too hard and let out a hiss, pressing the heel of my palm against my head. "Ugh, brain freeze."

"I'll take it. Looks better than mine," Darlene says, grabbing the drink from my hand.

"No!" I snatch it back before she can take a sip. My face and ears heat in a blush that makes her eyes squint with suspicion. The last thing anyone needs is Darlene drinking one of Anthony's special drinks. "You won't like it."

Darlene arches one penciled-on eyebrow. "There's not a liquor on God's green Earth I don't like."

"I'll go get you something better," I insist.

Before Darlene can question it anymore, I pull Brendan toward the bar and ignore his guffaws of laughter. Anthony looks up from the blender he's pulsing.

"I need a drink for Darlene," I tell him.

He pours the blended mix into a line of five waiting glasses and scoots them toward the edge of the bar toward the dancers waiting there. "Darlene's had fifteen shot's worth of drinks already. I'm not making her anymore. Rut opens in an hour."

"Fifteen! How is she still standing?"

"Hmm… Looks like she's not. At least not without help," he says.

We all turn and gawk, spying Darlene slow dancing to a fast song with a bewildered and somewhat amused looking dancer. I shake my head. My phone chirps and a glance shows me a text from Nate saying they've shut the doors because they're at capacity. I tap his name and call him. He answers on the second ring, shouting to be heard over the loud music on both of our ends.

"Why'd you shut the doors?" I ask.

"Because we're at capacity?" Nate asks, confused.

"Well, open them."

"We'll get shut down by the fire department."

"That's the point."

"If we get shut down, nobody will see my show. It's a strip club. That's bad for business."

"And what do you think your line's going to be like tomorrow if the fire department comes and shuts you down tonight because of overcrowding on your opening night?"

I wait a beat and give him a minute to let the thought sink in. Nate's a smart man with good instincts, but he's new to night club management. He can do choreography in his sleep, but it'll take some time for him to develop a good business sense. The nightclub world is small. You have to stand out or you'll get lost, especially in a city like New York. I know he'll get there, though.

"You're diabolical," Nate says, laughing.

"That's show business, baby," I tell him.

"Open the door," Nate says to someone on his end, his voice muffled as he speaks away from the speaker. "Yeah, I know I said to close them, but now I'm telling you to open them. Pack them in. I've got a show they won't want to miss. I've gotta go. Bye, Vee."

"Bye." I hang up and open up a web browser, looking for the non-emergency number of the closest precinct. I tap the blue phone number and it doesn't take long for someone to answer.

"Sixth precinct, this is Officer Barnes. How can I help you?"

"Hi, officer, I'm so sorry to bother you, but I saw two alphas getting into a fight outside of some bar on Christopher Street."

"Where did you see this?" the officer asks.

"Outside of some new bar called… God, I hate to say the name. It's so trashy. It's that new one called Rut. Listen, you can hear in the background how loud and obnoxious it is."

"We'll send someone to check it out. I need to get your name and—"

"So sorry, my baby just woke up. I have to go," I lie and hang up before he can finish his question.

Anthony and Brendan both give me blank looks. "What?" I ask.

"He was right. You are diabolical," Anthony says with awe.

I shrug and pick up my drink, taking a sip now that my brain freeze is gone. "Just doing good business."

The rest of the night passes in a blur as everyone switches from celebration to work mode and our doors open at seven. An hour later, I get a call from my uncle. It's been a few months since we first reconnected. I head up the stairs to the office and swipe my thumb across the screen to answer it. The door shuts out the worst of the club's noise as I bring my cell phone to my ear. "Hey."

"Hey, Veronica," Uncle Brian says.

"Hey, Vee!" his husband Steven shouts in the background.

"We were calling you to say congratulations. We know this is a big day for you. How's the opening going?"

"Good." I smile to myself and stand at the windows behind my desk so I can watch over Rut while we talk. "The house is packed. Everyone's worked so hard to make it perfect. Don't tell him, but I'm thinking of stealing some of Nate's ideas and making it part of the Rut branding."

Each club should have its own unique flair, but the core of Rut should be the same. Still, Nate's idea for gilded VIP thrones was genius. Every omega wants to feel like royalty on their special day. It'll be easy to make it an add on for our packages.

"Our lips are sealed. Maybe when you're done, we'll drive up to LA and see it," uncle Brian says.

"I'm making him take me to Rut for my birthday!" Steven shouts amid the banging of pots and pans. It sounds like he's cooking. "We're gonna pretend we don't know each other so he can pick me up. He owes me for canceling our last three dates."

I pinch between my brows and close my eyes. That was way more information than I needed to know about my uncles.

"I had to work, honey," Uncle Brian sighs.

"You're always working," Steven bitches. "You're gonna die at that desk. Just have a heart attack and keel right over top of your paperwork."

There's muffled talking in the background, like he's covering the speaker, and then uncle Brian sighs again. "Veronica, I'm sorry."

"It's fine." My lips quirk in a wry smile. "We'd love to have you, of course. Let me know what day you're coming. Maybe we'll have the thrones by then. Steven can be our test subject."

"No, I meant… I'm not good at this sort of thing. Last time I met with my therapist she recommended making amends. I never know how to work it into a conversation so I'm just going to be awkward and say it. We never had kids, and I was young and stupid. Self-absorbed and desperate to climb the corporate ladder. We didn't give you what you really needed from us. I should have known better. You needed us to stick around and to pay attention even when you said you were fine. We weren't there for you. I wasn't there for you. I'm sorry."

My eyes water and I bite my lip to stop it from quivering. Uncle Brian must take my stunned silence as a void to fill because he continues.

"We tried to find you after they took you. I don't know if they ever told you. If you wanted to be found or not."

"You did?" My chest pinches and it's hard to breathe. The club beyond the windowpane blurs as tears swell in my eyes. "They didn't tell me."

"They wouldn't tell us where they placed you or let us contact you. We tried again once you'd turned eighteen, but your file was still sealed. Our private investigator hit a lot of dead ends and old addresses. I don't know if you were allergic to social media or something, but you were hard to find. By the time he found you, you'd opened Rut. That's actually how we did. There was a photo in the paper. You looked so happy and proud in that photo, and I... I was a coward. I thought that if your life had turned out so great without us that it meant you were better off without us bothering you."

He takes a breath. "I didn't know how to face you now that you were an adult and you knew how badly I'd fucked up. So I convinced myself that you were doing fine and didn't need us anymore and if you wanted to find us, you knew where we were. I'm sorry for that too. We lost a lot of time we can't get back because I was too proud and afraid. I'm really glad you reached out."

Without my pack's reassurances and support, I'm not sure I ever would have been strong enough to risk it. But Brendan was right. One way or another, I needed the closure. After weeks of thinking about it, I picked up the phone and dialed their old number with zero clue about what I'd say if they answered or even if the number was the same. When Uncle Brian started crying, so did I. We've talked once a week ever since. He's right. We lost a lot of time, and we could never get that back, but that doesn't mean our separation has to be forever. I'm not sure I'll ever fully forgive him for everything, but it's impossible to stay that angry when a grown man bawls.

"Me too." I brush the tears from my eyes before they can fall or ruin my makeup. "I'd like to see you guys. Let me know what day you're coming. We'll go out to dinner first. Anthony's uncle runs a cute little Italian place down the road. It has an old world charm."

"I love carbs! And wine!" Steven shouts in the background, breaking the tension. "And I can't wait to meet your mates. Just wait till you see the mating gift we got you." He cackles.

Chuckling, I tuck loose strands of hair behind my ear. "I'll see you then. And Uncle Brian… Thank you."

"I'll text you dates, short stack," he says. "Love you, bye."

"Bye." The call ends and I palm my phone, staring out the window. The new MC comes out on stage and the crowd's energy ratchets up as the first dancer comes through the curtain. I watch the routine, but I'm not really paying attention.

My phone chirps with a text, and at first I think that was a quick response from my uncles until I see it's from Nate. The fire department is at his club and they're being shut down. I sit at my desk and kick my heels off my aching feet.

As if my words spoke it into existence, a fight actually broke out between two alphas arguing over an omega who'd been seeing both of them and didn't expect to run into her boyfriend while she was out with her sidepiece. There's some broken glass from a thrown tray of drinks, but nobody is seriously hurt and, even more important, the club didn't take any damage.

I cackle and tear out of my office chair. It rolls back and hits the window. Brendan looks up from his phone. I'm not sure when he came in and sat down, that's how distracted I've been.

"They're being shut down," I tell him as I join him on the sofa. I throw my legs over his good knee and he palms them. "Just for the night. Oh, this is good." Everyone who's there tonight is going to be talking about it tomorrow. They're going to pick up their phones and text their friends and bitch to their girlfriends that they got kicked out of the hot, new alpha strip club by hot firefighters.

"Try to sound less happy about it," Brendan jokes, grinning. He might not understand why this is such a good thing, but he sees my enthusiasm.

I tap my phone against my cheek as I think. The publicity is good, but more is better. But we can't pull stunts like this too often or we'll lose the liquor license. We need to keep the cops happy for the most part, without being too boring. What we may need is protection.

Guess it's a good thing that one of my mates is very well connected. If things go south with the police and they make trouble, it shouldn't be too hard to call in some favors, although I don't want to take that leap too early, especially without talking to Anthony about it first. He's conflicted when it comes to his family, and I get it.

Plus the mob would expect a cut of the door and the margins will be too slim in the beginning to handle that. It's better to leave that ace up our sleeve and broach the subject with Anthony only if there's no other way.

Brendan is tapping away at his phone and, curious, I lean over to see his screen. "Who are you texting?" I ask.

"I went to college with a woman who works at a small news station in New York." After a few minutes, his phone dings with her reply and he grins. "She works in a different department, but she's going to text her friend who's a broadcaster. They'll send a van and it'll be on the news in an hour."

My mouth falls open in surprise, then curls into a smile. "Have I told you how much I love you?"

"Only four times today." He puts his phone down and looks at me with an expression of utter fondness.

"Oh, only four? How lax of me." His thumb digs into the ball of my foot, a knot releasing. I sigh and melt into a puddle in his lap, returning his fond look with one of my own.

"I thought so, but I wasn't going to say anything."

"How magnanimous of you."

"It's been a busy day for you. Building an empire, plotting world domination, lying to the police, instigating a raid. You've had your hands full."

"Mmm. I could get my hands full of something else," I say as I pull my foot from his delicious grasp and climb onto his lap.

My skirt rides up my thighs as I straddle him. His hands go to my ass to keep me steady. Or to grab a handful of ass. He's good at multitasking like that. His tie is silky soft against my hand as I loosen it, reaching for his shirt buttons.

Even after all this time, he still dresses like the auditor he was when he walked into Rut all those months ago. I wouldn't have it any other way. If there's one thing I love more than my buttoned up auditor, it's ruffling him up and seeing him messy, then peeling him out of his suit.

"Bad time for dinner?" Anthony says from the doorway. He stands there with two white plastic bags bulging with takeout in his hands, and my stomach clenches. It's Italian. I can smell the sauce and the garlic from here. He must have gone to his uncle Tony's again. Because he knows it's my favorite and Anthony's sweet like that. He pays attention to the little things.

Jamie comes up behind him, either on break or between sets. "That smells good. I'm starving."

Anthony unpacks the takeout on Brendan's desk, and I gawk at the portions. Did he order the entire restaurant? I slide off Brendan's lap, and we join them.

"I hope you're hungry enough to eat a horse," I joke as Anthony passes out plastic wrapped cutlery.

"I could never," Jamie says, his smile slipping into a look of devastation. He glances at the takeout with longing. "Horses are too cute."

Everyone freezes for a beat, and then Anthony shakes his head. "No horses were hurt for our dinner, babe. It's a saying, that's all. I got you chicken marsala with an extra side of broiled broccoli."

"Oh, okay. I like chicken." Jamie takes his takeout container and I lean on him for support as I go up on my tiptoes to kiss my sweet himbo on his cheek.

"Have I told you today how much I love you?" I ask Jamie.

"I don't mind hearing it again," he says, giving me a shy smile.

"I love you, Jamie. Now enjoy your dinner."

Jamie takes his food and sits down in his usual seat. Anthony holds my dinner out to me, then jerks it away before I can take it. He taps his cheek, demanding his payment upfront. I roll my eyes at his antics and stretch up to kiss him on the cheek, but he turns his head at the last moment and steals a kiss on the lips instead.

"I love you too," I tell him as I take my food. "Thank you for getting us dinner."

"Of course, baby."

Once we're all settled in our usual seats, Brendan turns on the TV I rarely use and often forget is there. He flips the channel to the news and searches until he hits the right station.

"What're we watching?" Anthony asks between bites of his lasagne.

"Rut NYC's gonna be on the news," I say, too giddy to hide my excitement. "It's getting shut down by the fire department and a fight broke out."

"Nice," Anthony says.

"Is that a good thing?" Jamie asks, looking between us. His forehead scrunches.

"It's a good thing, babe," Anthony says. "Everyone won't be able to stop talking about it."

"Exactly," I say. "It's the best publicity we could ever buy, and it was *free*." I cackle while I twirl my pasta around my fork.

We eat, and then a little while after we're done, the news segment is on. A reporter stands in front of Rut, the hot pink neon sign blazing over the pretty blonde's shoulder. She reports on the fight, the noise, the rowdiness of the patrons. Mentions that it's New York City's first all-alpha strip club, and the zoning issues we faced early on.

Tipsy, well-dressed, attractive clubbers stumble away from the building in the background as police corral them and a fire marshal cordons off the building's doors with bright yellow tape. I count how many times the reporter says Rut's name.

It's everything I ever could have asked for, and more. And as I look between my mates, I realize that it's still only the beginning of our story.

With a belly full of pasta, three handsome mates, and a club in the most densely populated city on the entire planet that just reached notorious status, is there anything more an omega could want?

No, I don't think there is.

Want to keep reading?

Sign up for the newsletter and get the free bonus epilogue
https://dl.bookfunnel.com/b21dox29q5

Author's Note

Thank you so much for reading Rut Bar! When I started this book the only thought in my head was an omega-run alpha strip club and a himbo dancer. Then, I thought it would be hilarious to have the entire book revolve around Rut's IRS audit. Anthony roared onto the page and demanded I make room for his panty-melter smile. Who doesn't love a good bad boy?

Jamie's cuckold fetish took me by absolute surprise and I thought, hey, that could the whole theme. Subverting dynamic norms and finding your tribe. Found family is such an important trope in the LGBTQIA+ community since so many of us lose family when coming out, myself included. Vee's prickly nature guards a wounded heart. I enjoyed writing about a bad ass boss bitch who was getting shit done.

I'm not sure what I'll be writing next! I have a few ideas percolating and a bunch of rough drafts in various stages of development. I'm probably going to flit about between them and see which one grabs a hold of me and refuses to let go.

If you've made it this far, please consider leaving a review. Reviews are author hugs!

For updates, new release alerts, teasers, sales info, freebies, and bonus content delivered to your inbox about once a month, join my newsletter. To stalk me on social media or visit the shop, you can find that at www.alexisbosborne.com.

-Alexis

About the Author

Alexis lives in New York with her wife and step-son and a small horde of furry beings. She began her love affair with books at an early age, and began writing for fun in High School and College. She fell in insta-love with the strange and unusual at an early age. When she's not reading or writing she can be found painting and making subversive cross-stitch. Her favorite fairy tale will always be Beauty and the Beast. Alexis loves all things fantastical, alien, and weird. She will never forget the gorgeous glory that was the late, great David Bowie.

www.alexisbosborne.com

www.ingramcontent.com/pod-product-compliance
Lightning Source LLC
Chambersburg PA
CBHW061531190726
48289CB00004B/1000